THE SILEN⊤ ⊔⊔⊤⊖R⊔

The Silent History was orig⋯
winning app before being r⋯
definitive text. It is the work ⟨⋯
Matthew Derby and Kevin Moffett.

Eli Horowitz is the former managing editor and publisher of *McSweeney's*. He is the co-author of *The Clock Without a Face*, a treasure-hunt mystery, and *Everything You Know Is Pong*, an illustrated cultural history of ping pong. His design work has been honoured by *i-D*, *Print* and the American Institute of Graphic Arts.

Matthew Derby is a writer and designer and the author of the story collection *Super Flat Times*. His writing has appeared in *McSweeney's*, *The Believer*, *Guernica* and *The Anchor Book of New American Short Stories*. He also works at a video game studio in Cambridge, Massachusetts.
www.matthewderby.org

Kevin Moffett is the author of two highly praised story collections, *Permanent Visitors* and *Further Interpretations of Real-Life Events*. His work has appeared in *McSweeney's*, *Tin House*, *American Short Fiction*, as well as in three editons of *The Best American Short Stories*. He is the winner of the Nelson Algren Award, a Pushcart Prize, and the National Magazine Award. He lives in California.
www.kevinmoffett.org

ELI HOROWITZ
MATTHEW DERBY
KEVIN MOFFETT

The Silent
History

VINTAGE

1 3 5 7 9 10 8 6 4 2

Vintage
20 Vauxhall Bridge Road,
London SW1V 2SA

Vintage is part of the Penguin Random House group of companies
whose addresses can be found at global.penguinrandomhouse.com

Penguin
Random House
UK

First published in hardback in Great Britain in 2014 by
Jonathan Cape

www.vintage-books.co.uk

A CIP catalogue record for this book is
available from the British Library

ISBN 9780099592860

Printed and bound by Clays Ltd, St Ives plc

MIX
Paper from
responsible sources
FSC® C018179

Penguin Random House is committed to a sustainable
future for our business, our readers and our planet.
This book is made from Forest Stewardship Council®
certified paper

THE SILENT HISTORY

PROLOGUE

HUGH PURCELL, EXECUTIVE DIRECTOR

WASHINGTON, DC
2044

I was twenty-two and desperate for work, desperate for any human contact at all, so when I saw an opening for a junior epidemiological archivist, no experience necessary, I applied on the spot. The listing was vague, just something about "our continuing efforts to better understand the scope of the silent phenomenon." I got the job on a Friday, and by Monday morning I was already out on the streets of the Charlotte financial district with a list of names and a scripted greeting.

My duties appeared simple—find people who had come into contact with silents and record their testimony. The streets at dawn were empty, which was mostly a relief, given the infamous state of the neighborhood at that point. My first interview was with a bird rehabber, a weathered man with a severed pinky, who I found as he was raising the steel gate on his shop. I intercepted a pastor ushering a crowd of churchgoers out of a storefront chapel. There was a boy in the square whose brother was a silent. Most of what I recorded was speculative thirdhand info, wispy urban myths about how silence was a plague, or a conspiracy, or some sort of vague metaphor. Some people were convinced it was caused by food-borne toxins, some blamed the parents, some suspected the kids themselves.

I heard the term "mutetard" a lot that day.

By late afternoon, after getting mugged and dry humped by a group of teenage girls in football uniforms, I was beginning to question how much I actually wanted the job. But I had one more interview subject on the list, a repo man who'd been hired by the city to orchestrate a resettlement of silent squatters from the buildings along Trade Street, where they wanted to put in a high-end artisan pet arcade. His name was Camara, but he referred to himself as "the Camara," and within minutes of me finding him idling in a tan Burgoyne outside a Pulp Hulk he'd already shown me his blowgun collection and offered to give me a Key West salad. He didn't know much about the silents, aside from a two-day sensitivity training course he'd taken as a condition of his hire. "You don't need to know much," he said, chewing on a cone of fruit meat. "People see the Camara coming and they pretty much get that it's time to move. Even just a shadow tells them this. Just a silhouette of the Camara passing by a window. You don't need words to tell someone they're not welcome." He didn't know why there were so many of them living in the burned-out center of the city, and he didn't seem particularly interested in the question. "So long as they don't have a grenade launcher, it's easy money."

We waited in the cab of his truck until the dispatcher called. We were to drive over to the Bank of America building on East Fifth, where we'd meet the contract crew that would go in and take the place by force once Camara had them assembled. I asked if it wasn't overkill to involve armed men in a resettlement operation, and Camara said, "A home's a home. That's basic info, DNA shit. Animal knowledge that even these silents have. When you've got a home, you're going to do whatever it takes to keep it that way."

We pulled into a lot off a side street about a block from the bank building. The crew of contract soldiers stood around the transport truck that would take the silents to a camp outside the city limits. They hung around smoking fakies and telling dick jokes while Camara spoke with the CO. They were to surround the building while Camara gathered the silents in the lobby. On his signal, they'd enter through the designated access points and get everyone zipped and dipped. The whole thing should take about fifteen minutes, Camara estimated. The CO nodded, and gathered his men to brief them. Camara took a suitcase from behind the passenger seat of his truck. I asked him if it was a weapon case and he made a little wheezing sound. "Hygiene kits, brother," he said. "Everyone loves a free toothbrush. You ready?"

We walked down the vacant block to the front entrance of the bank building. Camara carefully pried away a sheet of plywood, and we slipped in through the shattered revolving doors.

I'd seen plenty of silents before. There were two in my first-grade class—sullen, withdrawn kids who seemed to exist on another planet. They were eventually pulled from the system, and I think my classmates and I all felt relieved. There was a family down the street that had a silent boy, and another one who folded pizza boxes at a restaurant on the square. In college I'd heard rumors about silent enclaves, groups of them living in the wilderness or abandoned sectors of the city, but I assumed those were trumped-up tales by the same people who told me about the mad heart-eating cult in the financial district. But inside that decaying bank lobby I saw how wrong I'd been about them, about everything.

There must have been fifty of them in the cavernous space, but I'd never have known if I hadn't been directly observing them from my spot in the shadows of the foyer—they were that quiet. It seemed impossible that so many people in one place could generate so little noise, just the rustling of fabric and the occasional cooing of the pigeons that clung to the massive chandelier.

Camara and I stood in the shadows. I could see him taking a head count, whispering the numbers as he surveyed the area. They were all over, scattered among a curvilinear maze of beat-up chairs and couches that let out onto a circular gathering area underneath the frescoes of human industrial progress. Old whiteboards leaned against the walls, revealing indecipherable, abstract drawings that appeared to be the work of multiple artists. Reams of copy paper were used as a sort of crude papier-mâché to construct oblong containers. In one corner a man was sewing pants out of the coarse gray fabric from old cubicle walls. A young woman took handfuls of twigs from a canvas bag and passed them out to a group gathered in a circle on the floor. They seemed fixated on her. She knelt in the center of the floor and braided some twigs into a sort of rope. Then a man sitting behind her braided his bundle and bound it to the bundle she'd made. The next person did the same, and the next, until they had made a large wreath. They laid it out on the floor and ran their hands along its surface, like it told them some kind of story. The significance of that wreath still mystifies me even today, but at the time I was simply fascinated that they'd been able to collaborate on such a project at all.

Without warning, Camara strode out into the light, holding up a pair of hygiene kits. "Everybody, listen up," he said in a firm voice that shattered the cool stillness of the space. Everyone turned. "You may not understand me," he said, "but the Camara is here to help you. I understand that this is your home, but the city has different plans for this space. I am here to transport you to a facility just north of here, where you can live in peace. There is running water, three meals a day, and cots for everyone. I understand that it will be difficult for you to leave. And that is why I am providing you with these kits, free of charge. They contain a full day's worth of meal strips, vermin spray, first-aid gel, and a shelter bag." He turned to show the room the kits. The silents watched him carefully. They couldn't possibly have had any idea what Camara was saying, but they seemed to respond to him. As he displayed the contents of the kits, their fear seemed to dissipate. They appeared genuinely curious and interested, and began to congregate in the center of the lobby. Camara's act was working.

"Is everybody in here?" he asked. Again, they continued to stare. "I'm going to go get the kits for you. Do you understand? I'll be back in one minute." Camara scanned the people in the room, nodding encouragingly. They nodded in response, but did not move. "Okay? Just wait right here."

We went into the foyer. Camara winked at me and said, "Real bunch of troublemakers." He checked his watch and called the contract soldiers. "Okay, they're all in the lobby," he said. "Roger that," a thin voice replied, and we waited. There was a dull burst as four soldiers broke down the front doors with percussion cannons. They rushed in with gas guns drawn, right past us. I could hear them converging on the lobby from every access point, quickly and quietly, spreading out into the space like a rolling cloud. Their boots ground against the concrete subfloor as they secured all of the exits and moved in.

I waited to hear some sort of struggle, but the building sounded oddly dead. I ventured into the lobby and saw that it was empty, save for the soldiers frantically pacing back and forth, searching the rafters with Maglites. The silents were nowhere to be found.

"You had the place surrounded, didn't you?" Camara asked the CO, who nodded in irritation. There was no sign of an alternate exit anywhere. The soldiers began tipping over tables and kicking chairs. "Over here," one of them said, standing over a vent in the floor, which led down into darkness. Camara knelt and peered in with a flashlight. "I'll be shitcut," he said, scratching the back of his head. The hatch was no more than two feet wide. There was no way it could accommodate more than one person at a time. But somehow a group of fifty silents had managed to spontaneously coordinate an escape without being detected.

We quietly filed out of the building, and I walked all the way back to the sanitary district on the outskirts of town, my head still buzzing. The next morning I was back out on the streets. All summer I recorded more testimonials, seeking out communities of silents and observing everything I could. Up until that moment in the bank building, I, like most people I knew, had defined silents by what they lacked. I thought of them as hollow vessels, defective parasites feeding upon the speaking world. But in that lobby I saw them for what they might *possess*. What unknown abilities had filled this void? Was the world somehow brighter, more tangible, without the nagging interference of language? Was the absence of words actually a form of freedom? I've often tried to quiet that constant voice in my mind, to try to experience the world the way they might—but always the questions rush in faster than I can carve out a moment of true silence.

That September I was promoted to regional coordinator, and sixteen years later I'm still here, now the director of the project. For years my colleagues and I scoured the globe to interview parents, siblings, teachers, health professionals, law enforcement, faith healers, neighborhood-watch groups, businesspeople—a diverse chorus of voices touched in some way by emergent phasic resistance. Starting in 2021, we introduced Mémo, the ambient dictation application that allows key subjects to record testimonials at their convenience from anywhere in the world, expanding our reach even further. Every day we are learning more about this strange condition, and every day there are more questions—questions that are, themselves, bound by language, a chamber sealed so tightly that we can hardly even imagine an experience beyond its walls.

But, of course, it's this experience that waits for us all. It's inside our brothers and sisters, daughters and sons and lovers. This document presumes nothing about the future; it is strictly a record of the past, of what we looked like before, and how we got here. Are words our creation, or did they create us? And who are we in a world without them? Are there wilder, more verdant fields out beyond the boundaries of language, where those of us who are silent now wander? Each of us must find our own path through these questions. We enter and leave the world in silence, after all, and everything else is simply how we walk that middle passage.

VOLUME ONE

THEODORE GREENE

EL CERRITO, CA
2011

She already looked half-dead on the drive to the hospital, but I wouldn't admit this until much later. I was pretty determined, I guess, to remain upbeat. In all the classes we'd taken to prepare for the birth, that was the one thing the instructor kept repeating to the men in the room, the future fathers. "There's no magic involved," she said. She told us that what our wives needed most was our support. Our patience. The idea was—and I totally believed this—that a calm mother would produce a healthy child. It had a logic to it, and we had no reason to doubt the instructor. We were all first-timers except for this one guy who showed up to class with a wife half his age. He already had three or four kids, I think, from previous marriages, and the instructor pointed to him and said, "Mitch has been through this before. He knows all about the idea of support, right, Mitch?" Everyone laughed but Mitch, who just kind of stared back at the instructor with a look of bemusement. It was almost more of a—even though his wife was pretty attractive—more of a look of defeat.

There were other aspects of that day that made me feel

like something bad was coming. Things that made it hard to focus on the goal, that one task of keeping the birth free of panic and dread. First there was the humidity. Everything was drenched in it. By the time I got home from work my clothes were damp. I went inside the house and Mel was on the couch with her head back, sweating with the fan off. "Why are you here?" I said, and she said, "I stayed home today." I said, "What?" and "Why didn't you call me?" You know? "I would have come home." But she didn't say anything. Just stared at the ceiling with her eyes half-closed like she was drugged. I went to the kitchen and took off my shirt. I put half a box of noodles in a pot, and when I went back to the couch to check on her she was crying. "Are there contractions?" I said, and she nodded. "Are they close together?" I said, and she nodded again, and I was like, This is it. I put my shirt back on even though it was soaked, and I helped her out to my car. She had her full weight against me. I felt like if I let go of her she would just collapse into a pile. I tried hard not to get worked up. But then when I opened the passenger-side door the half-eaten taco from my lunch break slid off the seat and onto the driveway. I looked at the taco on the blacktop and I felt this, like, pulsing kind of terror.

Of fatherhood, yeah, I guess. I remember thinking, This is the car we'll use to bring Flora home. This will be her first car ride, in my ten-year-old hatchback with mismatched seat covers that smell like burning human hair. Mel's car was newer, but I'd blocked her in and there was no time. No time left to back out into a more respectable set of circumstances. I was working at a company I hated and wolfing down tacos in the parking lot of a strip mall down the road. It was not where I wanted to be, and anyway what difference would it have made? Mel and I were the people we were, and there wasn't anyone to blame but ourselves for how we lived.

I got Mel in the car and started driving, like I said, toward the hospital. The clouds were wild and dark like right before a heat storm. They looked almost like smoke from a fire, sort of billowing in reverse behind the cell towers at the interchange. I glanced over at Mel, who was doubled over in the passenger seat. Her eyes were rolling around under her closed lids and her skin was a sort of light gray color. I looked hard at the road and told myself that we were all going to make it through the day, but only two-thirds of that statement was actually true.

NANCY JERNIK

I started taking Ambitor about a year before I found out I was pregnant with Spencer. This was right around the time it first went on the market, and almost half the women at Yan Talan started taking it. I remember seeing this ad for it, a three-panel foldout in the front of *Fortune*. It had a picture of a woman sitting behind a huge wooden desk in a corner office with floor-to-ceiling windows. She had her legs propped up on the desk and she was sitting back—like, reclining in a big upholstered leather chair, smoking a cigar. She was in the middle of blowing a smoke ring, and the caption said something like *Call the Shots*. That was it, except for the Ambitor logo and the tiny text that described all the side effects, which seemed like a small list to me, as someone who had taken a bunch of different antidepressants and weight-control pills and stuff. I looked at this woman in the ad and thought, That's me. That's where I want to be. I want everything in that picture. Not in a shallow way. Not like, I want to have a big desk, or smoke cigars, or I guess anything in the actual picture, which actually was really not very well done. But more of a feeling like, I want to be in control.

So I started taking it, and suddenly I had this capacity to *do* things. I had access to a whole new reservoir of energy. It was pretty incredible, actually. I mean, I still think about what it was like to be on Ambitor, and I would probably be taking it right now if I could. If it was still on the market.

I found out I was pregnant in December, and Ron, who I thought would be scared or upset, given that we were just a few months into our marriage, was actually really excited. I can remember that first trimester being the last really happy time. Because I was made VP in February and put in charge of the whole Schick Quattro for Women account. And I won't bore you with the whatever hours I spent at the office or at Schick headquarters in Milford, but it had the effect on my marriage that you'd expect. I saw it all happening. Like, I could remember watching as my relationship with Ron sort of split apart like a dissolving glacier, but—and maybe this was the Ambitor doing what it did best—I saw things drifting, but I didn't really care so much. Or, I cared, but only in the way you care for the people in a movie, watching them as their lives go down the tubes.

I hardly remember anything about Spencer's birth except that it took forever. Forty hours from start to finish. In the end they had to do a C-section, because he just wasn't coming. Or I wasn't trying hard enough. So I was completely out of it for the actual birth, and I didn't know that Spencer came out without making any noise. Ron was really worried about that, but the doctor told him it was a myth that all babies come out crying. Of course, nobody knew at that time about

Spencer—about what was wrong with him. So Ron just sort of took the doctor at his word. If I'd been awake I would've said something. I wouldn't have let that go.

We took Spencer home a few days later. Ron had a week of paternity leave from his job and we were almost able to get back to that place where we were happy. But Spencer wasn't nursing. Nothing at all. They said that you should wait a few days before panicking, that sometimes the kid just doesn't want to nurse in the beginning. But by the fifth day of nothing we started to get really stressed out. Ron was going to have to go back to work the following Monday, and it suddenly seemed so small, the window of time we had to be all together. I didn't know what I was going to do alone in the house with this kid who wouldn't eat. We called the doctor and she asked if we'd tried formula. I was like, "You said we should never give the kid formula." And she said that normally breast milk is the best, but if the kid is not nursing, you try the formula, so Ron went out in the middle of the night to a drugstore and got this stuff. He put the nipple of the bottle to Spencer's lips and he immediately started nursing. I remember lying on my side in the bed watching Ron hold the bottle while Spencer was just nursing like crazy, like he'd been starving—which he was, I guess. And Ron started laughing with this mixture of relief and joy, because finally here was something, here was Spencer showing that he needed something. And I focused on Spencer—I tried to block Ron out of my vision, because I could see him glancing over at me, trying to get me to laugh about it or even smile, but I just felt sick, absolutely sick to my stomach. I couldn't see it as anything other than a line on the battlefield, and Spencer, this baby that had wanted so much to stay inside me that they had to cut him out, had just crossed over to Ron's side. I eventually got him to take my milk, but I couldn't rid myself of that feeling.

The three months of maternity leave were like being underwater. Everything was so still and silent with me and Spencer alone in the house. He'd cry when he was hungry or tired, but that was about it. He never made any of those little trickling sounds that babies make. He'd stare at me, but it was like I was some kind of complex math problem on a chalkboard. I don't know how to explain it, but it just seemed like he didn't need me that much. And if I'm being honest, I guess it irritated me. I somehow expected that when I had a baby, we would be connected by a golden thread. There would be this bond between us that I could feel, even if we were in separate rooms or cities. But I didn't feel any connection to him at all. He was like an alien in my house.

I went back to work, and it was like finally crawling ashore. My team had held down the Schick account in my absence, and within a few weeks we launched a huge online campaign for the new Quattro with Flex-Edge technology. I was then up to 750 mg of Ambitor a day, which was only slightly over the recommended daily dose. This was around the time that the article appeared in *Harper's*, the one that was like, Ambitor is dangerous, Ambitor has these unknown side effects. Ron encouraged me to stop taking it—at first he was sort of sweet about it, but he eventually turned belligerent. He started blaming the Ambitor for Spencer's behavior, which I thought was a little . . . I mean, no one was saying anything about birth defects. This was just classic Ron, making a problem out of everything. I was still hoping that eventually Spencer would just sort of emerge from the depths, so to speak. Like, one day I'd wake up to the sound of his babbling in the next room, and I'd go in and he'd look at me and smile and say "Mama" for the first time. But it never happened.

AUGUST BURNHAM

NEWTON, MA
2012

My name is Dr. August Burnham, and I direct the Center for Neurodevelopmental Services at McLean Hospital in Belmont, Massachusetts. I administered the M-CHAT screening for Calvin Andersen shortly after returning to Boston from the tour for my first book, *The Wide Empty Sea: Living with Childhood Disintegrative Disorder.* My publicist reminded me on more than one occasion that the tour was a success, but I couldn't help feeling like it had been a lot of wasted time. A lot of sitting around in hotel rooms just to talk for a half hour in a chain bookstore in front of a dozen people who seemed to have wandered in accidentally. Radio interviews with hosts who hadn't read the book. The awkward exchanges with parents of CDD kids.

When I got back to Boston I was completely drained. I hadn't expected it to be so difficult to get back to work. I'd lost interest in almost everything. This of course had an impact on my domestic life. My partner, Bruce, and I had recently adopted a boy from Honduras, a special-needs kid with a cleft palate and some mild developmental delays—a beautiful boy named Hector, which was the perfect name for him. Little warrior prince. Hector had just undergone his first cleft palate surgery and he needed a lot of attention, and I was already—well, I'd missed the surgery because of the book tour, and I think Bruce expected me to come back and be twice as attentive and supportive. But I just couldn't bring myself to the task.

All of this is to say that when I screened Calvin I was not in the greatest shape. Calvin wasn't speaking at thirty months, and his parents had driven him to McLean from Hadley in Western Mass. Their pediatrician had diagnosed Calvin with an oral-motor delay that she thought could be corrected with speech-language therapy. They worked with a speech pathologist who told them that she'd never seen a case as pervasive as Calvin's, where there was just no trace of speech development. They were determined to get a more satisfactory diagnosis. Apparently he'd developed normally as an infant, but at eighteen months, when typically the rudiments of language are apparent, Calvin had no words or signs. The thing that was most disturbing to his parents was that not only was he not talking, but Calvin didn't seem to want to communicate with them or anyone else. He seemed to have no desire to express himself in any way.

They came to me thinking I'd be able to detect this thing. As if I were some sort of medicine man who could commune with the spirit that possessed their son. Any validation from the medical community would be an anchor for them. It would allow them to move forward in whatever direction the diagnosis pointed. But they were—it was like they were not going to leave there without a diagnosis. I was already burned-out, as I said, and their determination only put me in a worse mood. But I went ahead and led Calvin through some exercises for the M-CHAT. I asked him to go over to the padded mat in the center of the room. He didn't respond to the command, but he looked at me when I asked him, which meant that he heard me and was acknowledging me. I pointed at the mat and asked him again, and he just fixated on my face. I pointed again and asked a third time, but his gaze didn't waver. I found this very curious. Not at all like a kid with, say, autism. I went over and knelt on the mat and he followed me there. He seemed interested in what I was doing, right? Again, this is not the type of behavior you'd typically see with autism or similar conditions. I made a face at him, a sort of clownish smile, and I asked him to make the face too. But he did nothing. I made a raspberry and asked him to make one, and he gave no response. No sound, acknowledgment that he understood what I was asking, but still displaying a level of attentiveness that would be odd for any child. Something cold and analytical about it, almost as if he was examining me.

In the end he came up short on a few of the critical questions in the diagnostic. There was something going on, but I had to tell Calvin's parents that I wasn't entirely sure what it was. It clearly wasn't childhood disintegrative disorder—which, frankly, I was sick of talking about anyway. But Calvin also didn't show any of the classic ASD symptoms, aside from the language issues, which were profound. I was at a loss, to be honest, but I was intrigued by Calvin, and I asked to see him again and run some more tests. I felt a charge inside, like something I'd lost was returning to me. It was exactly the kind of focus I needed. Exactly the sort of uncharted space I'd always wanted to explore.

MONICA MELENDEZ

HOUSTON, TX
2014

The parents drove their kids in from as far away as Odessa to take part in the study. Others registered online, sending video clips and testimonials. One man flew in from Oakland once a month with his daughter, a beautiful girl named Flora, who clung to him during the tests, burying her head in the crook of his arm. I got to know all of the parents quite well. They were so consumed—to the point of obsession, really, which was understandable. By the end of the first year we had twenty-seven families in our study.

It all happened very quickly. I remember hearing Dr. Reyes describing the symptoms to a colleague at a dinner party at the provost's house, and then a few months later we'd publicly identified the condition and had thirteen diagnosed cases at the center. It was almost as if the announcement of the thing caused all of these cases to emerge. But really, who knows how long it's been around. We might never find out how many kids were just misdiagnosed over the years, living with this condition that no one understood. I heard there's a team working out of Douglas Hospital in Montreal that's searching through medical records to try to find the earliest cases—apparently there's an account from the 1980s of a factory worker with permanent aphasia who led a relatively normal life in a small town near Ottawa. I'm willing to bet there are others, but the year we conducted the study definitely had the flavor of an epidemic. Maybe *epidemic* is too strong a word, but you get the picture. Cases started showing up across the country. It hadn't really broken to the press in a big way at that point, but the mental health community was, I remember, starting to become obsessed.

How it started was, Dr. Reyes had noticed these clusters of otherwise normal kids who seemed to have a total language impairment. They weren't on the autistic spectrum, they had normal motor development, and aside from the obvious developmental delays from the language impairment they seemed to hit all of the baseline cognitive markers for children of their age. She was interested in finding out whether there was a pattern to this oddball phenomenon. I was brought in, because at the time I was the only nurse practitioner in the Houston metro area who had experience with the Hoekman tracking device. The Hoekman is a STEM imaging helmet that can capture neural activity footage at six hundred frames per second, which allows you to get an incredibly detailed look at the whole human head in situ. You can watch a subject examine an object and see exactly what areas of the brain are processing that information. So we fitted the kids with Hoekmans and had them sit at a table in the exam room. We brought in one of their parents and had them sit across from the child. They would greet the child and ask whether it was day or night—you know, just an easy question, to see if the kids were processing the utterances as language or as pure sound. Then the parent would sing "Row, Row, Row Your Boat" and ask the child to sing along. Again, just to see what happened when the question was posed.

What we found was fascinating. The Hoekman showed us that there was a dramatic spike in neural activity in the areas of the temporal lobe where we process sounds and recognize faces, but almost no activity whatsoever in the perisylvian region, where speech is received and produced. Usually, even with a developmentally disabled kid, you'd see activity there. You'd see them trying to parse the language of the voice they heard. But the kids in our study showed no activity, even though the tissue was completely healthy. Even though there was nothing else about their brain that would cause this type of inactivity. It was almost like part of their brain had been unplugged from birth.

Once the condition had been identified, we began forming coalitions with other early-identifier doctors around the country. Avula in Richmond, Burnham in Belmont, Yu in New Haven, all sharing case studies. The data was exhaustive, but no matter how much analysis we did on the brain scans and the behavioral surveys, we couldn't answer the real question, the one the parents were afraid to even ask: Why? Why them, why their kids, why this? And just behind that: What did I do wrong? They didn't want to ask, which was a secret relief to us, because we had no clear idea.

Meanwhile, the parents formed coalitions of their own, support groups that met regularly outside of the study sessions. They weren't going to wait around for us to provide the solutions. They invited me to one of their meetings and I went because I felt I owed it to them. It wasn't at all what I expected. There were about thirty parents in the room—almost all of whom were taking part in our study—and they all took turns getting up in front of the group and projecting home video footage of their kids. Most of the footage was from before the diagnosis. Really normal stuff—toddlers on swings, kids running around the beach or sitting at the table mashing food with a plastic fork. If you didn't know what was going on with these kids, you might not notice anything unusual. But we could all see the signs hiding in plain sight. The absence of even babbling, the staring, the frequent disengagement— all of it was as clear as day once you knew what you were looking for.

The parent showing the footage would narrate, you know, "This is Joanie—I thought she was just shy." And the other parents would nod. That was it. That was the whole meeting. Later the women started a website where any parent could post this type of footage. When I went to the site, I was surprised to see hundreds more of these videos from parents all over the country. Hours and hours of footage, more than there were hours in a lifetime to watch it all—the only evidence they had of the days and months they'd spent with their kids before the diagnosis. The moments of joy and hope before the big change.

FRANCINE CHANG

OAKLAND, CA
2016

I suppose I shouldn't have been surprised that I'd have a silent student in my class. I was a first-year, so I only got one of them. I had no idea what to expect. I had no plan. Maybe I'd work one-on-one with him, give him some take-home assignments, and hope for the best. First day of class, during circle time, Colin—that was his name—sat still, and, while he seemed nervous, he wasn't wild or out of control. Really, I didn't want to think about my job at all. I wanted it to be this thing that I left on my desk, like my stapler, when I went home for the day.

"Please call me Francine," I told the children on the first day of school.

"Ms. Francine," one of the little girls said without raising her hand. "Do you have a stain on your shirt?"

Yes, I did. I held my shirt up to my nose to identify the culprit. It was yogurt, breakfast. I licked it off. I don't know which I disliked more: the little girl, for saying this out loud, or the other kids for trying to score points by telling her how rude she was. They all started arguing. You can't believe how long kids can argue if you don't intervene. I stamped my foot and said, "This is not the rodeo, you little barnacles." And then I laughed at the ridiculousness of it. They looked at me like I was insane. A blond boy raised his hand and asked, "Is this how you'll be like all year?"

"Apparently," I said. "Now who would like to take a nap?"

Wouldn't you think teaching kindergarten would be easy? Addition, subtraction, cutting stuff with safety scissors, story time, summers off. I didn't think it through. I didn't picture herding thirty-four six-year-olds, these little need-machines, kids already reading chapter books sitting next to ones who didn't know what an *h* was. They were all missing teeth and had these chaotically spelled names: Jaylenne, Beauxregard. I couldn't keep track of them. Are you the one who carries corn chips in your pocket and eats them in class? Are you the one whose dad asked me how long I've been in this country? You know that feeling you get when you're singing along with a song, but you only know, like, six of the words? That was pretty much my entire year.

I'm not a leader. I don't like being looked to or giving orders. I don't want to be the head of anything. I never played princess. I wanted to be one of the princess's maidens, who sat around while the princess did the work. But teachers can't do that. You have to look authoritative, even when you have no idea what you're talking about. Especially then.

I put Colin at a desk near mine. I actually rearranged the desks so that I sat at the back of the classroom and all the children faced the front. I spent a lot of time looking at the back of Colin's head. We worked out a mutual agreement— he could do whatever he wanted as long as he stayed seated. I wouldn't call on him or try to rescue him, and he could draw circles and rectangles on his graph paper and not make a sound. In the rowdy scrabbling of the morning classroom, there was Colin, silent, benignly silent. A perfect container for himself. He gave nothing, demanded nothing, and I adored him for that.

He liked being around other kids. He liked games, but he had trouble with the rules, which were always changing, sometimes midgame, and the kids stopped including him. He continued going outside, but he never interacted with the others. He sort of moved along the edges of whatever was going on. Pretty soon, they started teasing him—put stuff in his desk, ran away screaming "Zombie!" whenever he came near them outside. Pack animals.

Still Colin would try to follow along with what was going on, imitating his classmates. Watching him do that broke my heart. I guess it sort of soured me permanently on the other kids, as well. It made me want to have class for just Colin. We could both hang out and do our work, him with his circles and squares, and me with this series of soft-core Viking-romance novels I'd been eyeing at the public library.

A few months later he stopped sitting at his desk after the bell. He'd stand by the window, studying the trees. He lay on the floor during morning announcements. I blamed his classmates, of course.

In front of the parents we put on an enlightened face, but in the teachers' lounge it was less gentle. Mrs. Moten, who had the other kindergarten class, was always complaining. "Might as well put a jar of pennies in a chair and pretend it's a student," she said. "Or a long piece of rope."

"I feel sorry for them," one of the secretaries said. "Being deaf and mute and who knows what else. It's like when the Kennedys forced that daughter to do a lobotomy."

"They're not deaf," Mrs. Moten said. "Or mute. Just, there's a big part of their brain that's not working. And if you're going to feel sorry for someone, feel sorry for us. And the other kids."

I want to make clear: I'm not one of these reformers who takes a special interest in needy kids and makes it my duty to improve them. Who secretly dreams of the kid one day winning an Academy Award and saying, "This is dedicated to my teacher Ms. Francine, who believed when no one else did." No, give me a class of miniature adults and let us quietly learn about the solar system together. Let us eat lunch in respectful disregard.

Still, Moten was including me in this. I told her that I actually liked my silent. Ugh. "My silent." As if he were a dog or a skin condition. And *liked* wasn't the right word. I found myself irrationally sympathetic to him. In a way that I never felt toward the other kids.

He was becoming a disturbance, yes. He didn't learn anything the entire time he was in my class, as far as I could tell. But, you know, if I go down my rule board, he adhered to all but one of them. He was kind, or, he wasn't unkind. He was interested—in birds, in the tiles, in the texture of Melodeigh Carlson's hair. He was quiet when others were talking. He tried his hardest. He just didn't complete all work before going outside. But then again, I didn't assign him any work.

"Well, try having three in your class," Mrs. Moten said. "You're new still. You'll see that this isn't a race, it's a marathon."

Okay, I thought. Just kill me right now and slap that on my tombstone. I ate my lunch in my classroom for the rest of the year.

I've never been able to remember my dreams. That year, though, I began dreaming about Colin. Nothing too memorable, except once I gave the class a riddle, *A plane crashes on the border of Canada and the United States. Where are the survivors buried?*, and the other students go through the usual answers: Canada, the United States, the countries where the people come from.

And I turn to Colin, who's standing at the window watching for the robin that's nesting in the oak tree, and he looks at me and says, without moving his lips, he says, "You don't bury survivors."

Yeah, not too subtle. But that first year, my head was such a jangled mess—the dream was probably the closest thing I had to a clear thought.

He left my class over Christmas break. The principal took me to lunch before class started back, and he told me about it. He gave me a gift certificate for a one-hour mani-pedi, as a reward, I guess. I threw it in the trash of the women's bathroom.

Two months later I quit, right in the middle of the school year. When I saw parents of my students around town, I averted my eyes. I wonder how they explained it to their children. I bet they told them I'd gone to a better place, like what you say with dead hamsters and grandmothers.

EMILY ROARK

YORK, PA
2016

I didn't notice anything wrong for a while, and I think Mom and Dad liked it that way. So did I. I just thought Becca was a silly, smart, weird kid. Good weird. I mean, she is, she still is. Sorry. I'm nervous. Becca's two years older. I don't remember much from my first years, but lately I've been going through pictures, helping Mom organize them in albums. So it's like I remember.

A big thing I notice is that there's not a picture where her hands aren't somehow on me. Our mom or whoever only took pictures when Becca wasn't looking at the camera, or Becca looked away when she saw the camera come out, but she always has hands on me. Through the bars of my crib. Next to me at dinner. And in some I can't tell if she's smiling or just focusing really, really hard.

We shared toys and baths, and I wore passed-down clothes that smelled like her. Like scratch-and-sniff pumpkin. We shared a room. Two single beds with a pink nightstand between us. I remember that a lot of nights I'd wake up in Becca's bed with her. I used to dream about black mambas coming in the window, slithering over the ledge and falling into my covers.

I felt safe next to her. I knew no mambas would even dare try to come into her bed.

We played everything. I followed along, did whatever she did. Becca went through phases. The obstacle course phase, where she'd set up pinecones and other things and run through our yard touching trees and skipping in certain places, and I had to follow her. Then mythology, when all she wanted to do was go through picture books of monsters and gods. I'd sit beside her and look at the books, too. She could draw, like, anything. The minotaur. Hercules killing the lion. They were so good I thought she was tracing, but when I held the drawing over the picture it was a different size. Then cats. We'd come back from the library with all these how-to-raise-your-cat books. I guess she wasn't reading, but she would stare forever at their pictures. Then draw all the cats. Perfect cats, and each looked a little different from the one before, just like real cats. We still have the drawings.

I'm not sure what all else to say. I remember one time Becca and I were at the store, both trailing Mom. Becca was ignoring me, keeping her head down. Becca at the grocery store wasn't the same Becca. I'd heard Mom talking to Dad earlier about how she was having a hard time in her class at school and how she'd started to, in general, withdraw—I had to ask what *withdraw* meant. They said take away. Each time we went to the grocery store, more people had started to notice Becca and comment to our mom about her. Maybe they were more aware of silent kids, or maybe Becca was more noticeable.

The time I'm remembering, just as we were going into the store, an elderly woman said, "I'm so sorry," when she saw Becca.

"For what?" our mom asked.

"Oh, I shouldn't have said anything," she said before scooting off.

"I'm starting to hate people who mean well," our mom said.

After we were done shopping the woman behind us in the checkout line started talking to my mom, telling her how pretty both her daughters were, and so on.

The woman looked at Becca and said, "Wouldn't it be incredible if she just snapped out of it one day?"

"What do you mean, snapped out of it?" my mom asked.

"Like, what if a doctor figured out a word or a method that would unhypnotize them? Wouldn't that be amazing?"

"You should stop thinking out loud," my mother said. Yelled. Everything sort of stopped. The cashier clenched a bunch of trembling grapes. It was the first time I'd ever heard my mom yell.

Becca had her chin tight to her chest. She clutched my arm. I wanted her to speak right then, so the woman could see she was normal. Or draw one of her cat pictures. I wished a camera could record us when we were at home. So the woman could see what I saw—a girl who liked pretzels and mustard and superhot baths and kept her bed made. I still have those photos, but the longer I look at them, the more it looks like something's not right. Like the woman at the store was seeing something I missed.

In the car Becca gazed at her hands, which she kept folded in her lap. When we got home, I brought out the drawing pad and markers, but Becca just wanted to lie on the couch with her eyes closed. When she was like this, nobody could reach her, not even me. It scared me how easily she could detach. Mom brought her soup, and she ate it. I climbed up next to her. I wriggled around and talked like Solomon Grundy, but no matter how much I tried to force her to look at me she wouldn't.

I couldn't sleep that night. The reason was, Becca and I used to have this flashlight in our bedroom. Our dad bought it because of my nightmares. It was a small Christmas flashlight with different-colored lenses you could change out and rotate. Snowflakes and snowmen, reindeer, Christmas trees. Things like that. Becca was in charge of it. After Dad had read us a story and kissed us good night and turned out the light, Becca would shine the flashlight onto the ceiling and swivel the lens around. Green snowman, red snowman, blue. And then the next lens and the next. Always in the same order. Becca'd do it until I was totally asleep. And I never had to remind her to do it, and she never complained about it, and no one but us knew.

That night I waited for the flashlight, but it didn't come. I started crying. I was sad and scared and a bunch of other things. I felt awful. If we just stayed at home, the two of us, nothing bad would ever happen. I knew this. Becca wasn't the problem, other people were the problem. Just as I was almost all cried out, I heard a click, and then I saw the green snowman on the ceiling, then the next one, and so on. She went through all the lenses. I don't remember whether or not I slept that night, but the flashlight never turned off.

If that woman from the checkout line was watching this, she would see two girls under their covers, one with a flashlight, the other clutching a plush turtle and watching, and she wouldn't stare. Kids being kids, she'd say. She wouldn't give it another thought.

DAVID DIETRICH

DECATUR, GA
2017

Every book I read I always found some character I wanted to be. The donkey and the magic pebble: he sees a lion and accidentally wishes to be a rock, so now he's a rock. His mom and dad come once a year and eat their lunch on him. I wanted to be that donkey and that rock. I really wanted to be that rock.

In second grade all I did while everyone else filled out their math packets was draw seating charts and then lines attaching people together. The lines were for people who hung out together. Groups of friends. I wanted to figure out how they were connected. How these four made a cluster, and these three did, and so on. I had no one. Even the teacher rolled her eyes when I asked stuff like, Can you give mouth-to-mouth resuscitation to a dog? I made my seating-chart maps because I wanted to know who went with who, and why.

I first saw the silents on *60 Minutes*. That show always has the best commercials. The turkey-on-the-airplane one. Also the one with the thirsty dolphins. This episode was an exposé of this new breed of mentally damaged kid. Some thought it was one thing and others thought it was another. The doctors seemed more worried about categorizing the kids than about what to do with the kids themselves. They couldn't talk. They didn't know their names. They looked . . . I liked how they looked. They didn't care about anything. They weren't suck-ups or brownnosers. What I thought was, a few years ago these kids didn't even exist, and now tons of people were rushing in to help name their problem. Everyone knows, you give something a name and then it has power.

You're asking if I identified with the silents? I don't even know what that means. Probably. People talk too much anyway. A life of talking and you say probably three good things. Accidentally. I used to go to the library to take security stickers off of books and stick them to people's backpacks, and once I found a book called *Famous Last Words*. It was people's last words. Some of them planned for years what they would say and ended up with something completely different. "No, don't open the drapes," and crap like that. I spent a while thinking about what mine would be and came up with the best one ever. Picture me lying under hospital covers, all bony and gray, and I'm telling the doctor to come closer, closer, and then I whisper in his ear: "Blood fart."

I wanted to see what would happen if I stopped talking. At first I had to keep my hand over my mouth, but it got easier. I didn't talk in class or at home—my mom was too painkillered to even notice—and then the next day at school. Work, lunch alone, recess, walk home again. I did it four straight days. It was amazing. Barely anyone even noticed. By the end I had superhearing—like how blind people get—every tick and creak in my house, every noise in school. Our teacher, Ms. Cardiff, I could hear all her nasty stomach gurgles as she walked the rows to make sure we were being good little robots.

Then on the fifth day my mom woke me up early. "We need to talk," she said. I guess Ms. Cardiff was having me put in a class for defect kids. That's not what my mom said, but that's what it was. Did I have anything to say to that? I thought about it, then said, "Okay." It came out all crooked. My first word in four days. *Okay*. It sucked. It should've been an eagle terror-screech.

I finished the year with seven other rejects. A kid with Down syndrome who pulled his penis out through a hole in his pants when the teacher wasn't looking. Another in a wheelchair with cerebral palsy who talked about how happy he was, how much he liked stuff. I guess he was trying to be inspirational or something. I'd found my group.

Then we moved to Decatur. My mom didn't tell me why, I didn't ask. Temporarily we stayed in this run-down apartment complex, Lakebridge Estates, just us and a bunch of decrepits and an outdoor pool no one used. I swam there, and I got really good at being underwater. I let myself sink to the bottom and would stare up at the sky through the water. I could feel myself . . . changing. I wouldn't talk, and I'd sort of shuffle around underwater like I'd seen silents do on TV. I started to think, Maybe I'm becoming one. It felt natural to me, and what if it wasn't something you were born with always? No one knew anything about it. What if I was the first known person who had the ability to turn himself into one?

I rode my bike around town looking for silents. Well, looking for them and also sometimes I'd return groceries my mom bought and keep the money. Sometimes I'd ride around and pretend I was in a commercial for bikes, so I had to make it look really easy. I had no idea where the silents would be, but I knew there were lots of them. I could feel it. I wanted to find the park where they all played and introduce myself. Introduce like an organism does, not by talking. I wanted to be part of their group.

The school thing just happened, I didn't plan it. I was walking to class on the first day after the bus dropped me off, thinking how dismal my old school was, and by the time I walked into class I had my arms out and I was doing the underwater stuff. The teacher was young and she said "okey-doke" a lot, and when she saw me shuffling into class with bugged-out eyes she nodded very slowly and then clapped her hands together, way less flustered than I would have thought.

She changed my name card with another on one of the front desks, and went to check her roll book, maybe to see if there was a note about me. I didn't expect her to look so happy, but people don't always make sense. Once everyone was sitting she introduced herself, and then, right after that, me. I made a face like the lights were too bright. Mrs. Lipkin called me "a unique visitor." For the rest of the day, she didn't go thirty seconds without looking at me. I counted. Fifteen seconds, eight seconds, twenty-one seconds. She looked at me an average of once every 14.6 seconds. I turned the counting into part of my style, rocking in my seat while I did it. I had no idea how a silent would really act, but by lunch everyone in school was on board.

Some were extra nice, some clowned me. No one ignored me. They talked about me when I was a foot away, like I was out of the room. Was I dangerous? If they hit me would I hit them back? I had power. I cast a shadow. And all I had to do was nothing.

Not talking was fine, but not listening was incredible. In

Art I drew with charcoal on the wall, before PE I bumped some sports fiends into the lockers. Nothing happened.

I was surprised how long it lasted. Until just after Halloween. The first parent-teacher conference, Mrs. Lipkin told my mom how proud everyone was of me. I can imagine my mom—who'd become used to teachers saying things like, "Is David this way at home?"—saying, "Uh, why?"

Mrs. Lipkin made me stand in front of the class and confess. She was so mad she refused to look at me, and to the other kids I became double what I had been before. Zero times two. Just another part of a cold classroom, like the chalkboard, or Phileas, the terrarium turtle who soon would teach us about death. There'd be no diagnosis for me. After I confessed, I went back to being nothing at all.

THEODORE GREENE

RICHMOND, CA
2017

I did everything I could to trigger some kind of speech in Flora. It was my whole life. Time is constantly slipping away. The window is always closing. If you're not there for her, if you're not by her side for every waking hour, flooding her with words, you're not doing it right. She'll never talk, and it's because you failed to give her the things she really needed.

I was determined to live in the house after Flora was born, but it became impossible to stay there. My plan was to hold on to the place, I guess to try to keep the idea of Mel alive. I saw a point in the future where I would lead Flora from room to room telling her things like, "This is where your mom quilted your receiving blanket," and "This is where your mom and I made a hundred origami swans to hang over your crib." I couldn't handle it, though. Without that joy that Mel brought to things, I saw the house for what it was—a shabby eyesore at the end of a dangerous street in a bad neighborhood. We spent most of our time holed up inside, and the silence was just chilling. Every night I'd wake up with a jolt, convinced that I'd heard the front door smashing open, and

I would lie frozen in the king-size bed with Flora next to me in her Moses basket and wait for the intruders I imagined were in the house to climb the stairs and murder us. It felt like we were at the end of the world.

So I found a small finished basement apartment down by the highway. It was not the kind of place I ever thought I'd live in, but maybe that's what appealed to me about it. It had smooth concrete floors and little street-facing windows, and it was cool in the summer and chilly in the winter. I never went back to my job when my paternity leave was up. I just wasn't interested in seeing any of those people again. So I was in rough shape financially that first year. But then my sister's husband, who worked for the state, told me about these pallets of computers they auctioned off on a regular basis, hundreds of laptops and tablets from various state organizations that were only a few years old. I bought two pallets for cheap and started refurbishing the units to sell online. With about four hours of work I could sell a tablet for almost twice what I'd paid for it. At first I was storing so many boxes that the apartment became a maze of narrow tunnels, but gradually I worked out a system.

I put Flora in day care so that I could focus on the business, but when she still wasn't talking on her third birthday I knew I had to confront the situation head-on. Something was seriously wrong, and no one was doing anything about it. I decided to teach her at home during the day and work on computers at night. I cobbled together a learning regimen from posts I found online. Books, rumors, random suggestions— I had it all charted on an elaborate color-coded schedule. I tried everything, packed it all in, because I read that after three years it became harder and harder for a kid to learn language. I was hoping that whoever had made that observation was wrong.

Every day we went through the full regimen. There were flash-card drills, sign-language videos, vocalization exercises using audio playback and a mirror. Every couple weeks there'd be a good day, some detail I could latch on to. I remember that she got really skilled at identifying objects on flash cards. I'd put three cards out on the table and say, "Which one is the cat?" I'd point to the picture of the cow, and she'd look at me without making any expression. I'd point to the picture of the frog and she'd have the same look. Then I'd point at the cat, and she'd smile. I tried it with several different animals and with many cards at once, and almost every time she was able to pick out the card I'd said out loud. I thought I'd made this incredible breakthrough. I had visions of the two of us in that basement apartment ten years into the future, laughing about a prank she pulled at school, or naming all of the countries in Africa for her Social Studies test, or me just telling her stories about Mel over the table in the kitchenette. I posted a video of Flora doing the card identification exercise to the community site, and the parents went wild. It was real evidence that these kids could learn language.

There were other parents posting videos of their kids' progress, and we all went crazy with envy every time a new one went up. One woman posted a clip of her kid who'd been gluten-free for several months, and was uttering syllables—he was saying "chi chu chu chu chi" in response to his mother, and in a sort of sentence-like rhythm. So Flora and I immediately went on a gluten-free diet. When this didn't help things, I tried removing all plastic from the house, which another parent claimed was offgassing toxins that paralyzed vocal development. For a while we stopped eating dairy, and then there was a brief stint where I was making my own bread from a starter yeast I bought from this tax attorney in Bakersfield who claimed his kid was learning to read—somehow the enzymes activated comprehension neurons, or at least that was the idea. The bread was good but it didn't help, and neither did the root-vegetable cure that was floating around briefly. Nothing seemed to have any effect in the long run. Nobody was able to replicate the card identification exercise I'd posted, which made me feel a little surge of quiet pride until an anonymous poster pointed out that Flora wasn't looking at the cards—she spent most of her time in the video looking at my face. She could somehow tell when I was pointing at the card I wanted her to respond to. She had no idea that "cat" stood for a cat—she just wanted to make me happy. That was a dark week.

Time passed, and nothing seemed to work—the language wasn't taking root, and at a certain point I just ran out of steam. I called my parents to tell them that I was officially giving up on getting Flora to talk. I don't think I really believed I was going to go through with it—I think I wanted my parents to convince me otherwise. To, you know, tell me not to lose faith, to keep trying, whatever. But when I told them I was giving up, they barely even spoke. I think my mother said something along the lines of, "You seem so exhausted. It must be a relief, at least a little." They'd doubted me all along. Right from the moment Flora was diagnosed. And I just remember a sort of rushing sound in my ears. We were alone, me and Flora. I doubled my resolve to get her to talk. I was convinced, more than ever, that someday we'd have conversations about ancient Egypt and deep-sea creatures and the weight of Jupiter, and that no one but me could make that happen.

AUGUST BURNHAM

NEWTON, MA
2017

The urge to speak is deeply human. It's woven into our DNA, into the structures of our brains. In a very real sense, thought requires language. Without it, we can't do the kind of heavy processing required to perform any complex ordered thinking. Try to imagine making your way through a world in which nothing has a name. How could you do it? What would that world look like? How would you even know that you were "looking"? Some time ago I researched a case of a Mexican man who was born completely deaf. His parents treated him essentially like an animal. He never learned sign language, didn't learn to read lips, had no way to communicate until his twenties, when he was discovered by a psychologist who actually taught him how to sign. Throughout the rest of his life, he refused to describe the world he lived in before he learned sign language except to call it a time of darkness. He was literally terrified of it. I think about that case a lot when I'm working with these kids. They must be similarly terrified, or worse—they're not even aware of what terror is yet.

The thing that fascinated and troubled me about the phasic-resistant children in my study was that they seemed totally uninterested—or *unwilling* might be a better term—to adopt the necessary language skills, despite what appeared to be a normal, healthy brain. We can't really speak with any confidence about their intentionality, but the fact remains that these children made no progress toward basic language concepts through any of the established teaching methods we had at our disposal. They could laugh, cry, scream, make any kind of sound you could think of, but they just wouldn't cross the threshold into the world of words, no matter what we tried.

Of course, my first thought was that it must be some sort of environmental toxin. The blood work that ruled out that theory also led me to believe that the condition was viral in origin, but with very unusual characteristics. If it was, indeed, a virus, it didn't appear to be contagious, and in fact there was no easily identifiable mode of transmission. The strangest part for me, though, was that only the neural pathways governing language were affected. The rest of the brain was spared in every case and with alarming precision. And so my thought was that if I could somehow stimulate the dormant areas, I might be able to, in a sense, prime their language instincts—it would be the equivalent of jamming my foot in the door of a phasic-resistant kid's mind. Allowing them to peek through the narrow opening to the vibrant world beyond, the world of language, which I imagined would be a little like Dorothy landing in Oz. If I could just get in there somehow and trigger that activity, it might act as a way to jump-start the brain.

I developed an appliance that used remote neural-stimulation tech to apply gentle, focused currents of electricity to Broca's area—the region of the brain that typically produces speech. I managed to affect this area with enough precision to actually generate a set of reproducible utterances in the patient—not words, but a handful of distinctive phonemes. These utterances were paired with an image of something the patient liked but didn't have immediate access to. Calvin Andersen, my initial phasic-resistant patient, was the first child in the study to undertake this experiment. Calvin's parents told me that he was fond of fruit rounds, so when we fastened the appliance to Calvin's head and sat him at a table, there was a fruit round under glass just out of his reach. I switched on the appliance, which immediately caused Calvin to enunciate the phoneme /oo/. It didn't even sound as clear as I just made it sound. It was more of a throaty hum, but it was distinct and reproducible. When Calvin made the sound, we lifted the glass and slid the fruit round across the table for him to eat. We did this for two weeks. We wanted to see if eventually we could etch this association into Calvin's brain between an object and the means to indicate a desire for it. We thought that he would eventually utter "/oo/" when he wanted a fruit round, but Calvin was incapable of uttering the phoneme on his own. We couldn't generate any sort of voluntary neural activity no matter how hard we tried—and we tried very hard with several children using a variety of incentives. It was tremendously frustrating.

And yes, some of the children did eventually start making the utterances in their sleep. Sometimes for the entire night. There wasn't anything necessarily wrong with this. I mean, they were just sounds. But some of the parents were disturbed. They claimed that it sounded like their child was being choked all night long. Eventually we gave up on that approach altogether.

You asked to see a picture of my son from around this time. This is him in his soccer outfit. This was right before a match with Wakefield Middle School. Yes, I know, you can barely see the scar. But if you look closely here, you can see it sort of traversing his left upper lip. A little white crescent where the cleft used to be. We were never really worried about it. Dr. Anupam is the best craniofacial surgeon in the Northeast. But we obviously had to contend with Hector's speech issues, which were pretty serious. And, sure, as you suggested, that experience of working with a speech pathologist to overcome the challenges probably influenced my work with the phasic-resistant population. But those kids were not like Hector. The way he went from barely speaking at all to being able to read aloud with perfect diction in just a few years— you know, the way he attacked it. You could really see his dedication. He was going to talk like a normal kid or else. It was a huge inspiration for me personally and professionally, and I feel, for lack of a better term, blessed.

STEVEN GRENIER

NEW YORK, NY
2018

When Royce's big article on phasic resistance came out—fucking Royce, who was if you remember the dumb shit who "accidentally" shot his production assistant in the shoulder in Uganda—how he ended up doing a cover story for *Time* is beyond me, but the article came out and caused a sort of low-grade panic to sweep through the country. I think there were at the time only around four or five thousand cases in the U.S., but the way people were talking about it—there was a current in the air that this was just the beginning of something huge, on the scale of polio or something. The *Time* piece left a lot of questions unanswered, of course. And when people don't get answers they're going to seek out the claims of whatever charlatan is most persuasive. I knew I had to dig up that charlatan. I had to get there first. Royce could go fuck himself with his own spidery dick, if he could even find it. Thing is like a pho noodle. I'd even help him look for it if I knew how to operate an electron microscope.

An intern turned me on to this woman Kirsten Strang, who'd written an article in one of those leftist mothering magazines, if you can believe that there's more than one. The headline was something like, "Plastics Ruined My Children and Yours Are Next." Strident, over the top, just the worst kind of clichéd example of loopy overprotective parenting that was, as far as I was concerned, as much to blame for the silence as anything else. The article claimed that babies were getting exposed to a laundry list of toxins starting the minute they came out of their mothers' wombs, and that these toxins were to blame for the silence. The main culprit was a new plastic that was being used in medical equipment, toys, and kitchen products—this substance called E-11T, which was designed to biodegrade smoothly but apparently also leached small amounts of cyanide when it was first introduced. The FDA didn't even catch it, the amount was so small, but Strang heard "cyanide" and her mind was made up. In the article she stopped short of directly blaming hospitals for silence, but I saw that she was claiming this online and even offering "alternative care" out of her home, which included midwife services and vintage medical supplies made of glass and metal. I was like, "Bingo." Perfect fucking storm.

Banks and I went to Ridgedale to interview Strang and get a look at her twins, who were both silent. She greeted us on her porch, wearing an ankle-length dress and a waxed-canvas respirator, and told us that we weren't allowed to film inside the house. She said the camera emitted enough heat to offgas small amounts of mercury into the air. This was disappointing, but I agreed to her terms, thinking we might be able to sneak in some footage when she wasn't looking.

Inside, it was like a derelict's hoard. She took us into the kitchen, and there were hundreds of mason jars stacked on the table and on all the counters. Some were filled and some were waiting to be filled, and she was boiling something in a pot at the wood-burning stove. Everything in the kitchen was wood or glass or metal. She told us there were so many toxin-leaching materials in modern products, all getting trapped inside of people's houses because of the energy-efficient windows and walls and everything, that it's inevitable kids' brains are going to be affected. She knew that her children's might never be normal, but why keep poison in your house just because the damage has already been done? I shot a glance at Banks, who gave me that look, that smile without a smile. We had seriously lucked into something.

She led us into the living room, which had no television, of course, just a few wooden chairs with no cushions, because she told us that the foam they used to make the pads was incredibly dangerous. Even the lamps in the room, she showed us, were bought from a thrift store because of the fabric-wrapped cords and Bakelite fixtures. This woman had thought of everything.

Next was the twins' room. The kids were kneeling on the floor playing with marbles. We could just barely see them, because the shades were drawn and the lights were off. I knelt on the floor to try to make some sort of contact with them. They both wore blue dust masks, and they stared at me the way a doctor looks at a gunshot wound—with the utmost clinical resignation. Strang hissed and said, "You've ruined their artwork." I looked down and saw that I'd put my knee right in the center of a wild pattern of concentric marble rings. The kids didn't seem too broken up by it, but Strang took them by the arms, kind of stiffly, and led them out of the room. They stopped at the threshold and stared at Banks and me until Strang moved them along down the hall. When she was gone, Banks looked at me, and I nodded. He turned on the camera and started taking some quick footage of the two homemade beds on pine platforms, as well as the marbles and wooden blocks the kids had arranged in bizarre patterns. I pulled back the shade and peeked out over the fence to the next lawn, where there was another kid wearing a kerchief sitting on a swing, slowly gyrating with her head down. I saw that the roof of the house had been done over in slate tile and that there was no car in the driveway.

Strang came back, and I distracted her by asking how many other parents in the neighborhood were taking these measures. She started to answer but cut herself off to sniff the air. She shouted, "You were filming in here. I told you not to film in here and you filmed in here. You just put poison in the air." She chased us out of her house, calling us murderers. Some of the other families came out and watched from their porches as we got the hell out of there.

We produced the segment in such a way that ostensibly exposed Strang as a nutty extremist but also left just a little doubt in the viewer's mind, like, "My kid was born in a hospital, with all of this plastic stuff all around him, and now he doesn't speak—maybe this woman is right," you know? Just the suggestion of that opens the door for more compelling material. Strang, too, benefited in the end from the thing in that she became a sort of fringe hero for about twenty minutes, inspiring other weak-minded parents to take on her wacko ideology. I suppose we were all partners, in a way.

PATTI KERN

PACIFICA, CA
2018

M ost Benevolent Thomas gave us children when we became fully vested. Mine was a small mint cockatiel, and Most Benevolent Thomas told me not to name him, that words, especially names, were an obstruction to loving belief, the kind we're all aspiring toward. I still accept this. Did I think the cockatiel was actually my child? No, not in the literal way Most Benevolent Thomas encouraged me to. But I stared at my bird during emptying time, and centered my love on him. I believe there's truth in even the most divergent mentalities. I spent my twenties following figures with conflicted relationships to honesty, but no matter what, I always came out with a takeaway. And so now I possess a lovely bouquet of acquired belief.

I was drafted into existence to help people. We have so little time in the manifest world, and we spend most of our lives fortressing. Erecting personal walls because we are frightened. Often, when I'm out for a walk, or on my front porch waiting for a client, I'll see a neighbor or someone I don't know and I'll approach them and say, "Tomorrow is an impossibility. Today is our day."

I extend my hands for them to hold and look closely into their eyes and wait. "Any response is okay," I tell them.

They rarely take my hands. They move on, or thank me perfunctorily, but it's okay. A missed connection is still a connection. And my reaching out is what finally provided the foundation for contact with the silent girl.

Business was slow. I do personal consultations, life coaching, some play-based conferencing with children. I love my job. Advising others allows me a chance to advise myself. It centers me.

Her name was Amanda. Her mother lived a few streets over—she was someone I often called out to from my porch. I must've known she was the mother of a silent. I must've sensed it. If you spend all your life studying subtle alignments you're going to have moments like this. There was a knock on my door one morning and this woman, very open and soulful with a gingham headscarf, stood there with her daughter. I had never had the privilege of close proximity with a silent. I'd seen them on television, of course, and in public, and I thought they were wonderful, but nothing prepared me for Amanda. She looked about eight years old, but with none of the chaotic energy that most children emit. She was frightened, I knew this right away. Her eyes, which fixed very suddenly on mine, told me this. She was tired of being incompletely understood, and her tiredness would soon give way to despair. I also knew that she was intrigued by me and my meditative bearing, as well as my pleasantly eclectic living room.

The mother said, "Can you just help me with her for a little while? You seem so kind and patient and wise."

This is approximately what she said. Words are the least important part of this story. They both entered my foyer. The mother, too, seemed tired. She thanked me and gave me her phone number and left. I held Amanda's hand as we walked into the living room. She was a polite and sturdy and beautiful little girl. I poured her a glass of water without ice and gave her two flaxseed crackers.

Please don't ridicule what I'm telling you. If it helps, forget about anything that makes you skeptical. It doesn't matter. Forget how she got there. Forget the crackers. Forget me, even. I have my techniques, some learned, some instinctive. If I told you about spirit colors and constancy mapping, you wouldn't believe me about what came next, and it's important for you to believe me.

We sat facing each other on my couch. I held both her hands and I started breathing deeply—involuntarily, mind you—and Amanda stared at me and began reciprocating. In-out-in-out. We were imprinting on each other. I nodded very slowly and Amanda did the same. It moved me. I could feel my inner places hollowing out to make room for something.

"You don't need to speak," I said. "What bridges us is nameless."

Amanda continued to nod. Her pupils glowed with a pure ineradicable sincerity. Most of us keep our fires deep within our caves, but Amanda's burned in every blink of her eyes.

I extended to her a volley of fellow feeling. Amanda accepted the volley and answered simply. People are always asking me what it was she said. She didn't say anything. She emitted. She doused me with her inner stream.

When her mother arrived we were still holding hands. Amanda had fallen asleep, but we'd continued communicating.

"She's a medium," I told the mother. "She's the most beautiful thing in the world."

"What happened?" she asked.

I reached out and took her hands. "Love," I said. "Communication."

I'm not unaware of the effect I have on people. I know I alarmed this woman. It's just, I knew I had found what I'd been searching for. This kind of natural communion.

We have so much to learn from these people. You have to understand, words are just conduits. We invented them because we needed something to hook at the truth—but words have become an obstacle, a smoke screen. Even what I'm saying right now, it doesn't approximate what I actually mean. There was a time, not as long ago as you think, when we had no words. We were just pure intention and purpose and spirit and feeling. An open fire. These children were put here to return us to those days. Watch them, understand them. Meet them with love. Listen to all they're not saying.

PRASHANT NUREGESAN

ATLANTA, GA
2018

Isabelle, my niece, was diagnosed with the silence, and that was a real lightning rod for me, in that it really gave me the focus to come up with the design for the Chatter. If I see a need, the first thing I'm thinking is how to fill it. That's just me. That's how I operate. Cereal takes a long time to eat. Bang: Cereal Milk. I can't see in the dark. Bang: Light Jackets. I can't leave my cat at home. Bang: Pet Björn. I just came up with all of those concepts right now. I don't even like them. You see, though? I try not to waste too much time between the problem and the solution. That's where a lot of businesses flounder. I guess it's just my nature, you know, ever since my father. We grew up in Pennsylvania, an old industrial town, and my father owned a furniture store in an old mill building. In wintertime he noticed people weren't shopping for furniture. It was too cold out! They didn't want to leave their cars, so my father, what he did was add a drive-thru option. The store was named Nuregesan's but people called it Drive-Thru Nu's, and every weekend there would be cars backed up for blocks waiting to pass through and check out the merchandise. This was a big thing in our town, until the Raymour & Flanigan opened in Scranton and suddenly everyone wanted to go there, quality and service be damned.

I got a degree in engineering from Rutgers and started working for a company called TrendNest, which was a kind of think tank that produced patents for products that other companies would then buy and bring to market. My most successful product design there was the Dype, which I don't know if you heard of but it was an undergarment aimed at men in their early twenties who liked to party but who sometimes lost control of their bodily functions as a result. You might not think there was a need for that, but I saw many of my classmates soil themselves while at Rutgers, and it was a thing that tarnished their reputation, sometimes for good. The Dype was made with a superabsorbent four-way stretch material that was protected under a separate patent I also created. It could be branded with any sports team or popular video game or singer. Anything you could print on clothes. The cobranding is key for that segment, or really every segment.

Then Isabelle was born. An adorable little girl who had everything going for her until the diagnosis. I didn't understand much about the mind science behind emerging phasism, but I knew it was a problem for the parents and the kids and everyone else, too. I wanted to do something, to make a product that could help Isabelle and everyone in her situation. But I have a proprietary five-phase design process, okay? Discovery, Analysis, Strategy, Design, Implementation. And the discovery phase here was almost impossible, because how do you really know what these kids need? You can't know. You can't get this out of them, obviously. I had to fall back on the core principles that I apply to any product I'm thinking about designing, which are comfort, convenience, and safety.

If your product isn't somehow tied in to one or more of these, you might as well get out of the business. You've got to fill a need. Your product or service or whatever has to make someone's life easier. It's got to have some emotional tie, something that would convince a person they can't live without it. I spent a lot of time observing Isabelle, taking notes on her activities. I followed her around at the park and in the woods behind her house and at Rumpus Run, that restaurant with the illuminated treadmill. I gathered a ton of data, and when I ran it through VisChart the answer was as clear as day. The main difference between Isabelle and normal, talking kids was that they were moving their mouths and she wasn't. Maybe silent kids just weren't talking because they hadn't gotten enough mouth exercise. Just like how a weightlifter has to train for a long time before he can bench four hundred pounds, maybe these kids just needed to get their jaws and lips working a lot harder. Maybe if they understood what a mouth was for, they'd start to really use it.

So that's how I came up with the Chatter, which was a hinged mouthpiece made out of a proprietary silicone blend. The mouthpiece fit comfortably in the kid's mouth, and it would do all sorts of exercises—opening and closing, side-to-side motions, circular grinding, tongue positioning. I brought in consultants, expert people who knew the methods and techniques you find in speech therapy. And the Chatter incorporated it all. It had a bunch of settings that the parent could control via a small remote. You could technically leave the Chatter in all day and just put it on random, which is what a lot of parents decided to do, because it was so comfortable and easy to wear that the kids seemed not to mind at all.

Some parents got upset about the Chatter, because it didn't make their kids talk. But I never claimed it would do that. If you look, even on the front of the box, it says this. It's as clear as day that it was intended as a mouth exerciser. And in that spirit it was very effective. And I do think that kids got a lot out of it. And the parents, too, you know, because it did look, even at a short distance, like the kids were talking. Parents could take their kids out in public and not feel like they were being judged. I had many parents write to me thanking me for this. I don't need their thanks, but I accepted it anyway, and I feel privileged that I was, you know, that they thought of me as a sort of advocate. And I was certainly able to get my business off the ground as a result. The Chatter was just the first of many products I developed to help that community. Helping those people cope became my core competency, if you will. Right in my wheelhouse.

NANCY JERNIK

TEANECK, NJ
2019

Spencer got kicked out of school. Or, they dismissed him from the school, which apparently they had every right to do, because they were a private institution, which was—I mean, I was paying for the school and they still kicked him out? I'd been getting these papers in his cubby. Incident reports, they called them. They would be like, *The teacher's aide was removing Spencer's snow pants when he bit her and did not seem to understand that this is not allowed*, or, *Spencer punched another student in the back and didn't apologize or express remorse.* I specifically remember them using that term, as if he was capable of expressing remorse. And there was no more information than that. No suggestions for working on the behavior. No advice. What was I supposed to do? I couldn't monitor him day and night, and wasn't that the school's job? He got a lot of these incident reports, so many that I guess one day they decided they'd had enough. I'm sure they were just looking for an excuse to get rid of him anyway. I had this sense that they looked at him as a walking vegetable, just this mute kid silently sucking up all their time and resources.

They gave up, if you ask me. They just assumed he was never going to learn like the other kids. Never going to adapt. And I ran out of arguments to keep him there, because I think that underneath it all I essentially felt the same way.

So we had nowhere to put Spencer, which was pretty much the main thing that made me lose my job at Yan Talan. The HR person said it was just because of what had happened on Wall Street the previous quarter, but I know that it was because I'd lost so much productive time staying at home with Spencer. I'd worked out a complicated child-care schedule with Ron, but he had just joined the nanofiber start-up and he was away all the time, and it was impossible to find a special-needs nanny in the dead of February. With my job, you know, it's all about meeting with people face-to-face. Every day in the office was like a long conversation that started when you entered the building and didn't end until you were home again, asleep—assuming you could sleep. Assuming you had time to sleep. That's just advertising. That's how it works. You can't phone it in. Which I found out in a big way.

So then I was alone in the house with Spencer every day, from six forty-five in the morning to about eight at night. Ron was usually gone before either of us woke up, and he didn't come home until after Spencer was asleep, which seemed a bit too convenient, but whatever. I'd wake up and lie in bed just waiting until I could hear Spencer moving around in the next room. He used to come in our bedroom when he woke up. He'd slide up next to me and bury his head in the crook of my neck, and we'd look up at the ceiling fan and watch it spin. When he got kicked out of school, he stopped coming into our bedroom, though. I'd lie there waiting for him, craving the smell of his messy, unwashed head of boy hair, because that was the only time in the day when I felt close to him at all. It was the only acknowledgment he gave me that he cared who I was. But instead he'd just sit on the floor in his room, moving marbles around. It wasn't only that—Spencer changed in lots of ways once he got kicked out of school. He must have known, somehow, that he'd been rejected. He stopped doing things for himself, like getting dressed or brushing his teeth or going to the bathroom. I had to basically dress him myself if I wanted to go anywhere. He just seemed to be slipping back into a younger state, and it seemed like it was on purpose. Like he was doing it to me.

After a while of doing this—of sort of having to be his maid—I got sick of it. I had no part of my life that was really my own. Everything I did in a day was in the service of Spencer. I was feeling starved for some kind of space where I had control, something that was mine and no one else's. The idea to start dressing Spencer up came out of that feeling of desperation, I think. I had this beautiful yellow Shirley Temple dress that I wore when I was flower girl for my mom's second wedding, and I just decided to put it on Spencer one morning. He looked down at the dress and seemed to be—well, he didn't try to take it off, and that's about all I had to go on, so I kept evolving the project. I had a few other outfits I'd saved from when I was younger, and I put them on Spencer, as well. But I couldn't stop there. I became, I guess, fixated on dressing Spencer up and putting him in these scenarios from my childhood. Almost like I was a director or a set designer or something. I mean, that's really what I started to think of myself as. Like one of those famous photographers, like the woman who took pictures of those insane-asylum people. I put Spencer in these scenes and took pictures of him. And he let it happen, so I assumed he was okay with it. Looking back, I can see how I was starting to take it too far by going on all of those shopping trips, but nobody understands how hard it is to sit in a house and have your child's breathing be the only sound.

One day I saw that the horses from a carousel I rode when I was a girl were being sold off. I tried to get Spencer to go with me, but he wouldn't leave the house no matter what I tried. "I'm going to leave without you," I said, like you know how parents always say to get their kids to start moving? But, of course, he had no idea what I was trying to say. So I actually did it. I just left him there. I was only going to be gone a couple hours, and when I came back he was under his bed as usual, rolling marbles along the seams in the floorboards, wearing the purple jumper with the smiling cat pattern. He was fine, so I started leaving him in the house for longer periods. I was feeling, finally, like I was doing something important. I had these photographs, and I felt like I was learning something about myself. But one day I came back from an estate sale and there was a sheet of plywood nailed over the front window. I went inside and there was a cop sitting on our living room couch writing something on a pad. He told me about Spencer punching though the window with his bare fist. Apparently a neighbor saw it happen. He shattered the glass, and I guess when he pulled back his arm after the impact a shard just slid through him. I saw a big smeared blotch of blood on the carpet by the window, which is where the cop told me the neighbors had found him. The cop said that Spencer was at the hospital, that they were operating on his arm, which was torn up pretty badly. I asked him what was going to happen next, and he sort of shook his head.

DCYF put Spencer in Barrowbrook, which was an institutional facility out on the edge of Brooklyn—apparently it was the place where all those kids went. Because it was my first offense I was just put into a rehabilitation program for abusive parents, which I breezed through because I wasn't one of those people. If you want to call what I did "abuse," then I guess I can understand, but all I did was give both of us the thing we really wanted, which was to be as far away as possible from one another.

DAVID DIETRICH

DECATUR, GA
2019

I finally found them. Downtown there was an indoor grave-yard of airplanes called the Air Zoo. I borrowed my mom's MasterCard to buy an annual membership. They called it an interactive museum, but it was nothing but aerodynamic facts and seven-minute movies. I went there a bunch. The silents were always with families: moms all desperate, dads just blurry, brother, sister, and then a silent. They went there after school, like me. Seemed like their parents treated them the same as their brothers and sisters. Like they were hungry, interested. At least they treated them that way for a while.

I loitered every day until dinner. This was about the time my mom was dating the albino, and she forgot who she was. And who I was. The albino said he was a magician, but he never showed me any tricks. My mom listened to these pod-casts he gave her—*A drop of nothing from nothing is nothing*—and stopped eating anything cooked or red. Who knows what else they did. Probably some sex things. She never asked me where I'd been. I wouldn't have told her. At the Air Zoo I could pass myself off as a silent.

If Korean kids go back to Korea after being in the United States for a while, the other Koreans know. Doesn't matter what the Korean is wearing or how good his accent is, they can tell by looking at his face. When I first started, I only cared about fooling the nonsilents, because I didn't know any silents, so I overdid it. I wiggled my fingers, bugged out my eyes. Silents aren't silent, it's a dumb name, but my movements were way too loud. I wanted people to notice. It was embarrassing. With silents, it's all about their intensity. Intense concentration and intense calm and intense everything else. I've studied them more than anything, I probably know more than anybody. Intense eyes, mostly, and shoulders and arms and chest, legs, and feet. All over, I guess. I tightened myself, made it restrained. I stared in the bathroom mirror until I didn't recognize myself.

I've trained myself to do a lot. I can eat the same meal for months. I have. I do. Breakfast cereal, I'm not going to tell you which one, with rice milk on it. I went to the Air Zoo five days a week. I interacted with the silents. I fully occupied their space. I trained myself to forget which word went with which thing. I wanted to unword all of it. It got so I could look at my bike and manually separate those four letters from the physical object. I stared so long at words they broke apart. I wrote *fruit* two dozen times on my biology folder until it disintegrated into nonmeaning. It was freed. I did it with *donkey, school, mother*. With my own name. *David David David David David David David David David David David.*

At the Air Zoo there's a fake *Enola Gay* in a warehouse-size room, and the guard didn't bug me there. When I used to wander the whole museum, he'd kick me out, grab my arm way too hard, and call me "zombie" and "retard," but I sent a really good e-mail to the museum director like I was my dad and told them that if they didn't want a full-on silent boycott, to leave me be. I always saw silents in the *Enola Gay* room. Whenever I saw one I would walk up close to the family and follow them like I was with them. I was so good. The parents recognized what was wrong with me right away and commented on it, or nudged each other, and sometimes waited to see what would happen between me and their son or daughter. Usually nothing. Sometimes something. That something ranged from quick eye contact to other moments I have no interest in telling you about. I don't have to tell you everything. I'll just say that once or twice I was able to hold hands with one of the silents. Okay, I'll also say that another time one of them put her hand on my face. Oh, and one took Fireball Haley's helmet off of its stand and handed it to me and I put it on, and then the security guard kicked me out again, but gentler. And once a silent girl almost fell over an escalator rail onto some war planes and I stopped her. I held her body and guided her back up.

The parents and other people were fooled, but I had the feeling that the silent kids weren't. I don't know. Sometimes it seemed like they were playing along. I didn't care. It was one of the first times I had a permanent feeling about myself.

But more and more, I noticed that the parents started to seem annoyed. Not just with me but their own kids too. They pulled their children through the museum quickly, from exhibit to exhibit, and then they left. Lots of heavy sighs. They stopped pretending they were normal families.

And then they stopped coming at all. It didn't happen all at once. At first I tried to figure out where they were going instead. I mean, the Air Zoo's a pretty crappy spot. Maybe word had spread. Maybe they were at the Fernbank Museum or the park or something. It was like before, when I'd ride my bike around town looking for them. But I could hardly find one anywhere.

I went onto some silent message boards, where parents chatted and asked questions. *I know this is off topic*, I wrote in one of the threads about life expectancies, *but the Air Zoo is a really fun place for silents and their families to go. I'd totally recommend it.*

It didn't work. Turned out that the silents were being pulled from the schools. The parents were giving up. Sending their kids away so they didn't have to think about them anymore. Special residential facilities, they called them. First a few kids here and there, then a mass retreat. I didn't even want to think about what those places looked like, but I dreamed about them. Prisons. Windowless. One day the silents and me were all together, a rogue army, and then it was just me, again, riding around on my bike. Stealing chromies off cars just for something to steal. Trying to figure out why I always lost.

The last day I went to the Air Zoo I sat by the fake *Enola Gay* and waited, in case one of them might show. Fat tourists plodding around me. Before, I had been afraid of most people, but now I was starting to just not like them very much.

A pair of twins wearing matching hats laughed at the name of the airplane. They thought the word *gay* was funny. *Gay* didn't mean *gay*, I wanted to tell them. It didn't mean happy. It meant less than *Enola*, nothing.

On my way out of the museum I found the security guard eating pretzels out of a can, and I told him that I was going to come back with a whole bunch of my silent friends and we were going to burn the museum to the ground. While he was inside. They weren't gone, I told him. They were getting organized. They were silently plotting his doom.

THEODORE GREENE

RICHMOND, CA
2020

The day that our school opened was hard for me. I know
it shouldn't have been. I know it was the thing I'd been
working for, the thing that all of us had struggled to get up
and running. I can't tell you how many times we sat in those
city council meetings waiting to be heard. Flora sitting next
to me, drawing concentric circles in her spiral notebook. All
of that time we spent developing the curriculum, sorting out
logistics, an insane amount of work that we all did on top of
our regular jobs. Raising the money to buy the old bakery
on Myrtle and converting it ourselves. Everyone working
together, just pouring all of our energy into the place, day
after day. I was actually hanging sheetrock, which I had no
idea how to do. All of us were driven by that hope, you know,
that the school would save our children. I think that's what
made it come together so quickly.

Flora had been making progress in our apartment. There
was no actual speech yet, but she was engaging with the lessons, doing the activities I developed for her. I could get her
to open and close her mouth, to roll her jaw and move her

tongue from side to side. I even got her to make a few sounds, letter sounds that she was sometimes able to repeat. These were seen as great victories by other parents. They watched videos of her doing these things and got inspired. They started to contact me, asking for advice and techniques, and I told them everything I was doing. A few of the other parents lived nearby and we started to get together, and the idea of the school quickly caught fire.

But by the time the school was finished and ready for students, I felt like . . . I mean, it never came to the point where I gave up on Flora completely. I still felt like there was an answer out there. I knew her mind was active. But she just wasn't changing. Or, if she was changing, it wasn't in any way that was improving her condition. Physically she was fine, and she was even starting to help me out with basic motherboard repair, but she wasn't any closer to talking than she was when she was three. And so when I was standing out in front of the school, holding her hand, I felt a—I'm going to call it a sagging. Of the spirit. When you get that heaviness in your chest. It hit me suddenly that we'd essentially just built this temple to our own fears. It didn't have anything to do with the children. I mean, it did, of course. It did. We really did believe that our kids would learn there. And just having them be together—to be around other kids like them. All of that would help. But it wasn't only about the children. It was about us, the parents. The school building was this crazy clown house that we were using to keep us focused on the future, on this dream of the day when we believed our kids would be normal, where they could talk to us, tell us what was going on in their heads. Instead of the present, which was where our kids were sort of dead. Walking dead.

Or maybe it was just me who felt like this. All the other

parents did seem happy enough. And the Oaks building itself was warm and inviting. I walked Flora to her classroom, which had walls and countertops I'd built myself, and I brought her to her rug area on the floor and spread the marble works out in front of her. Her teacher Ms. Chang came up and put a hand on Flora's shoulder to introduce herself. I was sort of taken aback by her—not only because she was younger and more attractive than I'd expected from seeing her application, but because she instantly knew how to act with Flora. They seemed to bond in that first moment, and I felt a little better knowing I was leaving my daughter in the hands of this well-trained expert. And I walked out of the school and drove home to the apartment, and for the first time I spent the day there myself. Sitting with the piles of chips and optic fiber and other silicon junk. And I could actually hear her absence. The silence had a vacuum quality to it. I know it sounds weird, but I think my sense of hearing was actually different, more sharp or something, for having spent so many years with no one but Flora. Her presence had a warmth, a texture. I could sense, in this palpable way, from moment to moment, that she was not in the apartment. I remember almost laughing. Not that it was funny, but just because I'd worked as hard as I possibly could to build that school and all I'd done was send her away from me.

FRANCINE CHANG

OAKLAND, CA
2020

My first week at the Oaks School I went in with this vague sense of righteous indignation—like, it was me and the kids and together we were going to show all the skeptics how wrong they were. But that didn't last. At orientation I was given a binder of newspaper articles, diagrams of cortexes, anecdotal evidence, firsthand accounts, to show what we were working against. I skimmed them. God, it was depressing. Dr. So-and-So says the silents are incapable of what we would describe as thought. They possess no language, no symbolic vocabulary. And Professor XYZ declares that without some new procedure, or miracle intervention, these children will be profoundly retarded, if not permanently defective, by age eight.

I'd been without a job for a while, too long. After I quit teaching at Clarendon, I did temp work, walked dogs, waited tables. Then came the opening at the Oaks School, the first all-silent school in the Bay Area, one of the first in the country. I hadn't forgotten a minute of that terrible kindergarten year, but I remembered Colin and how he seemed different, so I decided . . . I don't know what I decided, exactly. Mostly I needed to pay my rent.

Two months into the school year, between Halloween and Thanksgiving, three of the four teachers at Oaks basically quit. They still showed up, they continued eating their microwave lunches in the faculty lounge, but in class they mostly sulked. The clay therapy, the massages, the marbles, the recognition exercises—none of it worked. It felt like praying, a big wish into an empty space. The others contented themselves with teaching the kids how to sit still, in alphabetical order, for hours.

It's ridiculous how long I held out. I won't pretend I was nobler or imbued with a higher purpose than the other teachers. Yes, English is my second language and I was made fun of when I was in elementary because of my pronunciation and how my mom packed my lunch with tins of putrefied kimchi that other kids thought was gross. It *was* gross. I'm over it now. Maybe I was just more stubborn than the others. In class, one day I'd think we were making major progress, like when I came in to find them all starting their recognition exercises without prompting, and the next I'd have to pantomime what I expected of them, or distract them from looking at each other instead of me. I was working against this ineffective new curriculum but also the novelty of them being together, more or less for the first time, with other kids who were like themselves.

But I was okay with it. I wasn't a savior, and the kids didn't expect me to be. I understood what it was like to flail at something. To fall short of other people's expectations.

One student, Flora, seemed the most receptive. I think she was used to the curriculum, and her dad was superinvolved, and maybe she's proof that you can be born confident, silent or not. If there was a leader of the classroom, it was her, not me, and when I was at my wit's end I'd gesture to her and say to the other seven students, "See Flora? See her? Act like Flora." Not my proudest pedagogical moment.

Item by item, we abandoned the curriculum. I didn't tell my fellow teachers—I wasn't about to marinate with them in their constant gleeful misery during lunch. But the clay therapy was stupid. It seemed like something designed for photo ops. I replaced it with Ms. Chang's Magical Musical Hour. I'd pull up some symphony or concerto over the speakers, and I—this is embarrassing, but I danced around the classroom and stood the kids up and invited them to do the same. And they did! They danced and hopped around and laughed. The other teachers acted like the kids were deaf, and their classrooms were total silence factories all day—but these kids were completely tuned in to noise, whether they understood or not.

They could pay attention when they wanted to; they could understand when I was mad, or frustrated, or pleased, and react to it; and they were intensely interested in each other. Once, during music hour, I noticed Keith and Laura, who were probably the two worst students in the class, marching rhythmically to Puccini and staring at each other, looking like . . . well, in normal circumstances, I'd say it was a flirty stare. I danced over to them, just to get a closer look, and they quickly stopped.

I saw this more and more, this intense mutual attention. Not just with Keith and Laura, and not just boys and girls. During recognition exercises, during recess. They stared at each other, I stared at them, we all sat quietly until 3:30 and then went home.

Meanwhile, the other teachers were burning out. When Mrs. Mullins quit monitoring lunch to spend more time nap-ping in the teachers' lounge, they needed someone to take the cafeteria. Mullins was a small-time tyrant, and she had created this lunchroom atmosphere that went past orderly into state-prison territory. I don't know how she did it. There were forty students in the school, and they sat in groups of ten at four big round tables, four circles of silents. Looking back, I think these round tables did more for the kids than anything we tried in the classroom.

Anyway, I volunteered to do lunch. Mostly I just wanted to get away from the other teachers. I sat at a table by myself, the cold dead sun to the four planets of silents. I drank coffee and read. In any other school I'd have a stack of papers in front of me to grade, but here I could just sit with a soft-core novel about interspecies love on a forbidden planet and relax. The kids ate purposefully and continued the staring and threw their food away when they were done. This is how it went day after day. Pretty soon I stopped paying attention. Months of pleasant oblivion passed.

Until the day of our annual self-study. Even though the principal, Mr. Haskins, said the study was just a formality, the other teachers were stressed. Turns out, as much as they complained about their jobs, they had no desire to go back to a normal school, where they'd have to actually teach.

Mr. Haskins was touring the lunchroom, so I had to abandon my novel for the day. Sometimes Haskins seemed almost human, other times he was this ugly remorseless machine of jurisprudence. He was in machine mode that day, making the kids get up from their chairs so he could check if the floor was clean. This is how it happened: he was crawling around under one of the tables, hunting for crumbs, and then I saw Keith slyly pouring out his chocolate milk on the other side. Baiting the trap. Mr. Haskins crawled around some more, wriggling around on the floor army-style because the tables were so low, and when he came back up, the front of his white dress shirt was covered in chocolate milk. He looked down at the shirt and let out this spastic huff of air.

I was staring at Flora, who kept glancing under the table. She turned to Aileen, a girl in my class, and I saw it . . . like a brief surface ripple across her face. Perceptible only because I had looked at Flora so much. And then Aileen smiled just short of laughing. Okay, I said to myself, that's new. I could feel my heart beating clear to my spine. Aileen glanced under the table just like Flora had. She looked across the table at Keith and Laura, whose backs were to me, and I saw something similar happen in Aileen's face. That brief ripple, like fog across a mirror. I couldn't believe it.

Keith and Laura smiled too.

This was it. This was the moment I knew. They had begun communicating.

VOLUME TWO

KOUROSH AALIA

OAKLAND, CA
2021

The discovery at the Oaks School only confirmed what we'd suspected all along—that our brains are much more flexible and adaptable than any computer or machine. Brain plasticity, we call it—seamlessly repurposing cognitive real estate depending on the needs and abilities of the individual. Blind people, for example, adapt their visual processing networks to process tactile information, and sometimes even develop qualitatively new skills like echolocation.

What, then, is the compensation when the individual is born without language? The language instinct is so fundamental to our self-conception that it's nearly impossible for us to imagine life without it. We can close our eyes or cover our ears and guess what it's like to be blind or deaf, but how could we begin to imagine ourselves without words? I'm not sure it's possible, and yet that is the daily reality for these silent children—children who, whatever their disability, must on some level crave communication and fellowship just as much as the rest of us.

So we see the collision of a profound hunger, a profound limitation, and a profound adaptability. And now for the first time, in these specialized schools and facilities, these children have found themselves in a community of like minds, minds as strange and hungry as their own. It's an unprecedented set of circumstances, an ideal starting point for an unprecedented flowering of alternative communication.

And this is what we've witnessed, first at the Oaks School and quickly elsewhere—a form of nonlinguistic communication with a depth and breadth that continues to surprise us. We are only just beginning to unravel the inner workings of the communication, but the central locus appears to be the children's faces—hence the inaccurate but understandably popular term "face-talking." The field of microexpressions has been gaining prominence for the past thirty years, generally via easily quantifiable, arguably gimmicky uses such as lie detection. The communication between these kids operates on similar principles, but at a level of precision and subtlety that quickly exposed the shortcomings of the FACS taxonomy. What's most compelling, perhaps, is not the strangeness of the phenomenon but rather the *familiarity*—the children are doing something we all do every day, gathering information from each other's faces and actions, constantly, intricately, and often to an extent far greater than we're conscious of. It's not a language—glares and smiles are not nouns and verbs—but it is a rich form of communication nonetheless, capable of conveying emotional nuance more accurately, deeply, and immediately than any proper language could.

Typical human thought processes are deeply interwoven with language, as we all know, and patients suffering from aphasia often also display difficulties with categories, memory, and other cognitive faculties that have been constructed around a scaffold of language. But remember, aphasia is about the *loss* of one or more functions of the brain. These silent children never had language to begin with, so their brains evolved from the start using a very different set of tools. *Tools* may not be the right word, of course—words in general are unreliable narrators in these attempts at explanation. The existence of these children and their unusual skills, however, does not depend upon our ability to explain them, and we must have the humility to accept realities beyond our understanding.

These children, then, have met the deep human need for social interaction by capitalizing on the brain's natural compensatory abilities—effortlessly and unconsciously, resulting in a form of communication we can only grasp through analogy. What does sonar feel like to a bat? What does a scent look like to a bloodhound?

This phenomenon represents the greatest opportunity for linguistic research since Nicaraguan Sign Language. I'm waiting eagerly for the charges against me to be dropped so that I can get back to my study of Bay Area silent schoolchildren. I'm not really at liberty to speak about my case at this point, but anyone who takes even a cursory glance at the evidence will see that I was living in the ventilation system of the Oaks School purely in the interest of science, and that I took great care in setting up the observation cameras so that the identities of the children would be kept confidential. Check the line-of-sight diagrams and you will see that not one of the cameras offered a clear view into any of the bathroom stalls. Only a deeply cynical imagination would interpret my routine fieldwork as any kind of invasion of privacy, which is why I'm hopeful that I'll soon be released from custody, and can continue to document this incredible, existential transformation, which is happening in real time, right before our eyes.

PATTI KERN

PACIFICA, CA
2021

No, I wasn't surprised to see the news from the school across the Bay. I'd already been conducting many silent communions of my own. Once, at the fabric store, I knelt down in front of a remarkable little boy hiding among velvet draperies. He was really experiencing these draperies, rubbing them against his cheeks and neck. I waited until he was done, and then, when he emerged, I reached out my hands for him to hold on to, and he did. I looked into his eyes, which were blue with bursts of green around the pupil, and I wordlessly conveyed to him that he could draw from my stream. He could have whatever he needed of me. And he emitted his deep appreciation of this.

I didn't realize it but the boy's mother was standing directly behind me. I stood up and opened my arms for her to hug me, but she was carrying a long bolt of gingham.

"He's going to teach us all so much," I told her. "He already is."

She lowered her free hand, and the boy took it. He was

still transfixed. He hadn't taken his eyes off me. "Please don't touch my son ever again," his mother said.

"I won't need to," I told her. "Our exchange of truths is complete."

There were other breakthroughs, many small ones orbiting a single larger reality. The parents never fully understood. How could they? They were so obsessed with teaching their children to speak, to normalize, to be like us, that they couldn't see what the children really were, couldn't hear what they had to teach us. The parents tried to lock their kids in those jails disguised as schools—but the silents were irrepressible. They used their confinement as an opportunity for a greater communion.

We're taught at a very young age that memories and emotions are somehow less valid than actions. I reject that. If you've ever made love in the backseat of a small car, and then, very soon after, made love on a blanket in a forest with warm rain coming down, you know what I'm talking about. Same action, more or less, but different energies, different emotions, so a manifestly different experience. I've spent years following various charismatic figures, each making one claim or another on me, and what they've all done is taught me the folly of mediation, the barriers between us.

The moment I first connected with a silent, I knew that we were on the cusp of discovering the true language. Call it heart-speak, call it universal communication. We were on the verge of understanding that words were waterlogged boxes—unsuited to contain the meanings inside. With the true language, intention and meaning and expression are all one.

Some recognized it as a new psychic language, others said it was involuntary facial nervousness. I watched their teacher try to describe what she'd seen, but she didn't have the words for it. No one does. All of the speculation was so misdirected.

I wished someone from the news would've asked me. No, I don't necessarily think I'm the one who started the silents communicating, but perhaps I helped project it further. Ideas are always breathed into life by multiple creators, and I was among them. Was it just coincidence that the breakthrough happened within twenty miles of my house? The moment I heard the news, I felt—not knew, felt—beyond doubt that this is where it'd all been leading me. I'm not a planner—I was taught you disrupt the natural rhythm of the day when you impose too rigid a structure—but I began to make plans.

The gatherings at my house were an organic occurrence. I talked about the silents to anyone who would listen, and also to many who wouldn't, and after a while a congregation of sympathetic individuals began to arise. There were about ten of us: massage therapists, disillusioned missionaries, an ex–merchant marine . . . but those are labels. We all united over a hunger for kinship with the silents. We met on Tuesdays.

We began to hone our own silent speech. Our goal was to be ready once we made contact with the silents, once we had that access. I tried to teach the group what I knew, not verbally, but through silent deliberative projection. We sat in a circle on the floor and stared intensely at each other. Women weren't allowed to wear any makeup or earrings, men had to shave their beards. I wanted our language to arise out of nothing, out of that pure well of nothingness, and be born. We didn't even assign partners, we just locked in on whomever we were getting the strongest tremors from. With me it was often Patrick, a freelancing spine consultant—I could feel an aspirational quality to his eye contact. We sat there for as long it took, and when we were done we shared our findings.

"I felt fondness coming from you," Patrick said one evening. "I was returning it, did you sense it?"

"No," I said, even though I had. "I was trying to convey a sentiment about tolerance."

The former missionary said to his partner, "Are you hungry? Were you trying to tell me you're hungry? I sensed a hunger."

"I am, now that you mention it," his partner said, excited. "I didn't even know it. The language was communicating without me!"

"Was anyone in here thinking about the St. Louis International Airport?" the massage therapist asked.

There weren't major communication breakthroughs at our gatherings, just little ones, and this was okay. We had no clue as to what the future would hold but, like I said, I began making plans. My landlord found out I'd been doing consultations at the house, which apparently was illegal, and so he was trying to evict me. But not only did I not need my house, I didn't want it. I began devising plans for a new community, a new way of life.

AUGUST BURNHAM

NEWTON, MA
2021

I was as surprised as anyone to turn on the news that evening and hear that phasic-resistant children were "talking." Maybe even more surprised than the average person, seeing how I'd been studying them closely for the previous nine years, probably more closely than anyone else in my field and certainly more thoroughly than a few schoolteachers. I'd spent over half of my professional career working with these kids every day, and that's long enough to know that what these self-proclaimed experts were calling communication—the evidence that supposedly revealed that these kids had some sort of "secret intelligence"—was perilously weak. But this is what always happens, isn't it? A few influential people see what they want to see and have the means to spread the word, and suddenly they've got everyone in the country believing in this fantasy.

The fact is, I'd already been observing these peer-to-peer facial tics for over a year before the incidents that led to this "breakthrough" were announced on the news. I'd even presented video footage of the phenomenon at NAN in Seattle. There were two boys in my study who would always pass each other in the waiting room when one's session was over and the other's was beginning. I saw that they spent an awful lot of time just looking at each other, lingering on one another's faces, and while the parents commented on how cute it was that the boys were so fond of each other, I saw that they were altering their expressions just slightly. Almost imperceptibly. I started to study the children in pairs after that, and then in small groups. I had plenty of kids in my study back then, a lot of really useful data. But then it became a news phenomenon and everything changed.

I'm sorry if I sound like a jilted lover here. That's not my point. What I want to get across is that even though this behavior might look like communication—and yes, phasic-resistant kids have worked out a way to pass certain types of basic information among one another—it just doesn't have the potential to escalate. All animals communicate—even the branches of a coral reef have a fairly complex weblike biological communication system. So it's not surprising to me that we'd eventually see these kids make contact with each other. But the level at which they're communicating doesn't have the structural underpinnings needed for a language, or at least not the kind of sophisticated language that would enable these kids to, say, discuss politics or write an essay. The human face just isn't expressive enough to accommodate an ordered system of arbitrary symbols, which are the building blocks of any true language. Look at it this way: our faces weren't evolved to convey language. They're just not the right tool for the job, just like you wouldn't use a hammer to cut a pane of glass. The only way these kids are going to be able to speak is if we find a way to restore the parts of their brain that process language. It's as simple as that.

Of course, this is not the kind of thing parents want to hear. They want hope, but more important, they want results. And the kind of hope I was offering at the time was too far off in the future for them. It was too long a road, working steadily toward a real systemic solution. I've always believed that this condition could be reversed, but when all of this talk about peer-to-peer communication started happening, many parents stopped thinking about a cure. Maybe they felt that after a few years of the SpeakNow curriculum or one of the other schools that were springing up, their kids were suddenly going to be reading and understanding Shakespeare. I understood the appeal of it. I understood why they stopped coming to sessions. They were more interested in the short-term gains of the schools, whatever that amounted to, and I let the first few go without argument. But after a certain point the hospital cut the budget for my lab, and I suddenly had to make do with half the patients and a quarter of the resources. And it was a struggle just to keep the remaining families in the program. It was ludicrous.

I still get angry when I think about that period. I had to play nice, to appear to the parents like I was exploring the facial communication therapy. I had to get into bed with the people who'd come up with this half-baked theory, even as they were slowly dismantling my credibility as a doctor. I had to do a lot of things I'd rather not have done, just to hold on to the rapidly vanishing funds that kept the lab afloat. It was a very caustic environment, and this was right around the time that Bruce left me, as well, so that wasn't helping things. He moved to Brooklyn when the resident he was fucking got a job at Brookdale. Which meant that I was always at the train station shuttling Hector back and forth. Hector didn't say much about it, but I knew it was killing him inside, to have to live two lives like that. Predictably, his grades started slipping and—you know how they say bad things come in threes? This felt like maybe nine or ten.

FRANCINE CHANG

OAKLAND, CA
2022

I couldn't control myself in front of the cameras. I twitched. I sweated. Did I think the silents were on the verge of speaking? Could I show the viewers at home what face-talking looked like? Or at least theorize about what they were talking about? The worst was when I went on the *Twenty-Four-Hour NewsHour*. They talked about the same thing they always did—plasticity, nonlinguistic communication, microexpressions, on and on. The host said something about "plumbing the emotional depths of these pliant youths," and I tried not to snicker.

And then my own face began to involuntarily twitch, and when I glanced in the monitor I could see a streak of black marker on my cheek, below my eye. I mean, I could *feel* it. So I started trying to subtly rub it off with my hand. Meanwhile, all the experts were agreeing with each other: the silents weren't just equal to us, they were probably better, maybe the best thing ever.

Which was fine and all, but there was a big black line on my cheek, like war paint. I don't know how it got there, but

I could see it clearly in the monitor now. And, plus, I looked feral. Like something that belonged underground. My lips were as shiny and moist as digestive organs. I was wearing a dress I bought at the mall, after asking a saleslady at a department store if they had any clothes that might look good on TV. After a long pause she said, "Oh, you want something *slimming*."

The host said, "You okay, Miss Chang?" I was rubbing at my cheek with my shoulder, trying to scrub the marker off.

"I've got something, marker, on my cheek," I told him. I could see both him and the communication expert, squinting at their monitors. "Right here," I said, pointing at my cheek.

The two men insisted that they didn't see anything. They sounded so condescending. I said, "Look, if I'm going insane, just tell me. Don't coddle me."

After six more agonizing minutes, the show ended, and I went into the bathroom and looked in the mirror—nothing. Not a mark on me. Either I'd successfully rubbed it off, or the mark was on the monitor, or . . . oh, I don't know.

I can't remember why I agreed to go on TV. In the aftermath, when everyone was so excited, skeptical, fixated, overreaching, plenty of people billing themselves "nonverbal communication experts" handed out predictions. Principal Haskins was one of them. He called what the kids were doing "Oaks School Face Language."

"We plan to study it," he said, "and develop a vocabulary, and in a year or two we'll be teaching fourth-graders long division with this exciting new language." He always concluded with the line, "We've finally found the key to unlock the mystery of these special children."

I didn't agree. Don't misunderstand, the kids were thriving around each other. After the discovery in the lunchroom,

I had a little pull at Oaks, so I lobbied to add a second recess and extend lunchtime, until the school day was half class, half nonclass. By the end of that first year it seemed like all the kids were communicating, the ones who'd learned early teaching the ones who hadn't. It was remarkable.

The face-talking—as I guess I too was now calling it—was new to me, but not exactly unfamiliar. Watching them I always felt at the edge of understanding what they were conferring about. The exchanges were a progression of familiar expressions—a look of rumination, then happiness, then reluctance, worry. The sequences were what confused me. Flora would squint at Daniel, who would slyly smile at her, and she in turn would return a different kind of squint, something I couldn't even assign an adjective to. It reminded me, this probably sounds crazy, of the wharf at dusk. This happened with a lot of their expressions, especially Flora's. I'd look up from my book and watch them and be reminded of a meal, a feeling, a memory, weather.

The Monday after the marker-on-face incident, I went to school in a funk. Feeling hollowed-out and filled with cotton balls and wasps. I sulked at my desk, torturing myself with book sixteen of the Erotic Time Travels series, this one set during the Civil War: love on horseback, love by campfire, amputations. By now I'd pretty much whittled my curriculum down to hang-out time and music time. Today, though, I was just gonna let music time pass by. It usually only lasted a half hour anyway, and I was way more into it than the students.

After lunch I continued reading. Stonewall Jackson had raided the home of Miss Millicent Franklin, who was hiding a Union general beneath her petticoat. She didn't have time to put on her underthings, and of course the Union general couldn't resist the "corky pong" of her you-know-what, so he began to expertly compromise her with his tongue . . .

I was distracted by the satellite radio starting up, which I recognized immediately as a waltz, "When I Grow Too Old to Dream." I love waltzes. I love how dance and song complement each other—you understand the dance and the song makes sense, understand the song and the dance makes sense. I put my book down, feeling chastened to be reading such trash, and watched as Flora and the others cleared out the desks. What were they doing?

Once the desks were cleared, all of them stared at me. It's impossible to describe the feeling when they were really paying attention to me and studying my face. I could feel the energy and authority of their shared understanding. When Flora stepped forward and held out her hand to me, I sensed that whatever they'd agreed on was a consequence of my beleaguered condition.

Keith went to the radio and restarted the song. Flora held out her left hand, and I took it. She was a lot shorter than me, so I hunched over and we danced with a respectful distance. Flora was looking at me with intense scrutiny, reading me. It intimidated me, to be honest, but her expression wasn't judgmental. It seemed more methodical. Diagnostic.

We went through two waltzes. One-two-three, one-two-three. When we were done, Keith came over to me and held out his hand. Someone started the song over and we danced. That day, I danced with every single one of my students. I went home feeling energized, satisfied, a little crazy.

I should've kept my mouth shut, but in the next faculty meeting I made the mistake of telling the other teachers what happened. "For the past year or so," I told them, "I thought they were discussing *things*. Looking around the room and matching expressions with objects. That's not what they're doing at all."

"What are they discussing?" asked one of the pre-K teachers, a woman named Shelly.

I thought about her question for a long time, so long that we'd already moved on to the next agenda item, and the next, by the time I had an answer. When the meeting was done, I took Shelly aside and asked, "How are you doing?" She said, "I'm okay," like you would if a clerk asked you that question. "No, *really*," I said. And she paused for a second and said, "Fine, I think," and I said, "Keep thinking about it." And she did. Before she could reply again I said, "Don't answer yet."

Shelly waited and I waited, and after a minute or so I wanted her to say something like, "The more I think about it, the less sure I am." And then I'd tell her, "*Exactly*," and prove something about how complicated the question was, and that was what our students were constantly discussing.

But after a while Shelly said, "You know, I really think I'm doing okay. I feel good. I just had a nice lunch."

And then I said, "*Exactly*," and Shelly looked at me like I was crazy.

THEODORE GREENE

RICHMOND, CA
2022

It came so suddenly, and I wasn't sure how to respond. Really I wasn't any more prepared to communicate with Flora than I was on the day she was born. Everything I'd done up to that point was focused on getting her to speak, getting her to use her voice or her hands. It hadn't ever crossed my mind that she'd have some other way. I probably made it worse, actually, because all that time I was staring at her, focused on her mouth, struggling to get something out of her, and meanwhile she was—I'm just guessing, but probably she was trying just as hard to get through to me, but in a way that I wasn't even picking up. I know it's unproductive to think that way, to think of that time as wasted. But those are years I can't get back. That whole stretch, I can never recover it. Whereas I feel like if I'd only known, I could have brought her so much further along. I could have taught her so much.

The teachers started offering an evening class for parents to learn about some of the facial muscles and the basic microexpressions that they could make. All the parents sat facing each other. I was the only single parent taking the class, so I had to pair off with Francine. I wished that I could have worked with anyone else, because there was something about Francine that was just . . . she was kind of very attractive in an almost hostile way, like a wounded animal, if that makes sense. But I didn't want the attraction I felt to transform into an obsession or anything, because I wasn't . . . I mean, I lived in a basement. I've never been the kind of person women were interested in, even way back before I met Mel. I didn't have a chance with Francine, and I wasn't sure I'd even want one if I qualified. I still felt the presence of Mel, even after eleven years. It was like a gravitational pull she had on me.

Anyway, I had to stare at Francine's face for several hours a week while we learned things like the difference between the zygomaticus major and the zygomaticus minor, and how tightening the lips was different from pressing the lips, and that certainly led me to start thinking about her more often than I wanted to. I couldn't help but be taken by the incredible uniqueness of her face. She had sharp eyes and a flat nose with a broad, heart-shaped bridge. And always a bit of a wistful look that the muscle exercises only made more intense. I didn't get to know too much about her during class. We were so focused on, like, learning to detect an inner brow raise as opposed to an outer brow raise. It was frustrating and boring at first, really intensely boring. But once you kept at it for a while, once you just sort of accepted the boredom, you could reach a new level, a deeper kind of seeing. You could see tiny differences appear, subtle variations. Nothing that really made sense, you know, nothing that you could remember from one moment to the next. But I could definitely see changes in Francine's face that I wouldn't have noticed otherwise. It was hard not to fall into a sort of . . . it wasn't love, but it was something. I spent so much time scanning the surfaces, the whole terrain of her face. I came to know it so well.

At home, Flora tolerated my attempts to communicate with her. She thought it was funny. I can't imagine how it must have looked to her. Like baby talk or something, nonsense or white noise. We would sit at the kitchen table, and I would start to make the expressions I'd learned the night before. She'd stare back at me with this look like she didn't know how to respond. But we were getting closer to the goal. Definitely closer to being able to have an actual conversation. It injected me with this new sense of hope. I felt like Mel could see us from wherever she was. I was bringing us together again, which was part of why the time I spent with Francine was so terrifying. I felt like it was some kind of test. I'm not a biblical person, but I felt like Francine was there in my life to test my mettle. To try my dedication to Mel and to the future I was working so hard for.

And then there was a social event at the school. The Spring Festival. A thing with games and food. I was looking forward to it, to being with all of the other parents. I knew Francine would be there, and I'm not going to say that didn't play into my excitement. But there was also just a general feeling of anticipation. We were all, the whole community, we were like astronauts or explorers, all of us discovering this new way of life. Nothing was going to be the same, ever again. The principal rolled the PA out of the storage closet and started to play music. The kids stared at it like they could somehow see the sound waves or something. An old song came on, "Money, Cash, Hoes," I think, and some of the parents got up and danced. I was sitting in a chair against the wall, and I felt a hand on my shoulder. It was Francine. She was trying to get me to dance. She looked straight into my eyes and arched her eyebrow in a campy kind of come-hither style, but I saw her eyelid twitching and her hand trembled slightly on my shoulder, like she was nervous, too. And maybe a bit humiliated at having to be the one to make the first move. I shook my head, but I guess I wasn't very convincing, because she took my hand anyway and led me out onto the gym floor, right underneath the proprioceptive swings, and I have to say that she looked kind of amazing. Her hair was up in a new way and she looked glad to be with me. No one had looked at me like that in a long time. I pulled her close to me and she put her head on my shoulder, and I felt about eighteen years old.

But while we danced to the song, I could see Flora sitting in a semicircle in the corner with her friends, and they were face-talking to each other. I saw them looking at her with those faces, and I saw her look back, and—I wanted to smash those kids. I wanted to really give them something to talk about. I mean, of course, I would never. It wasn't their fault. It wasn't anyone's fault. *Fault* isn't even the right word. But I hated them. I loathed the way they could just easily chat with my daughter, whereas I was like a flailing baby in her presence, just blathering outside the fortress of her mind. I got delirious with rage, with jealousy, to the point where I was about to be sick.

Of course, Francine sensed that I was distracted. I looked away and told her that everything was fine. We kept dancing for the rest of the night, but after that I stopped going to the classes, and eventually I started avoiding the school altogether as much as I could, which was, I guess, just as well.

KENULE MITEE

BROOKLYN, NY
2022

I had seen those kids, yes. Many times, just walking, like this, back and forth along the boardwalk. They would come to my stand and buy a single stick of Spray Ya Face, and I would see them go over to a pavilion and they would spray themselves and just lie there in the sand. Rapid Downhill Citrus was the kind they liked the best.

I knew there was something different about them. They had a way of walking, of carrying themselves. In Ogoniland, where I am from, there was a girl in the village. She never said a word. We were all scared of this girl, who was always walking far out to the edge of the village where our mothers told us we shouldn't go. She was like a wild animal. Her mother set a bowl of pepper soup out for her, and she would come when the sun went down and eat the soup and sleep on the hard ground. This girl never harmed anyone, but we were all scared. My friend saw a show on TV about a ghost that took control of people's brains and made them commit terrible crimes. We thought that this girl was a ghost and if we got too close to her, even if we just got her attention somehow, she would steal our brains. If I heard a noise at night, I would think, Oh, it is the wild girl coming for me.

These kids gave me the same feeling. I would come to work early, very early, and wheel my cart out onto the boardwalk, and pretty soon I would see them coming out of that big house, all at once in a large group. I asked my boss one day, I said, "What is that big house behind Lucifer's Hammer?" And he told me it was called Barrowbrook, and it was a place where those kids stayed at night—the silent kids, he meant. This Barrowbrook was like an orphanage, he said, but during the day they kicked them out. So I would see them in the morning coming out of that place. Always very quiet, those kids. If you didn't see them, you would not know they were there. And they would wander in packs of four or five, up and down the boardwalk, up and down, looking for food and money on the beach, in the trash, anywhere.

I don't think they stole. They handed me change only. Sometimes it was enough, sometimes not. They didn't seem to know how much money they had, and they didn't seem to care when they didn't have enough. Some days they had no money at all. They would just come and look at the selection. I would say, "Ya ye, flavor of the day is . . . Mango Knificide," because that is how I do it. That is my thing, and people like it. But those kids would just look at me for a long time. I would say, "You buy something or you move along," and they looked at me like I was a dog barking. Which was frustrating, because if anything, they were closer to being dogs! I never liked them. Especially that boy with the scar up his arm. A fat winding white thing that looked like an eel. Very unpleasant.

I don't know what Spray Ya Face does, but all young people seem to like it. I see them spraying each other with it, and then they become very calm. I can make good money selling this product. It is much better than when I was selling pretzels, because everyone had a complaint about their pretzel—not firm enough or too firm or too salty. I didn't make the pretzels—I just unwrapped them. But nobody complains about Spray Ya Face.

One day those kids were standing around my cart looking at the flavors. A bunch of rough boys came by and pushed their way through. The kind of young man who wears a sleeveless shirt and pants around his hips, you know? They came up and pushed the quiet kids aside as if they were not even there. As I said, I did not feel comfortable around those silent kids, but I also felt like they were my customers, you know? So I told these rough boys, I said, "Hey, hey, be easy." And the biggest one came right up to me and made a pretend punching motion, like this, right into my face. I just stood there. I could not have a scene happen at my cart. I couldn't have a fight with this boy. It would ruin my business and I might never be able to get my green card. I was sure there was going to be a fight, and I told this boy with the sleeveless shirt to go, to get away from my stand. I didn't want any of this happening. The rough boy relaxed his arm, and I thought it was over, but then he turned and grabbed the silent kid with the scar and put him in a hold. I came out from behind the cart and took the rough boy by the arms. I was trying my hardest to pry him off the silent boy, but he was strong like a vise. I finally had to hold my hand over his mouth and pinch his nose, and he finally let go. I threw him to the ground and shouted for him to go, and he scuttled off down the boardwalk. I was shaking. I stood back from the silent boy, who was on his knees, breathing rapidly, holding his neck. I handed him a paper cone filled with water and said, "You go now, all of you." The boy's friends helped him to stand, and they walked off toward the beach, looking back at me with that strange expression, like they weren't sure if I was their friend or their enemy.

I went back to Ogoniland after the uprising there to bury my uncle. I asked around about the girl without a voice. I found out that there had been a murder in the village. A woman had disappeared, and nobody knew why. One day the wild girl returned from one of her walks carrying the missing woman's wristwatch. She led a police officer out into the hills, where the woman's body was stuffed in a crack. The woman had been murdered by her husband, who found out she was having an affair with a man in Port Harcourt. A famous Igbo director found out about this story and hired the girl to appear as herself in a series of movies where she helped police solve crimes by finding bodies no one else could find. I saw one of these movies while I was there. It was a very funny and very entertaining film, which ended with the wild girl jumping through a glass window onto the wing of a plane, all done with special computer effects. I was happy for the girl, who as I said was treated like an animal all her life.

The kids at the beach, I don't know what they are up to. I don't understand why they don't kick a ball or throw a Frisbee to pass the time. My friends and I, at that age, were working jobs so that we could afford the clubs at night. We would do anything. So I do not understand how these young people can spend whole days wandering around without a purpose. Groups of them, roaming around, not saying anything, making everybody uncomfortable. What kind of a life is that?

STEVEN GRENIER

NEW YORK, NY
2023

Porter wanted me to do a story on the "phasic resistance transitional facilities." I'm using air quotes because there was nothing transitional or facilitative about those places. Dumping grounds for kids no one wanted to deal with, is what they were. But Porter said the board had urged him to assign the thing to me. They'd learned from some kind of inside channel that *The Braggart* was doing a huge spread on three families with phasic-resistant kids, real heartstring-tugging shit, and they wanted me to offer some kind of timely counterpoint using the facilities as an anchor. The kids at these facilities were the forgotten ones, basically feral, cut loose from or sometimes even put there by their parents, abandoned by the whole system, just roaming the streets in an existential limbo. I thought I could cast them as a sort of organized clan. I'd somehow ingratiate myself into their ranks to get a real slice of their life, something no one had captured yet. I just had to figure out how.

Porter tried to sweeten the deal by offering me any city I wanted. New York was overexposed at that point, and it was so much easier to get laid in Philly, so I started there. I got to South Street and, okay, first of all, the place is pretty much a shithole. It feels like a superexploitative gypsy carnival. Every store sold something I'd never even heard of, things made of that cheap, flexible plastic that won't break down for another twenty thousand years. Guys were selling old storage wafers and tubes of optic gel on bath towels laid out right on the sidewalk. And there were those weird virtual attractions that I didn't get. Like, why would you want to know what it's like to get thrown down a well? Why would you pay twenty dollars to experience that? Or the thing where you could temporarily deform yourself. This is what people want?

So I was wandering around trying to find the facility, but it was a hassle because there was nothing that distinguished it from any other building. I mean, looking at the place, when I finally found it—you'd never know what went on inside. Even the sign just said FLETCHER HOUSE. No numbers, no indication of any kind. I tried to get in, but the doors were locked. Of course, right? Because they shut it down during the day and let the kids just wander off and do fuck knows what. I could see a guy pushing a mop in the hallway, but he wouldn't look up when I knocked. Or when I called him a chooch.

I went down South Street on the other side. A Chinese guy was rolling up the metal shutters over the entrance to a virtual action booth called Gorilla Spill, and there were about seven or eight kids standing in a semicircle watching him open the ride. He'd look up occasionally as he worked and shoo them away, but they didn't move at all. Dirty kids, didn't look too healthy, but with a sort of emotive glow. The guy saw me and made a face like, "Help me get these kids to leave." I was like, "They want to go in, don't they?" and he shook his head and said, "No money." So I bought tickets for all of them. I was just winging it at that point. The guy sprayed a luminescent pattern on our hands and we went in.

We were all herded into a dark room. A timer was projected on the far wall, and when it got to zero we were suddenly in this cargo plane with about forty bull gorillas. The floor fell out and we all started tumbling through the air. I wasn't prepared for this, I mean, I must have looked like a fucking . . . I was just flailing in utter terror and probably squealing like a baby. It really felt real. These gorillas, tons of gorillas in free fall, punching at me in the air. It was scary as fuck. But the kids, I saw them in the periphery of my vision, and they were all chained up like skydivers. They were organized. Totally coordinated. I looked over at this girl, the one I called Persephone in the segment, and she had this way of looking at me that put me completely at ease. They drifted over to me and grabbed me, and I did feel safer.

We eventually dropped into the sea and swam for the coastline. When we got to the beach, the kids started hiking through the dunes. They slipped through a tear in the border of the environment and I followed them through, which wasn't, strictly speaking, allowed. The poly count went way, way down on the other side, but there was a massive field of low-res sawgrass that rolled away from us for miles. The place was totally unfinished and was probably never meant to be seen by anyone. It wasn't even set up with a shadow-casting light. And no sound track or anything. Not even the swishing of the grass. It was total silence, where you can hear the sound of your own blood rushing through your body.

The kids seemed to have been there before. They'd cleared out an area in the middle of the field, and they let me sit with them in it. We sat there for what felt like several hours. It was just incredibly, unendurably boring. I remembered why I hated doing stories on these kids. They just sat and stared at each other or at the cruddy skybox. But I suffered through it. I needed to do whatever I could to fully integrate myself into their schedule.

After, I don't know, forever, the Chinese guy showed up. He had an electric prod and he started flipping out, waving the prod in the air and telling everyone to get the hell out. The kids were quick—they beat it out of there in an instant. I was just sitting there sort of frozen in place, totally surprised, which gave the guy enough time to stick me with the prod. It didn't hurt, but I was immobilized for long enough for him to lift me by my collar and drag me out the door.

I walked up and down the street a few more times, but I couldn't find the kids anywhere. I was feeling like I blew it. I'd have to go to another city and start all over again. I was incredibly pissed and disappointed in myself, and then I saw the girl, Persephone, standing on a rooftop, looking down at me. It was just the most bizarre thing. I went around the back of the building and climbed the fire escape. All the kids from before were up there. There was trash all over the place. Empty canisters and chip bags skittering across the roof. Clumps of old water-damaged pillows and a few pieces of street-trash furniture, and mattresses that were stacked up like a house of cards by the elevator shaft. They had a whole thing set up there. A hangout, if you could call what these kids did "hanging out." Persephone came up to me and took my arm. She led me over to a wooden chair under a blue tarp and sat me down in the chair. She stared at me hard for a while, doing that face stuff. It made me really uncomfortable. Like, who knew what I was telling her? Who knew what she could see there? Whatever she saw, it must not have been too bad, be-cause she let me hang around with them for the next four days, pretty much continuously.

Then Porter called and said they needed the segment for a Wednesday night live-stream, so I went back to New York and Banks and I edited the whole thing in about two days, working straight through. I don't know what happened to Persephone or any of those kids after the segment aired. I sometimes think about them, yeah. I wonder what they're doing. I know that the Philly facility changed its policy about shutting down during school hours, but I also heard that a bunch of kids just left and started living in the streets. I hope that Persephone wasn't one of them, yeah. Of course. But those kids, they were pretty much goners the day they moved into that place.

DAVID DIETRICH

DECATUR, GA
2023

Mom left. She moved in with a tile salesman named Drake who worked at Drake's Tile, but he was a different Drake. He explained how it happened but I forget. He was bald and had uneven eyes. Once a week he took me bowling and we played the little-kid way with bumpers over the gutters. He asked if I'd ever had good sex and I told him I don't know, even though I'd never had any kind of sex. He said did I know how to tell when I'd had good sex? I thought about it, feeling like there was no right answer to this question. And then Drake said good sex was when you pee afterward and it comes out in three separate streams. That's how you knew. Two streams was okay, but three streams was good.

I went and bowled my turn and then came back and asked, "What about four?"

"Four's a different ballgame entirely," he said.

Mom said they were destined to be together.

She said I could stay in our old apartment until I graduated, but I'd already been plotting my getaway. I knew I wouldn't finish school. The weird thing about knowing this was that class started being fun. There was none of the old pressure. It was like paying to go to a movie and then sneaking into another one afterward. Even if it's halfway over, it doesn't matter if it's something about a girl and her special pony and then it dies but she gets a new one, because you look at it like a bonus. A few of my teachers actually said they could see improvement, but I was in remedial classes, so they didn't expect much. I got second place in the remedial spelling bee, though.

I'd been listening to the podcasts the albino had given my mom on an emulator, and one went, *The power of you is perpetual.* My new goal was to be a more natural person. I was tired of wishing and wanting. All I needed was a hobby, something to bury myself under, like guitar karaoke or rehabbing hawks, but I never settled on anything. The silents were always one or two thoughts away. I didn't think about them every second, and I didn't see them much, but I was always aware of them. They were like the track my thoughts rode on. I used to do Internet searches for silent stuff, medical sites and message boards and interactive chats with silent schools, and lose like five hours in five minutes, but Mom had the Internet canceled, so I stopped. But I knew all about the face-talking. I knew they were starting to show themselves.

After school, I would ride my bike around and look for things to steal. One day I took a huge bag of dog food from behind a feed store, cut the bag open, and left a drizzle from a bike path into the grass, down a hill, into the woods. I waited at the end of the trail for a long time, but nobody came. When I retraced my steps back to the path, I saw a girl walking an old rust-colored cat on a leash. The girl was a silent. I don't know how I knew, I just did. I could've seen a picture of only her forehead and known. She had long arms and a shirt with a rainbow around the stomach. Her cat was lying on its side in the grass, trying to claw off its harness. The girl hadn't noticed me yet, and I first thought I'd act like a silent, like at the Air Zoo, but something said, Don't. It said, Go and try to use the power of me to meet her and maybe something could happen. I'd watched the silents more than anyone, I knew them better than any scientist or researcher in the world. I could do this.

I went and stood in front of her. I knelt down and tried to pet her cat on the stomach. Before I did, the cat grabbed my hand with its front paws and bit down on the meaty part, right by the thumb. I yelped and sort of fell back. The girl swooped up her cat in one arm and came over to me and took my hand to look at it. I felt all the old longing coming back, but it was different. This time it felt good.

I didn't try to communicate with her that first time. I just stared for as long as she would let me, and she let me for a while. She had tiny bumps on the bridge of her nose and on her neck, and I wanted to run my tongue along them. I wanted to carry around a picture of her and show people. I wanted her to wear my clothes. I was so excited that I even told Drake about her. I don't know why I did it. He high-fived me and asked about her rack.

"It's pretty good," I told him.

She was there again the next day. With her cat. This time, I went up and pretended I was going to pet the cat and then raised my hands up like, "No way, not again!" She smiled. She had braces. I love braces. She let me walk with her a little ways down the trail. I picked a yellow flower from a bush and she put it behind her ear. The next day I'd made her a card with pictures of cats I drew, but she didn't bring her cat. She looked at the card, looked at each picture and then at me, and

I saw wrinkles pass beneath her eyes, and I felt thanked. I tried to signal "You're welcome," but she kept staring, like she was waiting for something else. I tried to signal "That's all I wanted to say," but she kept waiting. We walked down the trail to a man-made lake with these deformed ducks in it. Some had red welts all over their faces and beaks. The day after that she let me hold her hand. And the day after that, too.

On the fifth day she took me to a playground behind the closed library. She let go of my hand and I followed her to the playground, where two boys and a girl were sitting in sand. They were just looking at each other, and when the girl came up to them they all gestured toward her, and she sat down, too. I kept standing. They barely looked at me. These weren't the kind of silents I remembered. The guys both wore fake basketball jerseys over long-sleeve shirts. Like anybody. They looked happy and greedy for each other's company. What's the point of being silent if you're going to be like everyone else, I wanted to ask.

I walked away from the playground really slowly, in case she wanted to catch up to me. I guess she didn't. I went back the next day, walked all around looking for her, and the day after, and then a bunch more days, but I never found her again.

I ate dinner with Drake and Mom a few days later. Tacos. I was feeling awful. When Mom was in the kitchen washing dishes, Drake said, "All right. Now let me smell your fingers. I want to know if you've been getting some."

I didn't yell at him to quit burdening me with his horribleness. I stuck out my hand and let him smell my fingers. He said, "Outlook not so good."

Before I rode home, I took the cinder block he used to

block his tires and dropped it through the back window of his car.

On good days I think maybe there's something inside you that wants you to be happy. Even if you don't want to, it forms thoughts and tries to lead you there. On most days, though, I think it's the opposite. No matter what you do, or think, or tell yourself, you're going to end up in the same place.

ARTURO CORDERO GARCIA

The first rule of miming is, get the fuck out of my face, I'm fucking miming. But these kids would not get the picture. Coming right up around me in a tight circle so that no one else can even see. The people with money—*my people*, my livelihood, the whole reason I'm out there. They're there to see me and they can't, because of these kids standing right up close. I never had to deal with this before. Competition, I've had to deal with. The urban street dancers, the cattle-prod swallowers, that woman who puts herself in a box with a snake. Of course I'm going to lose business to those people. I already know that. I'm not miming for the fucking masses. I'm miming for the discerning upper middle class. The ones that matter, the kind of people who can tell the difference between Noh and Kathakali. If you don't know the difference, go fuck yourself with your own fucking ignorance, you fucking degenerate. I mean, if you can't tell me when Decroux wrote *Words on Mime*, you might as well be in diapers. I studied with Decroux the year he died. I fucking saw him become the wind, so who the fuck are you? I came out of

Decroux's class like some kind of mountain climber. Climbing up to the highest plateau of human achievement, where my body is in an act of pure fucking expression, not even recognizable as a body anymore but just a sculpture in time representing the entirety of man's struggle against the world, and if you can't appreciate that, go take a flying fuck into your mother's dickhole.

Those kids, they circled me, and they wouldn't take their eyes off of me. At first I was okay with it. At least they were watching me and not one of those ass-eaters down at the food court. But the way they stared at me, it was relentless. It was hard to deal with—I mean, it was almost an existential crisis I went through with these kids, because in a certain way that is what the artist aspires to, am I right? A fucking rapt audience, totally under my sway. But these kids, I mean, I knew that they were in essence completely retarded. Whatever it was they were responding to, it wasn't art. It wasn't what I was putting out there. I tolerated it, though. I was okay with it until they started trying to mimic me. I was doing some very intensely corporeal shit, fucking supertechnical nonrepresentational shit. The real deal. And it started with this one kid, a young man of about thirteen or so. He just started, out of nowhere, mirroring me. Now, I've dealt with this kind of thing a lot. You work the park, you work the boardwalk, you're going to get these fucking mooks who come along and try to break your concentration. They try to get you to talk, they try to humiliate you, they try to do whatever they can to bring you down to their level. Fucking primates. But this kid who started mirroring me . . . that's not even the word, because it was more like he was capturing me, or amplifying me. I have this passage in my act where I dramatize the life and struggle of the French composer Mustapha Boumedienne exclusively through the use of my trunk. It took me seven years to perfect this narrative. The Theatre de l'Ange Fou saw it and said that I had gone where no mime had gone before. And yet here were these kids, these little cocksucking street urchins more or less nailing it on their first try. But not just nailing it. Adding to it. Enriching it, rounding it out. It was an insult and an affront and it made my fucking blood boil.

So yeah, I started to get really fucking pissed. Who were these fucking kids, you know? And pretty soon people started watching the spectacle. A lot of people. I was in a precarious situation. Do I break down in the middle of my act to tell these kids to go jump into a fucking wood chipper, which is what I wanted to do, but which would be going against everything I believed about the art form and the sanctity of the live performance? Or do I just try to ignore them, finish the performance with my dignity intact, and just never come back to Ocean City? I decided to go with the latter. I decided to ignore the little pricks. But the crowd kept getting bigger and bigger. They were watching the retarded kids, almost like they were the act and I was the one taunting them! Looking back, I don't know why I didn't just stop.

What? Yeah, yeah. I regret that I didn't have the foresight to just put an end to it. I let it get really out of control. The first kid who started copying me, he somehow became the locus of all of my frustration. I was locked on him, getting so fucking pumped up with rage at this skinny prick in his thrift-store getup. I don't even think he was doing it to fuck with me. I think he was maybe just trying to understand what I was putting out there. In any other context, you know, I might have been fine with it and even flattered. But everyone's eyes were on this. Everything was at stake.

Yeah, so I lunged at him. It was fucking animal—like,

animal me coming out and taking over the human part of me. I felt this streaking rush of something and I concentrated all my power, all my energy and force into my fist, and I fucking popped the kid right in his face. I felt his teeth against my knuckles, is how fucking hard and fast I hit that little cocksucker. Of course, I was in a world of shit for a while after that. You know, coldcocking a kid in public. I'd never done anything like it before, I mean, I had no prior record, so I got off relatively easy from a legal perspective, but something like that's going to follow you around for a long time if you're a performer. And it haunted me for a long time. It still does, because I remember looking down at the kid after I hit him, and I saw that it was fear that made me do what I did. I was afraid of how easily he'd taken my life's work from me and made it his own. Like it was no big deal. Like it was, I don't know, second nature.

PRASHANT NUREGESAN

CHARLOTTE, NC
2025

You want to know about Twitch Rave. I'll tell you what I can, but I can only tell you so much. Because the appeal of Twitch Rave is that you can't know what it is. You can look at the Twitch Rave peripheral and say, "Oh, looks like that's a kind of headset," and you can watch a silent kid put it on and go, "Okay, yeah, looks like he's really having a good time there," but you can't really know what the good time is. You want to know, but you can't. That's my design. That was my plan, from the first moment I came up with Twitch Rave.

All the market research said you've got to think like teens to sell to teens, and I sat there for a long time just concentrating, trying to think like a teen. But how could you possibly think like a teen? You can't. But then I realized—because realization is what I'm essentially all about, you know? *Making ideas real*—I realized that lack of understanding had to be at the core of the product's design. I had reams of test data that supported this: the thing contemporary teens wanted least in life was to be understood. Literally, that was numero uno on the list. So while it was impossible for me to actually think like a silent teen, I was sure I could come close. If I could just manage to bring a product to market without ever understanding exactly what it did, I'd be able to tap into the silent teen demographic like nobody else had.

The basic Twitch Rave interface was left over from an abandoned prototype for the ill-fated PlayStation Escape, which gamers had completely trashed in focus testing. But what I did was, I built a randomizing routine in Twitch Rave that made sure that it behaved differently every time you used it, and there was no way to replicate a single experience twice. Teens can sense that kind of authenticity. It's primal. They just know when an adult has had an active hand in any product. But all I knew about Twitch Rave was that you put on the peripheral and it used "the motion of your face to create intense and life-altering technicolor visualizations that are cosmic in scope"—that's a direct quote from the box copy, which was written by my intern, Sasha—she's twelve—but the randomizer makes it impossible to predict what the product does. It might be dangerous, or wildly pleasurable, or insanely dull—you just never know what will happen.

This all sounds obvious now, but my investors were less than thrilled. Was it frustrating when they withdrew funding? Sure, but now I'm supergrateful, because it left me with no option but to hit the streets myself, to really grind with my customers, shake their hands and get up in their faces and whatnot.

I started up the West Coast, hitting some of the communities where I'd built connections over the years. I found I had a bottomless reserve of energy to burn—there was something about selling directly to real people, showing up at a silent school or a community center with a briefcase and demoing the thing. Really demoing the hell out of it. Watching the kids react to it. Watching them fall in love with it. People in the industry are always writing off the silent market, but I'm telling you—these kids are out there, and their parents have cash. If you need proof, look in my garage, where you'll find a Z8, a Nissan GT-R, and a concept blade scooter by Earl McGinnis.

But about three weeks into my epic road trip—which I was calling "the Nu Deal" to myself and to the ex-investors I texted after every sale—I rolled into Asheville, where my sister lived. My niece, Isabelle, went to a silent school there, Breen Academy. The school was one of the biggest in the Southeast, which made it all the more bizarre that there were only a handful of kids there. I set up my demo table in the cafeteria and I was just really creeped out by all the empty tables, in a place that was already pretty dead quiet, obviously. My niece was the first one to try the Twitch Rave, and while she was testing it out I asked one of the aides what the deal was. She said that over the last year or so kids just stopped showing up to school. It started with these two boys who went missing, she said. They disappeared one morning on the way to school, and the whole city got up in arms. There was a massive search for these kids, who an electrician finally found loitering around outside a condemned manufacturing plant. Turned out those kids had willingly gone—like, they ran away. There were other silent kids living in this plant, apparently. And even more kids who just hung out there during the day. She said that the school tried to round kids up, but they weren't staffed for that kind of thing. It was like trying to herd cats, she said.

If you show me a dead end, you're just pointing out to me the exact place where you became a quitter. That's not the Nu way. So I drove out to the plant superearly the next morning.

I had three things on my mind, which I'm going to tell you in order. One, I didn't want these kids luring my niece into some diseased squat, and two, I was just curious about what they thought they were doing. Three was, I had this hunch that the kids would be so blown away by Twitch Rave that they'd go back to their homes, back to their parents, just so that they could get the money to buy Twitch Rave, which would, as a sort of side effect, be pretty solid PR.

The building these kids were living in smelled like bad candy. It used to be a latex-house-paint factory, I think. You could literally taste the toxic fumes all the way from the road. I parked out on the street—the lot was all broken up and covered in weeds. So I'm walking up toward the entrance, and there's these two kids carrying an old sofa across the asphalt. I saw them first, and I made the mistake of jogging up to them. They turned and quickly put the sofa down and ran inside. I took off after them, but they'd shut the door tight. I knocked for a while, but I felt like an idiot. Standing there pounding on the door. I was like, "I'm not a cop!" I actually said that. I don't know why.

There was a window covered in plywood on the side of the building, and I pried it open to get a look inside. I saw a girl sitting at a card table doing some kind of sewing or something, with tons of cloth bunched up next to her. She glanced up at me, and I thought she would be frightened, but she just gave me this look like I was nothing, like I was a squirrel or a pigeon, and she was staring at me, waiting to see what I'd do next. Which what I did was one of the dumbest moves I ever made, to the point where I feel sick even thinking about it. I had the Twitch Rave peripheral in my hand, this superexpensive, irreplaceable, one-of-a-kind prototype, and I tossed it through the plywood slat, as close to the girl as I could throw.

I made this gesture like, "Go ahead, give it a spin." But she just stared at it on the floor there, like I'd just thrown her a dead rat. I know that these silent kids have had a hard life. I know that they didn't get a fair shake from a biological perspective, but come on. Here was this superadvanced nonlinear virtual ecosphere sitting right there within arm's reach, and this girl wouldn't even give it a try?

NANCY JERNIK

In order to be in the Prescott Group you have to read and memorize *Prescott Says*, and then you have to live it, which is allegedly the hard part, only none of it was hard for me because it was the exact thing I'd been looking for all my life. *Prescott Says* is three chapters, one for each step in the Prescott Method, which is how you achieve the state of Total Flow Productivity. After I finished the first chapter I was like, "That was easy, but I'm sure this next one will be hard." But it wasn't hard, none of it was hard, because all I ever wanted was to shed my distractions, gather my flock, and restore my mind eye. I was like, "Is this really all I have to do to reach my maximum potential? Could someone have maybe told me this before? Maybe twenty years ago, so that I could have just skipped over all of the bad decisions I've made?" Why did it take this long in human civilization for someone to come up with the Prescott Method? I think about that a lot, like how much further along would we all be if Prescott had been around when Plato was alive. Or the pharaohs maybe.

Ron and I were both recruited by Dutch Guston, who was

one of the founding partners at NanoGyne, where Ron worked. This was about two years after Spencer was taken away. We started out as bronze-class cadets, but Ron leveled up really quickly, because he's like that. He also didn't have to deal with Ambitor withdrawal, which I had to go through because of Step One, so you can't really compare our progress. Apart from the Ambitor, though, I barely had to work at all to shed my distractions, even though I had a lot of them. I'd built up a bunch of things around me by that point, just hobbies and activities, like taking pictures of objects that looked like faces and collecting old racist folk art. They started as ways to help me stop thinking about what happened with Spencer, but I just kept going. I kept collecting. I think I was waiting for someone to tell me to stop. And then Prescott said stop, and I did, on a dime. And I never even thought about them again. That's the thing about distractions. They're just obstacles you put in the way of your path to prosperity. Once you take them away you see how you were really just crippling yourself.

So when it was time to commit to Step Two, that's where I caught up to Ron. Step Two is gathering your flock, which means bringing your family close and tight. Prescott says that even the early humans knew that the family unit was like an arrow through time, and that the tighter the family was, the faster the arrow would fly. You can't reach TFP without a family, and having a family that's separated is like trying to shoot a broken arrow. Ron and I sat down with Dutch to see what could be done in our case, because we were legally prohibited from getting Spencer back. He was like, "Legally prohibited? To take back your son who you gave birth to?" He brought up that part of *Prescott Says* where Prescott says that there's no greater impediment to the achievement of total prosperity than the legal system. He was like, "The answer is simple. You take back your son. You just take him."

That night Ron plotted out a strategic timeline on his Catena while I packed some things in a little bag. We would arrive at Barrowbrook at dawn and confront Spencer. It was this incredible feeling, like we were, I don't know, Bonnie and James, outlaws for justice. We were just going to take him back. It was so simple. I don't know why we hadn't thought of it earlier. But that's the Prescott Method. There's always a simple answer. If you're not thinking simply, you're simply not thinking.

We started driving in the dark before dawn. The idea was, we were going to show up and wait around on the boardwalk until they let the kids out for the day. Then we'd follow Spencer around until there was a moment of opportunity. Of course, we were hoping that he'd just fall into our arms and start weeping, and we'd all have a good cry and go home. But we were prepared to get him out of there by any means necessary.

We got to Coney Island just as the sun was coming up. I remember how beautiful it was at that hour, and I felt like it must be a nice place for Spencer to wake up to. I started to get scared about what we were doing. What if he had no interest in us anymore? Maybe he wouldn't even know who we were. But at the same time I was thinking, Would it be ultimately worse for us to take him away from his friends and his whole world? It seemed like all of the options had some bad outcome. Prescott doesn't believe in bad outcomes, only in bad planning. But I couldn't think like Prescott right then. I sort of had a little breakdown, so I wasn't even looking when the kids started coming out of the facility. Ron was watching, but he didn't see Spencer. I had my head down in my lap, but I told him to look closer. He said again that there was no kid who looked anything like Spencer. We walked up and down the boardwalk all morning, and we saw a bunch of silent kids moping around, but no Spencer. We waited until a staff person showed up at Barrowbrook to open it for the night. Ron pretended to be a tourist—he had his wallet in his hand and he said he'd seen a silent kid drop it on the boardwalk, a kid with a big scar on his arm. The Barrowbrook guy just stared at him with this blank look. He was like, "You saw this happen today? I haven't seen that kid with the scar for months." We asked where he might have gone, and the guy told us that there was a warehouse down by Rockaway that some of the kids were living in.

So we took a taxi over there. It was dark out. The place was mostly unlit. And really, for the city, very quiet. You could hear the water in the distance hitting the dock or platform or whatever. Very still and empty, and the air was clammy. I felt really—I mean, I was scared. I was holding Ron's arm, and that was the only thing keeping me from shaking right out of my skin. We went up to these huge metal doors, the kind that slide open. It looked totally dark inside, abandoned. I was ready to leave, but Ron saw this huge heap of trash bags overflowing the Dumpster that were buzzing with flies. We got closer, and you could see that the bags were new. Which I guess meant someone was squatting in there.

I didn't want to go in. I mean, we were going on this one guy's word that this place was real, that there were silent kids living there. But it could've been anyone in there. It could have been packed with rapists. And I have this fear—my worst fear is not getting raped myself but watching Ron get raped right before I get killed. Like the last image I see before I die is Ron getting held down and raped by a bunch of guys. I don't know why, but that is much more terrifying to me than getting raped myself. So I was begging Ron, "Please don't go in there. We'll come back tomorrow. You don't have to go in there." But he told me to be quiet and that we came all this way, we weren't going to just turn around.

He pulled back one of the metal doors and it was dark inside, but we could see that it was clean, like somebody was tending the place. I remember you could smell sawdust in the air. And there were boxes lined up against the wall, it seemed like a hundred of them. I was so distracted by that stuff that it took me a second to notice the two guys that were standing totally still in the middle of the floor. Silent kids that looked like they were waiting for us. Ron said he was there for his son. I could hear this very slight hint of fear in his voice, just a little tighter than usual. The guys took a few steps forward, and we stepped back. Ron pulled up his sleeve and made this raking movement up the length of his forearm, like trying to say "Spencer." The guys stopped and looked at each other. I'd read about how they could somehow communicate with their faces but I'd never seen it before. It was weird, but not in the way I thought it would be. It had this familiar feeling, like a song from my childhood, where I remembered the melody but not the words.

The guys put up their hands to say no. Ron was like, "Are you trying to keep me from my son?" He puffed up his chest and moved forward, and the two guys got really close and it seemed like there was going to be a fight. They were—there was something just not right about them. Their clothes were all patched up. Like, the one guy's shirt was made out of three shirts. But there was an order to it, like it was intentionally done. Anyway, I guess Ron decided to back down. He said, "This isn't the end," even though they had no idea what he was talking about. It was the one thing he had over them.

It took us forever to get back to our hotel. I slept for a long time, and when I woke up Ron was packing his bag. I said, "What the hell do you think you're doing?" and he said, "Prescott's second thesis—ever heard of it?" This was so Ron, totally not getting what Prescott meant in his second thesis when he said that obstacles are opportunities to do the unexpected. The unexpected was not to shrink away in fear but to jump at this thing and take it by the throat. I told Ron I planned to go back to that place and sit out in front until I could see my son. Ron kind of snorted, like I was out of my mind, but I could seriously give a flying one at that point. I was resolved. I was going to get Spencer out of there no matter what.

JOHN PARKER CONWAY

MONTE RIO, CA
2026

That first mayoral election, while I was on the campaign trail, I knocked on every single door in Monte Rio, and if no one was home I came back. That first campaign was the best. I was a newcomer, a figure of pure anonymity, so I was able to step into their living rooms and have a real conversation about things that mattered, without needing to address some drummed-up allegations or whispers of malfeasance.

I talked to farmers worrying about the Korean pinot. Old hippies worrying about the Bohemian Grove. Tweakers just worrying. I met them all, listened to their concerns. All voices deserve to be heard. A vote is a vote, right? I was there to listen.

Because that's what I am: a listener. I'm not one of those stumpers who harps on about his beginnings, rolling up his shirtsleeves and trotting out poverty stories about how his mom shaved pets for a living and his dad accidentally fell into a Dumpster of asbestos and sometimes all there was for dinner was expired ketchup packets, but, hey, look at me now and isn't this country great? I want to smack those guys in their fat happy mouths. Frauds. Of course I think this country's great, you'd be a fool to say otherwise, but my own path has nothing to do with it. What makes this country great? We leave you alone. You live and I live and let everybody else live.

So these kids. I was making my rounds out on Moscow, just a man and a dream of civic whatever, and I stopped at the old Schofield place. My notes said *Occupant*, which meant the tenant was new. The house was in serious disrepair: rain gutters sagging, driveway rutted, just soggy everywhere. Between the river and rain and the redwoods, that'll happen. I was preparing my newcomer riff: Monte Rio, the mountains and the river, the best of both worlds. Think of all the other godforsaken places you could've ended up.

I knocked on the door and waited. Knocked again, waited. After a few minutes a bright-eyed teenage girl, maybe seventeen, came around the side of the house carrying a cardboard box marked *Property of Oaks*. I greeted her, took the box from her, and said, "Lead the way." She just stood there, not so much afraid as surprised. I'm a largish man, especially now, but I try to offset it by constantly softening my features just short of smiling. "Are your parents home?" I asked the girl. She was still staring at me, arms crossed, clear plastic gloves on her hands. I didn't mind at all—I could wait as long as she could. Then I looked into the box to maybe get a clue about this family, something I could use in my favor, and I saw that it was filled entirely with dried dog turds. I guess I lost my composure for a sec—I dropped the box, threw my arms up, and shrieked. The girl hesitated, then smiled the warmest smile at me. Not at all mocking or scornful.

I didn't ask her what she was doing with a box of turds. None of my business, right? Personal liberty—that's a constitutional dictate, especially out here in the woods. But my mind was putting the pieces together. Gloves, unkempt yard—she was cleaning the place up. The former tenants must've been dog people.

Three more teenagers, two girls and a boy, roughly the same age as her, came out to join us, and that's when I fit the rest of the pieces together. They started face-talking like they do. I'd only seen it a handful of times before, and never up close. I'd always thought it'd be stranger than this, like watching people read minds. But no. I'm a pretty intuitive person and I felt like I could almost figure out what they were talking about, like if I spent enough time around them, I could communicate with them. The one girl was telling the others about me dropping the box—I could tell she was reenacting my surprise. After they shared a moment, they looked at me and laughed. I did too. Whatever it takes to get your foot in the door.

The rest I gathered by deduction and guesses. I walked around with them as they moved in. There were six of them total, four girls and two boys, only one of whom looked to be of voting age. No adults, no chaperones. The electricity hadn't been turned on, and they had almost nothing in the way of furnishings—an old lamp, a cheap folding chair. I looked in the cupboards and couldn't find any food. Plenty of our citizens have challenges, but these kids . . . It was a new variety of challenge, and they weren't going to last long like this. The youth of today are the voters of tomorrow, that's what I believe. And everyone gets a vote, talking or not.

"Any new resident of Monte Rio is a friend of mine," I told them before I left. "We're all bonded by an investment in the community. I'm going to do what I can to help you."

I put one of my *Which Way? Conway!* promo magnets on

their refrigerator, and it was still there the next time I visited, to make sure the power had been turned on. And the time after that, to bring them groceries, and again, to help unload a cord of firewood. They never exactly thanked me, but they never complained either, and sometimes that's plenty enough for an elected official like myself. After we stacked the firewood together, I shook each of their hands. One of the boys stared at me for a long time, and I stared back at him, and I feel like we both looked good and deep into each other's souls. And we were both pretty well pleased with what we found.

"Is it all right if I put one of my campaign signs out front?" I asked.

My opponent called it "political opportunism," but he has a cynical outlook—a tool of the dying Bohemians. I just respected these kids as citizens, as residents, same as everyone else. And if they are a little different, why isn't that a good thing? A small town like ours can always use another distinguishing characteristic.

So I defeated my opponent, and one thing led to another, and one of my proudest moments of that first year was having Monte Rio designated an official sanctuary area for phasic-resistant citizens. The first one in the country. Sanctuary from what? Well, from whatever. Monte Rio is a place where people can be people—talk if you want, not if you don't.

I don't know exactly how word spread, but it did. So we rode that train. We sent letters to their schools, I made some phone calls. Come to Monte Rio, I encouraged them. We have the river and the mountains. It's quiet here.

FRANCINE CHANG

OAKLAND, CA
2027

The year that first class graduated from Oaks, we held weekly committee meetings, videoconferences with the other schools in our consortium, to set up some kind of postgrad program. Fellowships for them to assist incoming students and work as mediators, things like that. They couldn't just leave—they weren't ready. They needed us. That's what we assumed.

At commencement, Flora took the stage and addressed the students on the six brand-new macro screens NuCorp had donated, projected to the crowd of relatives, advocates, onlookers, fellow silents. I felt like I could just about understand her. At least, I sensed a general message of optimism and gratitude, a culmination of their time at Oaks. It was amazing to see the whole school communicating with each other—it was as if they were an orchestra and Flora was conducting them. For long stretches it didn't seem like she was doing anything up there, but the graduates and their classmates were still stirring. Staring at her, at each other.

I was, too. For seven years I'd been with this same group

of kids, and now they were no longer kids. The boys had stubble, and I could tell some lifted weights. The girls wore makeup. You could see a sort of alarming pucker to their lips. Everyone had changed into warm, nubile, fearless near-adults, and I'd changed, too, into a woman who brooded on her arm fat and who spent a half hour that morning plucking hairs from her neck, nose, upper lip, ears.

When Flora was done, her classmates stood up and applauded wildly, and everyone else joined in. It was the first time I'd ever seen my students clap.

Principal Haskins gave me the next year off. A gift. Full pay and benefits, a travel stipend if I wanted to go to conferences or visit other schools. It was awful. I stewed. I actually did an online seminar to adopt a Filipino war orphan, but I failed the personality test, the one where you try to estimate how much love you have to give. They said I had "low nurturing capacity."

I registered for a dating site. Destinationheartlink.com. I started by doing some of their online jigsaw puzzles, which may sound like the most despairing activity ever created, but is actually only the second-most, behind online needlepoint, which I also did. I spent hours making virtual pillow covers and then slowly transitioned to accepting some of the requests to grow my Heartlink profile and upload video quick-flicks and personality tests, which I filled out with pretend answers. I created a virtual gallery with artwork and found objects. I got some link-up requests, which I ignored, until a guy named Bastien Hvorecky sent me a quick-flick of himself smiling and gesticulating at an outdoor café in Bratislava and I realized how lonely I was.

We started with basic v-chats, talking like two people in a restaurant. I'd prep myself for almost an hour beforehand, putting on makeup, figuring out what to wear that didn't make me look like someone's sad online needlepointing aunt. I sprayed myself with perfume, just in case, I guess. I don't know. We scheduled our chats at 9:00 p.m. and at 9:00 a.m., and I went to bed pulsing and woke up pulsing. God, he was handsome. He had a thin tan face and his hair was dyed blond. He didn't speak English, which was perfect. His questions came through twice, once in Slovak in his voice, and then in English, brokenly translated by a v-chat robot: *So you live appropriately California and work concerning dumb children?* Close enough. He was an engineer, or engine repairman, divorced with two children—I think. In our v-chats there was a lot of dead time, and he was as content as I was to just stare. Heartlink would post randomly generated questions in both languages for discussion, basic first-date things early on, like *What is your most treasured memory of childhood? What's your favorite color?* The questions became more and more personal each time we v-chatted. After a few weeks they were *What turns you into a total horndog? What's your favorite color dildo?*

And then the questions became less like questions and more like . . . requests. At first we'd look down at them and laugh, but then we didn't anymore. One asked us to take off three items of clothing each, which we did. I took off my blouse, skirt, and sandals. He took off his socks, pants, and cravat. The two of us just sat there, stunned. When we signed off I drank three glasses of wine and did a five-thousand-piece basket-of-kitties online jigsaw puzzle.

We got used to the requests. The fact that Bastien didn't speak any English put me at ease. It made him seem more harmless. He looked like an artist, the way some Europeans do, and the bits of his apartment that I could see from the v-chats seemed book-filled and modern. We started doing this mutual self-gratification thing with one of the v-chat programs, where it would somehow gauge how close we were. Masturbation, yes, I hate that word. I watched him and he watched me, and we tried to synchronize our countdown clocks. Honestly, it was really . . . nice. It was certainly better than jigsaw puzzles or needlepoint. When we were finished we'd blow kisses to each other and say, "Good night," or "Have a good day," or nothing.

We did this for months. Then the notification came from Heartlink that said there'd been a security breach. They were contacting everyone who this Bastien from Slovakia had been chatting with—and he'd been chatting with dozens and dozens—to make sure they hadn't given out any sensitive information. Worse, he'd been recording the v-chats and posting them all around. Randomly sending them to people's profiles. The Heartlink people forwarded me a message with the subject heading *Asian Plumper Gives It to Herself Hard*. And attached was a video of me, giving it to myself hard.

I cried. I got my hair cut in hopes of disguising myself. I did a lot of things, and then I fled. With two bags of clothes I drove north to Monte Rio. I knew a few of the recent graduates had drifted up there and were all living in a two-story house among the redwoods. It sounded like a recipe for disaster, but that particular recipe was one I already knew well. I pulled up to the house, a crazy-looking thing—it seemed like each past owner had just added a new room rather than fixing up any of the old ones. I nudged open the door, and found much more than a few of my former students—they were sleeping six to a room, on the living room floors, in the bathrooms. It was insane, quiet and anarchic at the same time. They welcomed me, let me sleep on the couch. There was a lot of game-playing out in the backyard. Frisbees and croquet. It was oddly normal.

The locals had welcomed them from the start. Admirers from town came through daily with food and water and firewood. There was enough firewood in the carport to build another house. Someone had brought several cases of canned artichoke hearts, and the kids used them in every meal. I don't think they had ever cooked for themselves. The food was randomly generated, a confused mass of ingredients in a hellish swirl. They wouldn't let me work. They always served me first. I felt this immense gratitude from them, a protection. When I first showed up they'd all hugged me, everyone clamoring to get their arms around me, then they all looked at me deeply for almost a minute, showing their delight and also trying to read why I was there. While they might not have known exactly what happened, they could see what I needed. There's something immediately ennobling about a group incapable of thinking or saying the phrase "Asian plumper."

I couldn't stay forever, but it was enough for now. I recommenced watching them as I had back at Oaks. They interacted purposefully during the day, making repairs to the house and setting up tents in the yard. My own personal goal was to drink enough wine to fall asleep at night without remembering Bastien and his deceitful Slovakian penis.

Sometimes I fell into a dreamless sleep right away and made it through the night without waking up. Other times, I couldn't. I lay awake listening to the stragglers outside, cutting wood and throwing it on the bonfire, playing various instruments. I could hear everything at night. The outside sounds, house sounds, sleeping sounds, and, often, the sounds of my former students casually coupling. It was huffy, rhythmic, greedy. Familiar enough to keep me awake until it stopped.

PATTI KERN

MONTE RIO, CA
2027

I read about the Monte Rio compound in the *Russian River Gazette*, and by the next morning we were there, the van packed with bulk-bagged megavitamins, organic nonperishable yogurt leather, and ten cases of cucumber water.

Upon my arrival, my determination doubled. The silents had settled in the main house, a two-story with one of the least ameliorative floor plans I'd ever come across. Houses should aspire to echo the bardo, our path from birth to rebirth, but this one was all low closets and rooms leading into rooms leading into rooms. Sofas that smelled like cat sperm. I let myself linger on the bright spots: a wood-burning stove in the living room, the bathroom's beautiful mosaic tile, the large teepee-shaped tents in the backyard where a lot of them slept. When we arrived two girls came out to our van and I was so overcome that I hopped out and engirdled both of them with a profound hug. They were rigid with the kind of passive, long-standing distrust of nonsilents that I'd expected. I held firm and tried to relax them with an outlook conveying roughly, "You young people will soon be embraced like prophets." After a few moments in my arms they loosened a little, enough to slip away and help Patrick unload the van, and I followed them into the house.

There's an awareness that guides you when you do something spontaneous, something out of step. Some of us have inner songs, some have inner lights, some inner maps—it all serves to help rechart our destinies. My inner awareness was my own voice saying, On on on. Every few minutes, on on on, for seventy-nine days now. I didn't need to speak. I told this to Patrick as we drove north through the redwoods. Patrick and I had become involved, but he was in a more primitive stage of attachment than I was. He would nod to billboards and scenic overlooks on the highway and make comments on them. An attempt at bridging. It forced me to keep saying, "Let's withhold, Patrick. Let's not mistake vocalization for true communion."

He turned all huffy. At one point he said, "I guess I won't comment on the fact that there're about a dozen network transmitters over there shaped exactly like grazing cows." He turned on the radio and found a classic-rock station. He said, "I guess I won't ask you if this is okay."

Oh, squander. So often we use speech as plumbing. We redirect needless emotional waste and dump it onto others. One of our sixty-four goals was to make people aware of this. To rid us of this petty flushing.

That's what went through my mind when I met the teacher, Francine. She was sitting on a barstool in the kitchen while another girl waited for butter to melt in a sauté pan. I focused so intently on this girl, ignoring the teacher, whose clothes and demeanor projected an aura of harsh casualness. She was stout, not pleasing to look at. But the girl had a lovely open face, a calming and synchronous outfit, and an intelligence in her eyes that went beyond knowing. Francine asked if I was part of the town welcoming committee.

"I'm on a deeper errand," I told her. "Which I'll communicate with them when no one else is around. It's too important to disclose."

By this time the girl was watching me, ignoring the butter smoking in her pan, and so I turned and expressed fellowship with my mouth and admiration with my eyes. I said aloud, "Right now we are standing inside the seed of tomorrow."

"I'm actually sitting," the teacher said.

"I meant me and her," I said, motioning to the girl.

"Her name's Angela," the teacher said. "It's probably good to know the name of who you're standing inside the seed with."

Patrick, finished unloading the van, extended his hand to the teacher and said, "She's got great plans for these people. She's filled out three spiral notebooks already. She's a woman on a mission."

My inner reserves wilted to hear Patrick say it like this. He had a great gift for reductive summary. There in the kitchen I made a note to establish practice regimens for all the nonsilents who would be living among the silents. Something akin to a collective meditation that would place us in a common register. Watching Angela cook, I made more plans. Vegetarian diets. Permaculture farming and a barter economy and goats with bells around their necks. Hourly hugs. Meditation hikes. A smoothie barn. Rustic permanent housing for the dedicated nonsilents, and temporary housing for the curious ones. A focus on individual spirituality and worship of the seasons. Group laughing sessions.

Francine interrupted my reverie. She said, "It's time for dinner. I'd invite you, but it sounds like you're a pretty busy woman. With that mission and all."

Some use words like crowbars. I could tell that the teacher thought she was acting in the silents' best interests, so I nodded curtly to her and withdrew. I tried to exchange a meaningful stare with Angela, but she was dumping a can of artichoke hearts over what looked like cubed Spam. Stay strong, I thought. Soon you will be cooking organically grown stir-fries. The silents' compound was an extraordinary canvas upon which we could paint a vision of true communion.

Ten days later Patrick and I were living in a tent across the creek from the compound. My plan was to keep to ourselves, keep quiet, and wait. I could've waited indefinitely. But Patrick was impatient. With the silents. With me. He said he was having a hard time seeing what was so important and special about them. All they did was murder perfectly good songs on out-of-tune instruments, he said, and play Frisbee, video games, and some chase game he couldn't figure out, and drink the wine that he was sure they traded in our cucumber water for. They were no different from other kids their age, in other words.

"Some journeys require us to be blindfolded part of the way," I told him.

"I liked you a lot better before you knew everything," he said.

Shortly before our pilgrimage, Patrick and I had become intimate, but so far I'd resisted sexual intercourse. Inside the tent, I allowed him to give me sensual massages and administer cunnilingus, after which we stared at each other for hours. Something about Patrick's face, the tightness of his features, turned my mind inward. I retraced my spiritual path. All those missteps, or what I thought at the time were missteps: the head-shaving, the starvation quests, Most Benevolent Thomas, the suicide pact—I knew they'd been right and necessary, because they'd inoculated me against falseness. And then, right when I'd be near that stream of truth, just about to fill my pail, I'd feel Patrick slipping under the covers and his wet mouth trailing down my navel toward my lap, and my mind would go gray.

One night I had a vision. Not a dream but a waking foresight of the future. Someone else and I were holding hands, and we were leading the silents toward an open field. The farther we walked, the more this inner feeling of predestination grew. Suddenly we stopped at a place where a perfect half moon hung low in the sky, and I knew that we'd arrived. I turned to the person next to me, expecting to find Patrick, and instead it was the teacher, Francine. A man flew through the air on a motorcycle and a thousand babies cried.

KENULE MITEE

BROOKLYN, NY
2027

I'm telling you that I will never forget that week. Things were already crazy in my life even before those kids started to show up on the beach. I had met this girl, a girl from Kpor. I should have known not to get involved with a small-town girl. She was beautiful, but Anglican and very, very religious. We dated for several months, and I thought that things were going well until I found out that she had a baby with another man in Ogoniland, and her parents were taking care of the baby until it died from meningitis. She said, "I am going to Kpor to bury my daughter," and my jaw fell out. I was like, "How do you go around keeping secrets like this from me?" I was furious with this girl.

She had left on a plane the day before. I was still mad in the morning when I got my cart from the storage locker. I had a feeling of utter darkness toward this girl who had deceived me. I remember that I was acting like a small boy. Angrily wheeling the cart up and down the boardwalk, shouting out, "Fat bread, fat bread, fifty bucks a stick." Like I wanted to hurt a man.

Oh. Yes. That was the other thing. They had just taken Spray Ya Face off the market about a month before, because of some boys that died. My boss said to me, "Now you will sell fat bread," and I was out the next day, selling this new product. I did not want to eat this thing, but I had to taste it so that I could know what I was selling. I found the sour filling to be awful. Maybe the worst thing I had ever put in my mouth. Those silent kids, they were not happy about fat bread at all. They had bought Spray Ya Face from me every day. They were my most loyal customers. I tried to tell them, "Look, it's not me. They took it off the market. It's dangerous. You shouldn't be messing around with it," but you know these kids. The things you say make no difference to them. They were very angry, and they did not come to my cart for many weeks. They would do whatever they could to avoid me. And I have to say that it hurt my feelings a little. Because those kids, they were part of my every day. I took great comfort in their presence, you know. With everything going on in my life, they were the one thing that didn't change.

So all of this made me very angry and sad on that morning. I hated this girl with her deceiving ways. I hated the fat bread. I hated its smell. I hated the people who bought it. I was pushing the cart down the boardwalk and I saw a group of kids standing by the entrance to the roller coaster. They were silent kids, I knew because of the way they moved, but I had never seen these ones before. That was strange to me. And there was one boy climbing up over the fence. I don't think they knew that it was closed down. I don't think they could read the signs. The yellow tape meant nothing to them, so the boy was climbing over, I don't even know why.

I wheeled the cart toward them and I said, "Hey, that's not safe there." They turned around quickly, and the boy on the fence fell right down on the other side. He started to groan, I mean, it must have been a ten-foot drop, you know? Onto his shoulder. The other kids, they ran away and left him there. I called after them, but they were gone. I was alone with this hurt boy. I asked him if anything was broken, but he had no way to tell me this. I climbed over the fence and jumped down the other side. He was breathing like there was no air in his lungs. I didn't know how to help the boy. I couldn't carry him over the fence, and the gate was locked, and there seemed to be no other way out of the coaster area.

There was a small hut where they must have sold tickets to the coaster at some point. I went inside to see if there was a key in there, but it was dark and empty except for some trash, empty beer bottles and wrappers and things. I stood there thinking what I should do next. I felt responsible for this hurt boy, but I didn't have a single idea of how to solve the problem. I was just standing there like a statue, frozen in thought, and the girl called me. Right then, of all the times to call. She was sobbing. They had just buried the baby and she was in a state. I don't know why she chose me to turn to. I said all the things that a man should say in this kind of situation, but nothing more. I knew right then that I would not see the girl again, that small-town girl with her church and her secret affairs. I did not want to waste a single extra word on her. I hung up the phone and sighed. I had already had the worst day a person could have.

I came out of the little hut and I couldn't believe it. There were about a hundred of those kids standing on the other side of the fence looking in at me. They started to climb up, two at a time, a whole wave of them coming up over the top. They got down and made a—I don't know the word for this—a temple out of their bodies to lift the boy up. They worked together to bring him over the fence. Like ants carrying a leaf over a hill, maybe, but really I had never seen anything like it. When they had gotten the boy up over the fence, a young woman came up to me and offered to lift me over the fence the same way. I waved my hands at her to say, "I'm okay, I will climb." For some reason I cannot describe, I just didn't want them to touch me. The girl turned around and climbed over the fence with the rest of them.

I stood watching through the wires as a group of those kids carried the injured boy to the beach. I could see that there were more of them farther down the shore, just sitting there in the sand, and they all gathered around the boy who had fallen to comfort him. And even more of those kids, not one of whom did I recognize, started to form a line in front of my cart. Many, many more of these silents than I had ever seen in one place. I said a prayer to myself then, which was, "Let nothing else happen today but that I sell all of this cursed fat bread."

EMILY ROARK

QUEENS, NY
2027

When Becca moved to that tilting pink house in Jackson Heights, I followed her there. Not right away. First I worked on Mom for months, told her how useful I could be to Becca and the other silents who lived in the group home. I could give Mom up-to-the-minute briefings so she'd know Becca was okay and the house wasn't being condemned and demolished while Becca sat around playing her vibraphone. I moved there in June. Most days Becca and I woke up early and took the train into the city. We'd sit facing each other and exchange smiles when someone came on screaming about sulfur lakes or how the police stole all his white blood cells. We'd play the drawing game like when we were kids— she'd start with a line or a few circles and give it to me, and we'd pass it back and forth until it was finished.

That's what we were doing the morning the man came and sat down next to her. He wore cutoff corduroys and had a high forehead. He looked at us, and right away I knew he was silent. I spent so much time with Becca that I felt I could almost communicate with them. He was facing us, friendly and probing, but I could tell there were other layers beyond my reach. Becca, though, was clearly interested. They went back and forth for a few minutes, and then seemed to settle the matter. I took the drawing from her and worked on it a little, added an alligator, some splashes.

At Bryant Square, Becca didn't climb the stairs like usual. Instead, we followed the guy with cutoffs to the D train and took it all the way to the end of the line, Coney Island. Or, I mean, Becca followed him, I followed her. Out of the station, past the condemned shops, down a crumbling boardwalk. Then, farther along the old midway, on the beach, a throng of people. I could hear the ocean rumble, crazed birds calling to each other, but down on the beach hundreds of boys and girls Becca's age were standing, sitting, watching. I stood there with my hand over my mouth. Becca was scrutinizing me, waiting, waiting, and then she smiled. She skittered down the stairs to the beach, and I followed.

I tagged along with her the rest of the day. We found a spot by some purple sawgrass and sat in the hot sand with our backpacks. Becca pivoted to a group of girls to the left of us, and everyone interacted for a while. At one point Becca gestured my way and all of them looked at me and I gave a half-hearted wave. They found this hilarious. We left our packs in the sand and followed the girls up to the boardwalk. There were funnel cakes and weird games, but mostly everyone just seemed excited about the sheer fact of it, of each other. The only sound was the sand on the wooden planks.

When we returned to the beach, some boys had come and claimed our spot. Two of them, sun-fried and ratty. As we got closer, I saw they were rooting through our packs. Becca ran over and tried to yank away the bags, but the boy who was holding hers wouldn't budge. His whole neck was tattooed with green snakeskin. I don't even remember what was in my pack, probably just some pens and gum and my subway card. They could have it. I wasn't going to mess with those guys.

Then down the stairs came a few more boys, no less terrifying—reinforcements, I assumed, but this new group ignored us and stepped up to Snake Neck. The one in front eyed him with almost no expression—but only almost. He didn't blink, he didn't move. It was stunning. He was stunning. He had this stern but animated face, big brown eyes. He and his friends wore tank tops and weathered work pants, and he had raised red scars on his arms. Parallel like a claw scrape. Snake Neck handed the pack to Becca, and the other guy handed mine back to me, and the two of them walked up the stairs and down the boardwalk and, I have no doubt, away from the gathering forever.

The main boy waited for Becca to search through her bag and make sure everything was there. When she was done he nodded to us, and the boys walked off. Becca was transfixed. She stood there stunned for a few minutes, then took my hand. We followed the gang around while they roved around the beach, then up the stairs to the boardwalk. Beyond one of the barbwire fences, a pair of boys were trying to rip planks off the old wooden roller coaster, which was about ninety percent demolished, and the gang intervened. A girl with a huge sun hat sat on one of the benches crying, and they gathered around her. Becca hovered at the edge of their group, and I hovered at the edge of hers.

Eventually Becca and I went back down to the beach, where we found some friends of hers from the home and others

I'd never seen before. Becca kept looking behind her to make sure I was still there, and the girls would wave to me every so often, like I was a baby or a pet bird. The sky began to darken, but I knew from the look of calm glee on Becca's face that we wouldn't be going anywhere for a while.

THEODORE GREENE

RICHMOND, CA
2027

I woke up in the middle of the night with this terrible heartburn. The doctor had given me a medicated throat mist that was supposed to help, but it barely had any effect anymore. I went out into the hallway to get a drink of water and saw a blue glow coming from the living room. I walked in there and Flora was sitting at my worktable again, watching the news feed on the wall. Just sitting completely still in the darkness. I could barely make out her face, lit up by the wallscreen, almost hovering there without a body, like a spirit. I knew what she was looking at, because I'd seen her stealing glances throughout the day. Everyone was covering it—you couldn't go anywhere without seeing some mention of the thing. Tons of silent kids sort of taking over the beach at Coney Island. These faraway shots of a sea of bodies. You might not even know they were silent kids if you—I mean, I could tell they were silent by the way they were acting, but you might just look at the news and think it was some sort of mass prank. A bunch of kids decide to meet up at a certain place at a certain time, the kind of dumbass stuff I used to do with my friends in high school. But the reporters were like, "The jury's still out on how these uniquely abled young people found each other or what it is they're doing on the beach."

I stood in the hallway watching Flora. The heartburn was killing me, but I didn't want to move. I *couldn't* move. I had an urge to go in and shut down the feed. Like the news was a kind of poison floating through the air, and she was inhaling it just by sitting there. I didn't know what those kids on the beach were doing, but I had this sense that it was something I needed to protect her from. What kept me from just going over there and shutting it off? Well, I had this other notion that if I took it away from her, she'd just be more curious. It would instantly become a thing. I'd just give it power by trying to hide it, so I just stood there—what do you call the thing when you can't make up your mind? I stood there doing that, looking at her, wondering what to do next. And in that light, I could see that she wasn't a young kid anymore—that sounds, I know, like one of those things a parent says, or maybe not even a real parent but one in a movie, but you do really have these moments when you look at your kid and you think, Oh my God, this is happening so fast. So much has already slipped away. I had to face the fact that she was sixteen years old, fully capable of going across the country if she really tried. And that opened up a whole new kind of fear for me.

Mincing. That's the word. I was mincing, is what I was. Just standing there like an idiot. I finally couldn't take it anymore. I had to pick a direction. I decided that shutting off the feed was worth the consequences. I went in and said, "You need to get your sleep, sweets," and I turned the thing off. I tried to make it not about the feed itself, the content of the feed. I just wanted her to get her rest. But I was sort of trembling as I swiped the power bar. And when the feed was shut it was pitch black, but I could tell that she knew I was cutting her off. I could sense it in the way she stood up and went to her room.

The next morning we went through our customary ritual—she had graduated that spring, but Oaks had brought her back as a sort of teacher's aide. I packed her lunch in the thermal bag she brought to school every day. I put the boxes of cereal out for her to choose from. I sat at the kitchen table and waited, and she came in at the normal time. She picked the yogurt-drizzled Os. I put them in a bowl for her and filled a little pitcher with milk, and she sat down at the table and we ate. To me, it was like every movement had a weight to it. I felt like I was in quicksand. But she seemed unaffected. It was as if we hadn't even seen each other in the night. Maybe she had been sleepwalking or something, was what I started to think, because she just didn't seem any different. I started to loosen up and feel a little better about things. She was a smart girl. She could handle seeing those kids on the beach. They were kids like her, so of course she'd be interested in what they were doing—but that didn't mean she was going to go out to New York and throw her life away. Right? I felt kind of foolish for the reaction I'd had in the night, because she had everything going for her at the school. Those students she worked with were her life. She was just going to walk away from all that? I was a little embarrassed, actually, for even thinking about her running off to join a cult or something.

We got in the car and the news was on. I always had the news running in the car, just so she could have more practice hearing words. But, of course, that morning they were talking about Coney Island. The woman on the news said that there were over a thousand silent kids on the beach. They'd stayed overnight, which was illegal, but there were too many of them to drag off, so the cops just kept an eye on them. More and more kids kept showing up throughout the night, apparently, and no one really knew how they were getting there or what they were going to do. I sat in the driver's seat, listening with my hands on the steering wheel, and for the first time I found myself hoping that she really couldn't understand a single word. I started to have a mini–panic attack, because, suddenly, this thing I was trying so hard to drill into her brain, suddenly I didn't want it there at all. Not this way. I didn't want her to start understanding words just in time to hear about these vagrant kids and their big sleepover or whatever it was. I looked over at Flora and she was just looking out the window at the houses. Just like the day before. She wasn't getting any of it. I could tell the words meant nothing to her. The news report was just another sound to her, some strange boring music that her dad made her listen to on the way to school.

I led her to the primary classroom and gave her three hugs plus one bonus hug, which was what we did at the beginning of every day. I watched her go into the class and pick out a carpet square, and all of the little kids came up to her to see what the morning work would be. Outside in the hallway there were a couple parents talking about the Coney Island thing. Fred Prior said his cousin had a silent child who had run away to go there. He didn't have any real information, though. His cousin was just as surprised and confused by the whole thing as we were. The kid was just gone, apparently, and then they saw him in some footage of the crowds. Sejal Pranesh was like, "Your cousin didn't go and fetch him out of there?" And Fred Prior shrugged. Carolyn Crosby said, "Honestly, where are the parents in all of this?" We were all supposed to feel pity for the parents of the kids at the beach. The implication was that we knew how to raise our kids, and those other parents didn't. It felt comforting to frame it that way. It was convenient. But while we kept talking in the hallway there, I found my attention drifting again and again to the classroom, where Flora was kneeling in front of those kids, rolling sand dough in her hands, and I felt my sense of satisfaction evaporate into the air.

DAVID DIETRICH

BROOKLYN, NY
2027

As soon as I saw the gathering on the news, I took a thirty-six-hour bus ride to Penn Station and the subway to Coney Island. I didn't know how to work the transfers, so a woman in tight orange shorts traced my route for me on a map and I ended up sitting by her. She was going there, too. She had a face like this papier-mâché American cockroach I made in seventh-grade art class—we were supposed to come up with an animal to represent some ideal. Mine was survival. The reason the woman was going to Coney Island was to study silents—she was doing some research about them. I kept snipping off strands of things I wanted to say to her. I do this chant that helps when I feel like I'm about to start talking a lot to someone I probably hate—it goes, *Nothing in common but arms, nothing in common but legs*—but the woman, even though some college probably paid her actual money to study silents, was getting it all wrong. For starters, she said that they were assembling on the beach as a display of solidarity. She called it the silents' "imperative moment."

A pair of kids in the seat next to us were playing with one

of those stupid-ass sound wands, using it to make death rattles. I said to the woman, "I don't think that's what they're doing. It's not for you. Or me. It's for them. They have this living . . . thing inside, and now they're using it. Have you ever held a gun? It's like a gun."

I'd said probably two words up until now to her, so she was staring at me with her mouth wide open. She really did look like that cockroach—like she wanted a mother cockroach to come lay eggs in her mouth. I turned my lips down and shrugged my eyelids. It was my sorry face, but she didn't understand.

I said, "I study them too."

She pulled out a Catena and started scribbling in it, and she didn't look up again.

Make a rule, make an arbitrary rule for yourself. Now stick to it. That's from the impulse-mastery chapter on my *Body-Free Mind* recording.

I had a rotten mind-set when the train let us out at Coney Island. Thinking about how I either say two words to people or two hundred—it's never forty-four, or seventy-one. And how I act like I've achieved impulse mastery but I go right on breaking every rule I make for myself: no more beef-and-cheddar tub dinners from Captain Hat's, no more fapping to silent-porn sites—which were all fake and total boner-wilters anyway— no more pretending, no closing my eyes and picturing me playing upside-down drums on the song I'm listening to, no imagining myself being reborn as a silent. I broke them all.

I was so fogged I didn't notice the beach right away. At the back of my mind I was thinking it would probably be over by the time I got there, that's how it usually worked—but it wasn't over. The beach was shoulder-to-shoulder silents. Some vendors had shown up and walked around yelling about tank tops and lemon ices and dissolvable tattoos. And a group of sweaty protesters, some carrying homemade signs, some chanting things like "Speak up" and "We can't hear you." And plenty of gawkers, standing high up on the boardwalk, which was littered with rotting junk that people were too lazy to push into the ocean. But the real activity was down on the sand. I can't say how many there were, maybe ten thousand. I stood there watching them for so long I lost track of my body—it felt like the sight of them was slowly hollowing me out, getting me ready. What I wanted, what I thought, what I did—none of it mattered. Because here they were. I kept waiting for them to do something. To fight. To scream. But nothing. I wanted to be with them so bad, I bit the inside of my cheek every time I was tempted to run down and join them. But I wasn't going to ruin their gathering. Down there things were airtight, sacred. And, as I stared into the sea of them, I knew why I'd come. I was here to prove I could be around the biggest group of them ever without lurching out or clinging. I could protect them and make sure nobody did anything stupid. Starting with me.

But the first girl I saw, the *very first girl*, turned around a few seconds after I started staring at her. She did that upper-cheek wriggle that silent girls do that makes me want to pray and make promises. My first urge was to do my politely longing face, but I refrained. Today was their day. They didn't need me sidling up to them and ogling them.

It's just skin, I whispered to myself. *It's just tissues and muscle.*

Nothing ever works. I didn't last twenty minutes. I was going crazy. I looked at the ocean, which nobody was swimming in—there were huge signs posted with pictures of babies dissolving in the surf—and admired its calmness. I decided I'd go out to the end of the rotting pier and dive in. I would put a natural barrier between me and them, and master my impulses from there. I hid my bag behind a pile of discarded extension cords, took off my shirt, and dove into the low surf. Goddamn, it was cold. It was an all-over sting. But I got used to it. I can get used to almost anything. To warm myself, I swam parallel to the shore and then found a sandbar that I could sit cross-legged on, with just my head exposed. The water wasn't bad if I stayed low. Baggies floated by, some plastic chew toys, other trash. This was when I heard the men talking. They must've been about fifty yards away, but their voices carried clear across the water. Four griefers in this swan-bird paddleboat rigged with dull black megaphone-looking things. I floated closer, just my eyes and ears and nose above water, and listened to them planning their plans—something about a sound gun, something about "enforced conversation," something about "giving the silents something to talk about." "Bowel-loosening decibels of pure noise." I heard all of it.

I waited for hours, it felt like. I turned into a prune while the crowd of silents continued to grow. I sat motionless, the waves slapping my cheeks.

At the beach, the crowd swelled and contracted, like a giant breathing animal. I tried to imagine all the little transfers between them, all the exchanges of happiness. I felt shivers. It was the most beautiful thing I'd ever seen. I was also very very cold.

But inside, I felt good. I felt in control. The paddleboat started heading toward the beach, and I followed, simple as a machine. I swam faster than the boat, underwater the whole time except quick guppy breaths, and waited right underneath, in a hidden den made by the bird's plastic tail feathers.

"Wait for the signal," one of the men in the boats said. "Then we'll shock these fuckers out of their happy fog."

With all the force I could muster I pushed on the boat. It didn't tip over easily, and the four guys tried to paddle away, but I swam faster. I caught up to it, gripped on to the side, and used all my weight to capsize it. I swear I could hear all the speakers zip-zapping and shorting out. A guy from the boat came swimming at me with flailing arms, hitting me again and again, and I was unconscious for the rest, but I guess the silents were watching everything happen and a bunch of them swam out and saved me.

When I came to, I was lying in an ambulance parked on the boardwalk. An oily-looking paramedic was testing my vitals, asking me the most irrelevant questions, just talking, talking. The sirens turned on and the beach stayed behind.

PALMER CARLYLE

HOBOKEN, NJ
2027

I was at the Book Bash in Dyker Heights browsing the clearance bins when Tate called me to the beach for crowd control. Book Bash was selling off all of its physical inventory, and there were still some treasures to be found, like a London Magazine Editions print of Bukowski's *Life & Death in the Charity Ward*, fine condition in a near-fine dust jacket. I bought it for a dollar, and I challenge you to find a copy in similar condition for less than two hundred. Thing was just sitting in the bin, waiting for the chipper. I was at the register paying for a bunch of books, when Tate called all the patrolmen over to Luna Park. Apparently the mayor was getting nervous. Someone'd estimated over three thousand kids on the beach, and it didn't look like they were going anywhere. Everyone was waiting for some sort of demands, but no demands were coming, which made everyone even more uncomfortable. I asked Tate how he thought these kids were supposed to *deliver* their demands, but he just told me to hang my dick on a hat stand and get over there.

The bookstore clerk said, "Mutetards getting out of hand?"

and I told him all due respect, I didn't like him using that term, and by the way, I'd just bought about seven hundred dollars' worth of books from him, including a fair copy of the original Ace edition of Burroughs's *Junkie*, for twenty bucks, fuck you very much.

I parked the Interceptor at Surf and West Tenth, and I could already feel the weird energy pulsing through the air. There were guys from every Brooklyn precinct there. I saw Chao, a buddy from the academy days, standing alone by the human-target range smoking a fake cigarette. I asked what the scene at the beach was like and Chao goes, "A silent mob scene is like a hand job without the hand." I didn't know how to take that statement, because you could go either way with it. I could imagine a roundly satisfying hand job from a ghost, but maybe I'm overthinking it. That's what Tate says. "You're thinking too much, Carlyle." I let him read my novel manuscript, and he said it felt "overworked." He was like, "Thrust your hands deep into the lifestream, Carlyle. Don't be such a pussy." He's a hard man with a bullet still lodged in his thigh, so I've got to trust he knows what he's talking about.

Chao and I walked through the restricted area, where a tech crew was stat-gunning an inverted swan boat under a pair of LED floods, and stepped up onto the boardwalk. The beach was literally packed with these kids. I've worked crowds of almost fifty thousand before, so I was prepared to meet a mass of bodies. I was also prepared for long-shot taunts and jeers from hooligans hiding in the throng, maybe a couple piss-filled plastic bottles hurled at me, and the general rowdiness and panic that you get when a cop enters any crowd of young people. But there was none of that. There was no sound at all, apart from the water and the hum of the portable generators. You could see the kids outlined in the light from the coaster, which the park guards had switched on even though the thing had been closed for years. We weaved through rows and rows of heads extending all the way out to the water, but any sound the kids made by moving around was drowned out by the tide. They were like a mass of seagulls out there, quietly strutting around or exploring or just sitting. In a way, I guess I found myself longing for a couple sick epithets—some kid saying, "Hey, do you smell bacon?" or something. Some kind of pushback, no matter how aggravating. Something to remind me what I was doing there.

We came to a group of kids who were bunched up in a wild kind of scrum. Chao trained his Maglite on them so that you could see how slowly they were moving, almost as if they were reenacting something. I really couldn't even describe it to you, what they were doing out there, but whether it was sport or theater or some kind of lame clothed orgy, it was unsettling. They put up their hands to block out the glare from Chao's Maglite, but didn't scatter. "They've been doing this for days," Chao said. I just nodded. I didn't know what it was they were trying to do, and I wasn't sure I wanted to.

We waded through the crowd for about a half an hour. Chao said, "Seen enough?" and I said I had, so we climbed back up to the boardwalk and showed off the uniform. It was this weird mix of tension—I mean, who knew what these kids were planning, and how were we going to do anything about it?—this mix of tension and calm. So quiet, but somehow growing, preparing, readying. For what, I had no idea, and when, neither.

Chao and I just stood there, catching up and passing the fake cigarette back and forth. The most action we saw was some kid trying to climb up the side of the funnel-cake booth. Other than that they were just out there in the dusk. It became obvious to me that the mayor had sent us there not for crowd control but to assert our authority, to let the kids know that, whatever it was they thought they were doing out there in the sand, it was happening in our world. It was happening only because Brooklyn was allowing it to happen. But those kids just barely noticed us. They might have been squatting on city property, but they were going to do their thing whether we were there or not. By this point we were almost eager for the shit to go down, for the penny to drop, whatever, so we'd at least have something to work with, or work against. It was the waiting that was driving us crazy. These kids could do anything, but all they were doing was nothing.

And then, after all that, they just left. It was around three in the morning when it started. We were standing under the Astroland rocket and they just started streaming across the boardwalk in huge clumps. Ten and twenty of them at a time, passing under the portable halide floods we'd set up by the entrance. I looked at Chao and he shrugged. More and more of them kept coming up off the beach. A whole surge flowing past us, kids with bedrolls and canvas bags or sneakers tied together and slung over their shoulders. Some of them arm in arm, drowsy and buzzed, others striding solo with a kind of stoic purpose. The only sound was the padding of their feet as they crossed the boardwalk. A reporter stood at a distance, for some reason whispering into a mic while the camera captured retreating kids as they passed in the background like soldiers returning from battle. I didn't know whether they had finished what they had come to do or if they were just moving on to the next step. We just watched them all go by, powerless to do anything but gawk.

The sky was overcast, so dawn never seemed to come. The beach world just turned lighter shades of brown. Gradually we could make out staggered shelters and smoked-out fires dotting the beach all the way up to the end of the boardwalk. It was deeply peaceful there with the whole operation closed down. Chao and I were told to search for holdouts and herd them to a white bus that was parked across from the coaster. They were transporting the kids to an auxiliary gym at Kingsborough Community College, where they were going to figure out what to do with them next. So we went along the shore kicking apart the plywood lean-tos and makeshift pallet shanties. There were a few stragglers, half-naked kids entwined in hollowed-out drifts or loners determined to hang on for another day. We led them up to the bus, where they sat facing each other, doing their face thing, popping and rippling their muscles in tightly orchestrated tides. It was wild to see it for real, close up. The thing you don't get when you see it on the news is the raspy little clicks and puffs that are a by-product of those little expressions. And the sense of, I don't know, something familiar that's just out of reach. Like the way a certain smell can bring back a whole part of your life. You don't know what the smell belongs to anymore—you can't identify it no matter how hard you try, but you remember where you were, how you felt, what was happening in your life. That was what it was like to watch those kids in their face-talk.

The bus hissed and lurched away from the sidewalk and pulled slowly down West Tenth in the barren morning. There was nobody out on the streets. In the light of day the rides and booths looked acutely shoddy. I went home and read that Ace copy of *Junkie* cover to cover in a single uninterrupted session—it was only in fair condition, so I didn't feel bad about cracking the spine. I just felt this almost uncontrollable desire to dive headlong into the world of words again. I know it doesn't make sense, but it was almost like walking around among those kids had somehow drained the language right out of me.

VOLUME THREE

THEODORE GREENE

RICHMOND, CA
2028

We threw a party for Flora the night before she left for Monte Rio. Fred Prior let us use his lawn, because he actually had a lawn, and Sue Ng ran a catering service, so she donated a whole setup with a couple staff people. There was a big white tent and globe lights strung all around the yard. It looked impressive, almost professional, and lots of people from the school showed up. There were kids everywhere, running around in the dark, kicking balloons up into the air and head-butting them, doing forward rolls through Fred's hedges. It was like some kind of magic was loose in the air.

I somehow managed to twist even this happy event into an occasion for regret, because I never really let Flora run loose like that. I never allowed her that kind of freedom. I was so destroyed by Mel's death, and I let it overshadow everything. And then I used Flora—I focused on her silence with what I see now as a kind of rage. Not rage in a violent sense, except for maybe what it did to me inside. But I had so much anger to burn and no way to let it out except through my obsessive quest to get some meaningful phrase out of her.

Just get her to say something, anything, in any language at all. It was like Flora was a puzzle Mel had left me with, and if I could only solve the puzzle, Mel would come back to me. I really almost believed that. And of course, all I got out of all my obsessing was a girl who, I don't think, had ever actually had fun.

And the real stinger was that Flora looked so much like Mel. Francine Chang came back from Monte Rio just for the party, and she brought a photo-stream of Flora from over the years, from literally the first day the school opened until Francine left the school. There was a family tree that Flora and I had made at one point, and it had a picture of Mel in it, and everyone kept asking about that woman who looked just like Flora. It was true. Flora was the living embodiment, like an exact mirror image of Mel. Francine came by at some point during the night and put her hand on my shoulder. "I wasn't sure that was a good idea," she said, about the photos. She was worried that she'd stirred up old feelings. I said it was okay, and I put my hand over hers. I was half hoping she'd look up at me and we'd—you know, that something would happen. I mean, I had seen the video of her on the Web, like, more times than I probably should have. And that sort of changed the way I thought of her, but even before that, I'd always felt a kind of resonance between us. Just the, I guess, doughy lonesomeness that she projected was always attractive to me in a way I could never put into words. But she just patted my hand and went over to the bean buffet to talk to Sue Ng.

Flora sat under a big willow tree at the other end of the yard with her friends. Occasionally a Wee Three or a Sprout would come up and give her a hug or sneak up behind her and drop a handful of grass in her hair, and she'd turn and laugh and try to get them. I could barely look at her. I don't know how I managed to raise such an incredibly kind and beautiful woman out of the blackest rotting rinds of my gloom. It was sort of astonishing. I drank myself stupid and passed out on Fred Prior's back-porch glider.

Then it was morning and we were driving up along the coast. She had a light orange scarf around her neck that was tied into a kind of flower, something she'd made herself. It was a particular thing they were wearing that summer up at the Monte Rio house, and she wanted to show up with it already in place. The Coney Island gathering had changed her. Ever since she saw that footage, all those kids together in one place, it was like something had shifted inside her. Everything about her life in Richmond was structured, ordered, and safe, and I imagine it was beginning to feel a little like a cage. But there were people like her gathering on their own, without the guidance—or, I guess, control—of the speaking world. It must have been exhilarating to see that. So I guess I wasn't entirely taken by surprise when she came to me with a hand-drawn map of California with a path to Monte Rio. I knew that some part of her was already there.

I could have prevented her from going, but what kind of life would we have had? She wasn't an insect pinned to a board. I could've kept her in the apartment, with her bedroom still painted to look like the ocean at night with the big fucking— sorry—big crescent moon around the street-level window. But what kind of life would it have been?

We pulled up to the house in the middle of the afternoon. The weather was weirdly hot and uncomfortable, nothing like what I expected up north. The house was set back a little from the street, nestled among redwoods that seemed to go back forever. The exterior was in pretty bad shape. The whole place needed an overhaul. But it was tidy enough. And I had to admit that it had something on the basement apartment. I took Flora's bags out of the trunk and set them down on the driveway, and I tried to scowl but as always she could see right through—she could tell exactly how I was feeling no matter how I contorted my face. She grabbed my shoulders and looked into my eyes and went AU6C plus AU12D with AU43A, which was a raising of the cheeks with her lips pulled back and her eyes slightly closed, which might have meant something more than "I'm happy here," but I was just thankful for whatever I could get.

PATTI KERN

MONTE RIO, CA
2028

Patrick and I argued from the start. I had plans for the first intentional silent community in Monte Rio, and I needed someone to help me see it through. We'd start by building the communion center, right behind the main house, and then construct outbuildings that radiated like yantra petals from a mandala. Whatever we needed, we'd build. It was going to be our place, the silents and us, fully integrated, purposeful. Seeing the gathering at Coney Island, I could tell that a movement was brewing. A hungering for community. We'd provide the retreat, but not a retreat *from* anything. A retreat *to*. To knowing, to the true language. A place for the dedicated and the curious to live and work among the silents. A site of refuge, of constant serenity. We'd grow what we needed, abandon what we didn't. The silents would be at the heart of it all.

We bought Quikrete, hand tools, nails and screws, two-by-fours, and particleboard recycled from derelict chicken coops. We went to the dump and salvaged old street signs and fence posts. I wanted to construct most of the communion center in recycled materials, but Patrick kept saying it was going to collapse on everyone. His enthusiasm for the project was ebbing, so he viewed everything I said through his own smeared scope. What did I know about wiring? he asked. About plumbing? Support braces, foundations, wainscoting?

What did I know? Nothing. I had very little prior expertise, no blueprints. I'd built a doghouse once, but the dog found it oppressive and liberated himself soon after. My plan was to bring all the supplies to the back edge of the compound and let the work dictate itself. I was sick of heeding these mandatory voices, especially Patrick's. Lately all he did was smoke pot and read encyclopedias out loud. He'd borrowed them from the main house, and when he was stoned he found them mesmerizing. *Fuck, listen to this, Patti. There are over seven hundred different types of curry.* His voice was like a drinking straw with a hole in it. Every word made him smaller and smaller.

Sometimes he helped, usually he didn't. In the process, I discovered something extraordinary: I liked hard work. I pulled nails out of old boards. I measured and leveled a footprint of land big enough for the center. I used a solution of baking soda and rainwater to scrub the guano off the chicken coop particleboard all by myself. While Patrick was in the tent "taking a break," which meant clouding his mind with the bong, I sat on the bare foundation of the communion center and stared at the wall of redwoods that lined the edge of the property. A hot wind blew through me, and I closed my eyes and felt witchy and old, an all-body fatigue. My will was flagging. I was the only one sustaining this idea. Patrick thought it was ill-conceived, the silents pretty much ignored us, the teacher Francine considered me ridiculous. I didn't tell her that she was one of the spiritual foremothers of the plan, whether she knew it or not. "We don't always make plans," I said to her when we were sharing a bottle of red zin next to the bonfire. "Sometimes plans make *us*."

I told her this the night before. Francine usually ignored me, but last night she responded by telling me about Flora, one of her former students, how she'd just arrived and had called a meeting with everyone in the house. Something was happening, Francine said. The negative voice inside me said that Patrick and I would be evicted by the end of the week.

I looked down at the bare foundation, dismayed by how little progress we'd made. Patrick returned, cream-eyed, going on about how much money he'd pay for a crawfish sandwich right now, and I told him how much I hated it when he talked covetously about seafood. He picked up the saw and said, "Fried catfish. Danish lobster tails."

"Please, Patrick," I said.

"Seared scallops. Shrimp cocktail served with fish roe on a bed of crabmeat inside a giant smoked squid."

"*Shut up*," I yelled. I told him to just go back into the tent and finish himself off. Let me be. It was reductive language, but I needed silence right now.

Moments after he left I heard a snapping sound and looked over at the north wall-frame just in time to see it collapse to the ground. I put my head in my hands and sobbed my eyes out. That was it. As soon I finished crying I would stand and walk out of Monte Rio with nothing, just as I had from the dozen other places I'd deluded myself into thinking I'd been called to.

I stood up, determined to leave. That's when I saw about forty of them, the entire population of the house and the yard tents, standing all together, all facing me.

I felt the cables of a hundred different possibilities starting to make their way through me. I picked up one end of a joist and began heaving it into place.

Flora, I'd find out later it was Flora, moved first—she grabbed a hammer and a box of nails. Another woman picked up the handsaw. And then the rest of them found some part of the job to attend to, and soon we were all working side by side. We finished the frame for the north wall in a few hours, then the south wall. We connected the joists. Previously, I'd worked deliberately, nagged by a monologue I'd absorbed from some do-it-yourself show. *Build the back wall a foot shorter than the front wall. Be sure to add support braces every four feet.* With everybody working alongside me, that voice was silenced. The only sound I heard was Patrick, who'd rejoined us, and continued his exasperating food monologue: steak au poivre, steak Oscar, carne asada.

I insisted that he go back to the tent and fill it with as much noise as he wanted.

Were we going to win any architectural awards? No. Was the roof watertight? Not even close. But the revelation was how easily that inner voice died on the vine. I finished sawing a board, and before I looked up and thought, I need someone to take this over to the east wall, someone had already grabbed it from me. I felt pulled to where Keith and Flora were putting up drywall, and when I arrived I saw that they needed a third to nail it while they held it in place. Flow. Action and intention becoming one. I remember my first guru talking about the goal of extended meditation. First your family and friends leave your mind. Then your fears and inhibitions leave your mind. Then you leave your mind.

When we were done working on that first day, after we'd eaten and I'd had a little too much wine, we danced around the bonfire until late. The kids were all smiles. It was like the loaded prelude before a kiss, except unsexual. We stayed up all night, permeating each other, and when I went back to the tent, Patrick was mumbling in his sleep. Something about fantasy baseball. I grabbed my pillow out of the tent and slept on the communion center's concrete foundation.

JOHN PARKER CONWAY

MONTE RIO, CA
2028

It was in my third year in office, just after the men's bath scandal. Nonscandal, I mean. Biggest sack of trumped-up horseshit ever. Bathgate. It happened in the sauna at the new Monte Rio Racquet Club. I'm sitting in a cloud of steam and some Green Party mole comes in, and the next day he claims I repeatedly stroked his shaft. That's what he called it, his shaft. Like he's a goddamn airplane. Said I bit his earlobe and whispered nasty stuff. Listen, I'm ready to admit that I might've accidentally *grazed* the guy's dong—it's not like I'm wearing my glasses in the sauna—but my days of looking for action in locker rooms and campsites and movie theaters, neighborhood barbecues, airport bathrooms, Renaissance Faires, are done. Monte Rio's my full-time bride, my soul mate. Only reason I go to the baths is to relax. Can't two men sit naked together in a steam-filled room without all this tawdry innuendo? Hasn't anyone ever heard of the freaking Romans?

So, once the winds of truth came in and blew this calumny to pieces, I wanted to celebrate. A few months back all the silent kids had moved their whole operation from the old

Schofield ranch to Bohemian Grove, which had been abandoned a decade ago. It had fallen into serious disrepair—picked over by loggers and squatters and souvenir hunters—but it was way better than the Schofield place. What a hellhole that was, a warren of tents and homemade buildings that smelled like stewed chicken, everything connected by tarps and cast-off signs. A hobo beehive. I sold all twenty-seven hundred acres of Bohemian Grove to that Patti woman, the leader, the one who forever looks like she's on the edge of orgasm, for a dollar.

We'd planned to have a simple ribbon-cutting ceremony in early July, and, visionary that I am, I doubled the budget for the Independence Day celebration, threw in an extra ten grand to get the Bay o' Wolves to do a concert, and decided to stage the whole thing at the Grove. We'd cut ribbons, drink wine, spray the water curtain, watch fireworks explode, and listen to the greatest folk-rap fusion jam band since . . . ever. We'd celebrate freedom—mine, theirs, yours.

Well, I've long believed the credo that it's better to ask forgiveness than permission. So I planned the whole event without exactly consulting any of the commune people. Maybe I felt entitled to because I'd essentially given them the place. We arranged everything on the fly, scheduled it for July 3— the fireworks company charged less the day before the actual day—and mailed fliers to everyone in town telling them to come out.

Setup started the week before, and that's when Patti came into my office. Wearing a poncho thing, titties bobbing, her hair pulled back—she looked like a surgery patient. We couldn't do it, she kept saying. We were going to upset the equilibrium. We're doing to them what Monroe did to the Indians.

"Did Monroe throw the Indians a party?" I asked. "Did he bring out the whole town to celebrate them? Because that's what we're doing for you guys. Just roll with it. It's America's birthday."

They didn't want to be celebrated, she said. It was an incredibly fragile time. If the community was ever going to take root and prosper, we couldn't come barging in with our fireworks and fusion jam bands.

I told her it was too late, but I didn't want her to leave angry. I asked if there was anything we could do to make it work for everyone, and she said yes, yes there was. She would agree to the Fourth of July party if the town and I respected *all* the rules of the place while we were there. "Of course we will," I told her. "You have my word."

She left. And I pretty much put that promise out of my head until I arrived at the old Grove the morning of the third. I walked the half-mile trail to the entrance, beneath those towering redwoods, and looked at the new sign—FACE-TO-FACE: THE COLLECTIVE RETREAT OF THE WEST. Lofty. I liked it. On another sign were the rules. First one: no isolation allowed. You had to be around someone else at all times, except in the bathrooms. I didn't quite understand that one, but all right. Wasn't the craziest thing I'd ever heard. Next one: no cameras or recording devices. Okay. The Bohemians had that one, too, after a reporter snapped a frontal shot of Vladimir Putin pissing on the leg of his horse, who was just standing there, taking it. The next rule: no talking anywhere within camp property. I guess it was part of the whole mindset they wanted: They can't talk, why should you? And I'd understand it on any other night. But a no-talking Fourth of July? A no-talking Bay o' Wolves, a band lauded for their complex lyrical wordplay? Monte Rio is big on personal liberties, on live and let live, and I was positive that a mandate like this wouldn't fly.

I went to find Patti. First off, walking the grounds, I was impressed. They'd cleaned it up, torn down some buildings and renovated others. All this in a few months. Hammocks, fire pits, outdoor theaters, food gardens, sun showers, a climbing wall, an open-pit barbecue, and picnic tables. I don't know what I expected, maybe something closer to the hobo beehive. Or the Manson Family's outpost. But those huge trees and this little haven within them, it all felt miniaturized, perfect. I was sold.

I found Patti in what looked like a ballet studio, on her knees, eyes closed, apparently meditating. I asked how I could help her win the town over on this no-talking idea, and she glared at me, then motioned for me and Jenny to walk back to the entrance of the retreat. Outside the grounds. Patti smiled all serene and said, "You'd be surprised what people do when they sense it's the right thing. This place is hallowed ground already. People will respect that."

You know when you get to a party late and all the booze is gone, and you look around and realize you're never going to catch up? That's what it felt like listening to her.

The celebration went better than I thought it would. I looked around, trying to catch one of my constituents talking, even whispering, but I never did. Everyone was gathered in a massive outdoor amphitheater, about two or three thousand of us, and once Bay o' Wolves finished, the fireworks began, blasting from an open clearing over the redwoods, which was sort of illegal, but tonight was worth an exception. In the bursts of light I could see big groups of people staring attentively at each other, townspeople and silents alike. It was the craziest thing. The whistle of the rocket, the explosion, and then this view of the town, united in silence. It felt like love. It shouldn't have surprised me—I mean, Monte Rio has always welcomed restless spirits, questing undecideds. But it did, it surprised me.

Sure, the drunker people got, the more they slipped and shouted "woo-hoo!" and "America!" and a lot of the little kids couldn't help but ask their moms and dads for more popcorn, no matter how much their parents shushed them, but I didn't see Patti or the teach or any of the others get angry. It was the principle they were trying to instill, the *idea* of silence. I might've had a little too much summer-ale homebrew, but I felt this great upsurge of pride. It was a privilege to be the mayor of the town where they settled. Not only had we made room for them, helped them get acclimated, but many of the residents actively revered them—treated them like royals. I saw the Tipton brothers step aside and let one of the silent men skip ahead in the beer line. At the line to the food tent, Shirley Easton, one of the vilest souls you'd ever want to meet, gave a little silent girl a double serving of potato salad. We were a sanctuary for these people. We fed off their presence.

It made me happy but also sad. I felt that stir of loneliness again, and I looked around to see if there was anyone worth pursuing. Worth taking a risk for. All of the men were too young, too happy. One of the silents caught my eye—he had well-kempt stubble and a prominent forehead—and I stared at him until he looked at me. He didn't return my smile but gazed at me with the most despairing look I'd ever seen. I felt confident that he was looking beyond my smile and returning my true inner expression. He was actually *seeing* me. I turned away to shake someone's hand, and then when I looked back he was still staring at me. I left quick, before any trouble could arise.

TERRY "BUG" DELAROSA

VILLA GRANDE, CA
2028

A bunch of regulars from the Elephant came out for the commune's grand opening. Piled into Carrie's windowless hydro van and followed the river line until the Equinox kicked in. We'd bought eight microtabs to split between four of us, so by the time we were in the parking lot of the old Bohemian Grove, things had slipped a dimension. Carrie looked cut out of crepe paper, and Bert was just rough scratch marks in the air, like something swatted to life by a cartoon cat in the beginning of a show. The thing about Nox, it always disturbed you differently. I don't mean like wine does you different from whiskey. It wasn't subtle. The first time you do it, you might find yourself hearing organ music for five hours, overcome on your sister's couch by wave after wave of gasm shivers, and the next time you dose, you're in the bathroom berating your own crushed-looking penis, getting angrier and angrier at how it wears a monocle and talks in a bullshit Irish accent—but if you took another tab you might totally change your outlook and become lifelong friends with that same penis all of a sudden.

Tonight it started with two-dimensional stuff. No problem. I could handle that. On the trail to the entrance, I unloaded some of my internal thoughts because I knew we couldn't talk inside. It was a big rule. Everyone said I talked too much, which I guess was true, but when I was quiet they always asked me what was wrong. I couldn't win, so I tried to do what came most natural, which, nothing really came natural.

"Four of them went in," I said. I do this thing where it's like I'm a voiceover for a movie. "But none of them came out. They thought they were there to celebrate freedom. They thought the silents would be friendly and harmless. But they were wrong. Dead wrong."

It was my way of saying I'm nervous.

"I will pay you to shut up," Bert said.

"One of them offered to pay the other to shut up," I said. "But that offer was declined."

Carrie interrupted by exclaiming how excited she was. She loved her some silents. "They're going to teach us so much!" she said.

"Like what? About what?" I asked, but Carrie was on a solo trip. I always pressed people when they got all lathered about face-talking. It was so amazing, like our truest essence making sweet love to someone else's true essence! Then why couldn't I learn it? Why couldn't I at least say hello? I thought the silents were fine, just shelled-up and sort of churchy-acting. I also didn't like the followers, who were these sun-dried turbohippies.

This new Grove, compared to the days when friends and I would hang there and smoke cigarettes and pretend we worshipped the devil, was unrecognizable. It was dim under the huge trees, but I could see as far back as the buildings where we used to paint pentagrams and bring roasted chickens to scatter the bones like offerings to Lucifer. The cabins sparkled with new lacquer, the trim had been repainted, roofs reshingled. They appeared to be candlelit from within.

Once the fireworks started, I had all three dimensions back, but there was a whistling, like a steaming kettle, and I felt like pretty soon I might need to ice-pick my own knees. I put my hands over my ears, but it wouldn't stop. Then I saw how many people were gathered—the whole town, it seemed—and the whistling got all train tunnel. We were mixed together, silents and not. No one spoke, but there was a weird energy. It might've been the Nox, but I sensed something would happen here, either very good or very bad. My internal sound track was going haywire as I scanned faces in the flickering light, just loose words zip-zapping around in my head: *fungible lezzie hat-trick noodles beehive.* I knew I was going to scream out "Origami sandwich meat!" if something didn't happen really soon. What were we waiting for? I couldn't see Carrie and the others anywhere—they were either hiding or, most likely, dead.

To my left, a silent girl, maybe nineteen, looked at me. I stared back. She was probably testing me, seeing if I'd look away, and then she would trank me and drag me out to the deep woods and steal my eyes. This was my thinking at the time. I gave her a sort of a snarl-slash-scowl, but she didn't look away. Then I fake-smiled. And she real-smiled. And then I frowned and she did, too. And I thought, Great. Mirrors. I was so misted I just kept eyes on her for I don't know how long, and then the whistling stopped and I was no longer paranoid, I wasn't thinking a damn thing. I felt like I'd come out of the cold. Like, being allowed to stare at this girl, for more than a minute, and not having to explain myself or challenge her or listen to that whistling or that voice, my voice. It released some vital heat.

They split us up. Two silents accompanied me and some others to a cabin with a yellow-and-red bar above the door and showed me my bed. I wanted to tell them I'd only be staying for two hours, so I held up two fingers and pointed to myself, but how was I going to tell them hours? What did an hour mean to them? They probably thought I was telling them peace out.

That night the silent girl from the staring thing came and visited me. I couldn't sleep because the Nox was still live, so I looked at the ceiling, remembering all the stupid stuff I used to do. Painting my fingernails, burning shapes in my arm with a hot coat hanger, acting Austrian, peacocking. The girl quietly came up onto my bed and sort of overwhelmed me. Helped me with my clothes and did everything. I didn't mind, no. It happened to others in our cabin, too, men and women both. A few hours later, she came back, at least I thought it was her. But when we were face-to-face, I saw it was a different girl. She was more aggressive—she stared at me so hard while on top of me—and I felt weird afterward, like I'd been milked.

I'd planned to stop by for a few hours. I ended up staying three months. The girls didn't visit every night, but they visited a lot. Without someone to talk to about how strange it was, it stopped being strange. I was tired all the time—there was alcohol but no uppers, or at least no one offered them. I watched people come for a few days and leave. One of my favorite things was the plays. The first time, I followed a crowd to the outdoor amphitheater. I didn't know what was going on, but I got drafted into it. Things there just sort of happened. Inside these boxes of Halloween clothes I found a Roman gladiator's costume. A dozen of us went out onstage, and the rest, silents, followers, townspeople, were in the audience. What was the play about? I have no idea. I walked over a bridge and came upon some lovers, and I pulled out my sword to attack them. Just as I did, a guy in a lion costume jumped on me and I fell to the ground. The audience clapped.

You probably think I stayed for the night visits, but that wasn't it. I liked the vibe there. I helped dig irrigation ditches, spread compost, danced, meditated, made chili for two hundred people. I wore commune clothes: white T-shirt and a pair of starched slacks. Three times a day, during group silence sessions, I'd seek out someone I'd never met and I'd stare until everything died away. The thoughts, the voice, the desire to join the two. I'd arrived somewhere clear.

Three months later, once I was back in Monte Rio, I didn't want to do anything. I especially didn't want to go back to the Elephant. But I did. My friends were always there, every night. Turns out they never even made it into the commune. They said I was creeping them out, so they wandered around the woods, then went home. I tried to explain what it was like—I left out the night visits—but it didn't translate. They said I was brainwashed. Fine. Sometimes, Bert or someone would come sit next to me, and, where I used to say, "You're higher than a skyscraper," now I just sat there and stared. And if Bert really was high, he'd stare too. We'd stay like that for a long time.

FRANCINE CHANG

MONTE RIO, CA
2029

It was at one of the Thursday bonfires—late, too late. I should've been asleep. Thing is, I was going a little crazy in my cabin among the redwoods. I hadn't spoken in six days, unless you count mumbling nursery rhymes in the shower. I had no books, nothing to distract me from my own puckered brain. So I and about seventy-five others sat on giant stumps around the fire. I was next to Dane and Michael, who I'd known since I'd taught them in second grade. We passed around a bottle of Denizen Red, from the first batch we made here on-site. It tasted like grape hand soap. Nobody talked, but, drunker and drunker, I became aware of a certain collective vibration. The silents mingled among the newcomers, people who came in RVs and rentals from all over the place. Followers, nervous and giddy. The silents opened bottles of wine and poured it into any glass that was empty, and then they'd engage the person until he or she realized this meant to drink deep from the glass. I was reminded of college, those post-soccer-game parties—the bonfire had that kind of atmosphere. A power structure, a tacit hierarchy. I saw it with

Michael and Dane, so nervous and aloof when they came to my class. But the way the two of them studied me now, then each other—I felt naked, prehistoric. I had the distinct feeling that they could read every past regret, every current delusion, and that they were peeking into my future and judging me unfondly.

By midnight people had started to pair up and leave. Just making eye contact, communicating intensely for a moment, and then walking off hand in hand. It was so simple, so overt. Dane stared into the bonfire and I followed his gaze and saw that it was Patti he was looking at. Aggressively peaceful berobed way-older-than-him Patti. Fire shadows moved across Dane's face as he communicated something pretty easy to decipher—a roll of the lips and lowering of the eyelids. Patti made a face that I still can't banish from my mind. Like a cross-eyed monkey getting ready to bite. Soon the two of them were headed toward the empty woods.

Yes, I was surprised. It looked consensual, but the ease with which they exchanged intentions—a look, another look, boom. It wasn't supposed to be that easy.

I didn't have much time to dwell on it, because someone seemed to have placed his hand on my sweaty thigh. I looked over, and there was Michael looking not at all beseeching or persuasive but . . . proprietary. Michael, who wore pull-up diapers in the second grade. Who drew lightning bolts on his folders and ate Cheese Nips he found on the floor and was scared of Slim, the class gerbil. He slid his hand back and forth on my thigh, and I caught myself thinking, Is that what all this has come to? All this work? I shook my head, roughly picked up his hand, set it back on the stump, and broke my six-day silence to tell him no.

In class, late from lunch, he would've given a contrite

frown. I was expecting something similar at the bonfire, but I sure as hell didn't get it. He shrugged as if to say, "Your loss," and walked over to a pair of women at least twice his age—they looked like fat storks—and soon the three of them were walking off together. Unbelievable.

The next morning, after meditation, I did the earlobe-tugging thing to Patti, which meant I needed to talk. She touched her lips twice, which meant that in a little while I should check the compost heap behind the cafeteria. It was one of the places she left me notes. No, not on top of the compost where I could find it, but elbow-deep under gnawed apples and shrimp peels and beet greens. The note was scribbled on the top flap of an orzo bag. Directions, address, time to meet. I imagine she wanted me to eat the note afterward, or shred it into tiny pieces and set them on fire. How else did she think we were going to navigate logistics like fire-code compliance and mayonnaise invoices without talking every once in a while?

We met at the Rio Theater, a converted Quonset hut, which was showing something called *Up in Flames*. Patti was slumped in the front corner, right next to the speakers, and I sat next to her.

She said she felt bad about the thing with Dane but it happened organically. She'd been to enough intentional communities to know that this kind of thing happened early on, but something something something. The movie had started and I couldn't really hear what Patti was saying, no matter how far I leaned in. Guys in black leather rode motorcycles through a crowded plaza, and there was a lot of slo-mo of people getting flung into the air. I found myself transfixed by it and only caught snippets from Patti, like "expressing their loving natures" and "emotional connectivity."

"We can't just do nothing," I said. "They need some kind of guidance, or a task. They're starting to act like royalty, like entitled bullies. I mean, I'm not anti-sex. I'm anti . . ." Just then the motorcycle jumped a fountain, and the rider landed on the second floor of a building. "Anti-this," I finished.

Patti mumbled something. I leaned in closer and she mumbled it again.

"Speak up!" I yelled, and she said, "It's all part of the plan."

I'll spare you the verbatim conversation. Fast-forward past five minutes of on-screen kidnappings and stabbings through confessional lattice and Patti saying stuff like "facilitating their desires" and "promoting physical connectivity." Turns out, for the past few weeks Patti had been dosing the morning tea ceremony with yellow wolfsbane, an herbal "libido enhancer." She said she was just trying to get talkers past that "final hurdle," the walls erected by society and socialization and all that.

"Sometimes people need help submitting to the natural order," she said. "Evolution is a party, and we're all invited."

Everyone but me, apparently. I stood and walked out of the theater. And once I left the Quonset, I just kept on going— back to the Grove, filling a suitcase, then out to the car. Flora came up to me as I was going, held my shoulders, and regarded me with a look of precise concern and solicitude and sympathy—and I couldn't meet it with anything but brittle frustration. I ran back to my car, stumbling on roots and rocks.

Driving back to Oakland, I replayed our conversation again and again, stoking my righteous outrage. I missed my students, the pliant, docile kids who I stewarded at Oaks by doing nothing at all. By watching. I wanted that back. I wanted to care for them without complication. I guess I thought that

Face-to-Face would be the perfect site for this—like summer camp, all of us frozen in time.

Before I got home my outrage had turned to regret, like always, and there was a letter on my door dated two months ago saying that the sewers had backed up and there was a likelihood that my bathroom was flooded with my neighbors' "evacuations." I unlocked the door, opened it, and waited for the smell to come to me.

NANCY JERNIK

BROOKLYN, NY
2029

Ron left but he didn't leave me. I mean, he thought I was insane. He thought it was repulsive, you know, that I was going to go sit in the dirt in front of an abandoned warehouse in the shadiest part of a city I didn't even know. He called it an extreme measure. How is sitting an extreme measure? I was going to sit out there and wait for Spencer to take me back. And if he never took me back, at least I would be as close to him as possible. Even if I died out there. The birds would come and pick at my bones, and I'd be closer to Spencer than I had been for the last twenty years. I said all of this to Ron that night in the motel, and he nodded and thought about it and said I needed to go on this journey. He couldn't go with me, but he would support me from a distance. Some people might think that's cold, but I saw it as incredibly loving. Like, somehow that night all of the longing we both had for Spencer got transferred to me. Holding vigil for Spencer was suddenly my duty, and we both recognized it.

At the time, to be honest, I wasn't entirely sure of my motives. Was I trying to prove something to Ron? Or was I just trying to, I don't know, generate some kind of inspirational anecdote that I could one day tell to a reporter on Bloomberg, about how I put everything aside to get my son back? I think my initial decision to go on the stakeout had elements of all of those. But in the end I just felt like something was happening inside that I couldn't ignore any longer. If I went back to New Jersey without Spencer—I mean, nothing there seemed to matter anymore. I couldn't think of a good reason to go back to that life. So the next morning I said goodbye to Ron, bought some meal bars at one of those Korean convenience stores, and took a cab out to the warehouse. And that was the last money I spent for a long, long time.

Of course, it started raining almost immediately. But I just thought to myself, This is the rain that will wash away the past. I sort of couldn't believe I was thinking that way, you know? A few weeks before, it would've made me gag. But I thought the thought and it made sense, so I went out to the entrance and sat there. My whole body was soaked after a few minutes. The rain was going sideways, like a monsoon, and I was getting pounded by these massive sheets of water—not even drops anymore but sheets. I just kept focusing on the past, feeling it all leach away from me. And slowly—I know this sounds dramatic, but I really did feel it—even the guilt and shame that I guess I'd been harboring for all those years about essentially abandoning Spencer, that all cracked and dissolved, as well, and when that was gone all that was left was a sense of pure yearning. Just a simple sensation, totally disconnected from everything else in my life, like, I don't know—a bell ringing in an empty room. I looked up into the windows of the building and I could just barely make out Spencer's face through the rain. He was looking out the window at me without any kind of expression, just a dead stare.

I'd put myself into this situation where the next move was his, and the fear of that, of not being in control anymore, was crippling. But he knew I was out there.

The rain eventually stopped, and I kept sitting. I had some bottled water and a few meal bars, but I honestly didn't expect to be out there for so long. So by, I think, the sixth day, I was starving. I had nothing left inside, no energy or will or even thought, really. I was completely empty. Everything got really bright and I sort of fainted. When I woke up, there were three silent kids standing over me, and one more who was kneeling by my head, mopping my brow with a rag soaked in cold water. They dragged me inside the entrance of the building, where it was a little cooler, and gave me some water and left me there.

I think they expected me to go on my way when I felt better, but once I was in I was staying in. They were going to have to drag me out of there. I rested for a long time, and eventually a girl came with some bread and honey on a chipped plate. It was the most incredible meal I've ever eaten. I wondered why people ever ate anything else.

I started doing everything that they did. I accepted that the area by the entrance was my space and that's where I slept and waited, and I didn't go any farther inside the building. Anyway, there were beehives everywhere—I've always had a really intense fear of all swarming insects. It was safe at the entrance and that's all I needed, so I just made my little home there. When they went out, usually at night, I followed them. We went way out, deep into the city, looking for food. They led me through this secret city within the city, the underbelly—the spaces between and behind buildings, or the tunnels and passages underneath. The roofs and fire escapes. The kids knew their way through all of this. It was almost impossible to keep up with them on the first few missions. I'd be completely winded by the time we got to the first bank of Dumpsters.

I thought I was going to be disgusted eating garbage, but do you know what people throw away? We'd get inside these Dumpsters and there would be whole meals, completely uneaten, sealed inside foil or those paper cartons. Perfectly edible food. Just tossed aside. I found that I really loved the idea of reclaiming this stuff. It was like what I was trying to do with Spencer, but on a much smaller and more achievable scale.

Spencer never went on the Dumpster runs. I barely ever saw him. I knew he spent most of his time on the second floor of the building, because I could see him through the window at night when we'd come back from the Dumpsters with loads of food. He never made eye contact with me after that first day, and I was fine with it. I understood that this was what I deserved. It was enough for me to just be close to him. We spent the better part of a year leading this very simple life, together but apart.

Then one morning I woke up and a guy in a leather jacket and khaki pants was standing over me. He seemed really upset and scared—he was swearing, I remember, and palming his chin, raking his fingers across his cheeks. He was the owner, he kept saying in this really agitated voice. He was the owner of the building and what was I doing there, looking like a dead person on the floor, ruining his property value? It was such a strange thing, having someone fire all these words at me. Apart from a couple phone calls to Ron back during the first few months, I hadn't really had anyone talk to me. I tried to tell the guy to stop, just for a second, so that I could explain myself, but when I opened my mouth I found I could hardly even make a sound, let alone find any words to say.

Even the words in my head, I realized, had a kind of a different shape to them.

I ran down the hall to find someone. My heart felt like it was about to explode. I knew that everyone was asleep on the second floor, so I sprinted up the stairs, even though that's where the bees were. And I could hear the sound of the bees getting louder and louder as I got closer to the landing. I was panting with fear, and I got to the top of the stairs and I could see the bees going crazy in the air, a big whipping cloud of them tearing around in circles up by the rafters. I was trembling, trying to force myself to move forward even though I was sure I was about to be swarmed. But suddenly there was a hand on my chest. A palm right here, pressing against my chest. And I looked up the length of the arm, which had long scars running up and down, and it was Spencer, staring at me in the darkness. I had watched him from far away for so long that I thought I would be prepared to see him close-up. But when I saw his face so close to mine, all I could think of was the boy he used to be, hiding under his bed, rolling marbles up and down the floor. He was a grown man, without my help. He looked at me with this sense of—there were layers and layers, and I knew that he knew who I was and why I was there, and that he wanted me to be safe, and that he might someday be able to forgive me for what I'd done to him, but not yet.

YARIV BASSANI

FLORAL PARK, NY
2029

I come out of the attorney's office and there's Fatima sitting in the Blade, and she has this look like, "What did you expect, Yudchik?" I knew that I was going to get screwed in the will, but an abandoned warehouse? This is the revenge my father takes on me, from the grave, no less? To saddle me with this burden? It was worse than nothing at all.

I sit in the car and slap the picture of the place on the steering wheel. Big huge warehouse at the Brooklyn Navy Yard. This crumbling piece of worthless junk. Fatima asks me, "What is this place?" and I tell her the whole sappy story about my grandfather and his import business. How, when he moved to the States from Israel, he missed the taste of true Jaffa oranges so much that he had his brother ship them over, and he started distributing them to grocery stores all over the city and eventually the whole Northeast and beyond. The mission of my family's business was to "bathe the world in Israeli sun," but it was all a bunch of bull. My grandfather was not interested in spreading the joy of Israeli culture. He was a cold, calculating tycoon who worked his family to the bone and gave nothing in return. My father, if you can imagine, was even more shallow and vile. I don't want to go into the ways he made life hell for all of us, my mother, my sisters, the whole brood. Suffice it to say that on the day he died I sat in the darkness in my living room and drank champagne to his corpse.

Fatima put the picture on my lap and squeezed my thigh. She knew it was because of her that my father put this damned millstone around my neck, while my sisters came out with four hundred thousand dollars between them. Because in addition to being a fake Israeli who did not care one iota for the people or culture, he was a rotten bigot who, on the day that I announced I was going to marry Fatima, collapsed— literally collapsed from a panic attack—into his potatoes at the dinner table, in front of Fatima and her mother and sister, and stuck me with the ambulance bill. Every time I saw him after that he would say, "Yariv, I died on that day. You assas- sinated me on that day. I was like Kennedy, with my brains sprayed all over your mother." He never looked at our twins. Never once picked them up, never even congratulated me when they were born after twenty-two hours of labor. When I told my parents about the struggle we went through, he nod- ded his head as if to suggest that it was somehow God's will that I was being punished for breeding with a Muslim Cushi.

I couldn't sleep that night. I couldn't stop thinking about this place, this warehouse. I wondered what was inside. I fool- ishly thought maybe there was something valuable inside— maybe it was all some big practical joke. My father was not a funny man, so it made no sense that he'd play a trick on me. But I hoped. I stayed up most of the night praying that this was true. My sisters with all the family money and me with this curse of a building? No man, I thought, would be so cruel as to do this to his own son.

The next morning I took Fatima and the twins out to the warehouse. It was a mess. Paint peeling off the brick face in long ribbons. Rotten window casings and broken glass. Multiple beehives plastered to the overhangs. There was some crude half-finished graffiti on the wall by the entrance, like some kids had tried and given up, half a head with just the eyes and nose. I told Fatima to wait in the Blade with the girls. I wasn't sure what I'd find in that place.

I went up to the entrance and pulled back the sliding door, and immediately I saw this woman spread out on the floor. An older woman with hair the color of dishwater, all in clumps like some sort of derelict. She was wearing old clothes stitched together with butcher string, and I thought, Oh, no—you know? This is the icing on the gravy—a dead woman on my hands. I cursed and the woman's eyes snapped open immediately. She jumped up, suddenly completely awake and alert. She opened her mouth like she was going to howl, like she was some sort of banshee. But instead the sound she made was a weak sort of hiss, which was, in a way, much more terrifying than if she'd screamed. A scream, I was prepared for. But a hiss? Was she part of some snake cult? That is what I was thinking, silly as it seems now. This woman could've had a knife or a broken bottle or who knows what? I'm a virtual conference coordinator—I don't know what goes on in the streets, and I didn't want to die at the hands of some middle-aged urchin. But the woman ran off down a dark hallway and disappeared.

I followed her down the hall, moving as slow and careful as I could. The place reeked of some combination of organic stenches that I hope you never have to experience. Imagine an orange rind slowly rotting in the folds of a fat man's jowls over the course of his entire lifetime and you have some inkling as to how bad it was. The woman went up a stairwell, and that's when I heard the bees. This insane chorus of them, like a hundred power tools running all at once. I crept up the stairs, and when I reached the second floor landing I saw the woman standing there with a young man who was maybe in his twenties, wearing a gray shirt and pants that were worn down to threads, but with what looked like brand-new wingtip shoes. Behind them, though, was this—I don't even know if I can accurately describe the state of the place, which looked like something out of a bad dream. Mattresses, tons of them, set up everywhere like a house of cards—like, end on end, carefully balanced. All arranged around a big circle in the middle of the floor with all kinds of junk strewn everywhere. Pillows, broken chairs, a giant purple bear like the kind you win at a roadside carnival. And in the back there were the packaging machines and orange juicers, and the bees covering them to suck away the residue, swarming over the entire surface. There were a dozen or more kids hiding behind some of the mattresses. It was just me in the building against this fleet of hoodlums.

The young guy approaches me and I get a chill down my spine, the coldest, most awful feeling, to the point where I start actually shaking. My knees are quivering, because this guy is coming at me and who knows how many more of these people there are living in this place? It might as well be an army of the living dead, is how I'm feeling. The guy comes up to me and holds out his hand. I jerk back like he's going to throw a grenade at me or something. I'm ready for the worst, but I look at his hand and there's a wad of cash sitting there in his palm. He holds it out to me, like I'm supposed to take it. I go, "What is this?" and he doesn't say anything, just sort of waves it at me. I'm like, "You want me to take this money?" He just looked at me like I was talking nonsense. It was a little like how, when I go to visit Fatima's family in Rabat, it's like I'm a baby again, is how little I can communicate with her relatives. I know now that he was one of those silent kids, sure, but at the time I wasn't thinking rationally. I thought he could be anyone, a terrorist or a prankster or someone else, who knows? But I could tell he had no idea what I was asking him. I took the cash—why not?—and counted it. Four thousand and change. I wanted to make sure I understood what was going on, so I pointed at him, then I went and slapped the wall of the building, and then I made a movement like I was taking the cash from him. And he smiled. That was our handshake. That was the start of a rewarding and mutually beneficial relationship. I don't know where this kid got his money from, but he paid me every month, on the nose, from then on. I was earning cash for nothing. The warehouse might as well have been a gigantic ATM. God was smiling down on me, despite my rotting father's best attempts to tear me apart.

AUGUST BURNHAM

RAHWAY, NJ
2030

There was one in Newark right next to the Jackson Street Bridge, and another off 280 where kids were living in retired school buses. There were a few in Elizabeth and a huge one in Bayonne in the old Manhattan Chocolate & Nuts building. In Jersey City there was a condemned ballpark where a small group of them made a home out of the concession area. I'm just thinking of some of the places I'd visit most frequently. And of course there were a bunch more in New York City. I tried to get out to each of the larger communities at least once a month. Some of them I visited more often, if it seemed like they needed extra medical attention. The place at the Brooklyn Navy Yard was a real concern because of the bees. I couldn't believe that those kids were living in that space with what looked like hundreds of hives ready to drop from the ceiling at any moment.

If I didn't have the burden of running the viviplant facility in Rahway, I would've visited more often. And, of course, if I'd been able to keep the EPR clinic open, I might have had some influence over how these kids turned out. But the public wanted to believe that the silent community was capable of supporting itself without assistance. The silent people they saw on the news all seemed so content, so confident. They stopped viewing EPR as a serious issue. But those kids squatting in abandoned malls and underground tunnels and grain silos—they're the true face of this condition.

I still believe that there's a cure, and I'm determined to find it. Viviplant Central was a necessary rest stop, not a dead end. I just needed some income while I worked on my proposal for more research funding. And I needed to maintain close ties with the silent community in whatever way I could.

I remember the sound of that warehouse. Even standing outside, you could hear the bees—more of a low rumble, something you sensed more than heard. My partner Raph had been doing apitherapy to treat his MS for the past decade, so we always had bees in the house once he moved in. Raph kept them in a matchbox and he taught me how to administer the sting, so I wasn't scared of them. But there was something powerful about all of those bees together in one place. Some genetic reflex, if you will, that made me a little skittish whenever I approached the entrance.

I had a little spiel that I did with the silents whenever I was trying to gain their trust, a sort of play-acting where I showed them what I was there for, how I just wanted to check up on their health and provide any care I was capable of. If all my years of study were worth nothing else, I could at least communicate with those kids. Most of the time they let me in without an issue. I'd just set up a card table in the corner of whatever space was available and wait for them to come to me. I could tell the more organized communities from the truly desolate squats because there would be a group of lead-ers who'd urge the other kids to get checked out. The Brooklyn warehouse was more organized than many, but that didn't mean the kids there were any healthier. Everyone had head lice, everyone. That was the most common affliction. I always brought packets of dry shampoo for them, and I demonstrated how to apply it again and again, but either they weren't keeping up with it or they weren't using it at all, because every time I'd return they'd all be infested. Of course, the piles of mattresses and ratty furniture they had arranged as corridors and rooms were rife with bedbugs, so they had bites pretty much all over their bodies. Their teeth were also in rough shape—I don't think they brushed with any regularity, if at all. I don't know how or if they bathed. They each had their own incredibly acrid odor, but they didn't seem fazed by this or interested in any of the hygiene products I left for them. Were any of them depressed? That's almost impossible to tell, but it haunted me. I mean, the whole thing haunted me. The public had this idea about these kids living in their own separate little world, far from the rest of society. Out of sight, out of mind, you know? But the effects of this kind of isolation are unknowable. These kids were just not getting the kind of care and support that they needed, and no one was looking out for them. It was abominable.

One day I got a call from the man who owned the warehouse. He seemed nervous on the phone. He'd read an article on my traveling clinic in the local paper and wanted to see if I was looking after the people squatting in his building. I reassured him that I was going out there as often as I could. He seemed genuinely worried about the state of things in the space. I asked him why he let it go on and he said that he had an arrangement with the silents there. I wasn't interested in his affairs, so I didn't pursue the issue. I told him I'd swing by the following weekend, which was the first opportunity I'd have to get out there.

So the next weekend I showed up and found the girl with the stings. They had her lying on a rug in the center of the big circular communal room where they seemed to spend most of their time. I walked in and I saw immediately that her left arm was twice the size of her right arm. Her eyes were rolled back and her mouth was slack. She'd been stung, I think it was thirty-two times, the report said. She was barely breathing when I got there. I don't even know how she was still alive. I administered some epinephrine, which didn't seem to do much. She was on the edge—she needed a drip or she could be dead in hours.

I took out my phone to call an ambulance, but this young man reached over my shoulder and grabbed it right out of my hand. I turned around and it was the guy with the scars on his arm. He'd always encouraged people to see me for check-ups, so I was shocked that he'd do something so drastic. I still wonder what his purpose was. Was he trying to protect his tribe? Did he think I was trying to call the police? How would he know? I made a series of desperate gestures to show that the girl was going to die, and he just stood there holding the phone away from me. I saw on the display screen, though, that I'd somehow successfully dialed 911 before he'd swiped the phone from me. So I shouted out, "Please, there's a girl dying from anaphylactic shock at the Brooklyn Navy Yard, get an ambulance out here immediately." He looked at the display on the phone for a second, and then he hurled it against the wall. I wasn't frightened so much as concerned about the way things were turning out. I tried to ignore the episode with the phone. I knelt down and tried to remove the stingers from the girl's arm, just praying that someone had heard me. Some of the stingers had actually been drawn into the skin by the inflammation. It was just an awful scene. The girl was going to die right there. And I became acutely aware of all the kids standing around me as I tried to pull out those stingers. Just watching me with their mouths hanging open. I never felt as much concern for the silents as I did at that moment, because it was just so clear that they were chronically unprepared to take on the challenges of the world. I mean, I had no idea about the bigger mess to come, but I knew that this was just the beginning of their suffering.

DRAKE POPE

We received a call from the district commander. Paramedics on the scene had reported a standard refusal-of-services, but the resisters were really digging in their heels, barricading themselves in. Backup was brought in from the local precincts, which meant that before long they had managed to butterhump the situation into a full-blown standoff. Which is when they called us.

I drove up to the warehouse in a Badger 110, which if you don't know is an urban crowd-containment vehicle, like the kind they used in Pusan. It's no fun to drive but it makes an impression. I had a small handpicked team with me. We pulled up in front of the place in broad daylight and took our positions at key points around the perimeter, making our presence known. The day was uncomfortably hot. Perspiration pooled in the sockets of our tracer goggles, making them all but useless, and we drank water by the bucketful without pissing once. We were miserable, and I can only imagine what it was like in that building. But I wasn't naïve. Heat alone wasn't going to flush the kids out of there. They were living in a condemned wreck of a stronghold, wallowing in their own turds. These people were not going to be lured out on the promise of a pizza and a rim job. They practiced a particular brand of asceticism that laymen always mistake for laziness but which I've come to know as a disciplined rehearsal for hardship. The heat would grind at them, but it wouldn't break them.

You'd think I would be pleased to find that my suspicions about those people turned out to be accurate. But I'm too far along in my career to take joy in the fact that I know trouble when I see it. That would be a little like a baker expressing shock when his bread rises. It's an ability that just springs forth naturally from the work. I knew from the moment I saw those young silent people gathering on the beach back in whenever that I'd eventually be doing the same with them. I said to Reville, "Only a matter of time." And Reville says, "Only a matter of time until what?" And I say, "Until I'm talking them down from somewhere precarious." And Reville, "Pope, they don't talk." And that's what interested me. That particularity was a thing that drew me to the silents. How do you talk to someone who doesn't talk? How do you change the mind of a person who doesn't know what *mind* means? It made me want to study them, to know them down to the core. It made my job new again. Because I felt, the way an elephant knows where to die, that one day I'd be called upon to coerce them into doing something they didn't want to do.

I'd been training for this type of scenario for several years. I'd read all the available literature on the condition, talked to professionals, made field observations. I knew how these kids operated. I had to do a bit of wheel reinvention in light of the fact that the standard tools would not yield the desired effect. To wit, I knew that a megaphone would be useless and a sound system's effectiveness would be limited at best. We knew that our primary point of tactical leverage was their eyes, which made things difficult, since we couldn't legally deploy any directed energy beams after the incident at Columbia. We could deploy tear gas but that was always a last resort. And, this is just a personal thing, but I feel like lachrymators are, in general, clumsy tools used by men who lack vision. I had something better. A nimble little drone fitted with a screen that displayed my face. I sat in a portable booth behind the Badger and practiced a set of well-rehearsed expressions that conveyed both the gravity of the situation and the reassurance that everyone inside would, upon exiting the building, be treated with the utmost respect. Golebiowski and Watts pulled back a plywood panel and sent the drone inside the warehouse, and Kosari helped guide it around remotely from the cockpit of the Badger.

It took us a long time to even find one of them. The drone's AI wasn't sophisticated enough to recognize that the mattresses and other refuse the silents had piled up were functioning as walls. Kosari had to actually write several lines of code on the fly to help the drone locate a small pocket of silents crowded into a fissure about three feet wide. I saw them on the small screen in front of me as I performed the expressions I'd prepared. I showed them calm. I showed them order. I gave them my most vigorous rendition of justice. I watched them in the glowing green of the night-vision camera as they took in my message. The man closest to the drone, who wore a long unkempt beard and had a gray sort of homemade tunic, got down on his knees and put his face close to the screen so that I could see nothing but his forehead. I felt the hairs go up along the back of my neck, just like they say. I felt like I'd broken through some barrier, as if I'd somehow deciphered their methods of communication. I'd brought one of them down to his knees just by looking at him remotely. I felt a moment of pride at having accomplished this feat, but the sensation was short-lived. The man was only trying to find a way to shut the drone off, and when he failed to deactivate it that way, he tossed it through a broken porthole under the peaked roof. Thirty grand worth of custom R&D smashed on the blacktop.

I called Reville. "They took out the drone," I said. Reville told me to hold tight, which was not the response I wanted. I asked him when the bulldozers I'd ordered would arrive. He says, "I stopped the order on the bulldozers." I didn't say anything. Reville filled the ensuing silence by saying, "You're not using force. Not before force has been used on you." I explained to him the violence of all the wires and chips busted all over the ground like some infant's broken bones, but it did not move him. "This is not going to be a repeat of Columbia," he said. Fair enough. I respected Reville. In my estimation, they'd crossed a line, and as I saw it the only thing to do was to shift the line back across the sand until they had nowhere to go. But I followed Reville's lead.

That was the first day. Next we rotated through a battery of some of the more predictable PSYOPS techniques—blasting the sound of dying rabbits, placing high-powered floods outside all of the windows, blowing hot air in through the basement, helicopter flybys. The kids weren't showing us a thing. By the fifth day of the standoff everyone was weary. Everyone was nearing the breaking point. The sense that you're drawing ever closer to an asymmetric chaos event is palpable. I've felt it many times. At Columbia, sure. In Montreal, in

Bogotá. It's just something I know, the way you know when it's lunchtime. I felt the first shock waves of premonition fully a day before the end of the standoff. So, when those young people dropped the beehive on Kosari's Interceptor, nearly killing him in the process, I knew exactly what to do.

PRASHANT NUREGESAN

ATLANTA, GA
2030

I was at an IPI Deep Mind Persuasion training session when my sister called. You're not supposed to communicate with the outside world during IPI training, because of how it tends to break the illusion that you're a Bronze Age Wanderer, so I knew it was serious when the High Priest led me through the back door of the longhouse where the catering crew was making ceviche and handed me the phone. My sister was pretty hysterical. It was hard to figure out what was going on. At first it sounded like Isabelle was dead. I was already braced for it—the whole family knew that Isabelle was living in that warehouse in Brooklyn with a bunch of her silent friends, and we were all pretty nervous about something bad happening to her. It turned out she wasn't dead, but she was somehow trapped in the warehouse, surrounded by a SWAT team that was shooting at her through the windows and whatnot. It sounded surreal, but my sister just kept saying, "Do something, Nu, you've got to do something," on and on. And, of course, I was going to do something. Of course I would figure something out. Even though it meant I had to

petition the tribe to be exiled, which involved a stoning ceremony, which was just rubber stones but still, when a guy whips
a rubber stone at you full force, you're going to get a welt.

I met my sister at the hotel where she'd holed up during
the standoff. I sat in the recliner eating a meal bar while she
told me what was happening. I asked her, "Why won't she
just leave?" She said that Isabelle had finally found the community of people she'd always longed for. My sister had never
seen the girl so happy as she'd been in the past few years.
And this was a girl who'd been through a lot. Many bad years
where she was treated for depression, on all kinds of meds,
and at one point tried to kill herself by swigging a bottle of
cleaning solution. I said, "You really want her living in all
that filth?" And she said again, kind of resigned or defeated,
"I just want her to be happy."

When I realized what I had to do, it was like I couldn't
believe my good fortune. This situation called for the exact
kind of techniques I'd been training for. Deep Mind Persuasion is all about moving beyond the antiquated notions of
products and services and into the practice of pure insinuation
and seduction. Convincing another person to do something
using only the power of your own presence—that's really the
vanguard strategy for anyone who wants to do more than
tread water these days. So I saw the standoff as a perfect way
to test out my skills in a real-world scenario. We return to the
Bronze Age in Deep Mind Persuasion training because of its
dead-simple commerce model. You have to go back to basics
if you're going to learn anything new. So now I was ready—
I was going to go there and convince the cops that the standoff was a waste of their time. It was going to be tricky but
totally worth a try, from a risk-reward perspective.

On the first night of IPI training the tribe leader binds

your hands with leather straps and leads you down an unlit trail. All around you are the sounds of guys howling in pain. All you can smell is pine sap and burning meat. You have no idea what's about to happen to you. You've got to stay in Deep Mind or you'll go nuts. Persuasion begins with the self. If you can get yourself to believe something that isn't true, it's a snap to get someone else to believe something. So I convinced myself that I was going into a business meeting. This was a sales pitch. The cops were the investors and Isabella was the capital.

It was dark when I got to the warehouse. You could feel something in the air, like something big was going down. There were a couple of city cops at the outer perimeter of the place, and they stopped me when I tried to get around the Jersey barriers they'd put up. I handed them my ID and the cops read it in the light of the flares that they were shooting in high arcs over the warehouse. They were like, "Go away," and I said, "I've got a better proposition. What if *you* go away, go home to your families, and I'll take care of this?" They seemed amused, but not in a good way. Which was fine. My father always said, "Fail faster," meaning that every failure is just an opportunity to come back stronger the second time. I was brewing up an alternate approach when we heard someone scream. The flares revealed the heads of a bunch of kids peeking over the, what do you call it, lip or edge of the roof. There were two SWAT guys down below aiming these weird rectangular guns up at the kids. One of the guns had wires extending up from its nozzle to the rooftop. Later I found out that they were some kind of long-range Taser, those guns. I was just standing there with the cops, watching all of this, when the kids suddenly chucked something over the edge of the roof. A big chunk of something—it looked like a paper lantern—that sailed down in a slow curving path and hit the hood of a black truck that was parked by the entrance. The thing barely made a sound on impact, but a few seconds later the guy who was sitting inside the truck started shouting. He jumped out, and you could just barely see this cloud surrounding him, almost swallowing him. He was swatting at his face and chest, and someone shouted, "Bees!" It was an entire beehive those kids had dropped. The officer went down and flailed on the ground. The cop holding my ID tossed it at me and started sprinting toward the guy who'd gone down. A paramedic knelt in front of the guy and jammed an EpiPen in his leg while a whole bunch of cops and EMTs and other people wearing black outfits and masks rushed the building. There was a cluster of gunfire and I saw the white contrail from a gas grenade launcher go right up in through the top window.

Everything happened quickly after that. I picked up my ID and started running toward the entrance. I was about halfway there when I heard an engine start up. A big, low, growling engine, like from a tank, which was basically what the thing was that they started driving toward the doors of the warehouse. I ran as fast as I could, trying to catch up. The tank had a low profile, bigger in front than in the back, which was part of what made it so terrifying. It was about the same size and shape as the animatronic mammoths that wandered through the woods in the training sessions, so in my mind I just transposed the thing into one of those mammoths. That was my focus point, my Mind Metaphor. I charged the beast just like any man would who had to protect his tribe from a terrible threat. I came up behind the thing and jumped on it, spread-eagling myself across the sloping rear part, whatever that's called. My plan was to—well, in truth I didn't exactly have a plan, but I had this notion that I could climb into the cockpit, or whatever, of the tank and stop it from blowing down the doors of the warehouse. I did a Deep Mind Visualization of the scenario and I could see all of the possibilities, all of the outcomes. My plan was airtight, with one exception—the tank was way closer to the warehouse than I thought it was. I was just mounting the roof where the hatch was when the tank smashed through the doors, which knocked me back onto the ground. Some cops rushed in through the opening the tank had made, and then everything got superquiet. I got up and limped slowly toward the entrance. It was like the tank had punched a hole in the fabric of the universe and all the sound had gone out, because you could hear every footfall of every guy moving around. Every cough.

I peered in through the hole, and that's when I saw Isabelle. She was hanging there by her, you know—just, from the rafters. My sister said later that she probably did what she did because she thought they were coming to take her away. She just didn't think any other life was going to bring her the kind of joy or whatever she experienced when she was in that warehouse. So there she was, hung from the ceiling with an orange extension cord, and the cops were shining their lights on her body like she was a side of beef. I couldn't believe what I was seeing. I was just—what happened to my heart in that moment, I can't even describe to you. The cops were standing there, doing nothing, just letting her sway back and forth.

STEVEN GRENIER

PHILADELPHIA, PA
2031

I'd been trying to pitch *Twenty Years of Silence* for some time, but I couldn't generate any interest until the Navy Yard warehouse incident. That really crystallized the public's concern about the silents, I think. It gave their anxiety a shape. It worked out well for me—initially, all I was pitching was an hour-long incidental stream, but in the aftermath of the standoff, when the *Post* ran those photos of the dead girl, the hosting network actually shelled out for a five-part miniseries with synchronous distribution across fifty or sixty of the major markets. Which allowed me to really give the piece the depth and breadth it needed. Of course, they also wanted it fast. Things were changing rapidly. The public's perception of the silents as lovable quirky mystics was dissolving. It was harder to pretend they were harmless once they started tossing beehives at cops and killing themselves.

Once that hit the news—I mean, that photo of the girl swinging from the power cord, that was a pretty impactful image. It really changed people's opinions. And because the silents had no PR rep who could swoop in and course-correct, reassuring people that this was just an anomaly, the fear and apprehension just kept rolling. You started to see towns and cities reevaluating the funds they distributed to silent initiatives. Some schools started shutting down, and the social services and outreach programs dried up entirely. The silents who'd gotten driver's licenses using the new nonverbal tests had their IDs revoked. And the transitional facilities—which got all their money from state grants—contracted in scope to where they were really nothing more than detention houses.

I don't want to sound callous, but sometimes you have to call things as they are, and this whole shift gave me a lot of really great material to work with. The tension was already out there—I just had to harness it. So I went straight to the warehouse where everything got started. I got footage of the actual beam that the girl used to hang herself, with whitened streaks where the cord had eaten away at the wood. I interviewed the kid's parents and her uncle who was on the scene during the siege, apparently trying to save her. He kept blaming himself for her death and seemed pretty much destroyed by the experience. We also visited a school on the West Coast, one of the first silent schools. I talked to some of the teachers there who were trying to hold on to their jobs while the state deliberated on how much funding to allocate for the following school year. A sort of gloom pervaded everything in that place. The kids were unfocused and erratic in a way that seemed new to me.

What I really wanted to do, though, was track down Persephone, the girl who was the leader of that group of kids I'd followed around in Philly something like eight years before—the segment that won me the Rangar Prize. She always stuck in my mind, like the photo of the girl running from the napalm, and I thought it would be powerful to follow up on her story. To see what kind of woman she'd turned into.

Fletcher House was the name of the facility where Persephone had met her friends, but it had been shut down a few years previous and the building was converted into a pet-friendly gambling park. I had the names of some of the Fletcher House staff from the release forms they signed, so I tracked them down to see if they knew Persephone's whereabouts. The former personnel manager was working in a ladies' ammo store, and he told me he'd seen Persephone a bunch, standing with day laborers on the corner of Girard and North American. I took a cab out there the next morning and there they were, huddled under a statue of Don Quixote, waiting to get picked up. I recognized her immediately. The bronzed, chiseled face, the hard eyes—she was just like the girl I remembered, but more fully rendered, more clearly drawn. I got out of the cab a bit down the block and casually made my way into the throng. They spoke to one another in Spanish and Laotian and Ganda, and I picked up threads and fragments here and there, but mostly I focused on Persephone, who stood listening to a group of women complaining about their daily rate. Persephone seemed to be following along, nodding in agreement or shaking her head in disbelief with the other women. I even heard her cluck and hum when someone made an emphatic point. I was shocked—I briefly thought that maybe I had the wrong person. But my gut told me it was her.

An orange bus pulled up and all the women lined up to get on board. I stood in line with them, hoping to sneak on, but the driver told me to wait for the purple bus as he shut the door and pulled away. I hailed a cab and followed the orange bus to a hangar by the Delaware. This was one of those tabloid sweatshops where they paid people to look at uncountable hours of surveillance footage for any unsavory images of public officials that the AI software might have missed. I got there as the last of the women were filing in. I showed my press credentials and told them I was evaluating their service for *The Braggart*. I signed about forty NDAs and they let me out on the workshop floor. Persephone was over in a corner, scrubbing through footage taken at a traffic cam, frame by frame. There was a big head shot of the city solicitor propped on her workstation, and she kept looking back and forth between the footage and the photo. A supervisor came by at one point and put his hand on her shoulder. He told her she was doing a great job and asked what her favorite flavor of Slush was, because he was on his way to the vending machines and would she like one? She sort of smiled and tittered and went back to her work. He said his favorite flavor was Brownerator Brown, and she nodded. He said, "Oh, do you not speak English or something?" and she nodded again. She was pretending. She was actually trying to pass as a talker.

I waited until her shift was over and followed the orange bus back to the Don Quixote statue. It was late—must've been ten or eleven at night—and she was walking down North American Street without any kind of weapon that I could see. She ducked into a pulverized brownstone, and I waited outside to see which window would light up when she entered her apartment. She was on the third floor, so I went in and crept up the stairs, which were littered with shell casings and used condoms. I stood outside her door for a minute, listening. All I could hear was the shotgun sample from a Pho Hop song booming down the hall. I put my ear to the door, assuming it was locked, but it swung open and I stumbled over the threshold. Persephone jumped up from a table where she'd been crying, I guess, and we were standing face-to-face after however many years. Her eyes were blotchy and slick, but she knew instantly who I was. She didn't move aside to let me in, but I could see over her shoulder that there was basically nothing in her apartment, just a card table under a hanging lamp with a bowl and a spoon. White walls and white wall-to-wall carpet. It was the living space of a person who didn't feel she was really living. And, I mean, everything had more or less been taken from her. The squat she'd called home had been condemned and torn down. The people she'd lived with had scattered throughout the city, eking out a shadow existence. I stood there waiting for her to let me in. But I was also suddenly aware of the impossible distance between us, in every imaginable way. To her, I was nothing but an unwelcome reminder, the ghost of her irrecoverable past coming back for a final haunting.

AUGUST BURNHAM

RAHWAY, NJ
2032

As you can imagine, the Navy Yard standoff had a profound effect on me. I'd been working with those kids for years. The girl, Isabelle—I'd treated her for rickets and viviplanted a new molar for her. I sensed that she was suffering from depression—many of those kids were—but of course it's almost impossible to make a definitive diagnosis. In any case, I'd failed. I didn't do enough. I'd seen it all coming from a mile away, but I hadn't been able to stop it. Not just Isabelle, but all of those kids—the whole silent community. I was angry—partly at the system, a society that would allow a whole population to collapse on itself, but also at myself. I'd been coasting along, trying to fit my research in the periphery of my life, when what I needed to do was to drop everything immediately and get back to work—the real work, a hunt for a genuine cure for the silence. If I didn't, Isabelle's death would be meaningless.

I put my notice in at the viviplant clinic immediately. I had no idea how I was going to raise the funds for a new research facility, but I had to make a break with the past. I ate fat bread and Slush for the next several months while I developed a business plan and talked to potential investors. The real breakthrough was the Isabelle Foundation, which the girl's family had formed to fund exactly the kind of research I wanted to conduct. They gave me the support I needed to get off the ground.

By the time I was officially open for business, though, things were even worse for the silent community. The voting issue was a huge concern, naturally, and the slashing of the silent service programs at the state and federal level, but I saw it permeate all aspects of the culture, right down to a handwritten sign taped to the door of the gas station down the street from the facility that said *No Shirt, No Shoes, No Speech, No Service.* It was astounding to me to see things come undone to such a degree. To see people circling their wagons in the basest way against a threat that was manufactured purely out of ignorance—it boggled my mind. I think there was a very real sense in the public's mind that people afflicted with EPR were somehow less human. And that was precisely the sort of abominable, archaic thinking that I was driven to eradicate.

The new facility wasn't much to look at, but rent was cheap and I was so elated to move in and get back to the EPR research that I'd had to put aside for so long that I would've set up shop just about anywhere. I sat alone in the empty office space that first night, crouching on the floor, riffling through the old files, pinning charts to the bare wall, reacquainting myself with my own research.

The biggest obstacle at that point was simply getting subjects into the facility. I had the database from the old clinic, so I sent out an invitation targeted primarily at the families I'd worked with in the past. I figured the response rate would be relatively low, since the children I'd worked with were by now into their early adulthood. But within hours I was contacted by the parents of Calvin Andersen. Calvin was my first officially diagnosed patient, and his parents said that they'd very much like Calvin to participate in any study I was conducting. They were still located in Hadley, but they would make the trek down to Rahway whenever I was ready for them. They included several recent photographs of Calvin that revealed the earnest boy I'd studied, buried in the gaunt, bearded face of a man I didn't recognize.

I looked at the sequence of Hoekman renders, MRIs, and PET scans I took of Calvin's brain, from when he was two to fourteen. From frame to frame, the brain grows, but Wernicke's, Broca's, all the typical language centers remain dark and occluded as the night sky. It seems so obvious now, but at the time I hadn't quite realized the value of my data. I had literally reams of patient documentation that predated the research done by anyone else. Certainly people like Kimura and Goodrich had more resources at their disposal, and they were more widely recognized in the field, but my data had the depth. I had been thinking longer and harder than anyone about EPR, and it was time—I could feel it—to shift the whole paradigm. A cure, essentially, if I'm being frank. I held the scans delicately, like they were holy texts. I couldn't believe my good fortune—that Calvin Andersen and his parents were on their way to my office. I panicked, because the facility wasn't properly set up for me to perform the tests that I suddenly realized I needed to do. So I used the lion's share of my savings to purchase a refurbished Hoekman and a portable PET scanner from a Russian wholesaler in Elizabeth. My cred account was drained, with overdraft fees left and right. It was a huge risk, but I'd never felt closer to my goal.

Calvin and his parents arrived the next day. It felt strange to see them again. Their faces were immediately familiar, though I could see all of the tiny ways in which time and anxiety had aged them—crow's feet appearing whenever the mother smiled, and the father's hanging jowls like the dewlap of a desert lizard. They told me that when my clinic shut down they'd given up on trying to find a cure for Calvin. They focused on accepting him for who he was, and that had brought them some peace, but they were never really able to convince themselves of it. They were still haunted by the possibility that trapped inside Calvin was a man capable of the full range of linguistic expression that his talking cohort enjoyed with the unconscious ease of breathing. The Navy Yard incident and all of the aftermath had convinced them that their son deserved another chance at freedom.

Calvin seemed to recognize me instantly, despite the thick white beard I'd grown since I'd moved in with Raph. I felt an instant rapport. I tugged on my beard and pointed to his and we both laughed. I showed him some photographs of my son, Hector, who operated high-altitude surveillance drones for the CIA. Hector and Calvin had spent many afternoons playing together in the waiting room of my old clinic while I discussed Calvin's progress—or lack thereof—with his parents in my office. Calvin seemed intrigued by the pictures. I used my old symbol cards to say *Calvin + Look + Hector*, and Calvin grinned as though the cards were old friends he hadn't seen in years.

I brought out the Hoekman and placed it on the table between us. Calvin's face changed, and he examined very closely all of the parts—the buttons and snaps, the leads with their multipin terminals, the padded cavity where the head went. Here was a memory that Calvin clearly felt a little more ambivalent about. I asked him through symbols if he'd let me take a study of his brain. He thought about it for a long, almost interminable minute before taking the thing in both hands and placing it carefully on his head. I nodded and synced the device. I'd forgotten almost entirely how to work the Hoek-man, and even though the model I'd purchased was a few years old, it was still far more advanced than the one I'd used at my clinic. I stumbled my way through and within a few minutes I was looking at Calvin's brain in real time, watching the whiplash neural traffic surging through his cortex. I had a clearer view than ever before of the dark areas where his neurons failed to spark. What had seemed so vast and mysterious before was now constrained, finite. The darkness, finally, had a shape.

NANCY JERNIK

MONTE RIO, CA
2032

We spent the winter living in that Kazakh jetliner that had crashed into the Hudson during the Olympics protests. There were just six of us remaining from the warehouse—the rest had gone back to their families, or were taken back, or else they just wandered off to other squats. We never saw any of them again, and it seemed to really destroy people's spirits. I grieved with them, but secretly it didn't bother me too much. I stuck with Spencer, and that was all that mattered. The winter was harsh, and the plane was partially frozen in the ice, so the cold was almost unbearable. But we made a crude kind of chimney out of some aluminum piping and put it in the flight attendant's area, and occasionally the warmth made us forget where we were and what we'd lost.

Spring might have taken some of the pressure off of our mourning, but it never seemed to arrive. The morning chill hovered throughout the day, and everything that had died in the fall stayed dead and withered. The bleakness really seemed to be getting to Spencer, a hunch that was confirmed one day when he came up to me—actually approached me, voluntarily—with this photograph of the Face-to-Face facility in Monte Rio. It was torn from a permazine, and it showed a group of young people standing waist-deep in a jade-colored river with a colony of humble cabins standing in the background among a cool stand of redwoods. The figures looked healthy, happy, at peace—they had everything that we lacked. I held the picture out and looked at Spencer questioningly, like, "This looks like a nice place, but what does it mean?" And he put his hand to his chest and then pointed to the destination on the map. I pointed to myself, and then to him, and then to the map as if to ask him if he'd like me to drive him there. And he looked away and sort of nodded. I was so excited. The thought of us taking this trip, of making this colossal change—the thrill was almost like high school, as if Spencer had asked me out on a date, except not weird. Just that feeling of having the attention, finally, of the person you've longed for in your mind for however long.

Of course, I had to get a car. I had one in my previous life, a wine-red Megara 110. But Ron, when he moved in with that woman from the Handbag Network, had the title transferred to her. So I looked into cheap rental places, and it turned out that there was a car you could rent for a dollar a day if you agreed to have a chip injected at the base of your neck that made you thirsty whenever you saw a tub of Slush. I didn't know what Slush was, but they promised me the chip would dissolve to nothing after a month, and it just seemed like the simplest, easiest way to get us across the country. We went to the rental place, where a small man in a lab coat gave us shots that you could barely even feel, and we got in the car and took off.

The trip was hard for a lot of reasons. I don't think we

were really prepared for the harsh treatment we got. Things had changed since I went to live with Spencer and his friends. Back then, there was confusion and even some suspicion, sure, but it was mixed with curiosity and a strange sort of respect. Maybe even awe, a little. But now the confusion had become exasperation, and the suspicion was outright animosity. Wherever we stopped people gave us looks, or wouldn't fill our orders, or would tell us that a bathroom wasn't working, when in fact it was working just fine. They treated us like we were both silent because of the way we were dressed, and that made me both proud and angry—proud that we were seen as equals, even if the treatment we got was awful. The chips in our necks also made things difficult, because I didn't realize when I signed us up that there were Slush machines literally everywhere. So we were always incredibly thirsty.

But the weirdest, hardest part was just spending so much time alone with Spencer. For all the time I'd lived in the same place as him, I still didn't really *know* him. When we were all together in a group, I could successfully play the part of acolyte. It was a role I found easy to take on. But when it was just Spencer and me sitting side by side in the car, things changed. I started to feel restless. I wanted to be his mother again. I wanted him to look at me the way a son looks at his mother.

We rode through the remains of Cincinnati. We spent days carving through the farmlands and plains, past Borden Peak and the Badlands and Zap World. We got lost in South Dakota and ended up at Mount Rushmore, which I'd never been to before. We spent a long time just staring at those faces. Spencer seemed sort of entranced by them, and I wondered what he must be thinking. Who were those men up there, and what had they done to have their faces carved into the rock? There was no way I could think of to tell him, and anyway I was only really sure about two of the four heads.

Afterwards we walked into a souvenir shop, and the man behind the counter took one look at us and stopped the music that was playing on the loudspeakers. We'd barely set foot in there, and he'd already made his judgment. There was no one else in the shop but a family of four eating freeze-dried ice cream. The shopkeeper stared at us blankly from behind the counter, and then suddenly began squinching and stretching his face in a grotesque mockery of face-talking. Rolling his eyes and licking his lips, really pleased with himself. The family stopped eating their ice cream and looked at us, eager and excited, waiting to see what happened next.

I decided that I'd officially, right then, had enough. I'd suffered the last of a hundred little paper cuts of intolerance. I picked up a Rushmore snowglobe and hurled it at the cash register, where it shattered into a million little fragments of glitter and glass. I stormed out of there and went into the parking lot, and for the first time in a long time I just wept and wept. I got down on my knees behind the rental car and put my forehead to the blacktop and sobbed. And Spencer followed me—he knelt beside me and put his arms around me. The first hug he'd given me in I don't know how long. Fifteen years, at least.

We finally crossed into California, and that was the most incredible part of the trip. The scenery was unbelievable—I mean, after you've spent so much time living in, essentially, a trash heap, it really is like a completely different world. Even the air felt richer, clearer. Spencer seemed to be drunk with the beauty of it. He put his head on my shoulder and closed his eyes, and the weight of him against me felt like the most incredible accomplishment—like getting Spencer across the country was the one genuine thing I had done in my life.

We pieced our way to Monte Rio, across the bridge and down that long winding road, the impossible redwoods on either side of us, and pulled past a series of burned-out shacks into a clearing with a ramshackle but neat cabin. We got out of the car and a group of people came out to greet us. A handful of kids roughly Spencer's age followed by an older Korean lady. This one young woman stepped forward, and there was something about her face, something familiar. I couldn't figure out where I'd seen her before until the Korean woman, Francine, told me she was Flora Greene, the silent girl who'd been in that documentary years ago, back when Spencer was just a boy. She approached Spencer and took him by the shoulders to look deeply into his face. He stepped back, startled by her bold gesture. This was not how silent people greeted each other—at least not where we were from. She smiled a little at Spencer's bashfulness, and he smiled, and they both laughed.

They took us to a sort of geodesic dome made out of aluminum pie tins and Clabbershot. It was hot and damp inside even though the air temperature was cool. We crouched in the dome while someone went to fetch some food. I tried to protest—I didn't want to call attention to ourselves in this way, but Francine just shook her head at me, looking resigned. "This is just their thing," she said. We stayed in the dome for a long time. Our hosts sat around Spencer and stared hard at him with a disconcerting earnestness. Finally, a young man in a red apron brought steamed, honey-soaked lichen wrapped in tree leaves and a bitter red juice that had a mineral aftertaste.

After the ritual—if that's what it was—in the dome, we were encouraged to walk the grounds. Flora and her friends took Spencer down to the river, and I found a hammock made of old clothes stitched together with a rough, thick yarn. I watched them build a bonfire at the river's edge until I fell into a deep sleep. I dreamed that Spencer and I were back in the Kazakh jetliner, but it was airborne, and we were cutting through the clouds, trying to keep a fire going in the makeshift stove while the wind howled through the broken windows. Then we were falling straight toward the ocean, and Spencer took my hand and I felt a sense of calm, but when I opened my eyes it was the middle of the night, and a girl I didn't recognize was standing over me, tugging at my wrist. I sat up and saw a shack down the hill that was consumed in flames. Apparently some stray embers from the bonfire had landed on the roof and the whole thing went up in a single burst. Silent kids were throwing buckets of water on the fire, which they were passing up from the river like a fireman's brigade. Spencer and Flora were at the head of the line, tossing water on the blaze, barely making a dent in it. I joined in, passing the buckets up to my son. Flora went up and down the line, checking in with everyone, stepping in when somebody needed a break. Whenever I passed Spencer a bucket, he'd be looking at her, or looking for her. He hadn't shown a whole lot of interest in women before—at least not that I'd ever seen. So it was a bit of a shock to see him so enthralled.

We worked for what must have been several hours, and eventually the fire died down to a glowing heap. Everybody stumbled off into the darkness until it was just me, Spencer, and Flora sitting around the smoldering remains of the shack. I leaned back on my elbows and closed my eyes. My face was hot, but my back was cold. I thought about the Mercury landing, about how those drones had to keep moving to avoid the night or they'd freeze. When I opened my eyes, I saw Spencer looking into Flora's eyes, and I realized I shouldn't be there. I stood and wiped the dirt from my elbows, and Spencer turned and looked at me and I saw how happy he was, and it made me a little sick, a little dizzy, but in a good way, like a Tilt-A-Whirl.

I returned to the hammock only to find a large bearded man in sports briefs straining its seams, lighting a blimp-shaped bong. I wandered around the compound in the pre-dawn light. A mist had rolled in, making the place feel even more like a ghost town than it already was. Half-finished buildings—or were they half-wrecked?—rose out of the mist like ancient ruins. Everything was overgrown and wild. My gut clenched whenever I thought about Spencer—we'd just been closer than ever before on our trip across the country, and already he was drifting away again. But maybe that fear was actually a kind of communion—a communion with all the other mothers in the world, in history, who'd had to stand by with a stiff upper lip and watch their children go off into their own lives. And maybe that experience of the pain of letting go was all I'd been after the whole time.

FRANCINE CHANG

MONTE RIO, CA
2032

Mayor Conway called me in Oakland to say Face-to-Face had become "moribund." He didn't specify how. Some people from town had come in with cameras and filmed the retreat and shown it during a county meeting, and now a lot of them were grumbling about passing legislation to have it condemned. The mayor said, "Know that I'm your biggest advocate." The defeated way he said it, it was worrisome. Like it implied, if I'm your biggest advocate, you're in trouble.

So I went back, like I always did. I found clutter outside the cabins, toys, wire, random computer parts, creepy-eyed dolls. Abandoned clothes and bed linens. Down by the amphitheater were tents and blue-tarp tunnels. A dead raccoon feet-up and decomposing near a propane tank. A boy I didn't recognize sleeping on the dirt nearby with his arm over his eyes. Quite a few of the cabin windows had been smashed, and glass still twinkled in the dirt beneath. I walked to the main kitchen and found Dane and Cheryl scavenging in the pantry for food. Dane with overalls and no shirt or underwear, and Cheryl with shiny eyes and a mouthful of croutons.

In the cafeteria, only Flora came up and hugged me. She looked around at everyone else—it was just silents now, all the tourists were gone—and then at me, visibly disconcerted. The cafeteria smelled like armpit, scalp, decay.

I'd heard about the thing at the Navy Yard, the bus-pass riots in Mexico City, public opinion turning against the silents, but I guess I assumed Face-to-Face existed on its own separate plane, propelled by its own logic. I stopped by Patti's cabin, but when I knocked, then knocked harder, no one answered. There were black drapes over the windows, and I heard faint Christmas music playing—it was July. I wanted to turn around and head right back to Oakland, but I guess I still felt some sort of obligation to the place. Or to my former students. Maybe I just wanted to be needed. I felt at home there, in a fellowship of sluggish decrepitude. I decided to stick around for a week, hoping to help but secretly knowing nothing would change.

And then, three days later, they showed up—a boy around twenty and an older woman, both in the filthiest getups I've ever seen. They walked up the main path in these, like, muddy quilts turned into clothes. The boy had scarred-over slice marks on his arm and the mom looked road-burned but happy. Their first night here, the bathhouse burned down, which seemed like some sort of omen, but they were still here the next morning, and they never left.

Spencer followed Flora wherever she went, with the most transparent look of fondness on his face. He was handsome. Together they went off into the deep woods with the canvas berry bags and returned a few hours later, each with two or three kindling twigs in the bags and huge smiles on their faces. During meals Spencer gallantly cleared her plate and gave her his dessert and watched her eat it. At the nightly bonfires they snuggled together and laughed together and left together.

I'd visit them in Flora's cabin, an oasis amid all the decay rubble. Everything was neat and clean—some half-melted candles in wine bottles on a card table, stitched-together rice bags draped over it as a tablecloth. They insisted I use their bent-birch love seat and they sat next to each other on the floor and we spent hours together in silence. I'd always thought that the only thing less interesting than the content of someone else's dreams is the sight of two people in love, especially when you're not in love. Give me a nice tetanus shot, or chip my front tooth instead. Anything but lovers and their love antics. But I was so happy for Flora, who was always so composed and self-possessed, now giddy, basking in Spencer's attention.

One day the mayor came by with a group of townspeople to inspect Face-to-Face. He pulled me aside and said that things didn't look good for us. "Public sentiment is a cruel mistress," he said. "Do you follow me?" "No," I said. He winked and said, "Sure you do." And I said, "No, honestly, I don't." And we both stood there quietly, his eyes blinking very slowly, looking like a friendly toad. That's when we saw the group of kids come out of the cabins, pretty much everyone at once. One woman clutched her purse to her chest and said to me, "We don't want any trouble." Once they got closer, I saw that they were wearing clean clothes, even Dane. At first I thought they were doing the orphanage routine, putting on a nice show for the benefactors. But they walked right past us to the amphitheater, Spencer's mom in tow. The rest of us followed.

We sat in the back bleachers and watched. I'd seen their impromptu plays and dress-up games, but this was way more organized. Half of them sat on one side of the theater, the others on the other side. Nothing happened for a few minutes. They exchanged glances every once in a while, and then, all at once, they stood and turned around, toward us. "What's happening?" the mayor said. I turned around, too, and Spencer and Flora were walking up, holding hands. Spencer was wearing a thrift-shop suit that was too big for him, and Flora had on an orange dress and she wore two braids tied behind her head and held two white gladiolas. She looked beautiful. She and Spencer walked down the aisle, stopped at the first row, and turned around. It was a long ceremony. Spencer and Flora communicated something to each other, then they each took a side and went down the aisle, person by person, and had a lengthy exchange with them, one that ended with an embrace. When they were done, Flora and Spencer returned to the stage and the others started clapping rhythmically and the couple began to dance, a slow waltz. The others fanned out around them and encircled them, hiding them from view, while I remembered the day I taught Flora to waltz, back at Oaks, a lifetime ago.

THEODORE GREENE

RICHMOND, CA
2032

I always made sure the apartment was clean when Flora came to visit. I got obsessive with it. I wanted to destroy any evidence that I'd gone on and continued to live a life after she'd left for Monte Rio. Everything in the place was the same as the day she'd left. Right down to the notes on the refrigerator and the way they were arranged. I know it sounds insane. I'd be down on my knees, scrubbing the broiler pan under the stove, which I'd never even used, and I'd be thinking, "This is insane." But I did it anyway. Every time she came.

Then she showed up with Spencer. The two of them, standing in the doorway. He was tall and wiry, with a haircut that looked like he'd done it himself, with ragged bangs that were, like, off-center. And he was wearing a kind of a quilted vest-type thing that was all beaten and sun bleached. Flora, on the other hand, looked incredible. Radiant. So confident and satisfied, and her hair was shorter than it used to be, tied back with the same orange scarf she'd worn when I took her to Monte Rio. And then I saw Flora's belly—the unmistakable fullness there that hit me like a concrete block. So much that I couldn't even speak. I could barely move.

I stood back to let them in, my whole body chilled from the shock. I was so blindsided by it, by all of it—I just gave Flora a stiff hug and shook the guy's hand, although I think I would've rather wrenched it off and tossed it into the bay. Flora led Spencer over to the couch and sat him down and then went into the kitchen to pour some water. I stood at the threshold, looking into the room at the boy, who sat on the edge of the couch. He had his eyes locked on a blank area of the wall just over my workstation. Acting like nothing was out of the ordinary. I wasn't sure how I was supposed to respond. I took a seat at my desk, swiveling the chair around to face him. I stared hard, directly into his eyes. He looked back at me for just a second and then looked away, which was unusual for a silent kid. I could see that he wasn't as comfortable as he let on. And I guess a part of me was happy about that.

Flora came back in with water for everyone, in plastic duck tumblers. We sat there in the living room for a good while, sipping water. I was feeling a newer, deeper kind of knifing pain than I'd ever experienced. The sight of a woman's pregnant belly always tore me up. And to see Flora, looking so much like Mel with her hair pulled back and her head resting on the couch pillow, with the fabric of her dress draped over her belly—it dredged up all of the ancient grief like corpses snared in a dragnet. She held on to Spencer's hand. Their fingers were intertwined and she would occasionally give his palm a squeeze, like a heart beating. And he looked over at her—he had serious gray eyes and he gave her this look like he was her puppet, that he would sacrifice anything for her. And I knew the look and the feeling that went along with it, and I wished I could've warned them both about the fragility of it all. But we sat for a while longer and then I divided up the lasagna I'd made into three smallish portions and we ate in the kitchenette. I kept my head down most of the time, just trying to process it all.

That night I turned in early and stayed up for a long time, staring at the triangle of street light on the wall opposite my bed. I thought about the baby. I wondered whether it would be silent or not. I knew that there were cases where two deaf parents had made a hearing child. Was it possible that Flora's baby might be born a talker? I felt guilty for even thinking about it. Or maybe what I was most ashamed of was the spike of hopefulness that accompanied the thought. Because I definitely felt that. I definitely conjured a series of images in my mind of the baby growing up in the world as a talking child. I imagined myself teaching him or her to play chess, explaining each step, or, later, helping figure out how to ask someone on a date. All the obvious clichés—clichés that I never got a chance to experience firsthand. All of that in an instant, a single, forceful wave that gave me a sense of almost criminal guilt. I swore to myself I would never confess it, but I wanted that baby to talk.

The next day we went out to Expect Discounts to get supplies. This was something I'd always done with Flora ever since she moved out to Monte Rio—they never seemed to have enough of the essentials, things like toilet paper, toothpaste, all that sort of stuff. Now she had this man in her life, and a kid on the way, so the trip seemed more urgent. The whole way there, Flora kept showing Spencer all of the landmarks from her childhood. The day-care center she'd gone to before the Oaks School opened, the Cambodian restaurant we used to eat at, the one that was decorated to look like a real temple inside, and the dance center where she'd taken classes as a teenager. I watched them through the rearview mirror. Spencer absorbed everything with the wide-eyed look of a tourist on a Hollywood tour—he seemed to adore Flora in a way that, I have to admit, weakened my resolve to detest him.

We pulled into the Expect Discounts parking lot, and the whole front section was taken up by a traveling carnival—a thing with rickety old rides and midway games. A sketchy-looking Ferris wheel loomed over the various tents and inflatables, and Spencer and Flora craned their necks way back to take it in. I made a face at Flora like, "You've never been on a Ferris wheel?" And she smiled and laughed, as if to suggest, "You'd know better than anyone else." I decided they had to go on a Ferris wheel—like, right then. I went to the little booth by the cotton candy machine and bought a whole sheet of tickets. I watched them go up in the gondola or whatever it's called. They slowly climbed up and up, higher and higher, until I could just see their feet dangling. Eventually I realized they should probably have some privacy, so I went and bought a sour paw and ate it by the Haunted Mansion.

When I was done eating, I threw the husk in the trash and put my hands in the sanitizer, and when I looked up I saw Flora and Spencer standing at the shell game. The woman running the game had a sideways mouth full of curved brown teeth, but she knew how to use it to rope people in. She was fast and persuasive, and Spencer and Flora stood there mesmerized by the sight of her. She held up four fingers at them, and Spencer gave her four tickets. She moved the shells around and stopped, and Spencer pointed to the shell with the marble underneath. She gave him a stuffed crayon, but he shook his head and pointed at a shelf of Siamese fighting fish in tiny plastic globes. She said he had to guess three more times to get the fish. Spencer handed over all the tickets I'd given them. The woman shrugged and did the shell game, and Spencer guessed the right shell three times in a row. The woman was flabbergasted, but I saw that Spencer had been looking at her face instead of the shells. To him, the answer was obvious. She thrust the fish at Spencer and gave him a withering look, but Spencer just turned to my daughter and held out the globe, and she took it from him as if he was presenting her with a holy chalice. She put her arms around him and they stood there in the parking lot, totally oblivious to the screams of the kids on the Whiplash and the Double Penetration, to the ride operators coughing up their lungs and the barkers shouting down everyone that passed by, just swaying there in slow motion like they were alone on a dance floor listening to a song of their own.

PATTI KERN

MONTE RIO, CA
2033

I heard the news about Flora while I was weeping the fluid from the fiberlight all-body cleansing glove I'd been wearing. I'd been doing this every morning for the past three months. First I'd unscrew the small bung at the ankle, hold my gloved foot over a steel-cut-oatmeal can, and let all the viscid juice from the previous twenty-four hours drain into it. That took about two hours total. When it was done I used what was in the can and pestled together fenugreek seeds, ginger, thistledown, baking soda, elderflower, pulped wheatworm, and some ingredients I'd prefer not to reveal. Which I added to the juice. Then I filled the specialized baster, re-screwed the bung, and discharged all the tepid fluid back into the glove, at my collarbone.

The body glove was my attempt at rebirth, a cocoon for the new me, a personal confession for my trunk and limbs. I thought it would help me out of my rut. It didn't. The suit had become my punishment, the stone I was pushing up a hill and watching roll back down, and repeat, repeat, repeat. Punishment for letting outside parties spoil Face-to-Face, for losing sight of the pure mission. I should've been stronger, should've been braver and more devoted.

I was waiting for the rest of the fluid to weep out when Francine knocked on my cabin door. I knew it was Francine, because she was the only one who came around. I answered maybe once every tenth visit. This time I yelled, "Unavailable!" but Francine kept knocking. I swiped the volume up on my Irving Berlin record and waited for her to leave. She knocked again. She clearly wasn't going to stop, so I told her to come in. When she saw the dripping excretion, which was sort of white and pulpy, her shoulders crumpled in a retchshiver, but I assured her that she was witnessing something ancient and Asian—at least spiritually Asian, if not literally.

"Flora's pregnant," she said, just like that, without any ceremony or suspense. This was Francine's operating technique. She was guileless, uncoy, unaware of the effect she was having on other people. Mostly, I think, she was lonely. She covered her mouth, shivered, turned for the door, and said, "Spencer's the father." Spencer. The newcomer. The slender, dark-haired loverman.

Did I grasp the full weight of this news the instant she told me about it? Yes, I did. This baby, this fruit of the union of two native speakers, I knew right away what she represented. She—I was sure it would be a she—was a new start, a do-over. She'd be born and raised here at the retreat, and the first faces she would see would be those of her people. The first sounds she would hear wouldn't be words, blurring, disorienting—they'd be the unpolluted silent transmissions of love and trust and peace. A brand-new human to show us where we went wrong. And where we could go right. Flora's baby would be pure. She would be the first native native speaker.

I reached out to Flora immediately. I found her in the cabin where she and Spencer had been living. He was there, and so were about seven or eight others, who were visibly unwelcoming. This wasn't a surprise, no—I was no longer the leader here but a ghost wandering around a graveyard. And also— I didn't realize this until I looked at myself in the mirror later—I was wearing a sleeveless bathrobe over the cleansing glove, which was salt-stained and which probably emitted a difficult odor, though I was used to it. Flora was sitting on the edge of a cot, like a snake who swallowed a potato, skinny everywhere except for the belly. Seeing her made me all-over joyous. I'd wanted to bring her an item, something to wordlessly declare my sisterhood, but all I could find in my rush to leave the cabin was a deck of poultry-themed playing cards from a truck stop in Petaluma, where Patrick and I stopped on our way up to Monte Rio so many years ago. She accepted it with a grateful sigh.

Midwife seemed to be my logical role. We didn't want a whole lot of nonnative involvement—I mean, Francine and the other woman, Spencer's mother, had abandoned the no-talking rule, which there was nothing I could do about, but I discouraged them from talking anywhere near Flora. Babies in utero could tell a man's voice from a woman's—it was where they obtained the first lineaments of language.

I called a meeting with Francine and Spencer's mother to offer my services. We met outside, on one of the derelict picnic tables by the compost heap, which hadn't been aerated in months, I could see. I stressed to them how important this baby was to the native speakers. How all the damage they, that is, *we*, suffered over the years was about to be repaired, because we would soon be welcoming into the world this amazing, prelapsarian—

"We've already found someone to take care of everything," Spencer's mother said. "A doctor. A medical doctor. You don't need to worry yourself."

In my state of heightened alertness, I found her easy to pin down. She was an atoner, a penitent, a hollowed gourd with no room for hope. Her hands were creased and battered and her murky eyes hid a constricted sort of intelligence. I found her beautiful and scary.

She said, "You can keep your distance. Flora's life is hers alone now. And no one knows what's going to happen with the baby."

"It's going to be stunning," I said.

"We can't even know if it will survive the delivery," Spencer's mother said.

Who told her that? I wanted to know. Someone who practiced medicine with calculators and actuary charts?

Francine said, "You should get some rest, Patti. You look really tired."

Tired? That's strange, because I'd slept thirteen hours the night before. I could've slept longer, too, but if I didn't drain my cleansing glove, my entire body started to burn and itch. Undeterred, I went back to my cabin and set Irving Berlin to loop three times and emptied my glove again.

For the next two months, I worked behind the scenes. I went into town and hired a handyman to install reverse-osmosis filters at the retreat, and I dosed all the icemakers with folic acid crystals and bought gender-neutral wood-block toys. These were the more practical things I did. I also executed some lucid dreaming, which I hadn't done in years, and communicated with the baby that way. I was careful not to talk to her—I simply emoted the gravity of the moment.

I tried to coordinate my schedule with Flora's. Spencer

was always with her, holding her arm, fetching things for her. I tried to communicate to the both of them that I would never do anything to compromise them or their child. But maybe my body language was off or my face didn't express what I wanted it to.

In fact, everyone at the retreat was avoiding me, so after a while I went back to my cabin. I watched Flora from my window, watched her bump get bigger, then lower. Then one day, during an endless rain, there was a rush of activity outside, and then I heard an ambulance approaching. I'd been envisioning Flora having the baby at Face-to-Face, but they whisked her away so quickly I didn't have time to go outside and communicate my good wishes. By the time I put on the waterproof wrapping for my body glove, she was gone.

DR. MADELINE SORM

SEBASTOPOL, CA
2033

Ms. Greene was already in transition when she arrived at the hospital. The people who brought her in—a serious-looking Korean woman and a mother and son—initially didn't make it clear to the nurse on duty that Ms. Greene was in active labor, so she had them wait in an examination room while the birthing suite they'd requested was prepped. The mother returned to the front desk a short while later to inform the nurse that Ms. Greene was pale and bleeding. The nurse examined the patient and discovered that she was dilated to ten centimeters. The bloody discharge was typical of an in-transition patient. The nurse asked the family members why they were so late in getting Ms. Greene to the hospital, and they said that they themselves had not realized she was in active labor. Ms. Greene, they said, had spent the majority of the day lying still in a field on their property, not giving any outward indication of pain until roughly an hour before their arrival at the hospital.

Orderlies arrived and helped Ms. Greene onto a gurney, which they wheeled directly to the Alternative Birthing

Center. They caught us by surprise—Nurse Lashari was still preparing the bedclothes and I was filling out forms on another patient. As soon as Ms. Greene saw the bed, she slid off the gurney and made her way across the room without assistance. The orderlies rushed to her side to support her, but she didn't seem to notice them as she crawled up onto the half-made bed. I told everyone it was all right—if Ms. Greene was indeed in transition, I knew that we wouldn't be there for long.

She got into position on the bed, gripping the rails for leverage as she began to push, before anyone had given her any instruction to do so. I approached the bed and squeezed her hand. I spoke to her, knowing she couldn't understand me, but feeling the need to run through my usual speech of encouragement and affirmation anyway. I said, "I'm not going to deliver this baby—you are." And, "I'm just here to help in whatever way I'm able. You can even pretend I'm not here." But even as I said these words, I saw in her face a kind of raw determination that deflated the admittedly canned sentiment I'd intended to convey. I'd never dreamed that a patient might actually take me up on my offer to be ignored, but Ms. Greene was doing just that. She didn't need me. She was in absolute control of her body, and she was going to give birth no matter what. It was an extraordinary and humbling moment.

The room became very quiet after that. Ms. Greene was visibly in the grips of stage-two labor, but aside from her perfectly timed rhythmic breathing she barely made a sound. We were in the basement, insulated from the rest of the hospital by thick concrete walls originally designed to withstand a nuclear blast. The family had requested we turn the overhead fluorescents off and so Nurse Lashari and I worked in a sort of warm dusklight. The family members circled the bed and held on to Ms. Greene, whispering and clicking as they stroked her arms and kept her hair out of her face. We all proceeded through the evening in a reverent hush, as if we were observing a religious rite. It was so quiet that we could hear the ticking cycle of the HVAC system. The tall young man who was Ms. Greene's partner crouched close to her as she pushed, staring directly into her eyes, never blinking.

The baby, when he came, emerged without a hitch. I held him while Nurse Lashari offered the umbilical cord scissors to the father. The young man took on the task with perhaps a small excess of gravity that I found endearing. The child weighed in at a perfectly healthy six and a half pounds, and with a full head of hair. Nurse Lashari cleaned him off and handed him to Ms. Greene, who looked calm for some-one who'd just been through labor. Her face was glistening with sweat and her hair was plastered to her forehead, but this was the only sign that there had been any struggle at all. She seemed at peace, holding the baby to her naked chest while her partner kissed her temple gently and repeatedly.

VOLUME FOUR

THEODORE GREENE

RICHMOND, CA
2034

I was already awake when I heard Slash start whimpering, almost like my body knew the boy's moods in advance— like it was prepared at any moment to leap into action. I got up and slipped into the room Flora and Spencer shared when they visited me and scooped him out of the fruit crate they used for his crib. The boy was a light sleeper in those first months, and once he was awake there was no getting him to go back down except by taking him on long drives. I was happy to do it. I think Flora and Spencer felt like they were taking advantage of me, relying on me to whisk Slash away in the dark of night whenever he got out of hand. I sort of let them believe that it was a burden, but really I loved the ritual of it. I loved the look of the city in the middle of the night— how even the most gruesome decay was renewed somehow in the light of those tall gooseneck lamps. I loved this power I had in the dark, being the only person in the world who was able to silence the loud, finicky tyrant. But mostly it was just that I got to be with him, alone, without anyone or anything to bother or distract us. We gave each other exactly what we needed.

"Slash" is what I call the boy. I know it's not a perfect name, but it's something. I call him Slash because when you lay him out on a blanket on the floor he makes these slashing motions with his arms, like a knight hacking his way through hordes of infidels. It started out as a joke, but it stuck. I couldn't just go on calling him "the boy" for my whole life, and Flora and Spencer certainly weren't going to name him. I mean, maybe they had some special wink for him, but that wasn't a name to me. Not a real one.

I got Slash into his car seat and slipped through the front door. It was one of those airless summer nights where you sweat just by thinking about it, just like the day Flora was born. That suffocating humidity, Mel slumped in the passenger seat, ghost white. Slash was clearly uncomfortable as well, yowling as I hauled him out to the car. I snapped his car seat into the dock and he instantly calmed down. He knew by that sound that we were about to go on an aimless sprawl through the night. I stood at the open door with my hand on Slash's tiny chest, just like I'd stood on that night long ago when I'd buckled Mel into the car. It was still impossible for me to understand how I'd been so close to her, so oblivious to the fact that those hours were her last on earth.

We took MLK, which lets you get into the heart of the city for half the price of Telegraph. All you have to do is pass through the Trench, which is so burned-out at this point that it's not even really dangerous. I actually like driving through there, because even though most of the houses are gone and the street names have all changed, I can still recognize certain places where I hung out when I was a kid. I liked to play tour guide for Slash, pointing to a mound of rubble and saying, "That used to be a store called Asata's. That's where your granddad stole his Cheetos." Or we'd go past the rending pool where the park used to be and I'd tell him about how I got smacked in the head with a fence post by Jason Barber. You might say it was wishful thinking, but Slash seemed to really love my stories. As much as a nine-month-old can love anything, I guess. He sat calmly, peering out the passenger-side window, and it really seemed like he was listening. I told him things I'd never told anyone. Obviously he couldn't understand me, but maybe someday he would. The chances were slim, but they were there. A talking kid coming from two silent parents. I wondered what his voice might sound like, what it would be like to hear him speak, to watch his mouth forming the phrases I'd fought so hard to wring from his mother's lips. Would he sound like Flora would have if she'd been able to speak? I felt ashamed for even considering it. But it did cross my mind. So I let myself think it and then I put it away.

He was asleep by the time we made it downtown. I watched him on the dashboard monitor, completely slack in his car seat. Just holding his tiny foot in my hand made my eyes well up. I'd carry him around the apartment and watch his face as he followed every object. He'd look up at the ceiling lights with this spiritual reverence, his face just flooded with wonder. I was obsessed with every move he made, no matter how small or subtle. I'd forgotten all of it from my own bout with fatherhood, all of those details that come packed inside a new life, the tiny things that are gone in an instant. I had no memory of any of that with Flora. Maybe I'd forgotten, or maybe I had been so consumed with everything else that was going on that I simply wasn't paying attention. But with Slash I had the chance to notice everything, a second chance.

I drove to a drive-through autobariste on Grand. The place made decent coffee when there was no other option, and I was pretty beat, knowing that I still had the trek back to the apartment. I pulled up to the register and put my palm on the scanner. There was a monitor above the dispenser and the news was running. I don't usually pay much attention to those ad screens, but while the espresso dribbled into the cup I saw out of the corner of my eye this image of a man with what looked like a bunch of wires coming out of his head. I looked up and saw that the wires were attached to a sort of helmet, and that the man was moving his mouth in an exaggerated way. The caption on the screen was *Ending the Silence*, and that was the first time I heard about the implant.

AUGUST BURNHAM

RAHWAY, NJ
2034

I met Russell and Abigail Andersen in the waiting room on the morning they arrived to pick Calvin up. They usually only met with me in my office at an appointed time to go over Calvin's charts. It must have been strange for them to see me in the wild, so to speak, but I had something to show them. I shook hands with Russell and gave Abigail a hug and ushered them down the corridor, past the tunnel scanner and the vapor deposition station to the evaluation room where I'd spent the better part of the past six months working with their son. Calvin was sitting at a table at one end of the room, wearing the prototype—a white skullcap with multicolored leads dangling from the contact points along the scalp, which can be shocking, seeing your son wearing this menacing-looking bit of cranial tech. I assured them that it was harmless and asked them to sit down across from Calvin. They looked nervous. I told them there was absolutely nothing to be concerned about. I said the surprise I had for them was a good surprise.

The biggest challenge I'd faced in creating the implant wasn't activating the areas of the brain where speech is physically produced and parsed. It wasn't the construction of the implant, most of which I had outsourced overseas. It was the words themselves, those building blocks of language that my patients lacked entirely—the words were the primary obstacle. This is a gross simplification, but I had to essentially seed their brains with a foundational catalog of words and word categories, the basic set of tools that any three-year-old possesses, but which my patients couldn't access. I tried various methods of inserting this grammatical DNA into their heads, with little success until Paul Warner came out with his modular memory actuator, which allowed me to flood a patient's language processing center—again, I'm speaking broadly here—with every word that the patient had stored in long-term memory. The fact was, all of those words and phrases, all of the necessary grammatical architecture, they were *already inside* the patients. They just had no way of interpreting the sounds they heard coming from other people's mouths as a formalized language. What's more, these sounds were already linked to a complex array of emotional and neurological states, everything my patients had experienced but had been unable to verbalize. The memory actuator made all of this raw data available, and through a persistent networked exchange with the central data center, the patient could spontaneously create a nearly infinite range of expressions using only the words they stored as pure sound in their memory, correlated with their naturally occurring neural-emotional patterns.

The Soul Amp was still in its infancy at that point. I was waiting for the self-assembling docking pins, which were stuck on a cargo ship in the South China Sea for weeks until the trade embargo with Vietnam got cleared up, so I had to use the skullcap and an external power device and work in a whole slew of hacks just to be able to run the demo. There was also a mountain of legal paperwork, naturally, but I felt confident about the core functionality. I hadn't yet talked about the Soul Amp to anyone outside my immediate circle of advisers. Calvin Andersen's parents would truly be the first people to see the thing in action.

Calvin was looking out the window at a crane that slowly lifted rebar from a flatbed truck in the lot next door. I went over to the master deck and initiated the demo, which stirred Calvin immediately into a state of heightened alertness. Abigail drew a breath. I could tell they were on edge, both of them. I asked them to remember the first time we'd met, back at McLean, when Calvin was just a toddler. I reminded them that they came to me that day because nothing was more important to them than giving Calvin the power of speech. I remember Russell saying that he'd trade his own ability to talk for his son's silence because he'd already had "a lifetime of words to keep him company in the dark." I assured him that he'd never have to make that kind of sacrifice. I turned to Calvin and said, "Isn't that right, Calvin?" and Calvin said, as clearly as any healthy twenty-four-year-old man, "That is correct, Dr. Burnham."

His parents, when they heard his voice, completely fell apart. They slid off their chairs and knelt on the floor as if God himself had entered the room. Abigail hobbled across the floor on her knees, stretching out her arms to embrace Calvin. She was babbling and gasping in the throes of disbelief. Russell seemed stunned, just paralyzed. He stared at Calvin, who was laughing along with me in delight, because we'd both worked so incredibly hard to make it happen. We'd put in months of grueling twelve-hour days fine-tuning the algorithms, hardening the logic, perfecting the physical enunciation modeler.

Calvin had been speaking coherently for over two weeks. I'd already become so accustomed to hearing his voice that I no longer thought of him as a silent. But his parents' reaction instantly reminded me of the magnitude of what we'd accomplished. We'd done it. We'd broken through the silence that had crippled Calvin. His parents suddenly faced the challenge of familiarizing themselves with a son they'd never fully known.

Russell started to ask Calvin a question and then stopped. I've showed the footage of this event a few times at conferences and panels, so I know the moment well. He paused, almost as though he was terrified that he might shatter the illusion if he asked the wrong question. You can hear me in the background saying, "Go on, ask him anything." And Calvin giggled a little with pleasure and said, "Yes, Dad, you can ask a question and I will try to answer it." And then we both laughed, and Abigail and Russell began to laugh too. Russell struggled to say something, but he was alternating between laughing and crying. Eventually he managed to say, "Calvin, we're so glad to meet you," and he gave Calvin a bear hug, overturning the rolling cart with the master deck in the process.

I called the implant the Soul Amp after a poem I heard once at an EPR conference in St. Paul. The poet's son was silent, and she wrote the poem while sitting by an open window, listening to some kids playing in a park across the street. She wrote something to the effect of, "The whiplash songs of children flare and fade / this house a silent witness to the sound of the soul amplified." That phrase just jumped out at me, and I wrote it down on the back of my nametag—*the amplified soul*. A whole being, an inner landscape as rich and varied as any of our own, just too quiet to hear. I hadn't even conceived of the basic implant at that point. But when I saw Calvin Andersen speak for the first time—on his own, using his own words to express his own desires—it suddenly made perfect sense. My mission wasn't just to give the silents language—I had to give them back their souls. And Calvin Andersen was the living embodiment of that quest.

STEVEN GRENIER

NEW YORK, NY
2035

I remember we surged out of the press conference like the fucking bulls at Pamplona. We were all on our devices, trying to get through to our bureau chief or our agent, or already composing our pieces on the fly as we streamed out of the auditorium where we'd just seen a silent talk for the first time. This was a moment I never thought I'd get to see in my lifetime. A cured silent, Calvin Andersen, standing there behind the podium talking to us as calmly and casually as I'm talking to you right now. He told us what it was like to grow up without language, which he described as being stuck on a rubber raft that was being towed by a cruise ship—he could see the lights on the deck and hear the music playing on the dance floor, but he couldn't ever come aboard. He was among Dr. Burnham's first patients, and he told a funny little story about how, when he was a kid, he thought Burnham was a magician in training, and that he was the test audience. He said, "I always wondered why his tricks were so bad. I didn't know that he was just showing me flash cards." We all laughed—he actually had us *laughing*. Not only was this man able to speak, but he delivered it with personality.

The day after the announcement there were people lining up outside hospitals to register for the trial cycle, as if they were waiting for the opening of a new theme park or something. They didn't seem to care that this wasn't how you got on the wait list—they just spontaneously started gathering in the courtyards and on the front steps. I'd never seen anything like it. A few weeks into the trial there were dozens of implanted silents who were treated like superstars, doing rounds on the news-feed circuit and appearing on late-night clips, where they were probed about their past and asked what it felt like to be suddenly capable of all the freedoms afforded their talking counterparts. They weren't always able to put their thoughts into words, and nobody could blame them. It must have been overwhelming and exhausting. But their faces were everywhere—on billboard screens and sky ads and bus wrappers. And the hype they received only drove the crowds waiting for implants into more of a frenzy. There were families on the waiting list whose kids hadn't even been born yet—they were just saving a spot for themselves in case the baby turned out to be silent. Others were signing up just to sell their spots to the highest bidder. It was a real circus.

A couple months in, there were almost three thousand successful implantees walking around, and that was when reality set in. Talking silents were no longer a science-fiction novelty. They were a real segment of the population, a growing minority with a unique set of pressing needs. Most of them were kids—kids who'd been in silent schools with nonlinguistic curriculum, heavy in math and physics and arts. These were smart, high-achieving silent kids, who were suddenly reclassified as illiterate talking kids. That's when the federal commission was set up to develop a specialized curriculum for implantees. Adults who got the implant were in an even stranger position. They'd been toiling away for many years at mostly menial jobs, repetitive tasks not requiring speech or much interaction, and suddenly a whole new world of possibilities was available to them. They found themselves competing with their natural-talking counterparts for jobs, and there were subsidies for businesses who hired implantees, so the whole market shifted.

This amazing medical story was quickly becoming a societal story, and within the first few weeks everything had been done to death. There was the spotlight interview with Burnham that extolled his lifelong search for a cure, and there were dozens of columns that followed the family of some silent kid into the hospital waiting room where every anxious wringing of the hands and daubing of the eyes with a crumpled tissue were drawn out in excruciating detail. Gail Rhee-Sanders at *Bullrush Magazine* actually found a little Venezuelan girl who was saving up all of her centimos so that her brother could get a Soul Amp. Just the typical obvious crap. Not my style. So instead of waiting for a story to appear, I decided to make one of my own.

First, I got access to the implant wait list through a friend at the NIH. There were thousands of families on it, pages and pages of names—ten years' worth, it seemed like. I decided to pick an unsuspecting family at the bottom of the list, and go in deep and gritty, firmly embedding myself in domestic life to get the real slice-of-life desperation, and then, whenever it all seemed most doomed, I'd reveal the true purpose of my mission: to give little Frida or Diego a free, no-strings-attached implant operation. And if the camera happened to catch the family's subsequent tears of joy and gratitude, well, that would probably make a compelling credit sequence, wouldn't it? I had inroads to Burnham since the *Twenty Years of Silence* miniseries, so it was easy to get him on board. I randomly put my finger down on the last page of the list and landed on the O'Connell family in Wauwatosa, Wisconsin—Judy and Clay, parents of Ampersand, an eleven-year-old silent girl.

I flew to Wisconsin with a bag of underwear and a tooth-brush and let myself in to the O'Connells' house. They were as shocked and appalled as you'd think they'd be, having a stranger barge in and set up camp in a corner of their living room behind the recliner, but that was all part of the plan. I sat down on my sleeping bag and told them about my meth-odology, that their sacrifice in keeping me on as an uninvited guest would help silent children everywhere, and eventu-ally they sort of just got it. And that was the first day of a two-month stint where I did literally everything with the O'Connells. That type of total immersion is the only way to really get at the truth. For example, would Judy O'Connell have told me that she'd felt sexually abandoned by Clay ever since Ampersand was born if we weren't both getting a Bra-zilian wax at Locks & Awe? She hoped that if Amper-sand was cured, she'd be able to rekindle the flame that had brought her and Clay together at the bowhunting convention where they'd first met. And I never would've seen Clay shed the single tear that rolled down his cheek as he let me in on his dream of reading the Cabela's fish-and-game catalog with Ampersand if we hadn't been perched in the canopy of a mas-sive northern pin oak waiting for a buck to wander into view. He never let on, but he was devastated by the fact that his daughter would be twenty-three before she'd make it to the top of the implant list. "Her whole childhood, just gone," he said, drawing a bead on a magnificent twelve-point that was gnawing on a jack pine branch in the distance.

I spent most of my time with Ampersand, who was an incredible kid, very talented for someone in her condition. She competed in statewide Junior Misses Silent MMA tournaments, and I spent hours with her every day after school, sparring with her and holding the heavy bag. I rented a van so that the whole extended family could go to the state championship in Madison, where Ampersand owned her division, placing competitively in three different categories. I also did the special effects for her school's Noh performance of *Terminator 2*, where Ampersand played one of the T-1000s in the future sequences. I became a sort of third parent to Ampersand, much to my surprise, because I'd never been a first or second parent and in fact always sort of hated children. But she was a real diamond in the rough. Never let her silence get in the way.

At the end of the eighth week of my stint, I rolled up my bag and tossed my laundry in the kitchencinerator and waited for the family to come downstairs for breakfast. I had an envelope ready on the table, and when they were all assembled there in their morning clothes I asked Judy to open it. It was so quiet in the kitchenette you could hear the autofocus servos whizzing as the cameras recorded everything. Judy scanned the certificate twice before registering any emotion at all. I've never seen anyone in such a state of disbelief. Clay sidled up to her and put his hand to her shoulder, and when he read the certificate he whispered, "Sweet Christ almighty," before collapsing into Judy's lap. Ampersand watched the whole thing, not sure what to make of her parents' behavior. I went up and gave her a hug and showed her in the best way I could that something big was about to happen. A week and a half later, even though the wait list was already bloated with dignitaries and jai alai stars and underage models, Ampersand was out cold on a gurney in the operating room with Burnham standing over her, guiding the nanocapsule along the spline toward her left perisylvian region, where it would take root and change her life forever.

PATTI KERN

HAYWARD, CA
2036

I felt stray voltage the moment I walked into that medi-park, an ugly ecstatic clamor. A miracle, everyone said. Hook all the native speakers up to machines, snuff out their instinctual language so that they can join the great jabbering din. Never mind that what they're communicating can't be translated into words, that it'd be like trying to reproduce a sequoia with popsicle sticks. A night sky with yellow crayons.

I left Monte Rio for Hayward after I heard about the lottery at Nu Ware. Buried my kombucha mother, blessed the baby from afar, and set out on foot—driving would've been too easy—all the way down to the East Bay. I stuffed hamburger wrappers in my shoes to reroute the discharge from my heel blisters. Twice someone yelled, "Put some clothes on!" I was still wearing the cleansing glove, which was pearl white with a flap in the back for solid-waste evacuation. From a distance I guess it made me look naked. I was honoring the baby's immaculate birth by reverting to my most natural state, physically reacquainting myself with my body. Which of course can inspire fear in self-estranged individuals.

After three days of walking, I arrived at Nu Ware Systems. The parking lot was full of parents nervously clutching their applications. Nu Ware, the war profiteer, was holding a lottery to determine who'd be accepted into the phase-two trial for their new prototype. A trial! A farce. I was emitting waves of righteous energy. The security guards at the medical park wouldn't come near me. Neither would their dogs. Neither would any of the gathered parents, some of whom had brought their poor, oblivious infants in hopes of somehow erasing their native consciousnesses right then and there. I was witnessing the early moments of a psychic genocide.

One implant says, "My plate is empty and I am full." And the other implant nods and says, "Yum." And you call that a miracle. But you can't fathom all the nuances of fullness, and the dozens of degrees of yummy. These two have spoken but they haven't communicated—they've said what's necessary, but not what's sufficient. And this is the simplest of exchanges, nothing like actual heart-communion.

I wanted to talk to as many of the parents as I could, to let them know some people out there haven't given up on finding a harmonious coexistence with the native speakers. But no one wanted to engage. I must've looked pretty irregular after my walk. Plus, the body sock always caused a mixed reaction.

"Please. Honor your children," I said to the women in the parking lot. I pushed my way through the crowd. "They're not defective. The only implant they need is love."

What did I see in their collective faces? Fear, misplaced trust, future humiliation. I didn't spite them. There was love in their hearts—they'd just chosen the easiest path. And the easiest path is almost always the incorrect path.

"Even if you end up winning the lottery," I said, "what you'll hear when they turn on those things won't be the true voice of your child. Believe me. Go home. Turn off everything and just look at your children and listen with your eyes."

One of the security guards finally approached me and grabbed me roughly by the elbow. He walked me to the edge of the medical park, asking me all sorts of questions. Why was I bothering all those sleepless parents? Was I the one who'd liberated the rats in their sensory deprivation lab a few years back? What was up with my idiotic space leotard?

All my unreciprocated love finally congealed into something more fleshy, and I just hauled off and smacked the security guard across the face. He let go of my shoulder and held his palm to his chin. I said, "Leave me be or I will grind your craving-fucked samsara-dwelling ass into a chunky paste and smear what's left of you across a brick wall somewhere. And then I'll lead every stray cat and dog I can find to lick it clean." My voice wasn't mine. It came from somewhere black and true. The security guard scuttled off.

Clearly my campaign of love needed to travel in an armored carriage. The next day was a blur. I allowed my plan to evolve on its own. I bought a few things: a rope, votive candles. Then, at a junkyard, I found a length of reinforced chain, the kind used for hauling trailers, and the oldest, fattest, ugliest padlock I'd ever seen. I unlocked it and threw the key out over a stack of flattened motorcycles.

Back at Nu Ware, I waited until the sun went down. By now the crowd had doubled, tripled. The whole parking lot was filled with tents and people, cooking meat on portable grills, sitting in collapsible chairs, coveting. I felt a rush of pristine emotion.

I slowly made my way to the doors, the lock and chain thrown over my shoulder. The news of my arrival traveled quickly, but I was quicker. I made it to the front doors of Nu

Ware, which were tinted black with guilt, and before the security guards could arrive I'd wrapped the chain around my body and through the door handles, then again so that I was wedged against the glass.

The same security guard approached with his gun drawn. I held up the lock for him and everyone to see, threaded it through the chain, and clicked it closed, and then he shot me.

I awoke who knows how long after that. Apparently his gun was a cattle prod or something, because I was as alive as ever, more alive, successfully blocking the entrance to the lab. The crowd didn't look as angry as I thought they would. Maybe the parents knew that I was suffering so they wouldn't have to. Maybe they were already grateful.

The parking lot wasn't as bustling as it had been earlier. Then I noticed the remaining crowd was filing off forty feet to my right. Apparently the building had another doorway, where the parents were assembling. Smiling, excited, deluded. "We won, we won," some of them were saying. A few of the older brothers and sisters of the silent infants came up to me and poked at me with branches. They dumped crumbs out of their potato chip bags so squirrels and crows would root around by my feet.

I was where I needed to be. I wasn't going anywhere.

CALVIN ANDERSEN

NEWARK, NJ
2036

D r. Burnham turned on the prototype, and then he said my name. "Calvin." It was a sound I recognized from before the implant. Maybe more than any other sound. But all my life I had thought of it as a song, or part of one. It was just a note that people would sound out whenever they aimed their faces at me and made the timbral breaths that I now know are sentences. But when Dr. Burnham turned on the prototype and said, "Calvin," it wasn't music anymore. It was a force, a thing, a heavy weight in the center of my mind. "Calvin" was a sound-picture that other people could use to represent me even when I wasn't in the room. It was a name. My name. I knew this instantly, somehow. Early on, in the first few tests, I would sometimes hear a word before the Soul Amp could catch up, and it would sit there in my mind, this unknown thing that was part music, part abstraction. I don't have the means to describe it. But "Calvin," I knew immediately, was me, and I was it. We were inseparable, my body and this idea that could be transmitted through the air on a human breath. Dr. Burnham said, "Calvin, can you understand me?" And I could understand him. I saw his brow arching to a peak and his lips slightly parted and I knew what he was asking, and when I said, "Yes," it came out so suddenly that I nearly choked on it. I laughed, and Dr. Burnham's face showed a great cloud of anxiety passing.

The time of discovery that followed was overwhelming. Dr. Burnham would take me around the examination room and have me name all of the objects. He'd hold up a notebook and I would say, "Notebook." And he'd point to the clock and I would say, "That's a clock." I'm at a loss to tell you how it felt to look at a thing and know its name. The power of it rippled through me. I felt like I'd been running all my life in a deep trench, only able to see the mud walls around me, and that the implant had lifted me up above the treetops and allowed me to soar freely in the sky, where I could take in the whole endless horizon. Everything had the feel of magic, which scared me. I told this to Dr. Burnham. He just expanded his entire face and then contracted it, and told me I'd understand in time. He told me that the joy of discovery would fade, and that I should just revel in the newness of the world for as long as possible. It was an easy thing to do. The world had sharpness, edges, handles. The connections between things became clearer. The categories, the relationships. Everything was vivid. So much so that it sometimes hurt my head. But in a good way. I was reveling. I reveled.

At the end of the first week Dr. Burnham suggested that I try out the Soul Amp "in the wild." That was his term for downtown Rahway, a place I had never visited. It was not actually very wild, but still it was amazing. I walked down Cherry Street, listening to the conversations happening all around me. There was something so easy about the way people traded their thoughts with one another. It was frightening and exhilarating both at the same time.

I went through a door and sat on a stool. A waiter with a shaved head and a bushy beard approached and leaned his head toward me. I opened my mouth and said, "Tek 9." I wasn't entirely sure what a Tek 9 was until the man placed the highball glass neatly on the bar and poured in the shots of Pisco and tritium flakes. It was the same drink that my roommate at the assistance house served at parties. Without even thinking about it, I had gotten the thing I wanted. I drank it quickly and asked for another.

After my second drink I saw a particular talking woman across the room. I have had intercourse only with silent women and I have always wanted to see if it is different to be with a woman who talks. I've always been attracted to women who talk, because they are much more difficult to read than silent women. Their faces are always working hard to keep something hidden, whereas when I look at a silent woman's face it is like all of her insides are spraying out from every pore in her head. This woman in the Rahway Gizzard Gulp had very expressive, perfectly symmetrical cheeks that flushed to punctuate her thoughts. She looked like an apple with eyes. I watched her from across the room for a long time as she talked to another woman, who had recently lost someone important to her. The woman I was observing examined her friend's expressions with the same level of scrutiny. She seemed capable of great depths of empathy, which I found powerful and stimulating. I would have been happy to just sit there watching, but I knew that Dr. Burnham would be disappointed if I didn't approach her and strike up a conversation.

I waited until the woman's friend excused herself to go to the bathroom. I walked up to the woman and attempted to tell her how much I admired her compassionate restraint in dealing with her friend, whose relentless self-pity seemed to frustrate and depress her. But what came out was something along the lines of, "I bested your wellness clinic, you fellow."

My cheeks became red. I might as well have been urinating in my pants, was how vulnerable and exposed I felt. She broadened her face and pulled back to give me room to try again, which I thought was more generous than I deserved. I tried again to explain myself: "I was granding over there and I foreshortened your Calypso style." I knew the things that were coming out of my mouth were wrong, but I couldn't find the right words. I raced through my mind to try to dislodge a phrase that would express what I felt, but I couldn't find any stable platform for the ideas in my head to land on. I could see in her face that the woman was prepared to give me yet another chance to explain myself to her. She was that forgiving. But I backed off and stumbled out into the night. Dr. Burnham said I would eventually hit my wall—he called it a wall, which was a metaphorical limit of what the Soul Amp was capable of. He said that it would learn as I went through my days. He said it would adapt and improve. I wasn't worried, but I was anxious to put the memory of that woman behind me.

Do you want to know a funny thing? I have even begun speaking in my dreams. Recently I had a dream where I was standing in the middle of a dirty pond and a crocodile was swimming toward me. There was nobody else in the vicinity. I was very scared of the crocodile, but I didn't dare move. I simply shouted, "Go away!" and the crocodile burst into a flock of birds that flew up into a dark cloud in the center of the sky. Isn't that a great dream? Its meaning is that I now have the power to do things I never thought I could before. Did you understand that when you heard the story as I told it?

PRASHANT NUREGESAN

REDWOOD CITY, CA
2037

Looking back, the creation of the implant seems almost inevitable. After I found Isabelle hanging from the rafters in that warehouse, I disappeared. I left the country for about a year and a half. I lived with my cousin in New Delhi for a spell and then went on to Barsana, where I secured a job working as a customer-support specialist for Chiller Industries, one of my own companies in the States. I had a one-room apartment with a single window that looked out on another building that had a nice view of Shri Radhikaji's temple, and I sat in a folding chair with my headset on and solved the technical issues of my customers with a prowess that was unstoppable. All of my grief at having failed to save Isabelle, at having failed my entire family, not to mention myself, I kept that tightly wound inside of me, and like a clock spring it kept me going. I lived on rice and street trash and thought of nothing but whatever task was directly in front of me.

My cousin visited me when I was in this condition, and I saw the horror on his face when I greeted him at the door. "You have to confront this, Nu," he said, taking me by the arm. "You can't keep hiding." We went straight to the temple, where he enrolled us in a course in vipassana as a way to, I guess, cleanse my soul. For ten days we took a vow of silence. Total, numbing silence. I wasn't much of a traditionalist, so it didn't bother me that the temple was being used for such an infantile bastardized form of meditation. What did bother me was the silence itself. For the first day, I admit, it had a leveling effect on my consciousness. I felt the great expanse of my mind unfurling before me, so much real estate that I hadn't yet occupied. So much ripe, open terrain to leverage. But by the second day this elation settled into a sort of dull pulse, and on the third day I felt I could actually hear the paint on the walls. Five days in, the silence consumed me. I literally felt as if my body had caught fire. I no longer knew which way was up. I had no idea what my hands were anymore. This was much more alarming than when I'd drunk opium tea with those two hot Belgian transfer students at Rutgers. I was no longer able to identify the world I inhabited. Even my own skin—I saw it as this blanket that some distant god had spread over my bones to keep me warm. The course turned me into an idiotic space infant, and the moment I stepped out of the damn temple I knew my calling. I knew that everything in my life had happened for a purpose. Isabelle's death was not my fault. My failure to rescue her was not rooted in some personal flaw. She died because of silence. It was the silence that made her tie that cord to the rafter. And if there was one thing I was put on this earth for, it was to find a cure. A real, lasting cure. This was my future. This was my destiny.

I'd saved nearly everything I made from working the support line, so I was able to get the next flight back to New York. I showed up to work the next day in an old suit of mine that was two sizes too big for my shrunken frame and got the ball rolling on the Isabelle Foundation. Our mission was to find a cure at any cost. To find a cure within a decade. There was nothing else inside me but the desire to extinguish the silence. It coursed through me.

So you can imagine how I felt when I partnered with Burnham to bring the Soul Amp to market. He did all the heavy lifting, and I shielded him from the rest of the world, using the Foundation to build up an incubating wall of capital so that he could do what he did best in a stress-free environment. I made sure the guy had anything and everything he needed. When the news of the Soul Amp hit the streets, he was the one who got all the interviews and accolades. He received all of the awards. Rightfully so. I never wanted or expected any kind of praise. I never have. I just want to get a job done, and the wave of excitement that flooded the country and then the world when the Soul Amp came out was a reward beyond anything you could imagine. Before, you'd walk along any main street in any town and there'd be at least one disheveled silent, a ward of the state, clinging to the rim of the fountain in the park, peering into the basin with a vacant look in his eye. But once the federal integration policy went into effect, all the silents in transitional facilities got the implant and the places shut down. People who'd never been able to work before were suddenly given this incredible second chance. And the response from the community at large was just completely inspiring, the way these new members of society were welcomed without a trace of fear-mongering or bitterness. Every kid I saw on the street with the little telltale port behind his ear—I'd look at that kid and think, "I'm in there. I'm actually inside that boy's mind. I've literally changed the course of that kid's life."

Once the implant had an install base of almost a hundred thousand, I decided it was time to roll out my next innovation—a suite of user-configurable mods that would allow anyone with an implant to customize their speech—or the speech of their children—to suit the individual context. The accent mod would allow you to pick one of several thousand regional dialects, and you could insert a second dialect and set the blend however you wanted. There was some controversy surrounding the content-blocker mod that allowed parents to gate their children's speech, which, okay, some people abused, but you're always going to get hackers and griefers no matter what you release. You can't let that stop you from providing useful services to people who are desperate for them. Once we had all that, the obvious next step was to release a pack of famous voices from history, which people went crazy for. You actually started to see natural talkers getting jealous of their formerly silent peers. And who could blame them? There were times when I was working on the mods and I'd listen to our QA testers talking to each other like Napoleon and Kenny Rogers and Mother Teresa, and I felt the same way. Maybe if Isabelle had been around to get one, she'd sync to a Pocahontas or Nina Simone, or whoever she decided she should sound like, and we'd have sat on the glass platform of my trimaran and talked about a future that, for her and me both, was suddenly much, much brighter.

KENULE MITEE

BROOKLYN, NY
2037

I soke is thinking about having one of those devices put in her head. There is a glass jar under her side of the bed, and every day there is more money saved in it. I have been watching it carefully. I don't know what to think.

People look at Isoke and they say, "Oh, Kenule, how is it you have taken such a beautiful young bride?" and then they find out she is silent and they don't ask any more questions. As though they suddenly discovered that I found her in the damaged goods aisle. I know they are saying behind my back, "Yes, she is pretty, but any man can win the heart of a cripple." I don't let it bother me. In fact, it makes me laugh, because I have a relationship with Isoke that is deeper and more unshakable than any of the so-called marriages I see around me. At night we are like pearl divers, knifing through the depths to explore each other's bodies, always finding something startling and new. These men who judge me, they are just children. Boys who throw stones at a squirrel because it can climb so well. They simply have no idea what love is. They do not know the language of the soul, and in a strange way I feel sorry for them. I see *them* as the cripples, not my wife.

I have seen this device up close, because I have six silent men working my fleet of food carts in the Astroland Mall—all of them I have known since they were young boys, gathering around my cart to buy fat bread. They have all gotten the implant in them, which has been good for my business, without a doubt. Before, when they were silent, I was earning just enough to buy the slurries for the next day. My carts were the least desirable in the mall. They were the carts people went to only when there were long lines at the other vendors' carts. Customers tolerated my boys, but many people felt uneasy about having to deal directly with a young man who took their money and gave them change without a single "hello" or "thank you" or "enjoy your day at the mall." Some customers refused to indicate their desired product with a gesture or nod—they insisted on words and nothing else. My boys were obstacles, problems. It's sad to say this, but people are cruel. That is the everlasting truth.

Now my boys are very well-spoken. Gentlemen, all of them. They make their customers feel appreciated. And the money I am earning now? I never dreamed of it. I will soon be able to put carts in several other area malls. I have my eye on a property in Bushwick that has, if you look out the window just right, a view of the sea. I have gained so much. But sometimes I still miss the past. Not the fat bread days, never that. But, well, it is strange to say but sometimes I miss those boys. Even though they are still right here.

One of them, Ezekiel, recently turned twenty-four. He is a great young man who spent many years in an orphanage until he was adopted by the wife of a popular jazz musician here in Brooklyn. I took all of my boys out to a nightclub near my house to celebrate Ezekiel's birthday. I thought we could just chill to the Afrobolly music they were always playing there, but these boys only wanted to have a conversation. They couldn't stop talking, showing off their new powers, the way a wealthy man might drive an expensive sports car to the grocery store. I thought it was silly, but I joined in with them, because, as I said, I love my boys. I would do anything for them. They asked me to tell them a joke, and so I leaned in and told the joke about the missionaries and the bedpan. When I got to the punch line, where the passing soldiers see the missionaries pouring the gasoline from the bedpan into their jeep and say, "Now that's faith!" the boys nodded gravely. Ezekiel said something I could not understand for the life of me, and they nodded again. I changed the subject, trying to start up a conversation about the things men talk about, you know, the secrets of a woman and things along these lines, and they seemed interested, but again, whenever they tried to speak, it was like another person was interrupting their every word. They didn't seem to truly understand each other either. It was very awkward. They are very gifted at saying the expected things, but they cannot seem to just relax and have a nice chat. I prefer the old days, where we would sit and feel the warmth of the alcohol and listen to the tunes. Those were good times.

I look at my boys sometimes and I see in their faces a new thing—a weight of some kind, like they are carrying a great yoke around their necks. A normal person might not even see this, but I am so used to reading Isoke's face. And so now I must admit, I am nervous about Isoke joining them. Because what if she changes? What if we can no longer communicate with our bodies the way we now do? What if, when she can speak, she decides that I am no good? That I am nothing but a breadslinger, a small man near the bottom of the food chain? She is so radiant, I am sure that if she could talk she could attract the attention of a wealthy, powerful man. There is no question of this. The way she is looked at on the street, it is almost scandalous. I know she is motivated to get the implant so that she can be closer to me, but what if the thing that is supposed to bring us together only flings us apart?

PERSEPHONE GOLDIA

PHILADELPHIA, PA
2037

I was implanted four weeks ago tomorrow. Some begin to talk instantaneously after the anesthesia wears off and some require an elongated unlocking period, and I must have been one of the primary threats to the osprey's nesting habitat. Must have been one of the latter ones. Very quickly I felt I could understand what the doctors were saying to me, but I could not reply to them. The doctors told me what I was experiencing was similar to the sensation of your mind waking up before your body. To me it felt itch-crippled, like trying to unlock a door with four different keys all together. Usually the surgery takes just a few hours, you don't even have to spend the night, but I was in the hospital for three days, working with two different therapists. Adult implants are still more difficult due to our diminished brain plasticity. I did the breathing and the projection exercises while they made adjustments. My first real sentence was, "Back porch bitches beat front porch bitches at they own tricks." The therapist told me this was likely a thing I heard on the radio towers killing songbirds. Heard on the radio and internalized.

I had wanted the implant ever since the surveillance-scrubbing company fired me for failing their language test. They offered it in English, Spanish, Hindi, Mandarin, and I failed them all. They had figured out I was a silent months before, but I guess they just liked watching me babble incoherently in four different tongues. After that I worked in one of the ag towers downtown, picking and sorting fruit under blistering hydroponic grow lights. When I sorted two hundred pounds I was done for the night. I worked on the twenty-seventh floor, strawberries and blueberries. I worked hard.

One woman I sorted beside would talk to me for at least ten minutes each time. I listened to her and watched her face trumpet and scowl. She was easy to read—most of her talking was about the boredom of the work. I frowned and nodded. She had a dry snuffed lantern face. It was all-over calming. Even now, after the implant, I have difficulty stressing the importance of photosynthetic algae. Difficulty explaining why I was so drawn to talkers. Once I had sorted my two hundred pounds I would wait in the break closet for someone to come in, and then would try to hold them there as long as possible. Even though the work was emptying I liked the ag tower more than the surveillance company because there were more stillbirths. More talkers around. When our shift ended another began. I would have slept there if they let me. I tried, but they did not let me. Then the ag tower was raided and all the employees were interviewed and I was fired.

So once the implant became available, I didn't need to wait two times. And I was excited to get right back into the world, but the rehabilitation doctors recommended delaying six weeks before applying for a job. They also recommended I do the at-home reentry exercises for no more than two hours a day. The rehabilitation involves simple recognition, sentence forming, philosophy, training yourself to withhold. I did the exercises twelve hours a day, and in under two weeks I was applying for recognition under the Endangered Species Act. Applying for every job I could. I interviewed to be a docent in a museum of medical oddities, to be a hostess at a restaurant specializing in tea parties for little girls. I tried to follow all the hints from the rehabilitation. *Allow yourself two seconds before responding to another speaker. Don't dwell too long when answering perfunctory questions, especially ones about your well-being.*

I do not know how I seemed to the interviewers. I could understand their questions pretty well, but I had difficulty deciphering what I myself was saying, even after I had said it. The interviewer at the tea party restaurant asked me what my biggest weakness was, and I counted to two and told her that I have never liked how my name is shaped. When she asked me to elaborate, I said, "It makes me feel . . ." And my pause was longer than salubrious, and they thanked me and told me they had a tough decision ahead of them. "Me too," I said, trying to be empathetic. They decided other than me.

Finally I was hired at the SS *Muir*, a zero-impact conservationist day cruise out near East Lansdowne. We set sail inside a high-ceilinged warehouse with surround screens on the walls. It was really just a long movie with two meals in between. I was hired as a junior hospitality technician, starboard side. My first day, I woke up tight in my upper body with brittle percolating happiness. I arrived in my khaki safari uniform forty-five minutes early. I stood outside memorizing my script and fact-supplement and shivering with white ache until the manager unlocked the door. "Jesus. It's freezing out here," he said. "You could've just knocked. I would've let you in."

I said the line I had rehearsed on my way over: "I am very happy to be working here today."

It came out perfect. "Well, all right," the manager said, and that was the beginning of the extinction cycle. Beginning of my first day.

Once the cruise goers boarded and we were headed out of Iquitos and down the Amazon, I went around to my section and asked for drink orders. I had an exact script: "Much like the pea aphid in the dry season, you are probably thirsty. What can I get you?"

When we arrived at the Pacaya-Samiria National Reserve, I asked if they wanted refills, and, if they did not, I said, "An adult crocodile can survive two years without eating." Then I paused to allow it to sink in. "But I bet you can't." Wait for laughter. "I'm happy to answer any questions you have. Our giant panda burger is delicious—it's one-hundred percent panda-free." Smile, wait for laughter. "It's made from red beans, smoked wheat-meat, and reengineered photosynthetic algae."

My shift was twelve hours long. There was not much downtime to meet and talk with my coworkers. I did fold silverware into napkins next to an older woman named Callie, who told me, "The script's a real pain in the ass at first, but you get used to it. Shit, I like it now. I just smile and veg out and don't say anything I'm not supposed to say."

If the customers were hostile and abusive, the script called for conflict avoidance. Smile, try to establish physical contact with them. Put your hand on their shoulder and say, "I'll come back in a few minutes. I need to go milk the oxen." There were a lot of other latent predatory—a lot of other quips. Menu jokes, trivia questions to see who would be the one to wear the toucan mask during the Gathering of the Birds. And also the SS *Muir* motto: "The first *S* is for *Satisfy*, the second is for *Smile*." And then, "Make Understood Inconvenient Realities."

At the end of that first day, I smelled like the hot jungle stench that was pumped into the warehouse. My mouth hurt from smiling. My neck hurt from nodding and tilting my head at a sympathetic angle. I had never talked to so many people before in my life. I swept out my station feeling laundered—I mean, scooped dry.

Callie invited me out with a few of our coworkers. We went to a bar with paintings of naked clowns on the wall. When the waitress came around, I pointed to something on the drink menu and she said, "That's my favorite." Then I heard her say it again about a different drink a few minutes later. While we waited, one of the floor managers tapped my knee and said, "So, your first big cruise, huh? How you feeling?"

I was so tired, so overdrawn. I wasn't thinking about any of my rehabilitation hints. All that mattered was me coming up with a satisfactory answer to this question, for him, for me. I closed my eyes and considered it. I took my mind fully inward and thought about the various flavors—the strands—the colors of my inner . . . I sighed. I felt an answer, a slippery fish I could touch but not hook.

"Relax," he said. "Have a drink, you'll feel better. If not, have another." The woman next to him laughed, and he turned and asked her the same question. She said, "Beat."

When he turned back to me a few minutes later, I said, "I'm beat, too."

His face swelled with a satisfied bloat. I sipped my drink, tried to think the words for how I was feeling, and then ordered the village elders to empty the cistern. Ordered everyone off the beach because of red tide. Ordered another.

SENATOR RANSFORD SWEENEY

DES MOINES, IA
2038

The worst kinds of tragedies are the ones you could've prevented. He was a six-year-old boy, Isaiah, last name withheld, out shopping with his stepmother and two half sisters. They're at an artisan mall in Muscatine, the one where you make everything yourself. Isaiah walks a few feet behind his family, but they're used to it. He looks slightly confused, bereft. He's a silent. Watch him for a few minutes and you see how he stares at people too long, trying to find someone he understands, someone who understands him. His stepmother barely tolerates him, his uncombed hair, his searching eyes. His half sisters steal his food and blame him for broken windows and missing toys.

The four of them are walking to the place where you can make your own flavored toothpicks, when Isaiah gets distracted by a wig-shop window. All these long-necked mannequin heads. When the boy looks up, his family's gone. What can he do? He doesn't know where they were going, can't tell anyone their names, or his name. He's smart enough to find an adult with a nametag and uniform—an old janitor. The boy's pointing and frowning and sighing at the old man, who deals with this kind of thing several times a week with silents. Did they lose their money in the candy spinner? Were they just confused? He never knows. He had a job to do, and ambassador-to-wayward-silents wasn't part of the description.

All this was observed by another man, a man who came to the artisan mall to look for a victim. He noticed Isaiah by the merry-go-round and pegged him for a silent immediately. He watched the boy go up to the ticket-taker and try to tell her, or express to her, what was going on. The man smiled when she waved him off. She probably thought Isaiah'd lost his ticket. No ticket, no ride.

Isaiah tried one more person, who put his arm around the boy and was apparently walking him toward the information kiosk. The man saw his chance. He ran up to them, embraced Isaiah, and said, "There you are. Had me worried sick." No recognition from the boy, no relief, but there was so much he couldn't understand.

The man hustled Isaiah out to the parking lot, into his van, where he handcuffed him to a cleat in the back. Gagged him with an old dishrag.

The boy was missing for thirty-nine days. After a week the nature of the search changed from a missing persons to a homicide. The family lit candles. Churches prayed. I met with local and state officials. Then one morning the boy walked into a gas station in Sioux City, the other side of the state, and collapsed there in front of the cashier. Dehydrated, nearly starved, visibly abused. A wreck. But alive. He was reunited with his father and stepmother and half sisters the next day. In borrowed clothes, clean, but still terrified. I went to his house and met him and his family. Everyone was trying to smile for me and the cameras, they knew that's what was expected, but I could see his parents were still just ravaged. The father was stone-faced, and he kept saying, "We should've gotten the implant. We just . . ." and then would trail off. Because what more could he say?

He was punishing himself more than anyone else ever could, but the more I looked into it, the angrier I became. To be honest, I didn't know a lot about silents before Isaiah went missing. I was aware of the implant but didn't know all the specifics. When it first came onto the market, it cost roughly $225,000, and most health insurance companies only covered the hardware and anesthesia. Way too expensive for most families. But as of last year all but some negligible lab costs had been subsidized by matching grants from the federal government, in partnership with Nu Ware. And the father *knew* this. He'd received notice in the mail, had been contacted by Nu Ware representatives, had heard about it from his doctor. The procedure was on par with having your wisdom teeth pulled. Isaiah could have gone in, and after a week or so it'd be like he'd never been a silent at all.

The father had learned his lesson, but my staff did some digging and discovered he wasn't an isolated case. It was staggering that parents would allow this to happen. But I guess the only way you're going to get full compliance is to actually force people to do it. It was the same way a hundred years ago with the polio vaccine. You can show parents a million pictures of polio children swimming in public pools, tell them how easy the vaccine is. But there will always be holdouts.

Isaiah's ordeal shows that the implant is no less vital than a lifesaving vaccine. If you're a parent, think about all the work you do, and then imagine never once hearing your child say that he loves you. Can you feel it? All that emotional investment, those sleepless nights, and you'll never hear those three words? Plus all the others? This amazing invention is a blessing, American ingenuity at its finest. To not take advantage of it would be nothing less than child abuse.

Which is why I proposed Isaiah's Law in the Senate. Essentially, the law made it mandatory for every child under the age of seven to be implanted, going into effect on the first of the year. Isaiah's was a cautionary tale, and surely not an isolated one. Think of all the voiceless children out there, think of their stories. These are children who, with the flick of a switch, could have their lives enriched and augmented, safe and thriving among healthy society.

The bill also allotted more funds for the distribution of the implants, and set up a subcommittee to oversee and expedite the implantation process, especially in underserved urban and rural communities. The law passed both houses by a wide margin, and the president signed it into law soon afterward.

Isaiah's story does have a happy ending. Some of my senior aides worked with his family to get him implanted, and the surgery was a complete success. Once Isaiah had completed his rehabilitation, he was smiling a lot more, telling everyone how happy he was to be alive. Plus, he was finally able to recount his nightmarish tale, providing the necessary information for police to find his attacker, a retired accountant from Waterloo named Sander Dougal, who kept kids locked in a storm cellar while he brutally assaulted and then drowned most of them, seven confirmed. Isaiah had managed to escape through a heating vent. And, thanks to the implant and Isaiah's testimony, Dougal is now in prison for life, where he'll probably either commit suicide or be murdered.

This law will be Isaiah's legacy. "Remember the silents?" people will say years from now. Some will, the younger ones won't. And before too long, the whole sorry story will be forgotten.

ZANE NOERPER

Ever play *Big Buck Hunter: Open Season 3—Unfenced* on jimson? When I got to Face-to-Face, I was pretty much exclusively doing jimson and playing *BB:OS3*. It's such a classic. Really the best, most realistic open-world hunting adventure game ever. I know the terrain like the back of my hand. I don't even play for score anymore—I'll just shoulder my rifle and climb to the top of a rise to watch the migration patterns of the Aniak caribou. Breathtaking doesn't even begin to describe it. And on jimson, you look at a caribou charging across the snow and you're like, "Is that a snake with legs?" Which is sort of what a caribou really is, if you think about it but not too much. That's what jimson can do for you. I ran a fan site, BigFansOfBigBuckHunter3-Unfenced.com, where you could access a cracked version of the game with all of the geobounders removed. It wasn't, strictly speaking, totally legal, but the people who ran Face-to-Face didn't seem to mind my installing a server farm in one of the old Quonsets in the backwoods behind the compound. They didn't really bother me at all, in fact. Just kind of kept to themselves. A chilled-out people, those silents. Super noble and soulful, like how I'd imagine the early Native Americans, or maybe Mayans. Or the Druids? Anyway, looking back, I took for granted how sweet life was in those days. My schedule was, get up, check the *Buck 3* forums, tend to my jimson patch, get as ballistic as possible, and spend the rest of the day wandering around in the game, watching a family of badgers tunnel for field mice, or maybe happening upon a whitetail doe getting studiously boned by a sixteen-point buck.

Over time, though, things started to go slightly downhill. When I first arrived from Cupertino, the compound was pretty packed. There were people wandering around at all hours of the night wearing nothing but a smile and a linen ascot, and fuck if you could tell the silent people from the talkers. Everyone was riding this whale-dick-size wave of togetherness. But then there was some sort of mess in New York, and that seemed to harsh the overall vibe of the place. It wasn't one specific thing you could really put your finger on—but I could definitely sense that something was finished. An era had passed. People were like, "I'm done with this scene," and the crowd started to thin out. It was cool for a while, in that I didn't have to constantly worry about some noobs wandering into my jimson patch and having some kind of silent bukkake fest on my crops. But eventually it got so that nobody knew who was in charge, or if anybody even wanted to be in charge, and that's when things started to slide into a big mess.

To be honest, I hardly noticed at first, but then it started to creep up on me. Last week I came out of a jimmy fog and I was like, man, I need a sauna like no one's business. You have to do fever therapy to come down safely off a jimson high or you go really crazy. Sauna, then hot tea, then friction rub—it's vital. I went to the sauna, but the top was all caved in, like completely buckled, as if someone had dropped a bowling ball on it. I went to the sauna guy's cabin to complain, but he was gone and there was a big hole in the front of his cabin where a tractor was parked. It looked like it had been there for a while—there were critters living in the wheel wells and little deer-shit pellets all over the guy's porch. I was like, Why didn't I get the memo that the sauna guy left? I went to the main house to complain, but there wasn't even an office there anymore, just a countertop with a Post-it note stuck to the front that said *Back in five*. I was like, Wait, was there ever an office here? I was confused and massively sad about the whole thing, so I just cooked up some more Sir James and got back in-world, where I crawled into a cave and witnessed a grizzly cub birth.

But even that couldn't last, because then a couple days later my servers went down. It was like standing at the edge of darkness. Total bone-cold terror. I went out to the Quonset hut where the servers were set up, and I found a bunch of goddamn saplings growing up through the middle of the floor. There were vines choking all the machines. I heard this awful sound, like the cry of a drowning baby, and I looked up and saw some kind of animal on top of the server rack. This grotesque thing like a cross between a cat and a weasel, and it was yowling and baring its teeth at me, and I was like, Man, it is fully time to get out of here.

I went back to my lean-to, got my pack and my vintage consoles, and headed straight out, just like that. I'd heard there was an off-grid community up in Bellingham that was made entirely from old moon bounces, which seemed worth a try. Down the trail that led to the highway I ran into this family of silent people who'd been at Face-to-Face for as long as I could remember. And the only ones still there, far as I could tell. A real unassuming bunch who generally steered clear of all the drama, back when there was drama. They lived in a raw-looking little cabin that had a sweet vegetable garden off to the side. There was an older woman with short hair kneeling in the garden, digging with a little hand-shovel thing, which I know has a name but I'm blanking. The woman paused to watch a little naked boy chase a goat around in circles. A man came up the trail from the river carrying two buckets of water, and his wife, who was wicked hot for a silent person IMHO, went down to meet him and took one of the buckets. We made eye contact, me and her, and I felt like I should apologize for taking off, but then I thought, These people probably don't even want me here. Look at this little thing they've got going on—they've got it pretty good. It was a real idyllic-type setup. As the woman walked in my direction, she picked two red bell peppers straight off the vine and offered them to me. They looked incredible, glowing, like the sunlight was inside them. Which I guess it was, when you think about it.

I looked up from the peppers into the woman's face, and I saw in her eyes that she wanted nothing but to wish me luck on my journey, and it was—I mean, the jimson was fully out of my system at that point, but still I felt a little dizzy, just from the sheer reality of it all. Face-to-Face was some kind of bombed-out summer camp at this point, but this group had managed to stake out a whole little world for themselves in there. I was speechless and sort of completely disoriented, so I just waved to them, took a bow, and headed off down the road, second-guessing my decision the whole way to Bellingham.

FRANCINE CHANG

MONTE RIO, CA
2038

I left Flora and Spencer and the baby to their domestic bliss and returned to Oakland. I thought about writing a book about my time at Oaks and Face-to-Face, but all I could muster were placeholder notes: *waltz lesson, redwoods, Flora's wedding. Bonfires. Asian plumper. Despair.* I became a shut-in, a cultivator of nostalgia. I took long food-induced naps and woke up gasping like I'd been buried alive. I had a pen-pal lover on death row. I played a game where I chatted with technical support about a minor appliance and tried to keep the technician online as long as possible.

After the implant, former students would call to thank me for everything, tell me how excited they were about their new jobs, spouses, their prospects in general. They were happy. And I was happy they were happy. After a while, though, I stopped answering. I *knew* these kids, or thought I did, and their new voices just didn't feel right. "It's James," one call began, and I thought, No, it's not. As silents, they surprised me all the time. But these phone calls were like form letters. If the caller had been at Face-to-Face, I knew to wait for a pause and then something like, *burned down . . . good memories . . . rabid animals . . . empty . . .*

I hadn't been back. Every time I rushed up there to escape whatever personal catastrophe in Oakland, I came back feeling doubly jilted. I had enough at home to make me miserable. I passed the evenings rereading my pen pal Victor Torrance's detailed description of the three-hour-long sexual acrobatics he'd planned for us: he'd be wearing nothing but ankle weights, I'd be strapped into something he called an erotic bungee—he sent me detailed sketches of it—and we'd break every so often for blackberry daiquiris and hot pecan pie.

Every couple months I'd go visit Patti in Hayward. She'd been chained to that door for . . . God, it had been almost two years now, and she looked as awful as you'd expect. She'd start chattering when she saw me, like we'd been in a conversation all this time: "Man comes to dump me food and I don't think some's even *food*." Her breath smelled prehistoric. She was badly sunburned, wearing a frayed full-body leotard. Said she didn't intend to leave, ever. She sucked the end of a dirty lollipop stick and tried to stretch her leg far enough to retrieve a gravel-pebble-looking thing on the sidewalk. Her arms were stretched awkwardly over her head, chained to the handles. I wanted to leave it all behind.

But one afternoon Theo called me, and after five minutes of awkward, halting conversation, he told me the boy, who he called Slash, was turning five—and would I like to carpool up to Monte Rio? I think he wanted to bring me as some kind of buffer—apparently he and Nancy had been bickering. I hesitated, tried to think of possible excuses, but none came. On our way up, Theo stopped at a toy store and I bought a wooden train set and Theo got a make-your-own-sock-puppet kit. He held the wrapped present in his lap as he drove and talked anxiously about Flora and Spencer and the boy.

What we found at Face-to-Face was both expected and somehow worse than expected. Overgrown, trashed, abandoned, scorched. Aggressively *over*. In the camp center, though, in a patch of sunlight, stood a single building, one of the smaller dorms, sided with materials from other buildings—I recognized the pecky cypress from Patti's old cabin, the green trim from the meditation center, and signs from the entrance, but the combination was strangely tidy. To the left was a big garden with zucchini and what looked like tomatoes coming in. To the right, a fenced-off plot with a few sheep and goats.

Flora, Spencer, the baby, and Spencer's mom were the last occupants. Flora was happy, breathlessly happy, to see me, and I felt ashamed for having stayed away. She rested her hand on my leg, just like she had in the old days, and looked from face to face while Theo talked to her. Nancy, who was sitting on the floor, greeted me and acknowledged Theo with a curt nod.

The baby was not a baby anymore—he was an actual boy, five years old, so big and curious. After he and Theo exchanged hugs, he stood with his elbows propped on his grandfather's bent knees and just watched. He was a dead ringer for Flora, and this started a nostalgia binge that clawed at me. Thinking about Oaks, the retreat, all my old students and their new lives. And Flora's family, staying here, staying true to . . . something. Patti's original vision, maybe. Making a blissful quiet home amidst the ruined camp.

The kitchen was filled with his homemade toys. Things made of wood and leaves and scraps salvaged from the camp.

There was a flat string-and-wood table that looked like a loom, or an abacus, with painted acorn beads on the strings. Another table with wooden shapes and drawing paper. Hanging from the ceiling were mobiles made with shale and avocado pits.

We all sat down, and he brought us things: two giant pinecones, a tiny pumpkin, a section of snake skeleton. He handed me or Theo an object, we passed it to each other, and he waited for our response, which, you know, I said, "Wow," and "That's a big pinecone," and so on. He must've handed us thirty different things. Watched us closely every time. I remembered the intensity from when Flora first started at Oaks, but never this forceful. Theo didn't say anything—he just looked at the objects, then at the boy, whose face was so composed it felt like at any minute he'd start speaking to us, which is just backwards, of course. It was like his expression was creating space for me to fill. Theo was happy, so nakedly happy. He patiently studied each pinecone and leaf and rock, seeming to find them all just as wondrous as the boy did.

When all the treasures were through, Theo raised a finger dramatically and then handed the boy his present. Slash stared at the package for a long time before unwrapping it, then tore it free and opened the box. Right away he reached in and slipped one of the socks over his foot. Theo uncapped a marker and drew big eyes and a curlicue mustache on one of the others and then pulled it over his hand. "Well, how do, Slash," he said, moving the puppet's mouth. "How's it feel to be as old as you've ever been and as young as you'll ever be?"

The boy watched the puppet, mesmerized. Theo took off the sock and slid it across the table. Suddenly Nancy scooped it up, holding it in a shaking fist. "I'm sorry, this has to stop," she said, in a choked voice.

Theo froze. "What?"

"Don't be coy," she said. She slipped the puppet over her hand and made its mouth open and close, then pulled it off in a crumpled ball and let it fall to the floor. "All you do is come up here and plant little poison seeds."

"What the hell are you talking about?"

"You don't see what this toy is teaching him?"

Theo leaped to his feet. "This isn't a talker toy or a silent toy!" he said. "It's just a *toy*."

"It's not just a toy," she said. "It's a message. One we don't want to hear."

"We?" Theo spluttered. "We? You and who else? Who's we?"

Nancy said, "No one here needs your fixing. They're not broken. Don't do to him what you already did to *her*." She gestured to the doorway, where Flora now stood, eyes wide and pooling.

Theo opened and closed his mouth, looking as if he might cry, then slowly nodded. He stood, went into the kitchen, past Flora and the boy, and returned with a paring knife. Which he used to carefully cut the eyes and mouth out of each sock in the kit, dropping the limp tubes to the floor. The boy watched him do it, grave. When Theo was done he panted for a moment, leaned over and hugged the boy, kissed him on the forehead, and then went outside. I heard his car start and then roll out down the pebbled trail.

I sat in that kitchen, sympathetic and vaguely horrified and mostly dazed, until the sky was dark, and eventually the boy led me upstairs to the guest room. The next morning I planned to catch the bus back south, but instead the two of us hiked up an old fire road, and I stayed another night. When I was hungry he brought me something from the kitchen. When I'd stare at him and then at Flora and remember the time I taught her to waltz in the class, he would crawl up into my lap and sit with me. He even fell asleep there once. I'd see him out in the yard with the goats, the sheep, his father, his grandmother. I stayed for a week, two weeks, and then I decided to stay a little longer. Each morning I'd come downstairs expecting someone to have cleared the faceless socks off the floor. No one ever did.

JOHN PARKER CONWAY

MONTE RIO, CA
2038

Look, I never claimed to be the silent savior. One of my opponents called me that because I welcomed them, tried to create a generally hospitable atmosphere, stimulate the local economy. I'd do the exact same for any large block of constituents. Loggers, truckers, Satanists, jugglers. All right, maybe not jugglers. That's not to say I didn't like the silents or respect what they were trying to create here. I thought their whole commune deal was beautiful. It failed, like most knew it would, but what commune hasn't? It collapsed about as nobly as it could've—no arrests, no mass suicide, just overgrown gardens and scorched teepees.

But this implant campaign was a new kind of mess. That morning, this little girl had fallen off one of those saddle scooters and shows up in the ER with a compound fracture. The nurses ask how she's doing, if this hurts or that hurts, and she isn't saying. They see the mom is face-talking with her, father's doing the same. Turns out the girl, age three, hasn't been implanted. Which is a problem, legally speaking.

In January, HHS sent notices to all hospitals and schools telling them the deal: mandatory implantation for all children under age seven. But some parents are dragging their feet. They must think . . . I don't know what they think. I can't understand why they'd delay. I've tried to see it from every angle, but I keep coming back to the idea of a kid being born blindfolded, with a little snap in the back where you can take it off. That'd be the first thing you'd do, right? Before you even cleaned him off? Hell, talking's *fun*. Same with listening. Why deny yourself that, missing out on all that music happening around you?

Even so, I'm not happy about how we're doing it. We're at the hospital, an institution based on dignity and compassion, and now you've got these nervous young parents, their crying toddler, three doctors, more nurses—a tense scenario regardless, but then the mayor's also there, me, a beloved civic figure, and also Dr. Ng, from the state public-health department, whose morgue-worker look wasn't really helping my easygoing atmospherics. At first the parents looked surprised to see me, but once the nurses wheeled their girl into the OR, that got their full attention. She was already anesthetized, all soft in the face, placid. Every once in a while a nurse or assistant looked up at us, standing like enforcers behind the parents at the observation window. Dr. Ng had his hands behind his back and was making sucking noises with his teeth.

The first part of the procedure was no big deal. The doctors worked on the kid's arm, fitting the bones back together. The parents leaned right up against the window. The father was small and stringy—I was sizing him up because I had no idea what he'd do when the doctors finished the arm and started the second part, which we hadn't exactly told him about. I mean, how could we? Mostly I was hoping he wouldn't even notice till it was over. The mother was just a girl still, a little turtleish and cave-mucked from being out in the woods so long. Her eyes, though, when she turned to look at me and Ng, were tropically clear.

I whispered to Ng, "Can't we just wait out in the hall and give them some privacy in here?"

He turned and regarded me with unconcealed impatience. His whole solemn bullshit undertaker act made me tired. "You can," he said.

So I left and went to the bathroom. I studied myself in the mirror, and I thought what I always thought: You are a fat motherfucker. I could've stayed there and killed time until the surgery was finished. Let Ng do the dirty work, whatever that involved. I made a conciliatory face, practiced how I'd look at the parents once everything blew over. Like, sorry about having to strong-arm you like this—it wasn't me, Ng's the bad guy. I did my reluctant smile, well honed from end-less council meetings. Staying in the bathroom would've mostly kept me above the fray. Whatever happened, I could act like I didn't know about it.

But, of course, my sworn duty is to uphold the law, whether I agree with the law or not. I took an oath to ensure domestic tranquillity and promote the general welfare and all that. To make sure that girl left the hospital as healthy as those doc-tors could make her. And after plucking a few nose hairs in the bathroom mirror, that's exactly what I was going to do. All of a sudden I felt a rush of adrenaline. Readiness for whatever was going to come next.

The doctors had moved faster than I'd thought, or else I'd moved slower, because when I got back to the observation room I could already feel the change. Mom and Dad were looking at each other inflamed and crazy, then looking back through the window. The dad rapped on the glass. The mother started to hyperventilate. Over her shoulder, I could see two doctors in blue scrubs and a nurse were working behind the girl's ear. Dr. Ng was calmly scribbling notes on a clipboard, real helpful.

I turned to the parents and said, "The doctors are here to heal your daughter." It sounded pretty good. Then I looked at them, they looked at me, and their faces were just exploding or collapsing or burning or . . . I don't have the words. I tried to talk soothingly. Told them how safe and nice the implant is. How their girl will be given opportunities that neither of them had. How they might want to consider getting the implants themselves someday, so they could talk to her.

That's when the father bolted for the door of the OR. I was ready. I wrapped him up and hugged him tight, and when he tried to wriggle free I kept hugging. I shouted for Ng to drop the clipboard, but he was already on his way over to me. He took a trank pen and poked it into the father's neck, and then went over to the mother, who was just standing there wailing like nothing I ever heard, and did the same to her. I felt the father wilting in my arms, so I set him on the ground as gentle as I could.

The girl actually woke up before they did—she was standing at her dad's bedside by the time his eyes fluttered open. He stared blankly for a moment, then realized where he was, who she was. He reached up and kissed the girl, and then kept his face within inches of hers. They both looked at the mother, who hadn't yet come to.

The girl took a deep breath, coughed, and said, "You look dizzy, Father."

Her first words. The father jumped back a little, and the girl said, "I can make words. Vertigo. I can make words," and he sat up in bed and brought his hand to his mouth and stared at his daughter making words.

NANCY JERNIK

MONTE RIO, CA
2039

Isaw two men coming up the trail from the intersection
with the county road. The mayor and someone else—a serious man with a coarse bowl cut, carrying a leather valise
with brass snaps. Nobody took the county road to get to the
compound, even when there were actually other people living
there. When it wasn't just us. So it was an alien thing to see
the mayor heading up the path wiping his brow with a handkerchief, accompanied by the bag-eyed man. So this was how
Theo was going to play it, I thought as I watched them approach the house. He couldn't make us follow the law, so he
was going to bring the law to us.

I dashed upstairs to find Flora and the boy. They were in
the bedroom, sitting cross-legged on the floor playing with
Spencer's old marbles. I took Flora by the arm and showed
her anxiety and the need to act quickly. There was a rapping
on the screen door. Flora's eyes went wide with fear. I put my
hand to her cheek and showed her that I would handle the
visitors, and that she should hide the boy. I knew that she
was upset at the way I reacted to her father at the birthday

party, and I guess I understood, despite how deeply wrong he was about everything. But now there was no space for ambivalence—the men were on our porch. She gave me a look of confused acceptance and took the boy into her arms.

I straightened my dress and went down to the front entrance, where the mayor stood knocking on the metal frame of the screen door. The other man scanned the yard with his hand visored against his forehead. The impact of the mayor's knuckles against the screen cut through the stillness of the cabin. I composed myself and opened the door. I hadn't spoken to an outsider in years. Almost since the boy was born, I think. Very few conversations with anyone at all. I sometimes chatted with Francine when we were safely out of earshot of the boy. And there was the argument with Theo. But I was not well practiced. I suddenly regretted having let that faculty slip away from me. The one power I had to protect my family from the rest of the world.

I let the mayor in, and he thanked me, stuffing his handkerchief in a back pocket. He introduced the other man as Dr. Ng. They entered the cabin, and the mayor looked around but didn't say anything. It was as if he'd searched hard and failed to come up with a single nice thing to say about where we lived—a place that I saw, suddenly through his eyes, for the crumbling shack that it was. I felt a moment of humiliation, immediately followed by angry pride. I asked them to sit at the table by the cooking area. The cabin was dead quiet. I didn't know what Flora had done with the boy. I just hoped they had enough sense to keep still.

"Nobody much comes up here anymore," the mayor said, and I agreed. "I mean, I haven't even been up here for a while. How long's it been, Nancy?" It was so strange to hear my own name like that, released into the air. I wasn't sure I even knew who that person was. I told the mayor I didn't know how long it had been. "Well, I was here for your grandson's first birthday—how old is he now?" I told him the boy was five years old. "Five years," he said, shaking his head. "It really just passes in an instant, doesn't it?" He snapped his fingers and looked at Dr. Ng, who didn't respond—he was too busy staring directly at me. "Unbelievable," the mayor said, accentuating his disbelief by making a high whistling sound through clenched teeth. "Is the boy around? I would love to see him— you know, how he's grown?" I told him the boy wasn't there. "Oh really?" the mayor said, almost as if he knew—as if he was honestly surprised to catch me in a lie so easily. He cleared his throat and said, "When you say he's 'not here,' are you talking 'not in the house,' or are you saying he's gone-gone, like in another part of the state?" I told him I didn't know. I said I was pretty sure the boy was with his mother. Which was true. "Flora? You think he's with Flora?" I didn't respond.

The mayor looked at the doctor, and then looked back at me. "Well, I tell you," he said, rubbing his thumb against his lower lip, "I, for one, really wish the boy was here. And I'm sure that Dr. Ng wishes that, as well. Am I right, Doctor?" He looked at Ng, who made no expression of acknowledgment—it was as if he'd been trained to zero out his face, freeze all of his muscles into a smooth unreadable death mask. "You see," the mayor went on, "as you've probably guessed, Dr. Ng has come all the way up here to diagnose the boy. And, well, it's been quite a trek. Not one that either of us is inclined to repeat. So if you could produce the boy, we could get the diagnosis out of the way and everything would become just much easier after that." I told them again that I didn't know where the boy was. We were all quiet then. I was about to say something then, but the silence was broken by a sound from above.

The sound of a marble hitting the floor and then rolling slowly down along a seam in the floorboards, passing right over our heads. All three of us looked up and followed the sound as it traversed the ceiling, coming to rest with a click at the other end of the cabin.

"You're sure he's not here?" the mayor said. He bared his teeth in a smile that barely concealed a frustrated rage. "You're absolutely sure he's not, I don't know, somewhere in the house, maybe even right upstairs?" I said I was sure the boy was gone. "Mind if I have a look around up there?" he said, and I said I did actually mind, because it was our house and he had no right. "Okay," he said. "Why don't you go up there, then?" I turned and went up the crude stairs to the bedroom where I saw Flora backed into a corner, holding the boy with her hand over his mouth, both of them tight-faced and trembling.

I went back downstairs. "Just as I told you, there's no one here. It's just me. You're welcome to wait—" but he interrupted me. "I really don't want to have to come back here," he said. I told him he didn't have to. "But you know that I have to," he said. "You know that I have to uphold the law." "What law applies here?" I said. I know I should have remained more neutral, but I couldn't help it. Dr. Ng chose that moment to speak. "The law protects everyone equally, Ms. Jernik," he said, and in the moment he uttered the phrase he was forced to loosen control of his facial muscles, so that I saw a glimpse of a man stricken with a terrible decay.

"You're sure this is the way you want to do this?" the mayor asked, getting up from his chair. I said I wasn't aware I was doing anything. "Don't patronize me, okay?" he said. He seemed genuinely hurt. "You think this is easy for me? You think I want to come out here like this and tell you—" but he didn't finish the sentence. He walked to the door, and Dr. Ng followed him. At the threshold he turned around and said, "I won't have you bullying me into thinking this is wrong." His neck was pink with desperation and rage. "This is—I'm trying to help—I'm the good guy here." I said I thought that was true. I could see that, of the two of them, he truly was trying to be the better man. "You know we're going to be back," he said as they stepped off the porch. "I fear it will be less cordial," he added. I nodded and waved stiffly, theatrically, the way my mother used to wave to my father as he pulled out of the driveway on his morning commute. I stood at the threshold and watched them disappear beyond the trees until it was quiet again.

I heard someone on the stairs. It was Flora, holding a duffel bag half-filled with her things. The boy stood behind her, peering out the screen door with a look of startled curiosity. Flora did not look at me but went straight into the kitchen and started wrapping utensils in a faded terry-cloth dish towel. I followed her in and separated the food we could take with us from the food we'd have to leave behind. My hands shook. In the end the pile of things we could carry was small. What of the old life was worth the effort to carry around? The answer was always less than what I'd predicted.

THEODORE GREENE

RICHMOND, CA
2039

I felt bad about leaving Slash's party even as I was walking out the door. I knew that with every step I took I was making things worse—just compounding the damage I'd done by cutting up his toy in front of him, in front of everyone. Everyone I cared about in the world. I could already taste the regret—I could see myself in the future, looking back and wishing I'd had the strength to take Nancy's criticism in stride, to act even remotely like an adult. But I walked out anyway and drove back to my apartment, where I ate a carton of pasta pudding and blacked out watching an Indonesian knife fight. I thought the regret would fade after a few days, but it festered and swelled. I had a dream where I drove an implant into Slash's neck with the whole family standing around me. My back seized, and I was bedridden for days. I couldn't eat. Without them, I had nothing.

Eventually I tried to get back to work. I went to the flea market in Fruitvale to look for old meshes I could refurb, and that's where I saw the game, buried under a pile of old storage drives. I could only see the corner of the box, really, but there was the logo with the big red question mark on the side and the montage of cartoonish faces, and I knew instantly that it was Guess Who?, which I'd had as a kid and totally loved. I remember I'd figured out a way to play it against myself by memorizing the faces of all of the people. I created names and these elaborate stories for each one. I saw the game and instantly thought of Slash. I thought about how much he'd love it. He'd take all the cards out one by one and lay them on the floor of the porch in some intricate pattern. I suddenly had to give it to him. Right then. The game was the bridge back to them. The olive branch, I guess you could call it. I bought the game and drove straight north to the compound.

I got there at sundown and hopped out of the car with the box under my arm, and right away I could sense that something was wrong. All the lights were off in the main house. Nobody was on the front porch. There was no sign of anybody anywhere. I went up to the front door and it swung open before I even touched it. I stepped inside and saw that one of the windows in the front room was smashed. A shock ran through me, and I stood there with clenched fists, barely breathing, readying myself for whatever was coming next. But as my eyes adjusted I saw that there was dust on the glass shards. The window had been broken for some time, a few days at least. The air in the room was completely still, and I was alone.

I'd always been nervous about them living out in that remote location, completely vulnerable. I felt like something bad was certain to happen at some point. My mind raced with all the sick possibilities. I found myself praying there had been some sort of accident rather than the other outcomes I was imagining, like a hate crime committed by some antisilent yokel up in those woods. Or it could have been one of those implant cops that I'd read about—federal officers who roamed the countryside with a portable implant tool in search of undocumented, unimplanted kids. As much as I wanted Slash to talk, I didn't want it to happen that way. I couldn't bear to think of him being held down by some thick-armed thug in a police uniform as he fired the implant into the base of Slash's neck. Especially not after the dream where I'd been the one holding him down. I wouldn't wish that on anybody.

I started combing the house for clues, taking panoramic footage of every room I entered so I'd have a record of the exact placement of every object. Everything was more or less untouched, though. I went into the kitchen and opened the fridge to find that it was empty. Nothing, not a single stick of butter.

I heard a car approaching outside. I went toward the door assuming that it was the police. The engine went off, and in the silence I heard a man and a woman talking. The woman said, "If they're gone, whose car is that?" and the man mumbled something. I opened the door and the woman was standing on the porch in a fuchsia microfiber dress and gold heels, holding a microphone. Behind her, setting up a floodlight, was a large man in a Steadicam vest—a local news team. They seemed perturbed that I was there, like I was the one trespassing on their property. "We got a tip that the last people had finally left this place," the man said. "So who the hell are you?"

I told them I was a relation, and did they have any idea where the family had gone. The woman made a little sideways smirk and said, "Funny, we were just about to ask *you*." The partner stepped forward and put his hand up to silence the woman. "For real, do you know where they might be? You'd know better than anyone, right?"

The impact of the news worked on me slowly, almost imperceptibly. I felt it like insects crawling all over my body. They crawled and my eyes blurred and the woman pointed the microphone toward me. "I'm going to take that as a no," she said, "but do you have *anything* to say about the disappearance of your family?" Even though her face was tight and serious, everything she said sounded like a joke. The man moved in with the camera. I could barely make out their faces behind the bright light. I shouldn't have said anything. I should've gotten in my car and driven off. But I didn't. I stood there, consumed with rage and humiliation, paralyzed. Every neuron in my body was on fire. "Them leaving like that?" I said, choking a little on the words. "They think this solves anything? They think they're not going to get caught? They think they can win?" I don't remember all of it.

I drove home in the darkness, stunned. You know when people say they're beside themselves? I actually felt that then. I felt almost like I was a ghost, hovering in the passenger seat next to my physical form. Did they really think I was going to force the implant on Slash? I just wanted to have a conversation about it. That was all. But now they were gone, and I was the thing they were running away from.

I got back to the apartment and found the news segment on one of the local streams. It was a thirty-second clip that contained almost no useful information—just a few seconds of Flora as a child from that *Frontline* episode, and then they cut to the footage they'd taken of me on the porch, shaking my head and weeping in the floodlight. I sat on the couch in the darkness with the Guess Who? game in my lap. I could barely make out where the box ended and where I began.

AUGUST BURNHAM

RAHWAY, NJ
2039

O n the way to the press conference Calvin admitted he was worried about the silent protest that we'd heard was being staged outside the hotel. Police were predicting four to five hundred demonstrators, and they'd staffed up in anticipation. I assured Calvin that there was absolutely no danger, but he spent the rest of the trip just staring out through the rippled glass of the horse-drawn carriage we were using to get around town, scanning the sidewalks for placard-carrying activists with Molotov cocktails tucked in their jeans.

We were ushered onto the forecourt of the hotel by a dozen or so black-clad officers in full riot gear. At the end of the gauntlet of officers a hotel employee approached us and asked for ID. "Ready for action, eh?" I said, nodding my head in the direction of the officers as I pressed my palm to the ID pad. "I wouldn't necessarily call it action," the man said, and when he stepped away from the buggy, I saw across the street in the park a dozen or so individuals in street rags trying and failing to hoist aloft a massive puppet. We watched them for a good minute or so as they struggled with the unwieldy effigy—

they seemed a person or two short, because the puppet's head lolled and slumped and one arm dragged in the grass. A policeman stood about ten yards from the troupe of radicals, casually reading something on his wristwatch. "There's your army of the night," I said to Calvin. "But Dr. Burnham," he said, "isn't that puppet supposed to be you?" I took a closer look and saw that it did bear some resemblance—they'd used cotton batting to replicate the corona of white hair that still clings to my head, and my spectacles were spot-on, but the facial features seemed to belong to another man. Had there been an additional protester to support the head, the overall effect might have been more convincing. But instead it just looked sad. I couldn't even laugh.

Have I heard the reports of silents refusing the Soul Amp for their children, or fleeing into the wilderness like the Greene girl? Of course—in my position, I'm exposed to all these rumors. But rumors is all they are. Don't get me wrong—I think it's barbaric for *any* parent to deny a child the proper medical treatment. But I don't think the implant resistance movement—if you can even call it a movement—will have any lasting impact, no more so than that cult in Seattle that administered lobotomies to all its members. We've seen time and again that unaugmented silent people just can't manage ordered, unsupervised community living. That's an unassailable fact. If you could point to even a single example of a group of silent people that thrived on their own, with no intervention from talkers, for more than a few months, I'd be willing to listen to you. But I've witnessed so much misery over the years, all stemming from the absence of language. So to deny the gift of speech to a child, to make that kind of choice for them, force them into a life of silence—I can't even imagine how you would justify it. I just can't even begin.

With the advent of prenatal testing for the viral markers of phasic resistance, parents are better prepared than ever to make informed choices about whether they can take on the responsibility of a silent child, and the implant all but assures them that they can. So who in their right mind would choose to cloak their child in a world of silence? I'm sure Calvin feels the same.

Fortunately, this so-called controversy seems to be on its last legs, as evidenced by the anemic protest. And the subsequent press conference itself went extremely well. We were unveiling the updated technology we'd been working on for the better part of a year, putting in ten- and twelve-hour days managing a team of seventy engineers and designers in three separate time zones. The name PhonCom started as a sort of inside joke—like something from a corny science-fiction film—but it was easy to say and even easier to remember, so we kept it. The centralized database that made up PhonCom allowed us to finally transfer the processing burden from the implant itself to our server farm, where we can more quickly process raw stimuli and produce infinitely more accurate and meaningful phrases. This service allowed us to significantly reduce the implant's size, especially the circumference of the external port. The impact of this development was huge—from that point on, all future implantees would be nearly indistinguishable from their naturally speaking cohort.

But bringing PhonCom online took a tremendous toll on Calvin and me. We were physically exhausted and mentally drained, and perilously close to our own individual breakdowns. Recognizing this, and wanting to do something special for Calvin, who'd selflessly donated so much time and effort to the cause, I got us tickets to the International Sacajawea Fellowship's annual conference outside Sioux Falls, which was accessible only via canoe or longboat. Calvin had never heard of Sacajawea, nor had he been in a canoe, so I thought, What better way to unwind than to follow Lewis and Clark's historic path to the Pacific Northwest and meet up with like-minded devotees of the world's most famous translators for some great conversation and debate? Calvin said he'd sleep on it, so the next morning I pulled up to his apartment complex in the carriage with an authentic resin model of a longboat strapped to the top. I tugged on Pinker's bridle to make her bray a little, and Calvin came to the window. A few minutes later we were on our way.

Calvin seemed uneasy on the water. He'd never learned to swim, and he didn't trust that the Instaflate lining of his period-accurate cloak would save him from drowning if the longboat capsized. He held fast to the rail and took shallow, rapid breaths.

"Let's play idioms," I said. Calvin was, at that point, the only silent in the world capable of parsing idioms with above-proficient accuracy, and we were both pretty proud of that. He nodded, still sitting rigid in the boat with his knuckles white against the rail.

"I'll start. If you can't see, you might be blind as a what?"

"Bat," he said. He cracked a tentative smile. It seemed to relax him.

"Okay, good. Now it's your turn," I said. He thought for a long time.

"Is this accurate, if I ask you to stop doing something fast, I might suggest you go cold . . ."

"Turkey. Good! Good job. Now, let's say I'm really good at playing cards. What am I?"

"An excellent card player?" he said. I reminded him that we were playing idioms. He paused, and I could practically see the activity meters flaring up at PhonCom. "Oh," he said. "You're a card shark?"

"Correct!" He was good. The best in the world at that moment. I had the world's greatest scientific advance as my passenger, and we were slowly drifting down the Missouri River in the crisp late-summer morning, and the cloud patterns were incredible.

As we approached Sioux Falls, though, things turned ugly. Unbeknownst to us amid our river idyll, a group of Lakota militiamen had set off a bomb outside the entrance to the Sacajawea Memorial Museum and Gift Shop in an attempt to shut the conference down. As we came around the bend in the river we saw the black plume of smoke rising through the trees, accompanied by shouts and gunshots. Militiamen were herding attendees out to the river's edge, and when they saw us coming they pointed and called out. Calvin held on to my shoulder with an icy hand and said, "What is the idiom for the kind of creek you are up when you don't have a paddle?" which was interesting to me, because I don't believe we had spent much time at all working on sarcasm or mockery.

DAVID DIETRICH

RICHFIELD SPRINGS, NY
2039

After Coney Island, I knew my destiny. I knew I couldn't just go back to Decatur and continue with a life of irrelevance. I found a group of silents living under a tarp on the edge of an algae farm in Jersey City. They were subsisting on sugar packets and vitamin patches and algae runoff. Under the tarp it stank like medieval abortions. I brought them four cases of amino-acid powder I'd stolen from a superstore loading dock. That's how I incorporated myself. First the powder, then I showed them my van, a twelve-seater, which I'd recently bought and reupholstered. I made it known that I'd take them wherever they wanted to go.

They almost never acknowledged me, but they let me drive them around, and for a while that was enough. Mostly food runs, places that trashed bread and pastries after hours—they led me there by pointing and punching me on the arm when I should turn. I drove them to random buildings and shelled-out stores, and they came back disappointed or visibly angry. After I dropped them back at the algae farm, I'd drive around some more.

Then I was pulled over for a busted taillight, and I'd never bothered to get a driver's license, plus I had some stolen camping equipment in the van. They sentenced me to six months of house arrest, which in my case was the van. Ambient motion sensors, Breathalyzer chip, the whole thing. I read, mostly. Biology, neuroscience, virology. Animal husbandry. I watched irrelevant people through the windshield. I figured some things out.

Once the six months were done, I went back to the algae farm, but they were gone. I sold the van, liquidated my savings, and two months later I owned a plot of land and thirty feral wallabies—a package deal. First day the herd jumped me, kicking and snorting and herding me into submission. Happened again the second and third day. The fourth day I got in a few punches of my own, and a few more on the fifth, and by the end of the month I was the toughest thing in the pen.

Most of them grudgingly accepted me as their leader. The ones that didn't, I killed and hung in the slaughterhouse. Butchered the meat, boiled the bones, and brought the brains back to an old shed I was using as my lab. I poked and prodded the wallaby brains. Zapped them with jolts to see what changed. Found a database of silent brain scans, stared at them till the cauliflower turned to scrambled eggs and then the eggs turned into worms. The virus was hiding in there, somewhere. Plenty of people had tried to kill it, searching for some misguided cure, but I was trying to *catch* it. I was done trying to be near the silents—I was ready to *be* silent. Theoretically, the right zap, targeted with precision at the language centers where the virus had to be living, could cause a mutation, activate the life cycle, set it contagious and free. But the logistics seemed difficult. Wallabies were simpler.

I never stopped moving. I knew if I slowed down, the wallabies would kill and eat me. I learned mixed martial arts, started running eight miles a day, always carried my buck knife. I mastered my perimeter.

The ranch was miles from a paved road, but ever since I put the FARM-RAISED WALLABY LOW FAT HIGH PROTEIN signs out on Highway 25 I had lots of knockers, mostly moms and their potpie kids who wanted to pet my "kangaroos."

"They're wallabies," I'd say. "And the only way you'll see one is to buy twenty pounds of meat, minimum." I'd pull some wallaby shanks from the deep freeze, mom and kid would blubber off. No matter how bad beef shortages got, no one was ready for wallaby. Never mind that it tasted like lamb. Wallabies were too cute to eat, they said. Pretty soon almost no one stopped by, which was fine. Then nobody did. Which was even better.

Well, not nobody—if a silent knocked, I'd let them in. As long as they respected my perimeter, my rules. If they didn't, if they were one of those implanted cows, I had my shambler—an electromagnetic pulser that temporarily scattered implant signals or just shorted them out altogether. I loved to see an implant waltz in all cream-eyed and ready to carp on like a ventriloquist dummy, and then he'd open his mouth and it'd come out all shambled—gasping and burping like, "Furason ermhorst, eebly eebly feebly."

Still, it was a little sad to look at my monitors and see Rosewater, one of the guys from the algae farm crew, trying to buzz his way in, now wearing a suit and tie and an awkward smile. I zoomed in and could see the small implant port, which was depressing but not entirely surprising, not anymore. I walked outside, feeling a bad mix of cheer and pity.

"I guess come in," I told him. "But don't try to talk. Won't do any good."

What a sad nutsack Rosewater had turned into. He carried a brown leather briefcase and had this perfectly manicured imperial beard. Pleated slacks, fake muscles. He probably sold tornado insurance or managed apartment buildings. In the old days, he'd been a king, hard-core, pure. Knew who he was, lived how he wanted. Guided by instinct. Uncorrupted. Like me on my farm.

Which I showed him around—fields, feed room, slaughterhouse, which was just a ringed area with a drain in the floor. I killed all my wallabies personally, and always in hand-to-hand combat. I didn't tell Rosewater any of this, of course— I just walked around the compound, gave him a few looks, and then paused in front of the meat locker. Rosewater paused along with me, looked at me in this unhesitant vomity way, and then spoke: "So, long-away friend, you actually *eat* these things?"

Motherfuck. I ran inside to turn on the shambler, but it was already on. I rebooted it. While I waited the ninety-eight seconds it took for full coverage, I oiled my sharpening stone and ran my buck knife across it. I had no plans to use it— I was just trying to shrink that loose-orbit feeling.

I returned and asked him to repeat himself. It'd be an extra pleasure to see his smug new face crumble when the shambled gibberish came out.

"My fiancée and I," Rosewater said, "we're pretty much pescatarians. We tried to do a macro diet for a few weeks, but it was torture."

His voice came out clear and unpinched. I pulled down a flank of meat from its hook and began randomly poking it with my knife until I felt able to speak. I said, "What in the shit-touching fuck is a macro diet?"

He started explaining, but I interrupted him. "Vacate," I said.

"Vacate?"

"I don't know what you've done to my shambler, but you have forty seconds to exit my perimeter before I do us both a favor and render your voice moot."

"Shambler? Old friend, you must not get out much! Shambler technology? Still? Seriously! There's nothing here to shamble." He explained the new improved centralized whatever—all I could hear was roaring in my ears and the sound of my knife sucking in and out of the wallaby flank.

Eventually I speared it on the end of the knife, lifted, and dumped the bloody mass on the counter in front of this polluted fop. "You disgrace," I said. "You and all your friends. Forfeiting without resistance. Letting the government geld you just so you can join the herd and get a job in middle management."

"Middle management? Friend, you're out here butchering overgrown hamsters. Alone, losing your mind. I was only trying to be friendly, maybe talk about the old days." As I sliced and sliced the countertop meat, he told me about what he called the silent underground. The last of the nonimplanted, the resisters, on the move in the Midwest somewhere. Maybe a dozen, maybe over a hundred. Most likely armed, lying in wait for the right moment to release their statement to the world. By the end of his speech, the counter was just a thick red smear.

"Me, I can't fool around like we used to, what with my new responsibilities," Rosewater said. "But I thought an outfit like that could probably use a guy like you."

I don't know if he was teasing me or what. This was the

trouble letting someone talk. Flattery and insult and yearning came out distorted a hundred different ways. I remember
that book of dying words I looked at once, what people say
when it matters. It was the same fake uplifting trash. *Let us
cross the river and rest under the shade of the trees* and shit. Don't
tell me to cross the river with you. Don't invite me to your sad
little puppet show.

I'd been out here for over four years, I'd mastered my terrain, and now I saw it all amounted to nothing. No perimeter
would ever be secure enough. No wall would ever be high
enough to keep out the chatter and lies. I had been selfish,
trying to heal myself just when the true silents needed me
most. I felt summoned. I turned and walked out to the corral,
leaving Rosewater alone at the meat-smeared counter. Two
dozen wallabies lazed in the sun, farting and snoring.

I didn't sleep that night. At dawn I went out into the
slaughterhouse ring, naked except for a thick smear of wallaby butter all over my body. I let out a blood-boiled war cry,
and it was echoed first by the slaughterhouse walls and then
by twenty-seven marsupial throats. They came charging into
the ring. I proceeded to grapple with every single wallaby on
my farm, even the dwarf ones, the females, even the peaceful
albinos. I left them with their necks broken, entrails flapping
loose. It was a fair fight, and they landed some good blows.
But soon there was only one remaining alive.

He was a male in rut, I could smell it. Our battle stretched
for hours. I gouged one of his eyes, and he bit my left nipple
clean off. He retreated and I advanced. He advanced and I
retreated. As the sun began to rise high and hot I lured him
close and flipped him into a sleeper hold. I choked him down,
and then passed out myself. The two of us awoke at the same
time, hours later, nestled together amid the cooling corpses

of his brethren. I nodded to him, and I believe he nodded back. I walked back into the house, gathered my money and weapons and lab notes, and loaded up my truck. The wallaby was waiting by the cab, snorting quietly. I opened the door and he jumped into the passenger seat.

We set out for the Midwest.

PATTI KERN

HAYWARD, CA
2039

Weeks passed. Seasons. Years, maybe. I remember lying in a freezing downpour knowing I'd die if I closed my eyes, which I did, which I always did once the arc lights of the lab parking lot winked out until morning, and their afterimage still pulsed on my eyelids and I prayed for that false light to turn into a tunnel, a sun door, star map, utter night. I wanted out. I wanted to dry up and flake into sediment and blow away. Sometimes I saw nature's real intent in far-off screams and bloated seagulls who perched on the eaves closest to me until I fell asleep and glided down to peck at my feet and legs. Testing my readiness. I awoke to the heat of my own breathing, covered in a reeking blue tarp. Rain continued to fall. Somewhere a car alarm cycled through amplified squeals and shrieks like an assortment of murders. Spring came. The grass beneath the air-conditioner window unit near me grew faster than the other grass.

A man with a wheelbarrow came and told me to close my eyes and he doused me in dish soap and sprayed me off with a hose. He was very old and he grunted when he carried the hose away. He came back and laid a towel just past the reach of my feet, and I struggled and struggled for it until I gave up. Then he came back and moved it a little closer, and I struggled again.

My arms were dead from the shoulder down, or shoulder up, since my hands were chained above my head. Early days I had flexed my legs and did Kegel exercises and toe rolls, but I stopped after long. Best I shrivel into kipper. Whenever I'd had a few nights without eating, I'd start to see what I needed to. I talked and talked to myself until I blacked out. I knew I'd been hoaxed into language too young and the only way to recover was to suffer. Suffer and persist until I was beyond pain and relief and thought and hope, and then see what was left.

I shouted at the ones going into Nu Ware and the ones leaving. It was mostly young children guided by parents. They looked so elastic and bright on the way in, and when they left they looked beige. The power gone from their eyes. Their real sentiments jigsawed into letters and words. It was tract housing, a war reenactment. "Come meet me," I yelled. The parents saw. They heard. Everyone knew my name. "I need just a minute with your happy little reborn camper there."

When they walked off, I yelled, "Mutality!" Or "Slapshod!" Or whatever came out. Sometimes I didn't yell anything.

I closed my eyes, ground my teeth, and willed the sequence to reverse itself. Parents backing drubbed chit-chattering children into the clinic for doctors to silence. Return them to their natural state of expression. Eyes closed, I could see the children back-stepping out of the clinic, cleansed, whole again.

This girl came up on me while I was sleeping. She nudged my shoulder with her hand. "Are you alive?" she asked. Even-toned, scoured of joy. I always dreamed of unattaching the implant with my teeth if one of them was close enough, but I couldn't even figure out where the wires went in, because there were no wires. All I could see was a nickel-size disc below her ear.

"Sit next to me," I said. Her father was in the parking lot unlocking their car, getting it ready to pull around. "Let me see what they did to you in there."

She stayed where she was. I saw she was holding a little bear doll that had a matching implant disc. "One of your teats is showing," the girl said. "And your eyes are all red and viscid."

"Viscid? My teats? Not even an hour with that thing and you're already . . . this isn't a teat." I peeked down at it, tapered, sun-withered. Actually, it looked every bit like a teat. Like something drooping off a hog. I stared at the girl again, tried to locate a spark and fan her flames as I'd done so many times. But she was already iced over, unreachable. Nothing, not me, not a million mes, was going to breach that new docile permanent frost.

"Go away," I said. "You're blocking my sun."

Summer ended. Three boys tried to set me on fire, but I wouldn't burn. A woman in a silver-thread suit kneeled next to me and made me sign my name to some papers. "My name doesn't mean shit," I told her. "I don't care if you use it to give people rabies." She wiped the pen off when I was done. The wheelbarrow man poured cold chai and water all over me and I sucked it out of my body sock. He brought me no-rinse shampoo and a thick hotel-room robe that stank of smeared pussy. He set a spackle bucket next to me and I filled it with my voidings.

I'd ask who he was, and he'd clear his throat and spit and tell me I was too near death for such idiot questions.

I lost hope. Then I'd think I had no more hope to lose,

and then I'd lose some more. Subsistence, existence, whatever you want to call it—it's a birthday candle. Someone lights it, you blow it out. You fight to rid yourself of wanting, but when they say make a wish and blow, you wish for a pair of leather riding boots though you don't own a horse, have never ridden a horse, you don't even *like* horses. What do you like? You like when Mom passes out early and you walk through the house with her makeup mirror pointed toward the ceiling and you stare into it and step over ceiling fans and lights. You like the clicks your dog makes dreaming. And when you see taxicabs or buses approaching from opposite directions and each driver holds up a hand as he passes. Life.

"You hear about them?" the man with the wheelbarrow was saying. I think he was smiling, but his face seemed to be encrusted in a hard shell of makeup.

"Yes," I said. Everything was a gasp by then. I was curled up tight to myself, shivering. I'd already died thirty-seven times. Metamorphosed into a crab, river rock, snake, flag, sunlight. My mouth was filled with thick saltine paste. "No," I said.

He talked about the government mandate, the forced implantings. "You're not alone," the man said. I noticed the black disc beneath his ear. "Right now three hundred of them have mobilized outside of Idaho. Led by that couple and their baby. In either Idaho or Ohio. Almost five hundred of them."

They don't need me, I told him. They have Spencer, Flora. They have vision. They don't need me. They have numbers.

I had chewed a hole in my lip. On the sidewalk all around me were puddles of secretion and filth in various stages of decay. He continued to talk, and his words maggoted themselves into mc. His story went on long after he'd gone. Long after the sun died again. And then he came by and drizzled

Slush onto the pavement around me. I'm done, I told him. I'm getting up. About time, he said. None of this was out loud.

I'd require bolt cutters and probably some long-term medical attention. But I needed to find that boy before anything else. The story wasn't over yet. The time for stoicism had run its course. Righteous action was now needed, and I was finally prepared to be the actress, the protector, the defender of the last hope for a new era.

I breathed in deep and decided to yank my hands out of the chains, but when I pulled I saw that my hands were right in front of me. I couldn't feel them but there they were. Plus, when I looked behind me there were no chains on the door. Just a bunch of pizza-slice-shaped coupons. Goddamn. I tried to shrug the robe tighter around my shoulders. It took me almost a day to stand up on my own.

I was filled to bursting with nothing. I walked.

NANCY JERNIK

ROCK ISLAND, IL
2040

We left Monte Rio as soon as we could. As soon as everyone was assembled. We knew the mayor would be back, or someone worse than the mayor. Someone without even the shred of compassion the mayor still had. We didn't have a clear idea where we were headed—just east. Just away from the coast. We started out in an old school bus someone had left behind, but the timing belt snapped outside Denver, so we left it by the side of the road and continued on foot, with Francine and I taking turns hauling our possessions in a wagon while Spencer and Flora carried backpacks filled with canned vegetables and cooking gear. I'd urged Francine to go her own way. I made it clear to her that we had no plan, that we were going to wander until we stopped, but she just shrugged and kept walking.

For the first few days the boy seemed excited by the notion of the trip. He would bound ahead of the group and then dart back, zigzagging in our midst, pretending to be a starship hurtling through an asteroid belt. Or he'd hop in the wagon against his father's protests and assume a primitive surfing stance, swaying dramatically to keep his balance. By the end of that first week of traveling, though, he mostly just slumped backwards in the wagon, staring out at the hills toward the world we'd left behind. The rest of us, too, even though we kept moving forward, heading directly into the morning sun—we had only the past on our minds. It didn't make sense to me that Theo would have sent Ng and the mayor right to us, and I didn't want to believe it, for Spencer's sake. But I couldn't put the possibility of it out of my mind. We'd narrowly escaped, but I wasn't sure we'd be so lucky a second time. Not that I knew where we were headed instead. A lifetime of hiding? I didn't know what the others were thinking, and I didn't say anything myself. We were all on edge, ravenous and scared, walking single file along the shoulder of the weed-flanked county roads that led us through Colorado into Kansas, a vacant, white-hot Möbius strip.

We were convinced we were being followed. We held our breath every time a weather drone went by overhead, fearing it would be followed by a squad of men in black padded suits who would surround us and bind our hands with zip ties. But no one appeared, except for when a gang of local boys tore past in a gold truck and hurled tumblers of Slush at us. I didn't blame them. It was just what they did in that part of the world. And the taste of it reminded me of driving Spencer out west to Monte Rio—how we were always so madly craving Slush, and everything was new and ahead of us still, nothing broken or burned. Nothing to run from.

Somewhere into Iowa we ran out of food. We started edging closer to larger towns and cities so that Spencer and I could forage in Dumpsters like we did back in our warehouse days, but the trash of these Midwestern people was more organized, more closely monitored. We'd vault the wall of a cavernous bin and find industrial garbage bags full of fresh bread, only to discover the bin rigged with motion sensors. One night we were climbing into a pair of big brown units, eight yards each, when I heard a pinging sound right next to me. A steak knife had just struck the wall of the Dumpster right near my calf. Spencer groaned and I turned to see a second knife stuck in his back near the shoulder. There was a man in a baseball hat standing in the cone of light cast by the parking lamp, rearing back to whip a third knife at us. I tugged at Spencer's sleeve and we ran into the woods, stumbling through the darkness until we were sure the man wasn't following us. I pulled the knife out of Spencer's back and tried to clean the wound with water from a creek. In our panic we'd drifted far from the camp we'd made, and it took us until dawn to find Flora, the boy, and Francine, who were out of their minds with worry.

When morning came I saw that the wound was beginning to become infected, red and firm in a widening splotch. We had to find a place with running water, a place where I could properly care for my son. Flora and I went into the town to look for help. It was called Rock Island, even though there was no rock or island that we could see—just a loose collection of fading storefronts and strip malls, indistinguishable from the dozens of other towns we'd passed through. I'm sure we drew attention to ourselves in our black rags and mud-caked boots, but I was beyond caring at that point.

We approached a motel called the Deluxe Inn Waterfront. Outside, a man was smoking a cigarette, and as we passed he waved and called out to Flora. I froze, taking Flora by the elbow. He came up close and squinted, said he knew her face, and was she famous or something? He seemed puzzled that we were shrinking away from him. I pulled at Flora's arm to steer her away, but she held her ground, facing the man, trying to express something to him. Then I saw the black port behind the man's left ear. He'd been implanted. He stared back at her and snapped his fingers. "Oh, you're that girl from back then, the smartest one!" He knew Flora's face from the various documentaries and articles she'd been in when they were both children. He was a sort of fan of Flora, I guess, and I could see his frustration deepen as he attempted to speak with her. His face moved from bemusement to shock to disgust as he realized that Flora was still implant-free. I stepped in and explained our situation. The man listened carefully. In the end he grimaced and stroked his chin. I could tell that he was not interested in helping us, but I pleaded with him until he took us to a room on the far side of the motel and let us in. There'd been a shooting there a month previous and the management hadn't been able to afford a proper cleanup crew. He told us we could stay the night there as long as we kept out of sight. Aside from a single geyser of dried blood flecks plastered to the far wall, it was no different from any other motel room in America, which is to say that for us it was equal parts prison, mausoleum, and safe haven.

VOLUME FIVE

AUGUST BURNHAM

ACADIA NATIONAL PARK, ME
2040

We moved the PhonCom data center out to the Acadia National Park bird sanctuary in Maine. Our team had outgrown the facility in Rahway, and the work we were doing required more sustained focus, but mostly, what a perfect environment to hone a language machine—up in the canopy in a glass building on stilts, surrounded by primordial birdsong, the elemental precursor to human speech. It's like waking up in paradise every morning. We are at peace here, fully engaged with the deep, complicated process of polishing that elusive final expansion of the Soul Amp's design, the features and enhancements that will forever end the debate about whether the device is a true cure for silence or simply a language emulator.

Don't ask me which one I think it is. Just look around. Just think back to the world before the Soul Amp. Think about what it was like back then, when you had this whole population of marginalized people who couldn't talk, couldn't work, couldn't learn. Human in form but incapable of taking part in human society—forgotten hordes who we locked away in transitional facilities or who languished in abandoned ware-houses and strip malls. Now look around you. Look at these able-minded, vocal citizens who are able to articulate their dreams and ambitions and who have the tools to make those dreams come true. When your dearest wish is nothing more than to lead the kind of productive, fulfilling life that should be the birthright of any human, and then you're given a simple tool that allows you to take part in society instead of simply taking shelter on its periphery, isn't that evidence enough?

Well, not for some people, apparently. This small but loud minority throws around reckless, inflammatory, and mislead-ing charges—that we're just piping canned phrases into the heads of silent people. Sitting up in an ivory tower some-where, cutting out sentences from old forgotten texts and broadcasting them across the network. Making people say what I want them to say. If this were true, how could it be that we have so many successful implanted actors, writers, and artists? Was it PhonCom that wrote the novels of Epistola Caridad, the Surinamese implantee who won the National Book Award for *The Empty Palace*? I wish I could take credit, but no—those verifiable works of art sprang from a creative mind *set free* by the Soul Amp. Is Harper Treadwell nothing more than my puppet? If so, how could she give so moving a performance in *Robocide 3* that she won four Critics Circle Awards and a Golden Globe? When you actually sit back and observe the evidence, the behavior, free of abstraction and psychobabble, you see that the critics have no legs to stand on. And, fortunately, the world at large seems to agree—the remaining doubters are becoming more marginalized every day.

Which is not to say that there aren't a handful of vital improvements still ahead. I can't show you the list for all the obvious IP-related issues, but I can tell you that, while the ultimate goal of facilitating the use of a truly infinite set of phrases is still a long way off, we're making real progress. The system is only as strong as its source, and we're still relying on the pool of phrases that we've already collected in our database for language generation. The pool is colossal—last time I checked we had over thirty-four billion unique phrases available. Even though the mathematical probability that any implanted silent would ever be at a loss for an exact phrase is infinitesimally small, it's still there. We've seen it already, in fact. Just a few instances in our data stream of someone searching for a specific description and coming up short, or trying to force another phrase into place, or just giving up and not vocalizing any phrase at all. It's much better than in the early days, but it's still not perfect.

I'm very sensitive about this issue—the one shortcoming that prevents the Soul Amp from reaching its full potential. There is an exceedingly small but influential resistance to my design on precisely these grounds. Fringe groups who have refused the implant and gone underground, and the talking sympathizers who have rushed to their cause. Even though their collective power is negligible, it haunts my dreams. I want to be memorialized not as a puppet master but as an innovator, a codebreaker who breached the steel walls guarding the delicate machinery in the human brain that creates pure language.

To demonstrate this commitment to silent empowerment— to silents determining their own fate—I've placed Calvin Andersen in the position of design director. Some people have found this coy, or political. I recently overheard some board members gossiping that I'd made Calvin my own personal peg boy, which I thought was in poor taste. My decision to promote him so aggressively *was* symbolic—I'll admit that. The silent community needs an icon of representation within the implant infrastructure. But I wouldn't have done so if I didn't think Calvin was up to the task. I've worked with the man for years—I know him better than his own parents do, quite frankly—so I think I can say with complete confidence that he's the right man for the job. The fact that we occasionally take kayaking trips and visit natural hot springs sites and enjoy collecting rare barks—what business is that of anybody's? And what on earth does it have to do with the impossibly difficult work of mapping the language code?

CALVIN ANDERSEN

ACADIA NATIONAL PARK, ME
2040

Do you know what is the worst sound in the world? The sound of a thousand tiny birds chirping directly into the inside of your ears while you are trying to just eat a sandwich. Actually, what is even worse than that, now that I think of it, is the sound of Burnham's voice shouting over the birds, trying to pretend like we are actually having a conversation, that it's not so loud up in this floating treehouse that I cannot even hear my own dreams above the din of birdsong. The sound of Burnham's voice drilling me with question after question, not because he is curious about my life but because he's testing his implant. That is the worst sound in the world, and every day feels like a slow death.

I finally got to the place where his constant testing of me was too much to take, so I decided to test him instead. I started calling him "Burned Ham" instead of "Burnham." "Good morning, Doctor Burned Ham," I said as I sat down next to him in the lab. He turned and gave a questioning half smile, but didn't try to correct me. I put the calibration helmet on, pretending everything was normal. When I locked the jaw plate into place, I said, "Would you mind passing me the spectron calipers, Doctor Burned Ham?" and he gave me the same look. He passed me the calipers and said, "A very funny joke, Calvin." I looked at him blankly, as if I didn't have the slightest idea what he was talking about. "You said my name wrong," he said, still maintaining that bastard half grin. "That's impossible," I said. "But you've just now said it wrong twice." I could hear just a thread of annoyance running through his voice. "That can't be true," I said. "All I've said to you was 'Good morning, Doctor Burned Ham' and 'Please pass the calipers, Doctor Burned Ham,' and certainly I said all that correctly—I mean, you just heard me." He dropped the smile and stared at me. He closely examined my every facial twitch and tic. I wasn't worried—I knew he had no idea how to read my expressions, so I was able to fool him without really trying. He sat back in his seat and said, "Say my name again." I said, "What? You want me to say your name again?" And he said, "Yes, again, please." I went, "This is ridiculous. You know how hard it is for me to talk with this helmet on. Are you trying to test me? Is this some kind of test?" And he just looked at me. "What's my name, Calvin?" he said. I stared right back at him, making my face as wide and innocent as a child's, and said, "I honestly don't know what this is about, Doctor Burned Ham." He shot up from his chair and began pacing behind me.

I just powered up the helmet, pretending nothing was wrong. "Who are we diagnosing today?" I asked. He went over to his tablet and scrolled hastily through the network map. "64.2775.243. Eloise Gibson." I entered the address and established a connection with Eloise Gibson's implant. "Okay," Burnham said. "Looks like the issue here is an inability to verbally express sexual desire. So please do whatever you can to provoke that in her." I loathed this practice—I had to use the helmet to massage a stranger's neural pathways in the hope of eliciting some kind of verbal response. This was how we tested the latest iteration of Burnham's translation code—the helmet ran on a local dev branch that had its own language bank so that it could operate independently from PhonCom. It was sick. I felt like a criminal, wandering around in these peoples' heads, vandalizing their thoughts. I sat wearing the awful pinching calibration helmet, with Burnham observing my every move, and tried my best to get hard for Eloise Gibson.

The next day Burnham uploaded a patch to the device and all of a sudden I could no longer say "Burned Ham" when I said his name. No matter how hard I struggled, I couldn't make "Burned Ham" out of "Burnham." He'd put some kind of block on that phrase. Everything he did from that point on, every word he uttered, made me want to crush him to a pulp. His constant posturing and preening for the media, his self-congratulatory quotes about saving silents from themselves—it was sickening. And the way he cavorted with implanted celebrities—like that novel-writer woman with the inverted eyelids and soft gray mustache who had become famous just for writing a few awful books—was too much to take. But the worst thing by far was the way he paraded me around as his shining trophy—the living, breathing, walking embodiment of his genius.

The greatest irony about all of this? The five-hundred-pound yak or however you say the expression, the thing in the room that Burnham doesn't dare contemplate, is that becoming his living experiment has in no way set me free. I am not a happier person. My soul is not singing. So I can banter with chattering fools—so what? Before I became this manacled freak, a sideshow curiosity, a party game, I had my room in my parents' house, RC boats in the county park, and cinnamon rolls on Sunday mornings after Mass. My life was a simple, beautiful routine. I was alone inside my own head, and it was a sacred place I couldn't even begin to describe to you. There are no words for it, because it was a place outside of words. It was pure color or—or a thousand folding sheets—or swirling wind. Before Burnham switched on the implant for the first time, I had no voices in my head—no roaring chorus that now plagues me from the moment I open my eyes to when I fall on the bed, exhausted after yet another day of intensive testing.

Does Burnham want to hear this, any of it? Of course not. How could a person possibly find peace without language? How could someone fully appreciate the glory of the night sky without knowing the names of the constellations? Who could enjoy the warmth of the sun without labeling its source? So instead of leaving me alone, he makes me the design director of this accursed device. It is a vanity position, in case you had any doubts about that. I do not design. I sit in the glass lab all day with the calibration helmet pinching my jaw, watching pigfilth sparrows as they flit around their bullshit nests and vomit into the mouths of their young. When Burnham takes his conference calls, I stream silent pornography on the wallscreen and slowly rub myself into oblivion until the workday ends and it is time for me to accompany him to another charity event, another radio interview, another industry booze cruise. The next version of the Soul Amp will bear my name in the credits, but instead of Director of Design my title should be something more like Puppet, Prisoner, and Lead Guinea Pig.

PERSEPHONE GOLDIA

PHILADELPHIA, PA
2040

It was defective, or maybe I was. My brain wouldn't surrender certain small-to-important items. There were glitches in the stream. Something daily, something hourly wasn't right. The bank dispenser asked me how I would die. How I would like, but I mean, my money—how I would die was what I was anticipating when she asked how I would like my money, sensible enough, and I said, "Twenty-seven exit wounds." The bulletproof glass, a pain in the lungs that wouldn't go away, a news moment I saw on the bus screens a few hours earlier. A manager came on and I told him tens, twenties, money was money. He paused for a moment, then dispensed my cash. My connections were often crisscrossed and time forfeited, and it was becoming worse not better. Worse. Rain delay.

The online rehab liaison told me I needed to stop torturing the undercurrents of the language and just allow it to flow out naturally. He gave me an address of a weekly conversation group for erstwhiles. It met in the back banquet room to a orphanage called—a Greek restaurant. Not an orphanage. I went after my shift on the day cruise SS *Muir*. Bled-out drained. Walking there from the bus stop with my head full of expired notes, tombstones: *remember extra blue cheese 86 crab bisque push summer rolls crocodile joke.* At the group we paired up or talked in small clusters, and at first I couldn't detect anything wrong in the others. One of my first partners was Trinidad, who wore a colorful robe and welcomed me and cackled my errors away. A lot of Trinidad was borrowed from movie trailers, but a lot of all of us was.

"You look perplexed," he said one night. "I hope someone hasn't been French-frying your gizzards, sister."

"No one's French—no, I'm okay. I've been a little I don't know lately. But I mean, under, feeling underwater. Deep. Shark-infested." I hesitated. It was always when someone asked me about me that I lost the cause. How I felt. How I looked. How I was. Simple questions. I tried to pin thick words on fast-sliding clouds in the span from birth to mouth.

Trinidad patiently fanned himself with a menu. I asked, "How would you say . . ." And then I just showed it, the way we all used to.

He nodded. He thought about it. He said "hmm" a few times. Then he said, "I wouldn't know where to . . ." He looked down at his menu for a moment, mouthing something. His face cycled through a few retorts. Finally he said, "Shark-infested isn't close, but it isn't far away."

Yeah, all of us had heard about Flora and the rest. From other erstwhiles, and on television. We watched a news stream called "The Last Holdouts," which showed Flora's high school graduation over and over and also the surveillance footage of the family from the Utah gas station, where Flora walked in holding her son's hand and they stood transfixed in the candy aisle, the boy studying each candy bar, trying to decide. He stands there for three minutes and thirty-seven seconds, the hours minutes seconds passing in the bottom right corner, until Flora lightly touches his shoulder and he selects a Honey Brick. I replayed the footage on my Catena and watched it on the bus to work, at home. "Brittle-outside-resilient-inside-hope," I said, trying to override the implant's close-enough shortcutting. "Curious-longing-dry-heave."

I talked to the others over the weeks. Our conversation began with an exchange of information. A popular icebreaker was telling each other our first words. Then we practiced transitional strategies, moving to a new topic, like, "Your sweater reminds me, I can't shake this wooly feeling in my throat. Bet I'm coming down with something." Then argumentative strategies by choosing movie trailers and debating which was better, and why. Then slang strategies. Everything would have been fine if not for me. Everybody would have bounce-housed from icebreaker to strategy to strategy. I asked too many questions, and my questions were icemakers. My favorite icemaker was, "How do you feel at night, those few moments before you go to sleep?" Also, sometimes I'd repeat back what they just said, and then ask, "Was that exactly what you wanted to say?"

It seemed like all of us had a deep inside itch. I just happened to come by and bother it. All of them were sad at night and hopeful in the morning and spent the day building up to solos that never came. Debating movie trailers wasn't fixing it. Trading slang—like, I'm 'bout to get cowboyed out in this fuckity—wasn't making anything disappear. No. We were building private stocks of unsayables, making substitutions, conceding.

Trinidad had heard that the resistance was mobilizing in an abandoned turkey slaughterhouse in eastern Colorado. They'd joined with a bunch of other unimplanted silents, and together they were assembling an army and no one really knew what they were planning. I asked Trinidad what he thought, and his face above the eyes softened and his chin ticked. "I think they are plotting around for a very loud statement," he said. "Something international. Perhaps similar to the trailer for *Blood Oath 6: Shanghaied by Vengeance*."

Others disagreed. One woman knew for certain that they were setting up another commune, something in the Black Hills, "where they can live close to the earth in peace." Another heard that they'd already bombed a Nu Ware clinic in Ann Arbor, but no one reported it because the government didn't want people inside—didn't want them to panic. I heard every possibility and I believed them all, because it did not matter. I kept watching the gas station footage, the boy, the woman, the hand, the choice. It was perfect. They were perfect. All I wanted was to be as fearless and pure as they were.

We started to meet more often—any night of the week there'd be five, six of us in the banquet room. We practiced our conversation over the next few weeks by talking about the underground. Argumentation strategies. Hypothetical and emotional strategies. Someone had heard someone who heard something. We each nursed along our own theories and fantasies. We just knew they were planning something huge, they had to be—why would we be talking about it so much if they weren't?

I practiced overriding the implant, staying silent as the language streamed past, waiting. Or repeating the same simple phrase a dozen times and seeing what I came up with. When Trinidad answered my questions with movie quotes, I made him try again. When someone said "fine" or "good" or "pretty much." I wanted them to hear what I heard.

One day I gave Trinidad a promotional hat from the SS

Muir. It wasn't much, but he liked hats, which he wore even indoors. He studied the hat and said, "Thanks, sister." I waited. I watched him. He stewed his nose and bowed his bottom lip. He said, "Okay, embarrassed-thanks, distracted-thanks." He coughed into his hand and added, "Sister."

On the bus ride home I watched the surveillance footage again, my sixth time that day, which was the maximum number of times I allowed myself. I imagined where they'd gone, pictured them sharpening tools somewhere, applying grease-paint, drawing battle formations on a whiteboard. Who knew what they were really doing. Mostly I hoped they were away from harm. My bus got caught in deadly crossfire, I mean traffic, so I watched the segment one more time.

FRANCINE CHANG

ROCK ISLAND, IL
2040

Nancy panicked for a moment when the motel worker demanded that we leave him some sort of ID, but for this bit of life on the run I was actually prepared—a fake gym-membership card that my ex-sort-of-boyfriend Niles had made for me. Niles, who I found out later smuggled living coral from Australia. He had made the ID for me as a joke, like ha ha, could you please be someone different? The picture on the front was incredible. Blond hair, mauve eye shadow, and lipstick. An aging Dallas hooker with my face and a different name. Tiffany Park. Nothing pretty, but then neither was the Deluxe Inn Waterfront.

All of us sat staring at each other in that crime scene of a room, greasy and bleary from the road. Defeated. Except the boy, who, even at this nothing motel, investigated every bit of newness we passed. The housekeeping carts, the ice machines. He followed me out to the Breeze Mart for supplies. I bought him a paddleball, and he patiently tried to master it on the way back to our suite, which wasn't a suite but two mirror-exact rooms separated by a doorless doorway. Farm equipment lithographs on the wall. The odor of chemicals used to cover up other odors. And, of course, the blood splatter on the far wall—faded, but with a violent spray that suggested . . . I didn't want to imagine what it suggested.

I stayed with Spencer's mom, who unplugged the television the second we arrived and lay down, eyes closed, rigid as a corpse. Any minute, I knew, she'd start talking in her sleep, mumbling "no no no" over and over. In the other room Flora tended to Spencer's wound while the boy sat cross-legged on the carpet in front of them, fiddling with a skydiving brochure. When he saw me, he came over and showed me what he'd made: a small tightly folded boat with two sails. He went and filled the bathroom sink with water, and set the boat in. It sank immediately.

I had to get out of that room. And where better than the Deluxe Inn Lounge, population four? I drank Singapore Slings next to a woman who eventually introduced herself as Evie. She was reading aloud an article on her Catena to whoever would listen. It was about the head of a cell farm who said he would give a prospective customer a second set of arms if the price was right. When she was done reading, she turned to me—she must have seen me listening—and declared, "Now that's some spider shit."

I laughed involuntarily. She dimmed her Catena and said, "Who I found myself talking at?"

I hesitated. Fuck it, I thought. Literally, a neon-pink sign in my head flashed *fuck it*. "Tiffany Park," I told her.

Where was I from? Myrtle Beach. What'd I do? Little of this, little of that. What else? Men are dogs. We drank another round. I told her that the biggest problem facing the world today was men who wanted me to be their mama. I said, "Come at me all strong and assertive and then I hear you talking in your sleep, like, Oh, Mommy, can I pretty please climb up in that womb? Tiffany Park is *not* your mama. Or your little sister or friend. Don't baby talk in my ear. Don't wave your little nightstick at me. Don't try to wake me up by slipping me your imitation crabmeat tea bag."

I wasn't drunk. I knew what I was saying—I felt it, directly. Francine Chang would've politely nodded to Evie and stared at the burst capillaries on her nose, her chipped front tooth. She would've felt scared and superior. But Tiffany Park did not care. She had some things inside needed saying. She had certain feelings. In the far corner of the lounge I noticed a karaoke machine, and so I interrupted Evie's story about slumlords and Irish wolfhounds and court summonses. It was time to sing.

Evie was reluctant, but after I knocked out a few songs, my standards—"Understand Me" and "Tornado Comin'"— she warmed to it. The half-dozen drunks huddled around the bar sighed and looked all constipated when we started our duets. To hell with them. I strutted around the lounge with the cordless mic, stopping at each of their tables, belting out the hits. The two of us didn't stop until the bartender blinked the lights and yelled for last call.

Walking upstairs, I felt like a bank robber fleeing the scene. I was whispering the chorus of "Slip Him the Pill," all hoarse from singing so much, when I noticed the boy sitting outside the room. Almost 2:00 a.m., and he's outside fooling around with a pair of earbuds Spencer's mom had given him. Just begging for the night clerk to come by and ask him questions. "You can't be out here," I said, shaking my head. He met my eyes, tightened his expression, and did the same thing. Not mimicking me but . . . appraising me. He was piecing my night together, it felt like. Going through the transcript. No thanks. I led him back into the room. The TV was on, muted. Flora and Spencer slept in the bed on the left, surrounded by pamphlets and brochures folded into boats and planes. The boy sat at the foot of the other bed and continued to play with the earbuds.

My room was full of Nancy and her tuberculosis snores. I went to the bathroom, balled up pieces of toilet paper, and put them in my ears, but it made no difference. I lay awake all night, my body humming, finally drifting off just after dawn.

I woke up surprisingly lucid. The others were already awake, faces grave and inert. What were we doing in Rock Island? What was our mission? Collectively, who knows. To hide? Till when? To prepare? For what? Individually, though, I knew what I had to do. Rock Island was where I'd cast off the dead weight of Francine Chang, hapless, plodding, middle-aged remorse machine. I'd revise myself for good.

I went to the Deluxe Lounge that evening, and the next. I liked everything about the place. The anchor-pattern carpet, the metal bowls of slightly stale cashews, the bartender, cross-eyed and unintelligible. I wore some new forestine-blue eye shadow and matching lipstick. I sat on a stool at the bar and talked to Evie, Ying, Sheila, Lee, whoever. I introduced myself to everybody. I asked questions and tried to provoke them. Who else has a thing for jai alai players? Paraplegics? Implanted silents? Toward the end of the night Evie and I would always hit the karaoke machine and everyone would groan, but nobody left the bar, now did they? Plus, Tiffany Park didn't give a red damn what a few slouchy old drunks in some prison town thought of her.

Lots of things happened there over the next couple weeks.

I laughed, I cried, I got into a hair-pulling fight with some troll who didn't like how I stared at her man. I told the whole bar about how Bastien Hvorecky tricked me into masturbating for the entire free world. I traded shots of whiskey with a man named Donald who drove a refrigerated truck. Then later we had subzero sex in the back of the truck. When we were done I didn't mope, didn't cry. I told him I was gonna have another drink and he could join me or not, whatevs.

One night I got a little drunker than I intended. Empty stomach, I don't know. I tottered around, singing "Ape Kiss" without the mic, arguing with people who all looked at me like they were getting ready to vote me off this talent show. I felt a hand on my waist. I looked down, and there was the boy. Christ. He reached up and took my hand.

"Who's this?" said Evie, who I didn't even realize was there.

"Great-nephew," I told her. "Plus, none of your goddamn business."

Of course Evie starts talking to him and he doesn't say anything, just stares at her. I look at him more closely and I see the tiny black implant port on his scalp behind his ear. Implant hardware. Christ, I think, how much time has passed? Then I remember the earbuds he'd been playing with, one of which he's somehow glued to himself. Evie's still trying to talk to him, looking at the implant. "Still hasn't mastered it," I said, and yanked him out of the bar.

He walked me back to the room. Before I opened the door, I smiled at him, held him by the shoulders, and said, "Everything's fine. Don't worry."

He looked worried. He held on to my hand after we'd gone inside, and paused at Flora's bed. Both of us watched her sleep. Her face twitched and jittered. The boy studied her carefully. I wondered if he could tell what she was dreaming about, by the way her face moved. I wondered if he liked what he saw. I just stood there holding his hand and watching until I felt like I'd throw up. Which, after I excused myself and went into our shared bathroom, was what I did.

THEODORE GREENE

RICHMOND, CA
2040

I knew a call would come eventually, so I spent the days and weeks preparing myself. I prayed the call would come from them rather than a policeman or a reporter or the morgue. But if I were being totally honest, part of me hoped the police would call telling me they'd been arrested and locked away. Even Flora, sure. Even Slash. And then, for once, I'd be the one who was free.

When the call finally did come, I was calm—I saw the blocked ID and lack of origin code, took a deep breath, and pressed Answer. The wallscreen bloomed to life, and there was Flora. It had been about five months, at that point, since I'd last seen her, not counting the security camera footage I'd found of her and Spencer and Slash at that gas station. She hunched her shoulders like an old arthritic woman, and the overhead tube lights shrouded her eyes with long shadows, which further muted any communication. She looked every bit as lost and hunted as she was.

I composed myself and stared hard at the screen. I wanted to show her I was relieved but also intensely concerned. She nodded and gave me a reassuring look. Just the sight of her face, as pale and thin as it was, put me at ease. I shuddered in the wake of the anger that had taken hold of me just a minute earlier. She looked at me curiously and I brushed it off, mugging in an effort to change the subject. I let her know I wanted to see Slash. She looked away, biting her lower lip as she tugged at a ribbon of hair that had come loose from the tortoiseshell band she'd worn since high school. Slash appeared in the frame, kneeling on the floor in front of Flora. I held my breath as he scanned my features, trying, I guess, to remember where he'd last seen me. It was only a split second that he didn't recognize me, but it might as well have been a decade. When he placed me, though, he broke out into a laugh and did an impression of me. I could still see some of Flora in his eyes, but it was clear—he'd changed. Unalterably changed, and he'd continue to change, year after year, the boy fading into the shadows of the man he'd become.

I put my hand up and he put his hand out and we gave one another a single high five. He saw that I was tense, and I tried my best to assure him that everything was fine. I tried to show him that I missed him, but he became distracted with something on the floor, out of the camera's view. I looked at Flora then, imploring her to come back home, come back from wherever she was. Come back now. She furrowed her brow in response and started heaving. She pressed her wrist to her mouth, and I was forced to watch her sob. I could do nothing but sit and watch.

Then there was a noise on the other end. Spencer burst into the room, followed by a man in a pressed shirt and tie. Flora stood and made a sound like a reverse shriek. I caught sight of a feathered spurt of dried blood on the wall behind her, and the nerves at the back of my neck burned. The man said, "I thought I told you never to leave this room." Flora glanced back at the camera. Spencer followed her gaze, locking eyes with me. The man rushed toward the screen. "What the—you're fucking making calls?" He slammed his fist against the wall and the call went dead.

I frantically hit the call-back button, but of course the number was blocked. I hit it again and again, striking the surface with more force each time, convinced that I might through sheer force of will shake the electrons to life and re-establish the connection. But the call was lost, my family was gone, and I was alone in my empty apartment once again.

I did a search for call-tracing scripts but there was nothing out there that could track down an ID for a call without an origin path. I sat at my desk and started roughing out a script of my own. I made some headway, but I was so beside myself with fear that I could barely write the code. I went back to my desk and played back the call. Frame by frame, I thought, there had to be something that I could use, some sort of clue to identify their location. I watched the images advance, scouring the blurred objects in the scene, but beyond Flora's face there was just the eggshell wall and the light tubes. The brown blood flecks. But then the man appeared. With the footage slowed down, I could see that he'd pushed Spencer through the door. There was a hand, palm-up, hovering behind Spencer for just a few fleeting frames. And then the man entered the room, and I saw that his shirt had a logo embroidered over the right breast pocket. I magnified the frame and applied a sharpening filter, and there it was—the Deluxe Inn Waterfront, stitched in navy thread, with the *W* stylized to look like a wave. I took a screenshot of the logo and did a search on it. They were in a crumbling motel on the border between Iowa and Illinois.

I went into the kitchen and filled a glass with water at the sink. I watched the water ripple in the glass as my hand shook. So this was what they wanted. To end up in some dingy motel room in the middle of the country. Fine—they didn't need me. That was clear. I wished them luck in all that lay ahead. And then I cursed the wicked way they left me behind. And then the sun was down and I was standing in front of the hallway mirror, perfecting the speech I was going to deliver when I saw them again, when they came crawling back. I wanted to keep my face entirely smooth. I wanted to show them nothing.

Two days passed like two hours. I paced the apartment, strong in my newfound armor. I envisioned the devastation and confusion I would leave in my wake.

On the third day there was a knock at the door. I steeled myself and turned the knob, but instead of my family there was a man standing on the concrete landing. A gloomy-looking Asian man in a dark suit with a clipboard tucked under his arm and a leather briefcase at his side. Behind him were six children, four boys and two girls, all wearing the same dark suits.

"Mr. Theodore Greene?" he said in a deep, clipped monotone. "I am an archivist with the silent oral-history project."

I told him I didn't need anyone recording me. I'd been using the Mémo for years to record my testimonials.

"Of course," the man said. "I am not here to record you, Mr. Greene. I am simply collecting census data. These are my assistants." He kept his eyes on me the entire time he spoke, and the boys and girls, all implantees, kept their eyes on him.

"You have a daughter—a silent daughter, am I correct?"

"Yes."

"And a grandson?"

"That's correct." I maintained the blank composure I had rehearsed over the past days.

"You must be proud. They're not living with you here, by chance, are they?"

I told him they'd moved out of state, and the man wrote something down on the clipboard. A wasp landed on his shoulder and one of the boys stepped forward to brush it away. "Which state?"

"Illinois. Rock Island. Some motel. Or, that's where they were last. I don't know."

He wrote something else on the clipboard and then passed it behind him. Another boy received it and folded it into a carrying case. "It must be hard having your family so far away, Mr. Greene. But their mistakes are not your responsibility. No one will blame you for whatever happens now."

I didn't say anything.

"We have everything we need," he said. He turned around, flanked by the children, and crossed the street to an unmarked white school bus.

I shut the door. I realized that I was shaking—my whole body was trembling. All of the rage I'd built up slowly fizzed away. I wasn't worried about blame. I wasn't worried about responsibility. My family needed me. I needed them. I sprinted into the bathroom, put my toothbrush in a bag, and headed out toward the highway.

DAVID DIETRICH

ROCK ISLAND, IL
2040

If America's a body, then the middle part's those in-between organs you don't know or care what they do. Spleen, gallbladder, pancreas. Pretend they're all vital and then when you carve them out nothing happens. I was looking everywhere for the resistance, but so far all I'd found were mumblers and smilers who, noticing me eavesdropping, would ask me where I'd come from, or where I was headed, and I'd say, "Are you writing a motherfucking book about me?" And they'd frown like I'd done them real harm, and I'd try to soften it by adding, "This is the part of the book where the main hero goes deep cover and rides around incognito. If that's okay with you, you groping mealworm?"

For two weeks I drove around Missouri because I found its shape calming. On maps all the other states look like weaponry and buttholes and tongues. I was in an anxious daze—all I'd been eating on the road were carob smoothies and these phosphocreatine supplement lollipops, which increased my core strength and messed with my decision making and gave me a permanent hard-on. I stared over the dashboard into the vaporized horizon.

I grew a beard. It was a sad beard that didn't connect all the way, like the mustache part thought it was all superior to the rest of it. I had a bunch of decoy hats that I wore. I flexed my wrist strengthener while driving, and lost ten pounds of stomach flab, which went straight to my biceps and triceps. The wallaby was still with me—I named him Wallaby, because I thought there was dignity in being named what you were—and we'd developed an okay repartee except he refused to shit on the newspaper in the bed of my truck. He did it wherever he pleased, and the only warning he gave me was he'd sort of shake his hind legs a little and then evict a handful of pebbly, foul-smelling turds, which I'd let harden in the sun before scooping out. After he was done, he'd climb back between the seat and the window, where I kept my knife pack and rope and *shuriken*, and sleep there—must've been too refined to nap next to his own droppings. He whinnied and snored like a drugged stewardess.

After two weeks in Missouri the closest we'd come to a lead was finding an unimplanted silent working an oyster bed near where we were camping. We followed him to a sooty group home and Wallaby and I peeked in the window, but the guy didn't do anything but play superchess on his Catena and then go to sleep. I heard about a militia in Joplin, but when I called and asked what kind of militia it was, the guy who answered told me to go to the nearest prison and get raped. I told him that actually I was headed to Joplin right now, and I was going to find his sorry ass and tie him up and take off his clothes and then I'd shave him bald and make him wear a blue swim diaper—then I stopped liking where my list was going so I hung up.

I used to think life had these points in it where you got to choose. You could decide, I'm gonna be the kind of person who does *this*, and then do it. I hadn't come across anything like that yet. Just vague yearnings and low impulses. At night I lay in my sleeping bag with Wallaby curled next to me and tried to will myself closer to the resistance. I knew I'd find them soon enough. And I knew something else: they were going to need me every bit as much as I needed them. I wasn't going to come to them all empty-handed and beseeching. I was ready. I was able. I remembered all these sentences from the old podcasts the albino gave my mom. *You are what you project.* And *Harness the power of an actualized you.* I finally believed it. I fell asleep with Mom rattling around my head, images of her sad in some hospital somewhere, and woke up to Wallaby trying to bite nits out of my scalp. We packed up, hopped in the truck, and continued to search.

We finally broke out of Missouri. Into Kentucky, whose every citizen should be mustard-gassed for parts, and Indiana, which smells like condoms and scorched birds. Indiana wouldn't leave me and Wallaby alone. Wallaby sort of captured everyone's heart there, and no matter how angrily I dismissed them they kept asking to touch him, photograph him, buy him. "He's not a goddamn pet," I informed them. They asked what he was and I told them, "He's a goddamn *companion*." That didn't sound right, so I started saying, "He's a goddamn *associate*." Didn't matter. They just laughed and snapped his picture, and sometimes mine, too. Which, because of the self-pulser I kept on my key chain, showed up on their screen as a white smear. A small victory.

I kept going. Every time my brain asked what I was doing, I sucked on another phospop to deaden its noise. I knew I had to lose myself before we could find what we were looking for. So I did, and then we did, at a pay shower depot outside Cedar Rapids. Wallaby and I were sharing a single booth to conserve money, which I guess was illegal, so the owner called the police. We came out of the dryer chamber and saw a pair of doughy officers waiting for us. "Is that one of those rabbit mutates?" they asked. I guess a blow-dried wallaby was the funniest thing to ever appear in Iowa, or maybe the prettiest thing, the way these officers were ogling him. I clenched my teeth, thinking of all the illegal knives in my truck.

"Must've been quite a wedding ceremony," one of them said to the other, who wiped the side of his mustache with his thumb.

"She seems like just the right height for—" the other one said, holding out his hands and lazily thrusting an imaginary boner. Two Iowa cops, bored out of their skulls. I was going to be the highlight of their week. I didn't buckle. I didn't crash. I just went blank. I hadn't really done it since I was a kid, but it felt right. I remembered all the flourishes, the nuances.

"Hey, sports fan," the mustache cop said. "We asked you a question. Does your bunny like it freaky or what?"

"If the perp don't reply, then the bunny does definitely supply," the first one said.

"Or is what we have here some kind of silent holdout?" the mustache one said. "Better watch yourself, bro—guy camped out at Shaver Park is looking for little silent kids. You're too old for his tastes, but you never know."

"Yeah. I bet Professor Undertaker and his little-boy army would love to practice their tricks on him."

"Too many bounty hunters, not enough bounty," said the mustache cop.

The first turned to me and spoke loud and slow, with broad irrelevant gestures. "Stay . . . away . . . from . . . Shaver . . . Park. Gloomy man want to implant you. Spooky . . . fucker . . . hunting . . . silents."

My heart flared, but I played it cool—just gave them my best dazed stare. Soon they lost interest and walked off, though not before telling me to have a nice life with my rabbit mutate bride. Ha ha ha. Fuckers. I will shave you both and fill balloons with your hair and give them to clowns. I will cut off your ears and feed them to Wallaby, but he's an herbivore, so he won't touch them, and I'll end up throwing them on some sidewalk, where they'll dry until a crow eats them and flies off and shits the remains onto the roof of your wife's long-dicked lover's double-wide.

As soon as they were out of sight, we jumped into the truck and circled around till we found Shaver Park. We crouched behind a swing set and observed: a school bus, a dark-suited man with a clipboard, a dozen children filing onto the bus like a special forces battalion. The kids were all stunned toothy mongrels—implants. Wallaby was sniffing the air like he could smell every molecule of their pollution. He looked back at me, shook his hind legs, and loosed a furious jackpot of turds onto my foot.

I took this as a sign. Wallaby knew. He was trying to tell me that the world's made up of two kinds of people, a few okay ones and a swarm of others, which is eternally chapping the ass of the okay kind. If the resistance was anywhere nearby, this school bus crew would be trying to murk them up with their fraudulence. Either way, for the first time since leaving the farm, Wallaby and I had some real purpose.

We waited for them to load into the bus and slowly pulled

out behind. Wallaby leaned out the window and sniffed the bus's off-waft. He had their scent. He was using his animal power to memorize them.

We followed the bus through the night like pilot fish behind a whale. I lost hope. Then gained it back. Then lost it again. I licked my supplement lollipops and tried to keep Wallaby away from my hard-on. On the road I peed into a baggie and took dozens of micronaps, just a couple seconds at a time. Whenever I opened my eyes, the bus was always exactly where I expected it to be.

BRIAN NG

ROCK ISLAND, IL
2040

We got their whereabouts from that sad old man and set out east, stopping only for quick readiness drills in feedlots and baseball fields. What I saw of the Midwest was all through the school bus window: birds, motor lodges, grain silos, can-you-eat-all-this buffets, Army Navy supply stores, police stations. Tire fires. It seemed nice.

Just before we entered Illinois, Dr. Ng motioned for the driver to pull over, so we could secure a special interdistrict exemption from the regional compliance board. Approval came through immediately, and we roared across the border. I was so excited to help that hobo family.

Dr. Ng had adopted me, signed my renaming papers, and implanted me, and then I was born. We were to address him as "Doctor" in front of the parents, and not at all when the parents weren't around. Once, after two days of implanting seventy islander kids who smuggled themselves into Oakland on a container ship, he shook my hand and then coughed. The cough sounded like *thanks*. The next morning there were twenty extra snack points on my meal account. I would have done anything for him.

At the motel he cross-referenced the guest registration with a housekeeping log, and then all twelve of us techs fanned out and searched the place. First floor, clean. Pool area, vacant. Supply closets, full of supplies. On the back side of the motel, second floor, overlooking the scummed-over pool, we walked past rooms 213, 215, then a sign that said NO UNAUTHORIZED PERSONNEL. Dr. Ng looked down at the housekeeping log, and then at the room, and back down at the log. I saw a smile appear on his face and then quickly fall. He only smiled like that when we were about to really help someone.

We assembled in a four-deep half circle around the door, just as we'd been trained. I was in the way back, with Anthony and Simon and the other losers. Simon slept in the bunk above mine at the warehouse. He sobbed at night, and I'd kick his mattress to wake him up and he'd say, "I'm not sleeping." Some runts splashed poolside while their parents waited to see what was going to happen.

We waited by that door for hours. We had a four-person battering ram in the bus, but I guess we needed a warrant to bust in the door, and Dr. Ng never did anything without the necessary papers. He led by example, by the strength of his calm.

Every so often one of the techs would try the knob. Melissa called out, "Hurry up in there and get your medicine!" Someone said she could hear whispering, then Karen banged on the door and the whispering stopped. The doctor just stood there with his eyes half-closed. He wore dark blue trousers, off-white shirt, and dark-blue coat. We did, too. I'd never seen him sleep or eat. One of the other techs saw him take a sausage link from the breakfast island at a gas station in Colorado, but who knows what he did with it.

Sad lodgers continued to stare out their windows, and we maintained our formation. Next to me, Anthony kept sniffing. "Smells like fear," he said. "Smells like someone shit themselves," Simon said. Just then a housekeeper pushed a cart slowly down the hallway. He wore mirrored sunglasses and had a reddish beard with lint and food and stuff in it, and he was muscular, especially his arms, which were ropey, covered with some kind of oil, it looked like. For someone who cleaned rooms for a living, he was strangely filthy.

"Fire hazards," he said. "All of you. Clear away, please. Back to your rooms."

He pushed his cart through the line of techs, into the center of the circle. Melissa looked at him, then his cart, and said, "You clear away. We were here first."

The man-maid put on a smile-grimace and said, "Sorry, that's the rules, little lady. Have to get through to clean the room."

"Go on ahead. Open the door. We'll make space, won't we?"

We nodded and eyed each other, waiting for something to happen. All of us wanted something to happen.

"You need to exit the walkway first," he said. "Otherwise, it's a serious violation. Of the code."

Just then Anthony shouted, "A bunny!" He pointed to the middle rack of the cart where, peeking out behind towels, I could see a white snout and small black eyes.

"It's not a bunny," Simon said. "It's a badger."

The maid looked down at the rodent, and then at the

doctor. I realized the obvious: this was no maid. The non-maid realized my realizing. Dr. Ng realized everything. For a moment all was still—and then we swarmed.

We came at him from all sides, three or four at a time, but somehow he warded off wave after wave—a mop handle to the midsection, a towel snap to the neck, a spray of industrial cleaning fluid to the eyes. Karen got a plunger rap on the temple. Simon was tossed over the railing, into the pool. I thumb-gouged at the man's testicles, but he didn't seem to notice. Clearly we were in the presence of an evil spirit.

Through the crying and yowls of my fellow techs I heard a voice. "Pardon me, sir," Dr. Ng was saying. "Sir?"

The doctor's voice was like someone at the end of a long tunnel. The maid looked up from our whimpering pile. Dr. Ng was at the top of the stairs holding the kangaroo under one arm. In his other hand he held the implant gun, which was pointed at the base of the kangaroo's skull, just like we had been trained. The kangaroo wriggled, and Dr. Ng squeezed more tightly. The man swallowed once, hard.

"Leave now," said Dr. Ng. "We have the authority to implant anyone and anything within the state of Illinois."

"What do you know," the man said, "about author—" and then Dr. Ng snapped the trigger. The kangaroo's eyes widened, then dulled.

The man didn't move for a long moment. Slowly his posture straightened. "The rest of you should run," he said, not looking at us. "Fast." He grabbed a toilet plunger from his cart. "Now."

We looked from him to Ng and back again. The muscles on his arm started to go all twitchy. We ran.

I scrambled down the walkway, the other techs sprinting behind. We tore across the parking lot and up the steps of the school bus. Melissa pulled the lever and the door slammed shut. We stood there for a moment, panting, dazed, craning our necks out the windows.

Up on the second floor, the demonic maid was standing over Dr. Ng, who was laid out on the ground. The maid was plunging the doctor's face, looking around, crying, yelling something. Dr. Ng had his hand gripped around the railing, screaming in a voice I had never heard before. His legs were kicking like someone getting heart-attack paddles. One by one we all turned away.

I looked around. Who was going to tell us what to do now? Who'd file the clearance forms so we could get our meal vouchers? I watched Karen and Zev, two of the oldest, stand up from their seats and make for the driver's seat at the exact same time. Karen got there first. Zev tried to fight his way over her, but she kicked him onto the rubber flooring, started up the engine, and we drove off.

PATTI KERN

ROCK ISLAND, IL
2040

Since releasing myself from the laboratory doors, I'd quit anticipating or envisioning or presuming anything past the immediate, physical moment. I had calm hands, tunnel vision, and a ten-wheel rig, permanently borrowed back in Cheyenne, which I drove all the way to the motel parking lot. Now, pulling into the lot, I was vacant. I expected nothing. I might've found the place reduced to sizzling ash rubble or a soft-focus Bethlehem with Flora and Spencer and the child wearing robes and nursing each other. I didn't peck around for portents and auguries. My rig was a rig. The highway was a highway. The motel was a motel. The young man I found huddled next to a defunct swimming pool was just a young man huddled next to a defunct swimming pool, except he was cradling a furry white animal.

He was shirtless, red from the cold, blubbering loudly into the animal's fur.

"Blue doctor," he said through the sobs. "Blue doctor messed my *life*."

I knelt in front of him—I'd expected to go straight to the

room Francine said they were staying in and shepherd them out of here, but it could wait a few minutes. This was just another necessary step toward. The man's features were big and unfinished, a distracted sketch. He had snot and tears in his beard. I took one of his hands between mine and told him, "Listen. Your life isn't a piece of patio furniture. So long as you're here, it remains intact. Stop crying for a minute and let's see what you have there."

"Scrambled eggs," he said, trembling with new sobs. He handed me the animal. "Smy *friend*."

Turned out it was some sort of small kangaroo. Little red-veined ears. A winsome squirrel face. It was beautiful. And very still, breathing but limp. It stared into my eyes and I stared into its eyes and felt a light knuckling down the length of my spine. The kangaroo was gently cooing, its mouth opening and closing rhythmically. I leaned closer, and its hot breath warmed my face. The man's weeping crescen-doed. I cradled the animal's head and felt some wetness on the neck fur, which I followed to a small black bump, the implant.

"Who did this?" I asked.

"Doctor Face-suck," he said, then gripped his hair and sobbed. On the front of his pants a wet mark began to form at the zipper and bloomed wider and wider. He looked down at his pants, then at me, and cried some more.

I had located the motel via Francine. She'd called me three days earlier, seven weeks into my walk. I was in Elko. She was drunk. The call began something like, "Patti, you dumb cockeye, I'm at the Deluxe Inn Lounge with Evie and I'm not even Francine anymore, I did some things, and we're getting ready to sing the shit out of some shit and where are you? I am so sick of—*Evie, shut up, I'm talking*—Patti, I hope you're

not a ghost. Why don't you come here and sing some—
Goddamnit, Evie—we're in a blood room, a crime scene,
number two-seventeen, except everyone else just *sits* there.
Nobody's any fun. Except the boy."

Then she must've dropped the phone, so I had to yell to be
heard. *"What town are you in, Francine?"* It took a few tries,
but she finally picked up the phone and said, "Is that you,
Patti? What're you doing on the floor? I was just gonna call
you. You're—"

"What town are you in?" I interrupted. "I need a town
and a street name."

"Town? Oh, hell. *Evie!* What's the name of this, what,
Rock. Rock Island. We're on the highway in the land of barking dogs. Hey, Patti, you remember when we—"

I hung up on her. I had what I needed. I hitched a ride
with a guy hauling house batteries in a sixteen-wheeler who
asked me to "polish his knob" for gas money, which I did,
twice, between which I watched and memorized how he
drove the truck, then I stole it after he'd parked alongside
the highway to scope out a suitable place for us to rut in outer
Cheyenne.

In front of me, the kangaroo panted more heavily. Room
217, I guessed, was up above, beyond the balcony overlooking
the pool.

I clutched the kangaroo, closed my eyes, and breathed
deeply to slow my heartbeat. The air smelled like animal protein: throat crust, urine, blood. Rancor. I could feel the kangaroo's suffering, felt the distressed cacophony in its skin and
muscles and tendons and bones.

It was simple triage. Before me were two suffering animals, and their mutual suffering was a pathetic vacuum. The
kangaroo gurgled, and the man was too far gone to realize

his arid wallowing just prolonged the distress. I put my ear to the animal's chest and listened to its heartbeat and the murky fluid-filled insuck of its lungs. I also heard something deeper and meaner and more worrisome, the beginnings of a warning. I was sick of navigating from warning to warning.

"Funmentally," the man was saying, "life's a dry piece of shit with a *tooth* in it."

That did it. I stood and lifted the kangaroo by its stout neck, gripped it tight with both hands, and twisted until I felt the last cartilage snap. I gently set the animal on the ground in front of the man and said, "Now cease your crying, dust yourself off, put on a goddamn shirt, pour some talc on your balls, locate some mouthwash, wait for me to find some important individuals, and get ready to hop in that rig if you're at all interested in getting beyond the present whatever this is."

He leaned over the kangaroo, bent close as if whispering something into its ear. The kangaroo, eyelids wide, tongue lolling, looked cartoonishly outraged. Its eyes had gone cloudy. Blood bubbled from underneath the implant. "I can't just leave him there," the man said. "He and I made a pact—we'd never desert each other."

Hooked to his belt was a big sheathed antler-handled knife. I pointed to it and said, "Get all the meat you can from him. That's his last gift to you. While you do that, I need to find the others."

He looked pitifully at the kangaroo, at me, at the kangaroo again, and said, "You came for them too? You're powerful. Strength recognizes strength, and you're like some kind of bird from under the ocean. You came to take care of everything."

I didn't like the foolish way he was looking at me. I turned and started toward the motel. "Start butchering those haunches," I said with my back to him. "We'll need them wherever we're going."

I climbed the stairs to 217 and pounded on the door. I tried to peek between the shades and the wall but I couldn't see anything. "It's Patti," I said. "Open up." I waited. There were smear marks on the ground, a single child-size sneaker, a toppled hospitality cart. I banged on the door again. "Francine, it's me. Let me in." The shade slowly moved aside, and I saw Francine's round face. She opened the door and let me in, held on to my arm tightly. "We, the kids, that woman. There was a war, we almost, they almost. Everything just."

"Save it," I said. In the corner Spencer, Flora, and the mother were cowering with the boy. It was the first time I'd seen him since he was a toddler. He was exactly what I would've expected if I hadn't quit expecting. He looked at me and I looked at him. I heard an audible click inside my head, heard it as clearly as I'd heard the cracking of the kangaroo's vertebra. "Gather any food and weapons and clothing and come with me," I told them. The boy shined a small flashlight beam at me, just below my eyes. I held out my hand and he took it, and the six of us ran to my big rig.

The man had just finished butchering the kangaroo, the blood eddying into the deep end of the pool. "You in the front and them in the back," I said.

We drove.

NANCY JERNIK

NEW LIBERTY, IA
2040

We huddled around the boy's bookworm flashlight in the back of Patti's truck. We should've been more careful. We should've struck out for the deep wilderness, where they'd never track us down. But we'd let our guard down in that motel, and if it hadn't been for a young man with a beard showing up out of nowhere and holding off that child army, the whole family would have been implanted. I was not going to let it happen again. We were going to keep moving until there were no more maps, no more roads, not a trace of talkers anywhere.

After what seemed like a day but was probably only a few hours, the truck stopped. We waited, each of us holding our breath, until the bearded man cracked open the cargo doors and slipped inside. We were at a gas station, he told us. He tried to calm us with his expressions, but of course Spencer, Flora, and the boy could tell he wasn't calm at all—they could see the swells and peaks of anxiety roiling beneath his wooden face. It was obvious even to me. He told us that he couldn't crack the key code on the truck's gas cap, so we left it by the pumps and carefully filed out one by one. There was a worn dirt path that led to a wooded area set back from the highway, and we followed it. When the path ended we kept going, pressing forward through the brush until we came to a high mesh fence that had rusted yellow warning signs bolted to it. We scaled the fence, the boy clinging to Spencer's back as he climbed over. There was a hill, and when we got to the top there was a small angled shed next to a concrete lot. Spencer and Mr. Dietrich pried open the door of the shed with a branch, and we went inside.

The shed sat atop a spiral staircase that led down to an ancient oxidized blast door. A missile silo. The door was half-open so we slipped through, feeling our way in the near-total darkness. Inside, the air was heavy and sour, smelling of chemicals and sweat. It was clear that many different people had passed through over the years. There was trash everywhere, decades of it piled and fused in drifts on the floor. Graffiti covered every surface, slogans and tags from different eras— *REAGANS A FAGG* was written in huge block letters over the second blast door, across from a massive clown face that was saying *Woop Woop*. In the bathroom there was a drawing of a vagina with eyes and the phrase *Vag Jobs Are For Pussies*. The boy managed to find a working outlet that powered a web of Christmas tree lights stapled to the ceiling of the control room, and when the space lit up we all felt a little tremor of relief. Maybe *relief* is not the right word, but I looked at my family in the dim glow of the lights overhead and thought, Here we are. We were home. It wasn't the pure frontier existence I was hoping for, but it would do.

We began cleaning up the place, tossing the debris down an open hatch. I made a crude broom out of a broken shelving unit and pushed the loose papers and balled dust clods and rotten condoms into the hole. There was a pyramid of old magazines in a corner of the control room, and when I took a stack from the top of the pile I saw a picture of a woman smoking a cigar with her feet propped up on a huge executive desk. The caption said *Call the Shots*. It was an ad for Ambitor—the same ad I'd loved back in that other life, the life I had when Spencer was born. Not even a life, really. Thinking about that period of time was like when you wake up in an odd position and your hand is still asleep. You know that it's part of your body—you know that it belongs to you, but it doesn't feel like you. I can just barely recall the sensation of paralysis, of time stopped, and the wishing away of days, weeks, months. I was trying to destroy myself, I think, for having brought Spencer into the world. For having made this being, this broken child. I was like one of those Spanish monks, beating myself with a leather thong to demonstrate the true depth of my penitence—punishing myself just for being alive, just for being human—only my whip was the Ambitor, and I had no God to watch over me and record my suffering. I was tumbling through the night sky without a parachute, thinking only that when I hit the ground I'd be as broken as Spencer, and we'd find some sort of kinship in our matching flaws. But, of course, there was nothing wrong with Spencer. Spencer was always Spencer, not a broken shard of a person but a whole being, alive in the world. I kept falling, never touching down, getting farther and farther from him until I lost sight of him completely.

That first night in the silo we all slept on the floor of the control room, Patti and Mr. Dietrich folded in among us, everyone under the fleece emergency blanket we'd taken from the cab of the semi. The next morning I woke up and the boy was gone. I disentangled myself from the pile of sleeping bodies and searched the rooms for him. I followed the faint sound of a chain rattling, which seemed to emanate from the top of the shaft. I climbed the spiral stairwell, and when I got to the landing at the top I saw the boy standing in the frame of the blast door. He looked at me with a sly sort of half smile and then leaped into the shaft. My heart, at that moment—it was like it burst into flame and dropped through my body cavity. I bolted toward the opening, where I could see that he was actually swinging on a thick chain that dangled in the center of the shaft. He broke into hysterical, giddy laughter and pumped his legs to swing in wider arcs. He circled the perimeter of the shaft, shrieking with joy as he clung to the rusted links on the chain. It must have been at least an eighty-foot drop to the bottom. I beckoned for him to come out, climb back up, but he just kept pumping harder, swinging more wildly. He was ecstatic. He had an exuberance that was so different from his father. Or had I just made a ruin of his father's childhood? I stood in the frame of the blast door for a while, watching the boy in the grips of all that unmediated pleasure, wondering what sort of life was in store for him. We were underground, literally underground in every way, and we seemed to be safe, at least for now—but safe for what? What kind of life was this for a boy? How much darkness could his little soul endure before it surrendered?

THEODORE GREENE

ROCK ISLAND, IL
2040

I'd seen the halos of pulsing red and blue light from the exit ramp, and already I sensed that I was too late. There was a line of squad cars curbed outside the motel, and cops were milling in the open doorway to room 217, tapping screens, snapping photos of the flayed pelt of some kind of white animal on the blacktop out front. The room was empty, from what I could see. No trace of my family anywhere, just a boy in a bloody T-shirt sitting in the backseat of one of the cars, holding an ice pack to his forehead, and a couple preteen girls sniffling on the curb. I'd been tearing from state to state in the Burgoyne, driving nonstop just to get to the motel, just to make it to my family. I ate only what fit in my hand, what I could carry from the service station door to the passenger seat of my car. I pissed in ditches, in bottles, from the steel girders of overpasses. And once I arrived at the Deluxe Inn Waterfront it was like my body couldn't stop moving.

I pulled up alongside the cruiser with the kid in it and got out. I was pretty out of breath. I approached the kid and he turned away and I saw the implant port in his neck. A cop came up to me, shouting for me to stand back. A woman with sleepy eyes and a dense, squared-off face. She waved me on, but I wasn't moving until I found out what happened. She asked if I was a witness and I said I was a relation. I demanded she tell me what had happened, and she clicked her teeth and said that distributing confidential information about the crime was way above her pay grade. "Who's that?" I said, pointing at the kid. She started to walk away. I said, "Can you just tell me, is my family safe?" and she repeated that she wasn't at liberty. I told her how far I'd just driven to get there, but she wasn't moved. I pointed to the animal bones and she just shrugged.

I parked across the street in the neon shadow of a Ham Cannon marquee and sat. I was just waiting for something to erupt from my soul. I craved some kind of external, physical counterpart to the clawing agony of having just missed my family. Once again, limping just a few steps too far behind. I struggled to fabricate a stream of tears, tried to will myself to regurgitate the bacon cheese sliders I'd eaten on the road, because if I was lucky maybe some part of my stomach or lungs would come spewing out as well. What I maybe wanted most of all was to turn myself inside out, to puke out a perfect inversion of myself that had all the most fragile parts on the outside where they could be most easily destroyed. But nothing came out. My eyes were dry and my stomach was settled. I sat calmly in the Burgoyne and watched the neon pig on the marquee repeatedly burst from the cannon and into the waiting mouth of a man in a cowboy hat.

I closed my eyes and tried to focus on the past. I wanted to conjure a memory of my family before everything came undone. It was hard. I was so fixed on the present, on my ridiculous quest, that I couldn't imagine the world I lived in before. The last one I could muster, we were all in the cabin in Monte Rio, just sitting around the kitchen table picking at leftovers, when Slash came stomping in carrying a carved wooden baton, swinging it around like some sort of marching tribesman. We started to goad him on, clapping and hooting in time to the beat he was laying down with his feet. Pretty soon we were all gathered in a circle around him, following his routine—even Nancy, who usually moved with the cold deliberation of a praying mantis. Even a weird tweaker who'd sleepwalked into the celebration from the woods. Slash would strike a pose and we'd all have to replicate it. Before we could catch our breath he'd be on to something else. Francine was Slash's star acolyte that night, and when she danced she radiated all the light and poise that had drawn me to her all those years ago. I'd backed off from her then, just like I had before, when she was Flora's teacher. I'd stabbed and buried my attraction, for Flora's sake, but what had I achieved? How had that—or anything else I'd ever done—benefited Flora? Now I'm alone, I thought, sitting numb in a shitpod of a car in the middle of nowhere, and Francine was with them, living day to day with my daughter and my grandson. I laughed out loud, a fake chuckle, as if it was some kind of rich irony, not just a fucking mess of a life. Everything I'd ever done for Flora had only set us further apart.

Soon there were just two squad cars left in the motel lot. And then there were none. The door to room 217 was still open, cordoned off with yellow tape. I walked up to the entrance and peered inside. I only caught glimpses of the place in the random ambient headlight glare of cars crossing the overpass. There was the dried bloodstain on the wall. There was the chipboard writing desk, the beds where they slept. None of it made anything clearer to me. No secrets were revealed.

At one point during the dance party, Slash had everyone take a turn in the center of the circle. You had to show him your wildest move. You had to really bust it out for him or he'd give you this comical look of disappointment. And no one wanted to let Slash down. We all had a go at it, with varying degrees of success. When it was Flora's turn, she did this crazy backwards windmill move, and when she landed it she knocked her headband loose. It went rolling across the floor toward the porch. Everyone was focused on Flora, clapping and whistling, but I was watching the headband, because it had belonged to Mel. One of the only things left of her. It must have been no more than a second that I froze, watching the headband wobble toward the door, but Slash saw it—he glanced at me and seemed to intuit right away what was wrong. He ran to the porch, grabbed the headband, and reached up to slip it on Flora's head. She took it from him, laughing, and put it on while everyone cheered. Slash gave me a quick look as if he was trying to see if he'd done the right thing. It all happened so fast. He'd known instantly what that headband meant to me. Even in the middle of all that joyful chaos, he'd known just what to do.

I walked over to the Ham Cannon and went inside. It was dark and narrow and there were just two men waiting in line for their meal. I asked the men how Ham Cannon worked, and they told me that customers stood at one end of a sort of bowling lane that had a ham cannon at the other end. The chef fired ham out of the cannon and you had to catch it in your teeth. It was free to try, but you got charged for any meat that fell to the ground. There was a great advantage, in other words, to a person catching the whole ham between his teeth on the first try. I asked the men how much they'd paid for their last meal there, and one said it cost four hundred dollars because he'd only snagged a bit of the shank. I must've looked surprised, because he quickly added that some people regularly paid over a thousand dollars. The other man just looked embarrassed and turned away.

I watched the men attempt and fail to catch the ham in their teeth. I consoled them as they paid for the meat, and they invited me to eat it with them at one of the square tables in the back of the restaurant. I politely declined, telling them I had somewhere I needed to be. I went back to the Burgoyne to lie down on the backseat and wait for dawn. I didn't think I'd ever see my family again, and it occurred to me that maybe we'd all be better off that way.

FRANCINE CHANG

NEW LIBERTY, IA
2040

I was on the verge of remembering something the entire time we huddled in that dank cavity, among the spent condoms and creosote filth. At first it was the ending of a movie my mom and I went to—I was way too young for it, but she never understood the ratings, probably thought R meant Really Good—at a drive-in theater out past Manassas. In the movie everyone in a small town was imprisoned underground where their body heat was used to power casinos and arcades, and I crawled into the back of our station wagon to escape it. My mom never left movies, no matter how bad or inappropriate. Then I was almost remembering the name of this long-necked girl in my first year at Oaks who spent the entire spring trying to free a thumbtack from a corrugation in her desk where it'd gotten stuck. Started first thing in the morning and didn't stop until the afternoon bell rang. She finally freed it on the third-to-last day of school, and I watched as she brought it closer to inspect it. The look she gave that thumbtack: sheer fatigued disappointment. She hated that her quest was over. For the rest of the day she tried to wedge it back into the corrugation, but it wouldn't go.

Caitlin. Her name was Caitlin.

We couldn't go, we couldn't stay. We were all perched on the crumbling tip of the present. The silo had one working electrical outlet, no running water, and for food we had to wait for big, buzzing David to go out and kill something. He was our hunter-gatherer. He took care of us all, and without him we probably would've starved. My thoughts were still muddy from weeks of mai tai Mondays and tequila shooter Tuesdays and whatever Wednesdays at the Deluxe Inn, so mostly I shivered in my corner of the control room, paying back every jalapeño popper and aperitif with an ice-blood shudder, while I tried to decipher where we were, why we were here, how one reasonable decision after another had somehow led to . . . this.

Spencer and Flora were the abiders, the hunkerers. They interacted only with each other and their son, holding his shoulders, casting messages deep and solidly into him. Flora even tried to prettify the silo, cleaning the walls and using the ancient shelving to build a cockeyed table, which made me so sad. Spencer's mother was their holy ghost. I don't even know what a holy ghost is—saying the words out loud right now makes me think of a very old dog—but she followed the boy around, gave him whatever he would eat of her food, brushed his teeth three times a day with pond water. Sometimes she cried in her sleep. Hearing it, I thought, She's doing it so we don't have to.

I was the factory of regret, and I was extremely efficient. Anything foolish enough to enter the factory was seized and converted: memories, plans, thoughts. I regretted things I'd done to get me here, things I would do once I was out, meals I'd eat and not eat, sentiments unshared, photos untaken, and when I was done I postdated a few hundred more boxes of general, yet-to-be-named regret. I found it oddly reassuring, almost divine. Yielding to a higher powerlessness.

David I watched for a long time. He was hard to pin down, and he didn't say much beyond "here" when he handed us food and "yeah" when we thanked him. At first I found his supplicant act sinister, like a Patti without the hugs. Also, he wore mangled track pants and a mesh shirt and acted terrified of the boy. He often left the room when the boy came in, or if he stayed he wouldn't meet the boy's eyes. His whole body clenched as if in the presence of a god. The boy seemed to sense David's unease—he walked over to him and either just stood there studying him, or he handed him things he found around the silo: a key, a doll's eye, a roll of electrical tape.

One morning I woke up to David and Patti arguing in the main hall. I quietly stood up and walked closer to listen. David was all frantic. He thought the boy was communicating to him, telling him to do something, but what? Patti insisted he calm down, what he was experiencing was explainable, nothing to get so lathered up about. "But I can hear his voice," David kept saying.

"It's your own voice you're hearing," Patti told him.

Their conversations continued. I gathered that David thought he'd been singled out to help. Patti repeatedly coached him not to do anything rash or stupid. This was a new Patti. At Face-to-Face, if I told her one of the silents was trying to communicate with me, she would've told me to listen with my enchanted magical inner ear, my heart-ear, whether they were telling me to kill the pope or put my head in a blast furnace.

The Patti here, now, had been harrowed, or maybe sharpened, a sharpened-bone version of her former self, the rest burned away—but she, too, seemed a little awed by the boy. She stared at him, and when he turned to meet her gaze, she either started to cough or smiled wanly and averted her eyes. One night during dinner I asked how she was feeling and she said, "Slightly closer to death than I was before you asked me that."

So, yeah, she and David were a billion laughs. One night I found him in one of the larger storerooms butchering a . . . well, it had no head or skin, but it looked like a medium-size dog. He sliced off one of the legs and looked up at me, paused, then sliced off another. He used the knife expertly, not wasting any movement as he trimmed fat and gristle and threw it over his shoulder into the center of the shaft.

"You think that's a family animal?" I asked.

David closed his eyes and stabbed his knife into its rib cage. He turned and regarded me with scowly impatience. "Not sure."

"Did it have a collar when you found it?"

He pulled out the knife and continued to cut. I was bored, I was tired of clumping around this metal hole, I would wait him out. No matter his age or his ropey muscles, he was still a boy. Beyond the hurt feelings and bewilderment was a boy who needed someone to listen to him, to take him seriously.

"All I wanted to do was find them and help them. I'm okay that it's only a few of them. I'm okay Wallaby's dead. If it's for a reason. But they won't even move. They've given up."

I asked him what he was planning to do, and he shrugged

and said, "I'm like an ant. I keep going till I get stepped on." He flipped the carcass over and began hacking at the haunches.

Like an ant. I could relate. Following a sticky trail of past students. Carrying crumbs of regret back to the anthill. Waiting for a foot to squash the whole thing.

PATTI KERN

NEW LIBERTY, IA
2040

We had tried, and tried some more, and the trying had become a thundercloud that found me and dumped on me in that silo. At night I dreamed I'd been found guilty of yearning in the third degree—for felony advancement of lost causes. My punishment was life in a cell with wall-to-wall mirrors and recordings of my own voice as I talked about the silents in the early years. *Language is a cage*, and *Listen to all they're not saying*. Words can't be unsaid, and I wouldn't even want to try. Thing is, someone had to be present for the beginning and present for the end—right here, under the earth, with Flora and the child and all of the others—and it was me. I'd wept, hoped, wished, plotted, decried, witnessed, lusted, rerouted, insinuated, suffered. And now I was old, god-damnit. Unsupple, inelastic, dry, cold, old, old. Hands like brittle claws, teeth filthy as a camel's. I thought about my nether areas only during bathroom runs aboveground, and even then the thoughts were in the realm of, Would there be blood in my voidings? There was blood in my voidings. I was dying. I'd always been dying, but now I was more. I could hear death coming like a distant sparrow wing beating ever closer in my skull.

I saw people, fragments. People from Face-to-Face. Friends. Men. Animals. I saw Amanda, the little silent girl who came to my house, the first one I met. She had come to me unsummoned, happenstance and inevitable, like everything. She started me, pushed me into the water. When I was done thinking of Amanda, I'd retrace my path back to the present, skipping over the bilge puddles of bad days. It took me hours. Those who say life is too short are mistaken. Life is long.

In the silo, we all sat huddled in our own orbits. Spencer and Flora, when I first saw them in the motel I hardly recognized them. Particularly Flora. She was still striking, more so than before. Her last traces of girlishness had burned off since leaving California, and all her charisma, allure, whatever you want to call it, had also burned down to a hard, barely aglow coal. I watched her and Spencer while we ate, waiting for some flicker of communion to pass between them, like the unguarded affection I'd seen pass so often between lovers at Face-to-Face, but I couldn't detect anything. I couldn't read them. Complete resignation was about all I could gather. They stayed busy fixing up the silo as best as they could, and spending time with the boy, but their usual glee was in hibernation. Which was okay by me. After the years chained to the door at Nu Ware, I knew I could survive this. I could slow down my heartbeat and mollify my organs and conquer hunger and self-loathing and lower my body temperature to ninety-four. I could survive anything. Except the obvious: life.

David smoldered with frustration, though. He was like some humpbacked warlock pounding away. He mumbled to himself, played with fuses and wires, sharpened knives, meticulously hacked-up animals. Years ago, if someone like him came to Face-to-Face with all that clenched fury I might've gestured for him to watch Flora or any of the others, to follow their cue. I might've put him in one of the more free-wheeling dorms, or slept with him myself and done my Kegel exercises with him inside me to allow a transfer of . . . I don't know what I would've called it. Devotions. Secretions. After I'd found him mooning over his broken wallaby—apparently it was a wallaby—he had been obedient, grateful even, and he still was, but he had a hard time contending with the child. When David told me the child was telling him things, I told him that he was confusing empathy for telepathy.

He insisted it was neither of those, that he knew his own mind and the silents and the sound of thoughts. He said he could feel the boy even when he wasn't in the room.

I tried to bring him down. I told him that the boy was a true silent, a double-silent raised in silence, maybe the first of his kind. "The first and now the last," David said—I had been thinking it too, but this didn't seem like the right time. But yes, all the empathy in that boy, plus all the expectations David brought along? Of course he was going to feel something. But David waved me off. He wasn't having it. He patrolled the edges of his own resolve too vigilantly for me to penetrate.

Our conversations took place in whispers. We were always awake before the others. I took thirty-minute naps every four hours and slept two hours a night. I'd yet to see David lie down.

"The end," he said one day. "That's what this is. All this planning and work. You steal a truck and we drive them to this bloody diaper of a hole in the ground just so we can freeze and die."

I said, "Things end. That's what they do. What choice do we have?"

He looked at me. His face was red and swollen. One eye drooped lower than the other and seemed to be trying to twitch itself back into place. He said, "How come they get to decide everything?" At *they* he gestured vaguely upward—I wasn't sure if he was referring to the aboveground world or a mess of malevolent gods.

He went on about how we needed to do something—*something* was as specific as he ever got—always in the morning, always in that rasping whisper. Once I might have listened, but by now I had heard too much. All my life I had been listening, following, grasping. First running after Most Benevolent Thomas to his cathedral tents in northern Idaho. Then the bobcat sect in Montana. Back east to a series of yogurt cults. Then boyfriends I used to stare at while they slept. Then the silents. I won't disavow any one of them. All of them had potential. All of them fell.

That's what I wanted to tell David: it doesn't matter what you do. Organize a parade. Fondle your aunt. Set a couch on fire. A force calls to you, you follow, but the tail you're chasing is your own. And, yes, David, that's exactly why you find yourself in this bloody diaper of a place. It's what you wanted. It's where you belong. Me too. I was here to see the end of our moment. This was the end—there was no doubt about that. But I just wanted to last long enough to see if all that straggly hope and aspiration and possibility made a sound when it winked out.

DAVID DIETRICH

AMERICAN HIGHWAY
2040

Have you seen pictures of trees and their root systems? Above are the branches and leaves and pinecones and birds and all that, but nothing grows if the roots aren't putting in work. Down below in the cold soil's where everything *happens*. Above it's all stillness and slowness and piggish nattering. Above's just a puked-up version of below.

Everyone had an area in the silo that was their own. My area was three or four flattened cardboards laid out end to end and a shredded shower curtain I pulled over my head for quick naps. Knives tucked into their hiding spots within easy reach, two phosphocreatine lollipops, a printout photo of Wallaby and me with shopped-in cowboy hats made like a *Wanted Dead or Alive* poster, a photo of me with Mom where her face is washed out from too much thumbing, just a ponytail and an eyebrow.

The old women had their cardboards too. Blankets. A water cup with some writing on it. Basics. Flora and Spencer had the boxes, the blankets, a nightstand made with broken shelving, and also a headboard for their cardboard bed, with columns and carved frog-looking animals on top of the columns. Plus a table for the boy to draw on, with a chair Spencer made from scrap wood. The boy had found some talc rocks and used them on the metal wall to doodle birds and bats and trees. They kept the area swept neat, and there was an understood perimeter around it—I always made sure they saw me and acknowledged me before I entered. They slept with the boy between them, each of them with a hand on him. They watched him even when he wasn't in the room with them.

The silo was awful, it made me want to pull out my chest hairs one by one, which I often did before nodding off—but it was necessary. Sometimes you need to be below things.

In Decatur, when Mom was in her last throes with the albino magician, she started coming home more, cooking for me, asking questions about school. She had essentially rejected me to move in with this dude, and now here she was stirring up tuna noodle gratin, saying let's go see a movie, let's buy you some new jeans or a bearded dragon lizard for the terrarium she gave me for Christmas two years ago, which I kept my change and stolen chromies in. She offered me a ride to the pool. Her lipstick was smeared. She looked so old and used up. A hook with the bait chewed off. I asked her what the old albino was up to, why didn't she buy some new panties and go over there and try to guess what card he was thinking of and make him a potpie or something.

She collected her keys and left, left for good. I saw the albino at the mall a few weeks later and he asked me how she was holding up, and I told him I had no idea, wasn't she still shacked up with him? Not anymore, he said. Not since . . . there was a little misunderstanding and she accidentally broke her wrist on his countertop and sometimes love burns bright but doesn't stay burning. Wink wink. Maybe she found a new love across town—he hoped she did. I just watched him walk off carrying his crappy fucking Foot Locker bag. I watched him without doing a damn thing.

What'd she distract herself with when she was lying in the hospital waiting for the doctor to reset her bones? I wondered. I wonder. Why didn't I just let her take me to the pool even if I didn't feel like swimming, let her be a mom for a little while without having to remind her of all the times she hadn't been one?

Almost all realizations come too late. Except, one afternoon down in the silo I was cleaning a schnauzer, which I had tracked for almost three hours, through briars and a tire dump and fields of headless wheat. I was coughing with frustration. I was angry at the others for being content to burrow like blind rodents. At myself for chasing what I thought I wanted, refusing to let up long after I didn't want it anymore. At the dead schnauzer for being so fast and skinny and making me jog eight miles for its stringy nothingness. So I was hacking and pulling and cursing and hacking, and I paused to wipe some blood off my cheek. In the room where I was butchering there was a plate-glass window that Flora had wiped clean. I couldn't see myself clearly in it, but I saw enough: beard, matted hair, butcher's knife, coveralls. What was I pretending to be now? Commando, mercenary, slave? In a world of frauds and impostors I was the fraud king. The best and the worst. Any other day I'd swing out and smash that glass and then I'd feel better and terrible. But that would be more pretending. I was tired of pretending. Tired of all the words and stories we hide behind.

I wonder if every kid starts out thinking he'll do something remarkable. I never thought that. Far back as I remember I never felt permanent about anything I did. I wanted to,

I tried to, but there was always doubt followed by shame followed by fury, refusal, shame again. But that's past. That's aboveground. Down in the silo, down below, I can see more clearly. I can be different. I can bring people together, make them stop what they're doing and pay attention and feel. It won't take much. I'm not scratching some dull itch anymore, not trying to fill a hole or scrambling to prove something. I'm so tired of the sound of my own voice. You've heard enough of these recordings. I feel warm. I feel like everything's been sucked out and I'm bald and ready to take flight.

I left the silo in the morning like I usually did, and I just kept walking. The farther away I got, the closer I felt to everyone there. All of them. And everyone up above, too. All those people living invisibly in their houses. A plan took shape in my head while I walked, and by the time I'd stolen a Venezuelan one-seater and was headed east, the plan was a certainty.

I will not dream about how anything I do will be perceived. I will not worry about how people talk about me after I'm done. I shouldn't even say it out loud. Saying it makes it less true. Saying anything. I love you. That's not true. I'm sorry. I'm not. All my life I have talked and talked, and it's been just a thin skate on the crusted-over surface of nothing. A babble blown dead by the wind. You, too. Aren't you tired of it? Now it's time to follow the end that's been there all along, waiting for me all the time I spent running, following, hiding. All that separates us is a tiny line. It's time to step over.

CALVIN ANDERSEN

ACADIA NATIONAL PARK, ME
2040

I was in the control room late at night when I heard the noise. It came from above and started hollow and shrill, like a marble slowly circling the basin of a copper pot. I was hypersensitive to any unusual sounds after hours, because team members weren't supposed to be in the control room past 8:00 p.m. Especially not if they were in the control room with the calibration helmet strapped on, randomly dialing in to people's implants and beaming neural patterns of self-doubt and whiskey-sick, which was my particular cocktail that night. Also, I wasn't wearing any pants, which was another thing that went against Burnham's *Principles of the Designer's Biome*. But the coordinated flat-front wool trousers we were assigned were painfully itchy, and so I'd taken them off to let my thighs get some air while I scrolled through the implantee network directory to find hapless victims to grief. Which was a third thing team members weren't supposed to do in the control room. So when I heard that noise I went rigid in my chair. Time slowed to a halt, and I felt thirsty and cold.

The sound came from far off, almost as though it was

occurring in another building, although of course that was impossible, because it was just the eight of us in that sprawling treehouse in the middle of goddamn nowhere. No matter how hard I focused on the sound, I couldn't figure out what it was. A mourning rodent? An old woman wheezing into a paper bag? And then, just as suddenly as it started, it stopped, leaving just the normal rush of the temperature regulation system and the sixty-hertz drone of the projectors that displayed the millions of phrases that streamed through the PhonCom data center every minute of every day—every word spoken by every implantee—a shifting white fractal cloud of characters set out against a blue background. This industrial hush was all I could hear for almost a minute, and then there was a percussive thud, loud and flat. It sounded like a server rack crashing to the floor. I checked the load balance and everything seemed normal, but I still felt a warping sensation in my gut. I stood and walked slowly toward the door, taking an old drafting compass from one of Burnham's Inspiration Vitrines as I went. I held the pointy end of the compass out like a switchblade and padded to the threshold, where I stood for a small eternity, waiting for another sound.

I heard nothing, but my stomach still churned. I shut my eyes and listened closely. Through the whooshing of the ventilation system I could detect a rhythmic clicking pattern coming from the server room. Click-click-click stop. Click-click-click stop. Again and again. It sounded like a person trying to open a combination safe or adjusting the settings on a power tool. I crept out into the hallway, naked but for my boxer briefs, an *Ask Me About North American Conifer Bark* shirt that Burnham had given me for my birthday, and the calibration helmet. I carefully made my way to the server room, everything inside me taut and alert. The compass was slick in my sweaty hand.

The door to the server room was closed but unlocked. To guard against hackers, the network was protected by a class-five self-randomizing firewall, but we were in such a remote location that it never occurred to us that the servers themselves could be attacked. The clicking sound continued as I pulled the door open and slipped inside. The space was illuminated only by the flickering red and yellow network traffic bars that surged and receded as waves of data passed through the system. There was a crude hole cut in the ceiling tile above the console, and a dark shape crouched in the center aisle. It was a small man with stringy muscles and a wispy beard, wearing forest-camo combat coveralls, a crude bone necklace, and what looked like a sheathed knife. I watched him unspool a length of multicolored cable from a black backpack and plug it into one of the RAID units. He unzipped the bag and started punching numbers into a keypad welded into the face of a green canister that looked like a scuba tank. I stood there silently, just watching him perform his tasks. He moved carefully and efficiently, as though he'd spent years in rehearsal for the event.

He punched in a sequence of numbers and the server rack on the far wall lit up as the units began to overload. The error tone played on the loudspeakers and the man looked up, surprised. He saw me standing by the doorway and froze in a half crouch, rising slowly with his hands up as though I was going to apprehend him. I saw that he had a bone-handled machete, but I wasn't alarmed. I was as calm as a midnight desert. I watched his face in the red light. Whatever he'd come to do, he wasn't going to be stopped—I could tell by the way he regarded me, his mouth turned slightly downward, his eyes focused at an apologetic distance. I returned his gaze to let him know I had no plans to interfere. There was nothing in that room that I cared to protect. I turned around and walked out of the server room, closing the door behind me, and turned down the hallway. I kept walking, past the control room, past the test chambers, through the lobby, and out the twin glass sliding doors to the observation deck. The canopy blocked the moonlight, so I had to make my way to the steel railing by intuition. I leaned out over the edge and listened to the screech and whoop of the birds, trying and failing to tell one species from another in their incomprehensible symphony.

Then the blast came—a low, concentrated thunderclap that took me down in an instant, knocking the wind out of me. A searing pain shot through my skull, so fast and hard that I remember thinking I must have been hit by a bullet, but as I lay with my hands clamped over the smooth surface of the helmet I realized that the pulsing came from the inside. My ears rang and I felt like my head had split open and all the words I'd ever learned were streaming out onto the ground. It was the pure, grinding sensation of losing my mind.

STEVEN GRENIER

CHARLOTTESVILLE, VA
2040

We know from the surveillance records that Dietrich entered the PhonCom facility at approximately 9:41 p.m., and that he used a Madrid Blacktooth demo saw, which he'd shoplifted two days earlier from a hardware superstore, to cut a port in the roof. He then crawled through the vent system, cutting a second hole to drop into the server room. He breached the firewall and installed a worm of unknown origin, most likely a pirate job from one of those sub-Saharan hacker cults. The worm bore through the PhonCom data set, completely tearing it to shreds within about a minute and a half. It quickly compromised all of the mirror server sites worldwide, so that by the time Dietrich blew himself up, taking the core servers with him, the PhonCom application was completely obliterated.

No one from Dr. Burnham's design team was injured in the blast, although Burnham himself hasn't yet come forward with a statement. The design director, Calvin Andersen, was missing when authorities arrived on the scene. Security camera footage shows him entering the server room after Dietrich had begun his operation. We're still waiting to hear whether there is any connection between Dietrich and Andersen.

Dietrich's remains are currently being scanned at a forensic imaging center in Kittery. The stolen vehicle he used to get to the facility was found in a parking lot in Acadia National Park. He'd carefully arranged a set of items on the passenger seat, apparently for authorities to find once he'd completed his task. They included the leg bone of an adult wallaby, a 1/144th-scale replica of the *Enola Gay*, and Huynh's two-volume *Encyclopedia of Microexpressions*.

Of course, nobody was aware of any of this at the time. I was in Charlottesville visiting a friend from the consulate whose implanted granddaughter was stepping up to middle school. We were sitting at the dinner table after the ceremony, passing around a second bottle of wine, when the girl came into the dining room holding a plush manatee by the throat. Her eyes were wide open and her pupils were dilated as far as they could go. She opened her mouth to say something, but nothing came out. The girl's mother got up to find out what was wrong, and when she did the girl crumpled into a fetal position on the floor and started flailing and grasping at her forehead as if it was full of hornets.

I rode with the girl's father to the emergency room. I've seen plenty of seizures and paroxysms and psychotic fugues before, but there was something about the girl's behavior that unsettled me. It was really like she was possessed by a spirit. She shook and flailed in the backseat, panting. Her father just kept trying to stroke her hair and whisper soothing reassurances, and all I remember of that trip was the streaking of the highway lights in the night and the father's hushed mantra of "I'm here, I'm right here." I heard a strain of desperation in his voice as he struggled to say something that mattered, something that might bring her back from the dark place she was in.

We rushed into the emergency room and saw that we were not alone. There were three other implanted children in the waiting area exhibiting the same symptoms. A young Asian boy squatted underneath the news monitor, covering his ears with his hands and quietly moaning. His eyes had the same wide, deadened look as my friend's granddaughter. Another boy was crawling underneath the chairs, barking out nonsense sounds and scraping his forehead against the carpet. An older girl looked passed out in her parents' laps, lolling her head back and forth and hissing. I told the father to sit with the girl and approached the receptionist.

"What's going on here?" I asked, and she looked at me like I was an infant. "This is an emergency room, sir," she said. "Please excuse us if it's a little hectic." I pointed to the kids in the waiting room and said, "Do you not see this? Does this not seem unusual to you?" She just asked me to sit down.

We sat there for a long time. The girl did not look good. She seemed to be in another world, nodding and twitching with her eyes half-closed. Whenever her father asked her how she felt, she just coughed and let out a low, gravelly sigh. He held her close to his chest and rocked her, and I told him I'd walk around and find a coffee machine.

In the hallway I called Bogdan and told him what was going on. He said, "Steve, what are you trying to do, get back in the game?" and I told him I didn't know. I said I just had that feeling in my gut. Seeing that girl in the throes of something, it just gave me that sour tingling sensation that usually meant a story. Bogdan said, "You're right about there being a story, bud, but you're a little late."

I went back into the waiting room and brought up a news

site on the overhead monitor. There was a shot of a school gymnasium in Manhattan that was packed with wailing kids who were gnashing their teeth and sobbing and slapping their temples. The ticker read *City silents racked by unexplained behavior*. The camera cut to a man in riot gear talking to an offscreen interviewer, but it was impossible to hear what he was saying over the animal howlings of the children in the ER.

AUGUST BURNHAM

PORTLAND, ME
2040

I admit there was a dark wisdom to the terrorist's plan. The worm bore a hole through the heart of the code base, and the destruction of the central server bank prevented us from dealing with the hemorrhage until it was far too late. PhonCom could easily have survived either one of those events in isolation, but the synchronized combination of the two did us in. Which is why I'm skeptical of claims that Dietrich was simply a loner with a death wish. He didn't just toss a Molotov cocktail into the server room—he carefully planted and detonated the explosive device in such a way that it sent a surge of considerable strength through the entire infrastructure, frying everything. It was a well-planned and well-executed plot, and it may be some time before we understand exactly what he was trying to accomplish. On the night of the explosion we just stood around the burning wreckage in our pajamas, stunned, while the worm spread across the globe, grinding PhonCom to pixel dust. Rendering the implant completely useless. Crippling the linguistic faculties of every implanted silent worldwide.

I spent the majority of the day after the disaster in conference with the NIH, the CDC, and representatives from about a dozen other state and federal organizations, all of us trying to figure out how to respond to the crisis. I had bad news for them. The genesis code for PhonCom had been corrupted—I couldn't even begin to speculate on how long it would take to get the system back online. I recommended the establishment of triage centers worldwide where we could assess the patients and work our way toward an interim solution. My vague sense of the possible effects of a sudden absence of language was validated by some of the early news reports—a vertigo-like disorientation, a perceived distortion of space and time, and a hypersensitivity to certain sounds—but it was impossible to say how these reactions would change over time. They could fade or flare, and there was no way of telling which way the wind would fan the flames. Containment was key, I told the committee. Close observation and the administration of pre-emptive palliative care were vital to ensuring that affected patients would endure the blackout.

Late in the afternoon I was taken by helicopter to a YMCA in Portland to observe the triage operation that had been set up there. As we lifted off I craned my neck to see the tops of the massive red spruces of Acadia National Park. I willed myself to focus on the beauty of the terrain and not on the fact that my life's work had been ravaged in less than a minute by a skinny brute with a death wish. There was an empty seat next to me that should've been occupied by Calvin. He'd surely been affected by the blackout, and had probably run off in fear, thinking that the whole thing was somehow his fault. I felt a crushing pressure on my heart when I thought of Calvin, but I put that aside, as well, so that I could focus on the blackout itself. Every decision I made would be critical to the survival of implantees everywhere. I had to be sharp. I had to project an aura of control and command.

We got to the gymnasium as the sun was setting, and the haze around the building seemed to contribute to the general sense of unease. Families stood in long, slow-moving lines through a maze of nylon cordons, carrying or restraining their children as they waited to be checked in. Parents who had already admitted their kids for testing lingered in the hallways, staring blankly at the trophy cases and team photos. The place reeked of foam and chlorine and it was hard to hear anything above the din of children hooting and grunting.

I was ushered into an examination area where a shirtless young boy with wild matted hair cowered in his mother's arms. Both were implantees. The boy rammed his head into the woman's chest again and again, and she bore the blows with exhausted resolve. I motioned for the mother to place the boy on the portable exam cot. She rose and tried to move the boy to the cot, but he started whaling on her with his arms and legs. Two volunteers stepped in, and the three of us were able to separate the boy and pin him down. All I wanted to do was check his vitals, but he struggled like I was about to murder him.

The boy was showing all of the classic symptoms of acute stress reaction. The volunteers gave him a sedative patch, which should've put him right down, but it had almost no effect. I tried to communicate with him using the flash-card method, but he just stared at me, gritting his teeth, while the volunteers held him down.

A young man in scrubs entered the exam area. He was a licensed pediatrician, but he looked like a teenager, with a landmass of acne spread across his left cheek. "I heard you'd arrived," he said. "Now maybe we can get some answers."

"Answers to what?" I asked. The man gave me a look like I'd just eaten my own feces, and turned to the mother to console her. She stared at her boy with a stoic grimace, as if she could project her strength onto him, somehow will him out of his hysteria. It occurred to me only then that children seemed to be more deeply affected than their parents at the implant blackout. It made sense. Children who were implanted as babies had never known what life was like without it. In a single instant, just like that, the voice in their head was replaced with static, nothing but a vacuum where their thoughts had once taken shape. The feeling must have been akin to a hand reaching down from the heavens and yanking their brains right out of their skulls.

The boy broke free from the volunteers and hoisted himself up to the top of the foldaway bleachers. The mother pushed past me and tried to go up after him, but he was too fast. He leaped from the bleachers onto the backboard of the basketball hoop, barking and hissing at the volunteers below as they tried to coax him down with foam batons. A thundering chorus rose in the gym as other children caught sight of the boy. With his long, unkempt hair and his shirtless back he looked like a young Tarzan. A group of children gathered under the net and howled as the boy climbed the suspension shaft to the ceiling and popped out one of the perforated acoustic tiles. He disappeared through the hole and his peers went wild, screeching and clawing as the volunteers tried to restrain them. The pediatrician stood dumbly underneath the hoop, staring up at the ceiling. I went into the men's room and ran cold water through the tap. When the basin was full, I dunked myself and held my breath until I could no longer feel my face.

GORTON VAHER

I was a sculptor back in Lithuania, nationally known, but after the purge the best job I found was chief of edible ice art aboard a fake cruise. The SS *Muir*, sixteen nights of entertaining children and child-brained adults with dessert-size replicas of famous ecosystems and oil spills, colored with flavored syrups. Does it sound fun? It was not fun. The other workers treated me like a piano-bar whore. Everyone called me Iceman—"Iceman, table sixteen wants lemon-lime condor nests"; "Iceman, some woman says her Nile basin tastes like cough suppressant." Everyone but Persephone. She called me Gorton. And once, Gor. It made my stomach leap. *Gor.* I loved it. Then on day three of the cruise, the implants fizzled out and Persephone stopped calling me anything at all.

I searched for her as soon as I heard the news, but she was nowhere. And then she appeared at dinner, calm and conscious but floating from station to station, smiling as if from a great distance. I saw her staring into a bowl of origami albatrosses, and I patted her shoulder like I sometimes did and asked if she needed help. She tilted her head and smiled with her eyes, and whether she needed help or not, I helped her.

The kids, the implanted ones, were immediately a handful. They couldn't tolerate the predinner movie minutes, which were only forty seconds long. A few had nasty stings from trying to battle each other with baby stingrays from the petting pool. Some parents demanded that the captain unlock the main doors, but he refused. The *Muir* emphasized authenticity above all else—not just ocean sounds and randomized storm patterns and ninety-eight simulated portholes, but also the door policy. Once the doors were closed and time-locked, you were setting sail on the open ocean for the duration. We'd had heart attacks, panic attacks, women going into early labor. There was a medical staff on board, but they weren't prepared for anything like this. No one was. "We're in the middle of the Pacific," the captain said. "The nearest port's eight hundred miles away."

"We're not in the middle of the Pacific," said one of the fathers. "We're in southeast Philadelphia. I can smell hot garbage and urine from my cabin."

Our info from outside was fuzzy, and I think everyone assumed the implants would come back online in a day or two. So we carried on like good sailors, ice art and all. I spent most of my shift avoiding the kids, stalling at a table of senior women who wanted me to carve the Patagonia bone fields out of their seventeen-inch slab. Meanwhile, moms and dads had to grip their children by the arm to make sure they didn't run off. I saw one mom holding an infant in her lap nursing a different kid, I guess the brother, who was way too old to be nursing. The mom said to him, "You full yet, sweetie?" and he just stared at her, eyes full of fuming hunger.

It got worse each day, brawling siblings, angry kids splashing around in the toilets, gleeful toddlers in the kitchen walk-in eating someone's four-tiered anniversary cake, eating and eating until they vomited all over the grated floor.

And mealtimes, the worst—shattering plates, flying food, shouting parents. Most people just stocked up on smoked crab buns and hid out in their rooms, waiting for the cruise to be over. But the staff had to soldier on. Upstairs in the Oasis Room, I readied my mobile ice station, refilled the sixteen syrups, made sure my liquid nitrogen was full and that the etching drill was sharp. I noticed Persephone at a table with five rabid beasts, doing her best to clear the dinner course while the kids tried to wrench away the porcelain butter frog. She held the frog high in the air, where they couldn't reach it. I was afraid they were going to go after her, so I wheeled my cart over to the table. Once I pulled up and started doing my here-comes-the-edible-ice-art whistle, the kids only had eyes for me and my nozzles and tubes.

I started with something simple, the Serengeti's legendary baobab in lime and chocolate syrup. The kids banged their forks, licked their plates, pulled hair, but I forged on, sketching out the trunk and fuzzing the leaves. But when I reached for the green syrup to give the foliage some depth, the nozzle was already unholstered. I followed the tube under the table, where a mule-faced girl was suckling straight from the hose, pure concentrated sugar. I snatched it away from her. Her top lip raised and I thought she might start bawling, but instead she, this toddler in a lace dress, she snarled at me. That's when my hoses fell limp. I looked down to see a boy with a ponytail slurping the syrup straight from the canister, with two others punching and clawing at him. I dumped the three kids and tried to push the cart clear.

That was when I heard my rotary drill start up, and I saw

that Mule Face was aiming it dangerously close to my *varpa*. I gave a shrill little yelp, I'm not ashamed to admit it, and leaped back, but my feet got tangled in the tubes and hoses and I fell. The girl came closer, and I frantically wriggled under the table, ready at any minute to feel something awful.

Persephone suddenly appeared between the two of us. She gave the kids a look that froze them where they stood, syrup dribbling onto the floor. I stared up at her, trying to keep my eyes from watering. I separated her face into quadrants, like you would a sculpture, but each quadrant seemed to be doing something different. Persephone yanked out the tubes and helped me to my feet, and we ran toward the kitchen while behind us the kids were still fighting over the syrup. At some point the scrum heaved toward Ramiro's flambé station, which tipped over. A paper albatross caught fire, and spread to the tablecloth. Parents were shouting orders, trying to corral their families, pushing others out of the way. Then the sprinklers went off, and pretty soon everyone was jostling toward the exits. Except, no one knew where the exits were.

I took Persephone's hand and yelled, "Follow me," to everyone, and headed for the employee exit beneath the kitchen. Behind us a propane tank exploded, a loud deep blast followed by a billow of white smoke into the hallway. I let go of Persephone in the sweaty swirling chaos but then found her hand again, and this time her grip was tight.

We made our way into the kitchen, through the prep station, and downstairs to the employee door. I kicked the emergency exit handle, and we all streamed out of the ship and onto the rainy sidewalk. Still holding hands, I turned to Persephone, except instead of Persephone it was a tall older man with serious-looking scratch marks on his cheek. He said, "Thanks for helping." I told him, "No need to thank me, I would've done it for anybody." I had done it for anybody. He continued to hold my hand while he sat down on a curb. In the distance I could see Persephone walking away, into the lit-up tangle of buildings and signs.

KENULE MITEE

BROOKLYN, NY
2040

I was fixing a flat on one of my carts in the storage bay when the policeman came rushing up at me, waving his baton. He said I needed to get out fast. Some of the wild children were running loose in the mall, and they were closing it down until they could control the situation. I was angry, because I had to make a living. My boys had to make a living. And we were being shut down because of a bunch of children? How dangerous could they be? I put my tools away and locked up the cart.

As I was leaving I saw Fish, one of my crew, laid out on the floor next to the Nachoteria. His cheek was swollen and bloody. I knelt down and saw that his face was really bad—there were teeth marks, and a flap of torn skin was hanging loose. Blood all over, and his shirt was ripped and stained. "What happened?" I said to him. He just stared at me. I kept forgetting that he could no longer speak, that his implant was just a tiny dead speck lodged in his head.

I lifted him by the arm and we headed toward the east wing of the mall, where there was a Wound World outlet. An evacuation notice played on the loudspeakers, and people ran past us in the opposite direction, holding their bags close. We saw two security guards hauling a fat woman out of the Zen Pond while her motorized wheelchair slowly sank to the bottom. The woman had a bite on her arm that looked like Fish's cheek, and she wailed as the men struggled to bring her on land. I thought of Isoke, at home in our apartment, eight months pregnant with our son, and I went cold with dread—I knew I needed to leave this place.

Farther down the main promenade we saw one of the wild children. A small girl, maybe nine or ten, clinging to the top of a palm tree. She had a golf club in her hand and she was swaying back and forth like a trapped animal, growling at a police officer in riot gear holding a net. The officer swatted at the kid as we went by, but she just knocked the net away with the golf club and then climbed up onto one of the rafters that held up the sky-dome.

We entered Wound World cautiously. Half of the lights were out and it was deathly quiet. I walked slowly down the dressings and splints aisle. Fish was right behind me. I was reaching for a box of bandages when something crashed to the floor at the end of the aisle—a box of metal scalpels that scattered across the linoleum. I jumped back, and Fish clamped his hand on my shoulder. He pointed down the aisle, and through the gloom I could make out three children huddled by a dialysis chamber. I let out a little yelp, a sound beyond my control. The kind of noise a frightened dog would make. The children hissed at us, and we turned and ran so fast, as fast as our legs would carry us. I did not care or think about anything else but getting as far from those children as possible. We ran straight across the promenade into the Sunglass Hut and hid behind the counter.

I found a roll of masking tape in a plastic bin beneath the register, and I wrapped this around Fish's head to stop the bleeding. He slumped against the wall and shut his eyes while I watched the children lurk inside Wound World. They seemed to be as anxious to leave as we were, but every time they approached the glass entrance they'd jerk back from some threat we couldn't see. There was a girl in cornrows and two white boys, and they kept taking swings at one another and scratching and making terrible guttural noises. Sounds of confusion and suffering that I had never heard before from a human being. It was a terrible thing to witness.

We heard a popping sound that I remembered well from my youth—the bursting of a tear-gas grenade. It rolled through the entrance to Wound World, spraying out a grayish-brown cloud of smoke as it disappeared into the store. Three men and a woman in respirators and padded black jumpsuits were sneaking slowly toward the entrance. One of the men held a long chrome tube with a nozzle that was attached to a tank on his back, and when the little girl emerged from the store, coughing and spitting, the man sprayed a tan foam at her— that kind of foam that hardens instantly, like what they used to hold back the crowds in the Pusan riots. The foam stiffened around the girl, stopping her in her tracks. The woman ran forward and dragged the girl in her foam cocoon onto a green metal caddy. The others went inside and sprayed the remaining children. I could see the fear in their faces as they were wheeled out of the store and down the promenade to the police vehicle backed up to the entrance of the mall. They were like animals that had found their way in but couldn't figure out how to leave.

When all of the kids had been extracted from Wound World, we darted in and grabbed a few boxes of bandages. I tore off the tape from Fish's face and drizzled antiseptic gel over the area. Fish winced as I wrapped a bandage around his head, and then we sprinted out of the mall and across the vacant fields to the medical center by the expressway, which was packed with people. Fish stopped me in the entranceway and put his hand over my heart, which I took to mean, "Go home to your wife." I hated to leave him there, but I was anxious to see Isoke. I embraced him and told him I would check on him as soon as I could. The words meant nothing to him, but he nodded.

I took a bus back to my apartment. The driver had to stop several times to avoid hitting children who were skittering across the street. It took almost two hours to go just a couple miles. When I finally got back to my apartment, there was a man in the doorway of the elevator holding his daughter down while his wife shouted into a phone. The elevator doors kept closing and reopening on the man and his daughter. I went up the back stairs and burst into the apartment, where I found Isoke in bed under the covers. I held her while we watched the news. An armored van pulled up to the local gymnasium, and a team of police dragged frantic children out one by one. I lay there stunned and numb, running my hand along the curve of Isoke's belly. I was breathing so fast. We were going to bring a new life into this crazed place? It felt like Isoke and I were the very last people on earth, living on a piece of land the size of a postage stamp, surrounded by a wicked and treacherous forest. There was no room for another.

VOLUME SIX

CALVIN ANDERSEN

ROCK ISLAND, IL
2040

I don't remember the night of the explosion very well. Only that when I woke up I began to walk. I walked through the woods in the darkness, away from the burning lab. I used the light from the fire to find my way, and then the light was gone and even the shrieking of the birds was done, and I was just walking in the pure dark. My mind was clear and clean. I was aware that words had once occupied some territory in my brain—I could sense the power they once had over me, but I knew that they were gone. It was impossible to imagine what they looked or sounded like, or how my tongue could be convinced to shape one. I did not feel exhilaration or relief. I just felt focus, complete focus on the task at hand.

The sun rose over the ocean and I was walking south on a coastal highway. I wiped the sweat from my forehead, and there was dirt and flecks of caked blood in my palm. I had no pants on, and I was still wearing the calibration helmet, but I felt right. I felt like myself for the first time in years. Something inside of me was newly aligned. I thought about

Burnham, and I could not understand why I had spent so much of my life trying to do what he wanted.

The brawl at the motel in Rock Island had been a momentary flare in the news stream. An isolated novelty, just barely worth reporting. But I understood the real story. The explosion at the lab was the opening salvo in a long war, one that I wanted to be a part of. The resisters were out there, living on the frontier beyond language, and they were thriving. I would find them, and they would teach me how to live this way, how to protect this quiet that I had forgotten I possessed.

I walked along the highway for many more hours. Eventually a trucker stopped and leaned across the cab to open the door for me. I saw that he wasn't wearing pants either. I backed away, but he looked at me reassuringly and said something that appeared genuinely comforting. His face suggested a casual confidence, as if he was just saying, "Hey, there's nothing weird about this. We're just two guys driving along the highway without pants on." He looked like a whiskey barrel with a Santa Claus beard. I told him where I wanted to go, but when I went to speak it didn't feel like a string of words. It was more like a song playing in reverse. But the driver seemed to understand. I climbed into the cab and buckled my seat belt. He found a Kazakh black-metal playlist on his dashboard, and we listened all the way to the Iowa state line. He bought me cheesequakes and bacon rings whenever we stopped at service stations, and all I had to do in return was sit next to him and hold his hand as the black-metal vocalists brayed from some deep hidden hollow in their throats.

The driver let me out on an overpass above the motel. It was smaller than it had seemed in the news footage. The rooftop was littered with bits of junk that had been blown from the road, hubcaps and rearview mirror casings and headlamp fragments. Two young girls crouched in the lee of a dryer vent that stuck out between shingles, sharing a glass pipe while a man in a jumpsuit nervously kept watch. Part of the marquee had fallen away, revealing one of the motel's previous identities as a horse-themed motor inn. There was a star-shaped pool cordoned off with yellow safety tape and a deflated bounce house at the far end of the parking lot, which was mostly empty.

I walked down to room 217, which was where they had said the family was staying. I stood at the door and tried to bring myself to knock. I even raised my fist, but somehow the idea of the sound was terrifying. Instead, I crouched by the window and tried to peer between the slats in the blinds. The room was dark and seemed deserted. The bed was unmade, the sheets wadded up by the nightstand. Empty beer cans on the floor. It looked more like a squatter's hideout than the cradle of the silent revolution.

I turned around and slumped against the wall. Everything since the explosion had been a long dream, and now suddenly I was awake, with absolutely no idea what to do next. There was a soft pink light pulsing through a window next to the reservations desk, and I got up and followed the light to a lounge, where an older woman in a purple sequined blouse sang karaoke on a small stage. I sat down at the bar and watched her, just so that my body would have something to do. The bartender placed a drink before me, and when I looked up he pointed down the bar to an old man with wild, matted hair. The man smiled and waved his hand over his head, mimicking the contours of the calibration helmet. I had been wearing it for so long that I had forgotten it was there. I'd just accepted it as a part of my own head. I stared at the man deliberately without expression. When he saw me look at him like that, his face changed. His smile faded by a degree and he crinkled his eyes a little, almost like he was about to wink at me, but stopping just short of it. I could tell he knew why I was there, and that he'd come for the same thing. There was nothing else for us to do but sit there for the rest of the night, slowly drinking ourselves to a state of blindness while the woman struggled at the microphone to hit even one correct note. I had to admire her courage.

THEODORE GREENE

ROCK ISLAND, IL
2040

The clerk initially wasn't going to let me stay in room 217, even though the cops had already scoured the place, taken all the evidence, and left. It made her nervous even to consider it, and she offered up a litany of excuses to dissuade me. She said the shower wasn't working and I said, "Don't give a flying one." She said there was blood on the wall and I said, "That sounds about right." She said bad things happened in that room, that it was unlucky, that nothing good had come of anyone who stayed there. I just stood at the counter, cleaning my nails with a complimentary refrigerator magnet until she sighed and gave me the key.

I went to the room and lay on the cold bed. I lay there for as long as I possibly could. I tried to visualize my body turning to ashes. I thought I might actually be able to burn myself alive using only my mind. My body would flake apart into a cloud of black fragments and drift in tiny eddies around the room, disintegrating in midair, nothing left of me in the end but a gray impression on the comforter. I thought about Flora lying in this same exact spot, just a day before, before she had slipped away from me yet again.

I woke up to the sound of a crowd cheering. The motel had set the monitor to automatically turn on at 7:00 a.m. I opened one eye and saw the screen smeared with pulsing garish colors, gauzy silhouettes of men in pitched action. I rubbed my eyes and blinked. It was the opening rounds of the Reno Invitational Bi-Continental Jai Alai Championship Series. Hartford had just beaten Des Moines. Three hours later I was still in the same position, still watching.

It was an intense day. The 11:30 match, Asheville against Tuscaloosa, was especially grinding. In a battle of a single point, Olabe, who as far as I could tell was Asheville's finest, finally got a shorter reply and flung a left side as a low *cortada* with outside placement, but the shot just hit too low. Olabe went ballistic. It was the first time anybody had seen him blow up like that, the announcers said. They replayed the tantrum again and again, frame by frame. They commented on the twisted look of anguish that spread across his face in ultraslow motion—they were surprised, but I knew that particular expression well, the dawning realization that the future will be pretty much like the past.

Eventually I sat up in the bed. The room listed and swam. I crawled to the quarter fridge under the desk and saw that it was full of tallboys. I could have as many as I liked for eighteen dollars each. I felt a bit like a fool for taking the first one, because I could've probably walked down the highway and bought a whole case for less than that. But it got easier and easier to pop them open as the day went on. By nightfall the fridge was empty, but the tournament was just heating up, so I decided to venture down the hall to the motel bar to keep the buzz alive.

The lounge was a dark narrow passage that let out on a trapezoidal stage area. A woman stood at the mic singing early Usher to an empty house while the bartender studiously worked at a quiz game on the counter. There was a high school skeleton police procedural running on the wallscreen, and I asked the guy if he could change it to the Jai Alai Network. He nodded, waving his hand until Olabe's noble profile filled the screen. I had everything I needed. I ordered a Blood & Sand and settled onto the leftmost stool, which afforded the best view. The color commentary was indecipherable through the karaoke woman's labored recitations, but I didn't mind—at that point I'd seen enough of the game to produce my own detailed mental play-by-play. Maybe I started saying it out loud, too, at some point. Maybe the bartender asked me politely to stop, and then asked again, later, and finally poured a liter of bathtub vodka on my crotch. Maybe I was eventually instructed to leave.

Somehow I made it back to 217 that night, and somehow I made it back to the bar the next morning. I did little else in those few weeks but get obliterated and watch jai alai. The tournament culminated in a blistering series between Tulsa and Orlando, which became increasingly hard to follow as the network kept cutting away to news reports of the implant lab blowing up, and then the kids losing their minds, running wild in the streets, hiding out in Dumpsters and treetops. Shaky footage of the kids swarming a grocery store, shots of parents shuddering in tearful disbelief. Head shots of concerned state officials. The significance of it all wasn't lost on me, but I felt it the way you might feel the heat from a distant star. Meaning, not at all. My focus was entirely on that fronton in Reno. Everything else was just an obstacle.

It was during the side-change of game 12 that the kid

wandered into the place. Not really a kid—about Flora's age, I guess. All the regulars stopped dead to watch him. Evie the sad karaoke fiend, Jeff the Aleutian bartender with a set of fake eyes, and two lonely truckers who had given up halfway across the country, I guess realizing that there was nothing waiting for them on the other side. We all watched him take a seat four stools to my right. He was filthy in a raised-by-wolves sort of way, and just dazed. Vacant. Implanted, wearing a conical helmet with a bunch of wires coming out of it, some sort of neoindustrial lab shirt, and no pants—just boxer briefs covered in cheerful script that said *I'd Rather Be Warbling!* He looked on the outside like I felt on the inside. I had Jeff pour the kid a dungeonmaster. He stared at the drink for a long time, then looked over at me. I raised my glass, gestured vaguely towards the screen, raised the glass again, and chugged it down. The kid did the same.

I got him completely wasted that night, handing him drink after drink, stuff he'd probably never even heard of. He'd just take the glass from me and pound it in a single swig, no matter what I gave him. I got a sort of sick pleasure out of it. It was a pretty hateful, ruinous thing to do, but it felt good, like scratching a rash you know is going to eventually spread. Meanwhile, Orlando came back from six points down to take a commanding 8–4 lead in the series. The kid was hooked—I mean, between the broken implant and the drunken haze, he couldn't convey much at all, but he seemed intrigued.

I hauled him back to my room that night, because I had no idea where he was staying. I put him on the bed and took his shoes off. It felt weird, taking another man's shoes off, but I found an odd comfort in the process of putting the kid to bed. The helmet I left alone. I sat down on the mattress next to him and put my feet up. He was snoring faintly, and I liked him more than anyone else in the world at that moment. Before I passed out I experienced a brief, lukewarm tremor of peace.

The next morning we were back on our stools by 9:57, just in time for the pregame show.

FRANCINE CHANG

We were all starving. David had left one morning with the cooler empty, and we waited like we always did for him to return with his bloody laundry bag of freshly killed drifter animals. But he never did. We kept waiting. Nancy ventured aboveground—I thought maybe she was hunting for herbs or meat or berries, but all she came back with was a long dragon kite, all moldy and shredded, which Flora and the boy went to work on, cleaning it and sewing it together with dental tape. Patti said maybe two words a day. She had rappelled down into the bomb cavity and found some rusted medieval-looking cans of albino asparagus and spiced apple pulp, and we split what the boy didn't eat between the rest of us. The boy filled up our jugs of water in a nearby creek and brought them back one by one. When he came to sit next to me, I'd point a flashlight at my jug, and together we'd watch all the silt or plankton or sea monkeys or whatever float aimlessly around. We'd do that for a long time. Afterward he'd stand and extend his hand and make me follow him out to this tree with a rotted platform built into it. It was almost as desolate outside as it was inside, but the fresh air always made me feel better. Sort of better.

About a week after David disappeared, we finally accepted that he wasn't just out tracking some particularly elusive poodle. Maybe he'd twisted his ankle. Or was tangled up in barb wire. Or was just tired of constantly providing for us. I decided to head out on a search. Someone had to. I started in the overgrown fields around the silo. Calling his name like an idiot, as if he'd just gone out for a weeklong game of hide-and-seek. I was hungry, sore, vitamin-deprived. I felt like I had a urinary tract infection. Plus, my eyes were clouding over, so I probably had glaucoma too. And shingles. Though I have no idea what shingles are. I kept walking south, closing my eyes against the blinding sunlight and picturing David in an oversize mousetrap. The humane kind, the ones that trap you but keep you alive. "David," I called out every once in a while, because it felt good to hear my voice in a big open space. He wasn't anywhere nearby.

I walked and walked until I came to a tram line. I found myself repeating what my mother used to tell me when I lost something, a Korean phrase which translated roughly to "Do backward what you did forward." Up the escalator were two arrows, one pointing to Cedar Rapids on one side of the tracks, the other pointing to Davenport/Rock Island. I got on the tram to Rock Island.

Whenever we went into a tunnel, I had to turn away from the window, because I couldn't bear to look at myself. The silo had turned me into a filthy, addled spider lady. On the tram were a bunch of single elderly men and greedy-looking teenagers and a few families. I expected stares and horrified looks from other riders, but everyone was distracted by a young girl leashed to one of the leather handholds. A man and woman sat next to her—mother and father, I assume—and they didn't even look up as she lurched and bucked around, trying to free herself. That face. I couldn't not stare. Muddled and seething. It was the face we usually point inward, and only when no one's looking. I had no clue what was wrong with her, no. She must've been implanted, but I didn't notice at the time.

The Deluxe Inn hadn't changed, but after three weeks entombed in the silo it seemed like a sultan's compound. Paint, windows, electricity, intentional plants. Largely deserted, as always. I went to room 217, which was locked. I looked in the window and saw a pair of beat-up sneakers, some crumpled boxer shorts, and cans everywhere. I washed my face and combed my hair in the lobby bathroom, then went to check the Lounge. Neither Evie nor any of the other female regulars were there. It was just Corporal, a craggy old river rat, Jeff the bartender, and two slouchers at the bar with their backs to me. They were watching jai alai, and one of them was wearing headgear, like some party hat of crisscrossing metal spiders. When the bartender saw me, he turned his back without acknowledgment and grabbed a bottle of Midori sour. I took a seat in the far corner with my back to everyone else. Dietrich was nowhere near this place. I knew it like I knew I wouldn't stop drinking praying mantises until I was sloshy and glum.

I heard one of the men at the bar say, "That jerkoff grabbed his cesta. You can't do that. You can't *do* that." Shout, actually. I glanced over and saw the other man, spider hat, lean forward and look at him confused, dismayed. He stared at the screen, which showed a replay of a catch and shoot, one of the players spinning around the other and whizzing against the wall. Helmet turned back to the man, slowly opened his mouth and closed it.

The man sipped his drink and said, "Everything tastes chafed. I could understand if it was one thing, or maybe two things. But it's everything." Staring at the screen, he said, "Will someone tell these crotch fleas to *protect* the fucking *blind side*?"

Now I turned fully around, because I knew that voice. I walked toward it, ignoring Jeff's arm outstretched with my praying mantis. I put my hand on Theo's shoulder, and he turned to me sidelong as if he'd been snagged from behind by a fishing hook.

Theo. Here. Improbable, inevitable, just like everything else. He was himself but crumpled. Stiff-necked, eyes orbiting loosely in their sockets. Drunk, intensely drunk, but intensely something else, too.

He said, "You," and inhaled deeply, and waited a long time to exhale. He stared, pivoting his body around so that he was completely facing me. His face was like a rough sketch. The other man turned to me too, tilting his head slightly. He looked right through me, nodding, waiting, his expression unclouding until it was perfectly blue, and he gave me the briefest flicker of a smile and nodded. Then he fell off the barstool.

Theo gently helped the man to his feet, and took one long gulp from his drink and emptied his wallet onto the bar—bills, change, crushed straw wrappers, and sugar packets. With one hand on my shoulder and the other on the stool to steady himself, he turned back to me, straightened, and said, "Take us to her."

PATTI KERN

NEW LIBERTY, IA
2040

The world goes away without much complaint. Then you do. All you need is the right crawl space, a place to get steady, becalmed, expectationless under blankets all day, huffing stuck air. I wasn't trying to extinguish myself—I just had no stomach anymore for food or water or lurching survival gestures. I was secure in my shell. I had to descend to ascend, had to lock myself up to free myself, get low to get high. And plenty of other necessary paradoxes. Months of days I spent in Hayward thinking I could eat air, leech nutrients from it. Months of nights I spent in the ground-pussy of that missile silo thinking I was back in Hayward. What the others were doing wasn't important—I heard them, smelled them, but their consciousnesses were arrested to me. The others, they could've been sun-rotted blood pudding. I don't mean that in a bad way.

Except one day the top hatch conked open, then mumbles and footfalls on the metal ladder—first came Francine, then a man crowned with a metal bird nest, then Flora's dad. I remembered him from Face-to-Face. I didn't bother with wonder or surprise at his arrival, but I did feel a slight inner gear tick, a recalibration to this added presence.

Flora's dad found her and Spencer in their happy domestic hollow. He and Spencer exchanged an awkward handshake. Then he and Flora stared at each other for a while, hugged each other, tentative at first, then less so, then held each other for a long time. Everyone around them waited. The dad looked pained while they embraced. But he wasn't going to let go before Flora did. Eventually they released, and he ran a flashlight back and forth over the heap of blankets and metal walls. He lifted the blankets where the boy had been sleeping, kicked through some trash, and went into the control room with the flashlight.

They'd brought supplies from above, and Francine, looking like a gleaming raisin, set a squeeze-brick of water next to my shoulder. Francine, always so sad and decent, so boring. But good. Good at keeping a lot of plates barely spinning. She used a plastic syringe to squirt a thick horse-nutrition paste into my mouth. Tasted like something I'd coughed loose from down deep.

I swallowed it and said to her, "Quit saving me, Francine. I can die anytime I want to. Paste won't stop it."

The one with the bird nest milled around with a can opener. I could barely see his eyes in the dim of the silo, but his mouth was curled at the corners as if he was drugged or mesmerized. I shooed him off and he tripped and stumbled over one of the metal floor bolts but didn't fall.

Flora's dad returned with the boy. Arm around his shoulders, the boy hugging the man's waist. This, more than the arrival, pulled me out of my stupor. I got the can opener from Bird Nest, opened up cans of lymph-colored beans, and poured it into bowls. The boy ate carefully, watching his grandfather watch him, watching me, then Francine, who was trying to get Flora and Spencer and Spencer's mom to eat the paste. I picked up my own bowl, poured its contents into my mouth, chewed, chewed some more, felt good at first, then felt bad, felt worse. I ran over to the empty missile shaft and vomited into it.

Nancy was wary, of course, but Nancy was wary of everything, and there was no sign of a platoon of black-suited soldiers—just these sad, rumpled hoboes. Theo had told Francine about David, about Maine, the bomb, the aftermath. David was dead. I sat with that for a moment, let it settle. The implants were now useless, defunct. The emergencies were isolated at first, then more widespread. Riots in Memphis. Fires in Sydney. Civilian patrols, government backlash.

Theo took out his device and showed us what was going on: some poor implanted boy shoots a mailman in Los Angeles, another runs off and drowns in Mexico City. One spur had a long report about a sheriff in Arizona who turned an old juvenile detention center into a holding pen. Footage of young boys and girls alone in dingy rooms, pacing and smacking the walls and looking scared and insensate. When Theo moved to turn off the device, the boy held his hand and wouldn't let him. On the screen a blond-haired girl stared at her reflection in a two-way mirror, an expression like sadness but all jumbled. When it cut to the sheriff, the boy rewound the footage and watched the girl again. He paused it as he'd seen Francine do, and stared at the girl as if trying to communicate with her, then unpaused it. When it was done, he rewound it again, and again. Studying it, memorizing it.

Later he took the screen and went to his corner of the silo. We all scattered to our blanket tents, leaving the father, Francine, and Bird Nest looking for somewhere to go. Bird Nest lay down right where he was, uncovered. Francine and the father went to one of the subplatforms and sat against a low cement wall.

That night I thought about David. His impatience, his purposefulness, him. Christ, how long I'd spent all glib and overstuffed in my shell, and meanwhile David had gone quietly headlong to what he probably thought was an honorable death. How pointless, I thought. How goddamn misguided and utterly pointless. I was so jealous I couldn't sleep.

Across the room the little boy's pristine bloodless face was still illuminated by the screen. I started thinking about all the false revelations and epiphanies I'd propagated. The leaps I'd made and landings I'd had to roll out of, and how each one sort of inoculated me against the one that came after it. Until, here I was. Here he was. The boy was *ingesting* the news, experiencing it along with the people on the screen. He looked sad, but lately he always looked a little sad, which seemed appropriate to living in a missile silo with a bunch of decrepit husks. But the news of the fried implants, it appeared to be wounding him. He squinted, tightened his lips, sighed through his nose, a vessel of pure intent and purpose. He couldn't stop watching.

I closed my eyes and tried to will back that feeling of openness and caring I once had. I used to be a cellar door, an empty cup. I used to salvage lessons from gurus, children, strangers, infomercials, smells, textures, snacks, songs, dreams, animals, wind chimes, wind. I used to feel things. Now? I was crusted over, stuck. I was room-temperature leftovers. I had no more space in me for the silents, the implants. Or even the boy, the double-silent, raised in face-talking from his first moments, never clogged with an implant to mute out that inner world beyond anything I could even conceive—and here he was, studying tiny pictures of his fellow humans with utmost loving belief, showing me how it could've been. Finding truth or meaning or beauty in that little device. Finding purpose. Actually, I don't know what he was finding.

But I could hear him manipulating the device all night. And when I woke up in the morning he looked spent, sadder. He drank water when it was offered. But he wouldn't stop looking at the thing, not even when the charge was spent and the screen went dead.

NANCY JERNIK

NEW LIBERTY, IA
2040

I woke up early to a strange sound, like a sheet of rain repeatedly hitting a tin roof, and then dying off. I sat up and saw Theo through the blast door, alone, hunched over at the table, spinning the rear wheel of the boy's skateboard with his index finger, watching the bearings whir. It came to a stop, and he took a sideways pull from a tarnished flask. The boy had found the skateboard in a drainage ditch one night on one of our food runs. I let him take it back to the silo, but he was only allowed to ride it in the lower hallway. I didn't want him riding it outside, where the pavement was cracked and crumbling, more or less a guaranteed accident just waiting to happen. I had this vision of him sailing though the air, landing on his neck, and going into a coma, and when I thought about that my hands froze with fear. And I'm not a superstitious person, but it did feel very much like the presence of the treacherous skateboard and the arrival of Theo were cosmically linked somehow. It was hard to deny as I watched him sitting there gazing at it in a drunken haze. Francine tried to convince me that Theo hadn't turned us in back at Monte

Rio, but all she had were his words, and since words were what put us in our situation in the first place, I wasn't inclined to ignore my intuition. I tried hard to let it go, for the sake of the family, but I knew that eventually we'd pay for this decision to let a wolf into our midst.

Theo stood up and placed the skateboard on the floor. He pushed off and skated down the corridor, waving his arms for balance. As he approached our dining table he crouched down, scooped the tail of the board with his back foot and kicked out his front leg, which sent him up onto the bench, hurtling forward, his arms out in front of him and his face pinched shut. He slammed chest-first into the table, toppling the bench onto his left arm. The boy, who I guess had been watching the whole time from under the covers, shot up from the floor and ran out to him. He ran to Theo and knelt down. Theo groaned and slid over onto his side and put his hand on the boy's shoulder. He said something I couldn't understand and started to chuckle. The boy started laughing as well. Theo struggled to stand, still laughing and wheezing. He put the board down and modeled the trick he'd just attempted. The one that had just resulted in him getting crushed by a piece of furniture. He showed the boy how to push down on the tail of the board in order to lift off. The boy watched him intently, taking in every nuance of his posture. Theo then slid the board out with his foot for the boy to try. The boy stepped on the board and then hesitated. He glanced back into the sleeping area and locked eyes with me. I held my breath. I didn't want to be the one to ruin this moment between the boy and his grandfather, but my disdain for Theo seeped through my every pore. The boy stepped off the board and looked away. Theo made a puzzled expression that quickly shifted into something else, something darker.

He stepped quietly into the room and knelt in front of me. He whispered—hissed, really—"Do you have a problem with this?" I told him I did. I said he was going to hurt the boy, he'd just proven how unsafe it was. Theo snorted and frowned. "Hurt? He's a kid," he said. "He's a goddamned kid and he's going to get hurt. That's what happens. That's childhood." I looked away. "You're serious about this?" he said. I didn't say anything. Anything else would've been a lie that the boy could see from a mile away. Theo stepped back, furious and baffled. He started pacing angrily. Spencer and Flora woke up, not knowing at first what was going on. Theo kept pacing, muttering to himself. The man who had come with him stirred in the corner. Theo rushed over to him and grabbed him by the shoulder. "Here," he said. "Here's a helmet. The kid can wear this helmet. See? That's safe. You'll let him ride if he wears this thing, right?" He gestured for the man to remove the helmet, which he did after some amount of prodding. Theo brought it over to the boy, who eagerly took it. The thing was covered in wires—it didn't look like a safety helmet at all. Everyone was awake at this point. Everyone was looking at me. I felt cornered. "You're not giving me a choice, are you?" He just stared at me without blinking. "Inside only," I said, waving my hand at the board. It was about as much as I could bring myself to say. The boy smiled and slipped the helmet on, yanking the straps to fit it over his ears. He laughed with anticipation as Theo fastened the straps under his chin. When it was on he turned and took a bow for us. Everyone applauded.

I faced the wall and feigned sleep while Theo led the boy through a series of basic maneuvers. The room was dead quiet except for Theo's voice and the grinding of the skateboard wheels against the concrete floor. Everyone was rapt. I boiled and fumed.

The next morning I woke up early and went out to the strip mall on 130 to pick through whatever the local junkies had missed. I filled half a bag with leftovers, fantasizing the whole time that when I returned Theo and the other man would be gone. But as I climbed the hill back to the entrance to the silo I saw Theo emerge in broad daylight carrying the board under his arm, followed by the silent man and the boy, who was wearing the helmet. Francine tagged along at a distance, looking nervous and awkward. I rushed up the hill through the brambles and came up behind them, trembling, my body as light and sharp as an arrow.

"I told you not to take him outside," I said to Theo, short of breath, not even trying to conceal my rage.

He waved his hand, not even looking at me, and put the board down on a loaf of broken pavement. I came up behind him and slapped him hard across the ear. He crumpled and shrieked, backing off sideways as he gripped his head. I moved in and swung at him a second time, clipping his temple. The silent man took me from behind and held me as I struggled. "You want them to find us," I shouted. "You know what they'll do to him. You've wanted this all along." The last words came out as a throaty hiss, barely recognizable as language.

He stood up, pressing the side of his head where I'd connected with my knuckles, and said, "So this is why you're acting like a fucking lunatic?" "So you admit it," I shouted. Francine rushed in between us. "Guys," she said, "this is not . . ." And then she trailed off. Theo was staring intently at something, and his face was so strange that I turned to look in the same direction. There was the boy, standing completely still in the high grass. He opened his mouth and closed it again, like he was popping his jaw. The helmet was enormous on his head, and his eyes were dull and far away, trained on some interior space. The silent man loosened his grip on me. He dropped to his knees and clasped his hands to his forehead. The rest of us were still.

FRANCINE CHANG

NEW LIBERTY, IA
2040

The sky was gray-blue and littered with clouds. Windy, an odor of far-off pig manure. Nancy and Theo had gone quiet, both staring at the boy. Theo's friend was on his knees, looking across the field, face still frozen in a queasy half smile. Everyone seemed slow and off. Except the boy, who was now wading in high yellow grass, wearing the spider helmet low over his eyes, strangely intent.

We followed behind him to a nearby oak, part of a windbreak along the edge of a field of straggly briars and shrubs and scrub. The landscape was so ugly it was almost pretty. The oak had a few rotted footholds, and the boy scaled them, all the way up to a tiny platform near the top. He stood on the platform, shadowed in the low light, king of the barren fields, holding a flat palm over each side of the helmet. I was cold, straining to see him. His features were pinched into a point, crumpling tight around his mouth.

Nancy was standing directly beneath him, hands fluttering, ready to catch him if he came crashing down. She called up to him to be careful, to watch out for birds and fire ants and loose branches. She still wore those immaculate scrap clothes—shirts patched together with blanket fabric and men's ties. Shoes made from other shoes. Theo's friend, meanwhile, was still on his knees in the tall grass, looking off at the silo, the empty field, the almost-collapsed barn.

The boy relaxed his jaw slightly, released his hands from the sides of the helmet, and sighed audibly. I thought I could hear a low humming sound coming from the helmet, but it might've been from the factory way beyond the fields, which belched out columns of pus-colored smoke. The boy's strained expression beneath the helmet softened. Sympathetic, almost. It went places. I watched him, and my mind went places, too. I realize I sound like Patti now. But this is how it was.

I cycled through old things. Mostly loose memory puffs I didn't bother grasping on to—pictures, bad dreams, my mother. She spoke almost no English when I was growing up. She'd take us to movies, to school plays and orchestra recitals and a thousand other things, without complaining. I watched her watch the movies sometimes, and wondered why she looked so content. So unconfused. She couldn't be understanding a thing, I thought. Maybe that's why.

I focused on the boy, and he seemed to be focusing on me too, even though he wasn't looking at me. One morning in second grade my mom dropped me off at school like she always did and there were no kids in the halls. I went to my classroom, but the door was locked. I looked in the window—the light was turned off. The desks were empty. I tried the classroom next to mine, but that door was locked, too. Turns out it was a school holiday. An obscure one, Flag Day or something. I slumped in front of the my classroom door and cried for probably a half hour. When I finished crying I stood up and walked around.

Back then, school was a terrifying dark box of hazards. Kids who made fun of my accent, a teacher who accused me of smelling strange and wrote a note home suggesting I start using antiperspirant, my own thoughts. Empty, though, the school seemed harmless. Even pleasant. Down the main hallway was a mural of kids scaling a giant rainbow. I'd never noticed it before. Everything smelled of paper and pine cleaner. I walked around until I found the door of the art classroom unlocked, and sat there for the rest of the day eating my lunch, sculpting snowmen out of clay. When the afternoon bell rang, I went and met my mom out front. I never told her what happened.

Theo called up to his grandson to ask if he was okay. The boy was somewhere else. His face was alive and his shoulders swayed slightly forward and the sun had just set. The ugly overgrown fields were cleansed in bluish light. It could've been a vineyard, a field of blackberries, except for all the plastic bags snagged on the briars. Some had happy faces on them and the wind drove them wild. A dozen or so bats flew over the field, formless, frantic. In the distance, the factory continued to sigh its reefs of smoke.

I thought of David out here, wandering around with his knives, looking for something to kill and butcher. Providing. Feeling close to things.

I thought of my elementary school and how after that day it wasn't so bad anymore. Empty, it had lost all of its menace.

The air was cold, and none of us had the right clothes. Up on his platform the boy seemed to wobble, so relaxed I thought he might forget where he was and topple down through the branches. The sky was dark and the branches were almost bare, and the boy's face looked faintly lit from within. He half smiled and opened his eyes and began swaying smoothly back and forth, back and forth. A bat burst from the tree and swooped low over our heads and out past Theo's friend, who had his back to the tree, still staring off at the silo, the empty field, the almost-collapsed barn. His pained rictus was gone and he was breathing deeply, and at first I thought something about that old barn must've soothed him. But he couldn't be seeing the barn, I realized—his eyes were closed, and his head was slightly tilted, as if he was listening to some far-off music. Then he started to sway too.

JOHN PARKER CONWAY

MONTE RIO, CA
2040

Right when I pull up to the sooty ring of houses, I see a young boy swinging around a little chain saw. He has greasy hair, walleyed, a face twitching with pure malignant delight. He and his mom lived in the hills, up in blue fog with the other commune leftovers—it was implant central up there. Dr. Ng and I had personally seen to it that every silent was properly outfitted during our compulsory county-wide drive last year. So when everything went haywire, I deputized myself so I could take distress calls—putting out fires, bandaging whatever granny got whacked in the head with a tree branch. Completing the circle. Mostly what I'd do is drive up, lower the passenger-side window, and shoot the kids with the trank. Which calmed things down for ten, twelve hours.

The boy swung the chain saw and carved through one of the beams supporting the roof over the carport, which listed against a redwood trunk. He looked around for something else to buzz. I couldn't get a clear bead on him from the car, so I jumped out with the trank. He scurried behind the house. I followed.

I could see the boy's mother in the windows, watching him maraud. She wasn't a silent. I'd met her before, part of the last wave that moved to Face-to-Face as things went south—a talker detaching from society for the good of her son. A martyr. Sad, kind of noble, but mostly sad. She saw me and looked down at the trank and seemed to sigh. She had that air of punishing gravity you see in moms of dead and disabled children. I walked around to the back of the house and found the boy standing on the corrugated metal roof of a dog kennel, bringing the chain saw down between his legs, idly chopping at the chain link, maybe trying to get at one of the four greyhounds in there, but mostly just sparking and squealing. He saw me approach and paused for a moment, then continued poking at the fence.

I kneel down to line up my shot, a 650 cc humane-dart of Deprasil. But as I'm aiming, I notice that behind the kennel is a deep ravine, so if I shoot him and things went how they usually did, after 4.7 seconds give or take he'd fall backward off the kennel into the ravine. Something to consider—but not necessarily a deal-breaker. He'd survive the fall, though maybe with slightly diminished havoc-wreaking capabilities going forward. At this point my thinking was, it's an issue of opening your eyes and admitting the inevitable. You can finger-patch a cracked dam here and there, but sooner or later something permanent's got to be done.

So I'm looking through my sight at the boy's knees and legs, scraped raw from thorns, at his torn T-shirt and scratched neck, and I realize he's stopped banging on the kennel. The saw's still going but he's got it dangling at his side and he's standing very still. I look at his face—even with the wild hair he's still handsome, his features simple and lightly drawn, baby fat not even burned away yet. He's just a kid.

Then I hear the chain saw fall. From his hand and off the kennel, bouncing into the ravine. The auto-shutoff silences it. Now the boy's standing in the center of the roof, swaying from side to side. He stares in my direction but doesn't seem to see me. He's gone ponderous and deliberate, like all those loose ribbons had been tied up into a bundle. I blinked, thought for a moment, and lined up my shot.

Then I hear a fast rustling whip by me and suddenly the mother appears in my crosshairs. She's hopped up on the kennel and is now cradling the boy, burying her head in the pit of his shoulder. The greyhounds were shrieking and pacing in their cage. I moved a few feet to the side to try to get a better angle on the shot, but it was no use—she had her son fully enveloped. The trank held four darts. I could easily just pluck off the mom, wait five seconds for her to fall, then pluck off the son.

Years ago I was the one who welcomed that first wave of silents into our community and smoothed the tracks for others. This woman embracing her son on top of that nasty kennel, all blurry with panicked dogs, she was probably here because of me. Staring at them, I felt a great upwell of pity and shame, so massive and contourless that I knew I couldn't do a damn thing about it except grind my teeth together and wait for it to pass.

The mother held him from behind while he swayed, buoying him lightly. They had the same big eyes. They swayed side to side while the greyhounds lurched and barked. She brushed his hair aside and I noticed her crying, not boohooing but just soundlessly producing tears. Streams of them. She held on.

The boy stopped moving and closed his eyes. I'd lowered the trank by now, and I didn't even bother to raise it. His mother let go, and the boy slowly turned around to look at her, still leaning close to him, still crying. I waited. The greyhounds, no longer barking, twitched their noses and looked upwards. The kid blinked awake, looked around, down at the dogs, over toward me, then at his mother, her face wet with tears. Watching her closely, he reached his hand out to her waist and touched her lightly. Like he wanted to make sure she was really there. Really her. She started boohoo crying then.

She nodded and smiled at the boy, and he extended his free hand toward her shoulder. He smiled back.

Halfway home, I realized I'd left the trank there in her yard, lying in the grass.

AUGUST BURNHAM

PORTLAND, ME
2040

I was sleeping in the back of a police trailer parked behind the Portland YMCA so that I could do around-the-clock triage on the affected children. The CDC had sort of taken over the place, converting the various fitness areas into safe holding pens, examination rooms, and lab facilities. It was the most advanced quarantine colony on the East Coast, but even with volunteers from all over New England we were still struggling to control the children's behavior. I hate to use the term "holding pen" to describe where the kids lived, but that was essentially what they were—handball courts padded with wrestling mats, full of stalking children. We had to sedate them with tranquilizer darts in order to check their brain activity, and it usually took a pair of volunteers wearing riot armor to extract them for testing.

At the time of the mass event, I had just finished examining a young redheaded girl. She was coming out of sedation, which can sometimes be a nasty situation. The nurse held the restraint cords to keep the girl down in case she started to buck and kick. I was standing at the portable desk, traversing the scan of the girl's brain, comparing its neural architecture against the brains of the other children we were studying. The girl opened her eyes wide and started breathing quickly, almost panting. She fisted her hands and dug her heels into the vinyl bed, straining against the cords. The nurse put a gloved hand to the girl's forehead and tried in vain to comfort her. The girl shrank away and tried to bite the nurse, hissing deep in her throat. When the nurse withdrew her hand, though, the girl stopped. She went completely still. The nurse looked alarmed, and I thought for a moment that the girl had done something to her. I stood up and saw why she was so startled. The girl's face was moving in slow motion, the mouth opening and closing and her eyes seeming to turn inward. We moved in to check her vitals with the wand—everything was normal. I took her gently by the chin and lifted her face toward mine, and as I did this I saw something—a flickering that passed across the surface of her face, an ineffable transformation of her features. It was as if I saw her go from animal back to human. I don't believe there is a word in our language, or perhaps any language, for what I saw on the girl's face. It was the primal spark of a mind recognizing itself.

We found out later that the same phenomenon was occurring throughout the facility. The children were all exhibiting the same odd behavior—a sort of rapturous torpor. We assumed it was a fluke, whatever that would mean, but of course minutes later our sister facilities in Portsmouth and Central Falls and Hartford were all calling up, reporting the same occurrence. Nobody could figure out what was happening, but when I ran a diagnostic on the redhead's implant I saw the signature of the Reiss calibration helmet time-stamped at 18:41:03. I checked the other children in our facility, and each one had the same time stamp. I'd assumed the device had been obliterated in the explosion with the rest of our gear. I couldn't imagine how it was possibly still active. But we traced the signal and located it in rural Iowa, and, as we now know, it was Calvin who had transported it there and handed it off to the unimplanted boy.

The device was designed to access specific neural pathways in silent patients' brains. The conductor of the signal—Calvin, back when he was my design director—would pass a predefined emotional impulse into the mind of a targeted subject and then record the vocalization of the impulse. We'd then assess the verity of the response based on the signal. We could pass out these impulses to a single subject or a hundred of them. But by all indications the boy had simultaneously accessed all possible endpoints—in effect, all implantees worldwide.

We're still trying to piece together exactly what happened. Because it took place in such a remote location with very few witnesses, certain aspects may never be clear, but we believe that the boy was able to act as a sort of neural beacon, broadcasting a signal of such strength and purity that it broke through the chaos of the implanted children's brains and established the kind of order and focus that afforded conscious thought. You see, the children who had been affected most acutely by the destruction of PhonCom were all implanted within the first year of life, and of course none of them had ever developed an internal consciousness that wasn't brokered by the implant. They hadn't *learned* to be silent. So when the plug was pulled, they had nothing—no organized way to process and categorize sensory information. Their erratic and sometimes violent behavior was the product of their minds desperately trying to make sense of the world, with no guideposts or map.

We can only guess at the exact nature of the boy's transmission, but scans show tremendous spikes along Bellamy's curve—the constellation of paths that process emotional content—in the brain activity of the children at our facility immediately following the time stamp of the device. It was just a moment, and just a simple signal—from a neurological perspective, anyway—but their brains must have seized upon it like a beggar to a crust of bread.

I wanted to study that boy. I had to. I needed to record his brain activity, map his neural architecture. It wasn't going to be easy—it would take weeks of continuous observation and analysis in a clinical environment to generate a truly high-resolution profile. And, of course, distilling all that data into some sort of answer was a whole other challenge. But this boy held the key to the silent world I'd been trying to access since the day I first observed Calvin back at McLean, and I wanted in.

STEVEN GRENIER

NEW LIBERTY, IA
2040

News of the zero beacon spread across the country in an elongated sprawl. Isolated status messages from parents that metastasized into local news reports in the major cities about kids going into a trance. Within the first hour it was clear that something huge had happened. "A synchronized reawakening on a scale that nobody was prepared for"—not to quote myself, but that's how I phrased it in the live-stream. By that time the kids had already come out of the fugue state, calm and alert. I had been in a holding facility interviewing a group of volunteers for a segment of *Night Watch* when it happened, so I saw firsthand. It was terrifying, and then amazing. We just knelt there on the floor next to them as they slowly awakened.

Bogdan called less than an hour later, so I excused myself and went outside to talk. The air was sharp and gritty, like a thunderstorm had just rolled through—everything was taut with a weird anxious energy. There were people clustered in doorways and gathered on stoops, everyone staring into their Catenas as the news rolled out. Bogdan was calling to tell me about the helmet—about how they'd been able to track down its location. He wanted to know if I was interested in riding out there with the recon team. I was like, "Where and when," obviously. I hung up and made my way to the rental car. There was a man standing at the threshold of his brownstone apartment, calling inside, "It's okay, darling. It's okay to come out." I could see the girl's silhouette in the hall, taking tentative steps toward the door. Driving down the street to the airport I passed a woman leading a pair of implanted twins, who were bounding down the sidewalk, staring up in wonder at the ailanthus trees that lined the streets, as if they were vaulted cathedral ceilings. There was a lone boy in the park, standing at the bow of a wooden pirate ship, balancing on one foot as he whistled into the clouds, while his father wept on a park bench. Many kids were still locked away in basements and vacant strip mall storefronts, and there were random packs of runaways living in peripheral space, hiding in construction sites and junkyards—kids who had no way of telling anyone who or where their parents were. It was a real mess for a while, but things were finally on their way back to normal.

I made it to Edwards later that afternoon, and we flew in a Peregrine 12 out to the location in Iowa. It was easy to spot the missile silo from the air. Just a disc of concrete cut into a scrubby wooded area. The driver barked something into his headset, and we looked out to see two men running across the clearing toward the entrance of the silo, which was a little wooden shed that looked like nothing. The pilot asked whether he should deploy the long-range Tasers, but I was relieved to hear the command from Durso come back saying no.

By the time we touched down the two men had run into the shed and down the spiral stairwell. We went down after them, one by one, descending into this black, wet, shit-smelling void until we got to a room lit with Christmas LEDs, where an old woman stood in the doorway, struggling to hide her terror. She spoke in shuddering fragments, like, "You . . . can't . . . my family." I told her to stay calm, that it was not a raid, that we just wanted to see the helmet. I told her what had happened topside, and she was dumbfounded.

It was a real desperate place those people had crawled into. Steel doors on steel drums for a table, crates sagging against the walls, stocked with salvaged cans and bottles. Everywhere the smell of rotten waste and fermenting sweat. The woman's family hid behind her, crowded on a collapsed mattress, shrinking back against the wall. I could see Calvin Andersen among them. He looked thin, gray—they all did, to varying degrees. I could tell which ones were silent by the way their eyes darted from the old woman to me and back. The boy was sitting in front of his father, who had his arms clasped tightly around the boy's chest. The boy had the helmet between his knees, and he looked at us with a disarming curiosity. I knelt before him and held my hands out to see if he'd give me the helmet. He turned it over and looked inside, as if he was trying hard to understand why I might be interested in such a beat-up piece of headgear. I took it from him and tried to put it on, but it barely fit. I made a face as I pretended to struggle to force it over my ears, and he laughed.

It took a lot of negotiating, but we convinced them it was safe to come out. We escorted them back to the Peregrine and headed north to Chicago, where a crew was preparing a hotel suite for them. I had already been informed that Burnham's team was on its way to the hotel to pick up the boy for a long-term neural analysis at Mass General, but I didn't mention it. It wasn't my business. I just sat and watched the boy looking out the window of the Peregrine as we swept over the

Loop, his eyes round with wonder at the sight of the minia-turized world below. Kind of amazing to witness—you know, to be able to experience that thrill again through a kid's eyes. I remember thinking that we were out of the darkness—that after what we'd all shared, nothing could be the same again. I guess I was right about that much.

NANCY JERNIK

CHICAGO, IL
2040

They put us up in a suite on the top floor. Flora, Spencer, and the boy in one room, Francine and Patti in another, and then Theo and me in the small alcoves that flanked the kitchenette. They said it was a secret location. They said, "To throw off the press." They told us we could spend the night and as many nights after that. We should think of this as our home for now. Even though nothing there was ours. Nothing but the helmet, which the boy left on the coffee table. The hotel sent up platters of food on wheeled carts. Fresh juice, fresh coffee. I hadn't had a cup of coffee in years at that point. I stood at the corner window that looked out on the skyline and drank slowly, reverently. Thinking about what to do next. I did not trust the people who'd brought us to the hotel. I knew we had to leave. I just hadn't figured out how.

There was a bus station across the street down below, and I watched the people streaming in and out. When Spencer was just a baby, I would sit by the window of the house we lived in and put him on my lap and make up stories about the students passing by. In the fall, with the window open, the white gauzy drapes billowing against Spencer's face. He didn't respond to the stories I told him, of course, and I think I was crushed by that. But he loved to sit there. He would hold out his hand and let the drapes envelop it, laughing uncontrollably at what must have been something like—I can't think of the word. Magic? That memory, as distant and opaque as it was, came to me as something new. It was not part of the story I'd told about myself. It didn't figure into who I thought I was. But it was there anyway. It had happened despite my best sweating. Despite my best effort. Efforts.

Theo joined me at the window, and he said an awkward something about the view. I nodded without turning his way. I still couldn't look at him. He'd finally gotten what he wanted. Out of the corner of my eye I could see him opening and closing his mouth, but he didn't speak a word. He turned as if he was about to approach the food cart, but then stopped and grabbed my arm. He said, "I just wanted to talk with them. I wanted to listen. I just wanted them close. You have to understand that." My throat tightened. Theo said, "Tell me you never once wanted to hear your son's voice." I opened my mouth, but there was no answer I could find.

A man in teal scrubs entered the room pushing a gurney. There was a fin-shaped apparatus sunk into the cushion with bundles of multicolored leads hanging from a port in its side, and what looked like a set of defibrillators.

"What is going on," I said, the words sputtering as I spoke them. The technician smiled sheepishly as he parked the cart in a corner. "What is that?" He said that Dr. Burnham would explain everything when the team arrived. "When the *team* arrives?" I said. I turned to Theo, who stood frozen in place next to me. I couldn't say what I wanted to say to him, so I just stared. I wanted him to see himself as I saw him, handing his family over to these people. He looked at me for just a moment and then turned away. But when our eyes met, I saw doubt and fear where I expected triumph. I saw that he was just as scared and confused as I was. Not just about the man in the scrubs and the imminent arrival of the doctor, but about every decision that had brought us here, starting with the moment we first held our children, these living bundles of unanswerable questions. Why were we given these children? Why *us*? We wandered through our days, groping for anything that looked like an answer, each of us living in monastic isolation with our boundless uncertainty. Picking through the despair for some kind of absolute truth. If only our children were more like us, we thought, we might find peace. But our children were not like us. They were nothing but themselves, and it was finally time to let them be. We had traveled very different paths to this hotel room, but now we were in the same place, and we both knew what we had to do.

"They should be here in a few minutes," the man in the scrubs said, propping the door open so that he could wheel another set of devices into the room. "You just make yourselves comfortable." He pulled the second cart into the room, and then brought in a cert—a set—a set of lights—like the kind you'd see in an operating room.

I went cold, all over my body. My breath caught in my throat. Theo leaned toward me and whispered, "Take them to the bus station. Send them to Canada. Whatever's farthest. Get them out of here." He pressed his credit swipe into my palm, and then quickly went over to the equipment. He pointed to the equipment and tried to start up a conversation with the man. He poked at the keypad of the machine and it made a buzzing sound. The technician grabbed Theo's wrist and pulled him away from the gurney. Theo glanced at me with a look that told me to move quickly, and then he leaned into the man and jolted him with his shoulder, and the man pushed back, shouting.

I rushed into the bedroom where Spencer was playing a marble game with the boy. He looked up at me smiling, but his face turned serious as I took him by the elbow and pulled him close to me. I tried to embrace him but he was like a giant in my arms. I could barely hold him. He got Flora up from the bed and the four of us slipped out of the room. Theo was straddled to—he was straddling the technician, pinning him to the floor while a woman in purple scrubs tried to pry him away. He reared back, sending the woman crashing into the gurney. Calvin stood in the doorway to his room, watching with confusion and maybe amusement. And then we were out and down the hallway and down the stairs and then outside.

In the bus station I asked the clerk how far away the bus went and he said there was one about to leave for Vancouver. When he said "Vancouver," it sounded like an animal noise, but I bought three tickets anyway. There was no time to negotiate goodbyes. I just put them on the bus and walked away. I should've felt some unbearable sadness, but I did not. Regardless of what I'd done to him—or what I'd failed to do— Spencer was strong. He was happy. He was the kind of person I'd never been able to be, and I could only see that as an achievement.

There was nothing left to do but wait. I sat outside the bus station. It was almost an hour before the police arrived, and by the time of the—interrogation—I found I could hardly put together a sentence. I had no idea what was going on, and of course they thought I was trying to protect my family by not responding. They thought I was faking. Until reports of other cases came, started coming, in. Today I can only talk in phrases and snippets. Words come in waves and seizures. Some mornings I am almost normal, and some afternoons I can't find the right name for a single thing. This testimonial I am recording is the result of hours and hours of focused effort stretched out across days. Everyone was surprised by my sudden condition. Nobody thought it was possible. A medical anomaly, they said. Until I wasn't an anomaly. Until I was just one of thousands of people everywhere, losing words one by one until there is nothing left to say.

JOHN PARKER CONWAY

MONTE RIO, CA
2040

Once the kids calmed down, for the next three days I was left cleaning up the mess—sometimes literally, like at the chocolate-covered-fruit stand out on Railroad Ave., but mostly it was a matter of herding up the lost ones who were wandering around town and beyond. They still couldn't talk, of course, so we had to bring them back to the station and figure out which kids went with which parents. We sorted it out, together, as a community, just like old times. Afterward I went to the Pink Elephant, feeling almost normal, but not so normal that I could just go home without stunning myself some.

Inside, I found a half-dozen regulars crowded around Bug. He was the de facto lord of the Elephant, a lifer who wore coveralls and drank nonalcoholic beer out of a giant gas-station mug. He was staring at everyone with his head slightly tilted, lips tight like he was storing something inside and couldn't quite figure out what to do with it. When I walked in, Lewis was insisting to one of the she-regulars that Bug had been drinking his usual N/A beer all night long, that he'd already been acting a little awry when he'd come in for his noontime chili dog. A moist-lipped roofer named Garrett piped up, "Probably he's dosing again."

Garrett waved his thumb in front of Bug's face and said, "How many fingers am I holding?" Bug smacked the thumb away and said, "Bone cows. Storm oxygen knuckles fall rousted dry dry dry."

"He ain't even here," Garrett said, shaking his head. "He's departed earth."

Bug, the overhead light shining off his bulbous nose, kept his gaze steadily focused on Garrett. Slowly, painstakingly, he pointed at him. He blinked and looked around and pursed his lips ardently and coughed, and finally said, "Foot . . . *fall*." He shook his head violently, banged his fist on the table, upsetting his mug onto the floor. "*Foot*," he yelled. Foamy spittle shot out at everybody. He shook his head some more and banged his fist.

"I haven't seen him this messed up in a long, long time," Lewis said. "Not since his morphine phase, when he carried around an empty guitar case and wanted everyone to call him Black Andy."

I knew I wasn't gonna be able to drink in peace until this situation was taken care of, so I walked over to the group and asked what seemed to be the matter.

"Did somebody hear something?" the she-regular asked. "Like a gnat, or a fly? Or maybe like a tiny lawn mower just for ass hair?"

I forgot to mention that none of the other Elephant regulars ever actually acknowledged my presence, except to each other, since that bad business with Dr. Ng and the implants. Others in town understood, but the Elephant had always been full of grumblers and silent sympathizers. I guess they still thought I was a monster. I think they even blamed me for the implants shorting out.

"Terrance," I said, edging in closer. Terrance was Bug's given name. "I would like you to please try to nod if you can understand what I'm saying to you. Or blink your eyes three times."

He blinked once but didn't nod. He turned to look at me, and his expression sort of caught and gathered itself. His face grew livid. He let out another string of words. Things like *cellroids prow lork, pelligran sapination.* Gibberish, but nothing was the slightest bit hesitated or slurred. The way he gestured when he spoke, it seemed like he knew exactly what he intended to say. But something was coming in to overdub the sentences with nonsense.

I stood up, paused while everyone's attention focused on me, and announced that something needed to be done. And if none of them had any idea about what to do, then I'd drive Bug to Sebastopol, where there were trained professionals who could diagnose and treat what was going on. I began an ad-libbed disquisition on community spirit and personal responsibility, when the she-regular cut me off, telling me to go ahead and take him but not to expect a special medal or campaign donation.

"I knew your father," I said to her. I don't know why I said this, I had no idea who her father was, but it kind of froze her for a minute as Lewis helped Bug out of his chair. I got him into my car and we started driving east. Up close he smelled kind of gamey, so I lowered the windows and opened the vents. It was about 10:30 and the roads were empty. I tried to keep Bug calm as we drove. I turned on the passenger console and told him he could play video games, watch TV, check the news, make a call, listen to music, whatever. He just poked at the screen forlornly.

I asked him questions, tried to prompt him to say something. What's your first memory, tell me three things not many people know about you—things like that. I even tried to talk to him in his gibberish language from the Elephant: "Big frozen holes tall neck undertaker?" Nothing.

Suddenly he began banging on the window. I looked out his side and saw trees, a mailbox, the old side entrance to the Bohemian Grove, more trees. "What's out there, Bug? You see a deer?" He turned to me, eyes wide, and pointed forcefully toward the rusty gate. "You want to go to the Grove?"

Bug's mouth opened and closed, and he gestured again towards the window.

"There's nothing there anymore, buddy. Believe me. It's all gutted and gone."

He coughed violently, trying to get something, anything, to come out. I turned in my seat and saw tears streaming down his cheeks. "Terrance, listen, everything's going to be fine. We're just getting you somewhere safe."

He swallowed, exhaled, breathed deep, and formed his hands together in a ball. I poked at the stereo, trying to find some sort of distraction, and landed on a show where you give them ingredients and they tell you what to make for dinner. By the time the first meal was finished, spaghetti with beans, Bug had given up trying to articulate anything. He lowered his head and held it in his hands and stayed that way until we pulled up outside the emergency room.

Inside, I asked for Dr. Shaw, who I'd worked with on the implant drive years ago. He came out of his office looking ragged. I started to explain what was going on, and the doctor looked at Bug, then at me, and cut me off. He said, "We have a problem."

AUGUST BURNHAM

CHICAGO, IL
2040

They were gone by the time I got to the hotel. Ms. Chang and Ms. Kern were there, sitting on the couch, looking tired but strangely amused, and there was a paramedic wrapping Mr. Greene's forehead in gauze, but the others—the family, including the boy, and Calvin—had disappeared. An officer informed me that the mother, Ms. Jernik, was the last to see them, and that she was in police custody but wouldn't respond to their questions. I'd flown all the way out there to study the boy, so of course I was frustrated and disappointed that he was gone. I was also extremely concerned about Calvin. It's a mystery to me how he ended up in the company of these implant resisters, who must be taking advantage of his disoriented state. They also stole the calibration helmet, which is puzzling—I'd certainly like to look through the logs to see how it's been used since Calvin saved it from the explosion of the PhonCom facility, but I'm much more concerned about his safety.

I asked to see Ms. Jernik myself—I thought I could take a gentler approach, explain to her the nature and importance of our research. They brought her back to the hotel. She was a frail old woman with hair like tarnished silver and a curious look on her face. I took her into one of the bedrooms and sat her down in the recliner. "Is there any reason in particular you don't want to tell us where your family is?" I asked. "Do you think they're in trouble? Do you think we're going to hurt them?" She studied me intently as I talked, but wouldn't respond. "If I assure you they won't be harmed in any way, would that persuade you to tell me where they are?" Again, she didn't say a word. Just scanned my face. There was no acknowledgment on her part that she understood anything I was saying. I thought possibly she'd suffered a head injury in the process of helping her family escape, or that she was on some sort of medication.

The portable MRI didn't pick up any sign of trauma, and the urine test was negative for intoxication. I asked her if she'd agree to a blood test, and while she didn't verbally consent she willingly put her arm out when she saw the needle. I ran the sample through the hemo scanner and everything came up normal—except for a spike indicating active EPR antibodies. Which, of course, was surprising, to say the least. We drew a new sample and ran the test again and got the same results. It didn't make sense to me, but there it was: she was infected with the EPR virus. We did a PET scan and confirmed that her brain activity was nearly identical to that of a typical phasic-resistant patient. Just like her son, I presumed. Just like her grandson.

Of course, Ms. Jernik's status as my Patient Zero was short-lived—there were cases emerging all over the country at just that moment, and we soon began connecting the dots. The progression of symptoms varies—some patients first lose their ability to process language, others can understand speech but are unable to produce meaningful phrases, still others can speak individual words but have no sense of grammar. In some cases, the total loss of language skills happens within a week, and with others it can take a month or more. But the basic facts soon became clear: the virus—previously a pre-natal risk only—had mutated and broken loose. It was contagious, and it appeared to be airborne.

We're still trying to understand exactly how this might have happened. The initial source of the mutation had to be the carriers, the silents, and so I instantly focused on the PhonCom meltdown, which had affected all implanted silents. The symmetry of Dietrich's attacks—the onset of the worm and the physical destruction of the facility—appear to have conveyed a small surge of electromagnetic radiation through the implants as they shorted out. This pulse, we now believe, stimulated the mutation in the virus, drastically altering its means of transmission. Whether this was an unexpected side effect of the suicide bombing or, in fact, Dietrich's actual intention is still unclear, although the possibility that it's some sort of cosmic coincidence diminishes with each new piece of evidence the authorities uncover.

By the time we understood even this much, it was too late to quarantine or control the virus in any meaningful way. The implanted silents are so widespread, both geographically and demographically, that almost the entire population, at least in this country, was exposed during that first week post-explosion. An early survey appears to confirm that roughly seventy percent of the subjects tested are now positive for the virus. The blessing, if you can call it that, is that in the vast majority of cases the virus appears content to remain asymptomatic, almost dormant—at least for the moment. We have made no progress in determining what prompts its onset. Currently only a small portion of the carriers are displaying symptoms of linguistic deficiency. How long that will last, we have no idea.

I spent several days with Ms. Jernik, studying her condition as reports of new cases continued to roll in. She did not seem to be terribly bothered by her absence of language. I gathered from reports by the other talkers who lived with her in the silo that she rarely spoke even when she could. That she saw talking as almost a vulgar act, never to be performed in the presence of her son. She now appeared to be almost content, even amused. I found it difficult to maintain a clinical distance from this woman who seemed so blithely accepting of a condition that will cripple her for life. I was consumed by the urge to reach across the table and shake her awake. It's one thing to be born without access to the realm of language, but it's quite another to be robbed of it. And for an entire civilization to retreat into this lonely and isolated space—a lifetime of solitary confinement . . . it's not something I can tolerate.

I am not a virologist, and I concede that I'm out of my depths on the work I'm now doing to map the neurological progression of the virus. But we *all* must contribute in any way we can, and we must do it immediately. When all of the men and women who are capable of fighting this virus are silenced, when our access to the great pool of knowledge is shut off, where will we be then? *What* will we be? How will we be able to go on living in communities, as nations? Can we then really consider ourselves human? I don't know the answer, and I don't want to know. But we cannot deny the reality of our circumstances, and preparations must be made. Like so many others, I too have tested positive for the virus. I too have no idea when the curtains will be drawn. Which is why I am attempting to translate Weise's *Encyclopedia of Microbiology and Virology* from words into simple pictographs that I believe I'll still be able to parse after the virus takes its toll, if and when that day arrives. It is a painstaking process, to be sure—I am currently only halfway through the introduction—but my own loss of language cannot be the end of my fight for a cure. Even if I can no longer benefit from that cure—even if I'm only fighting for some distant reader of this history. If we lose this, we lose everything.

KENULE MITEE

LAGOS, NIGERIA
2041

Akintunde was born so quickly—we barely made it to Columbia Presbyterian in time. Isoke went right up on the delivery bed and got on all fours, and she pushed the baby out before the doctor had even arrived. The nurses were very impressed. They weighed and washed Akintunde and wrapped him in a blanket. Isoke and I lay in the bed with the baby between us, and it was, just as they say, an experience like nothing else in the world.

We were alone for a very long time. After an hour nobody had come to check on us, so I went out to find something for Isoke to eat. The whole ward was quiet. There was just one young woman at the reception desk, who would not look up from her screen as she pointed me in the direction of the vending machines. I went down the hall and saw on the other side of the glass doors a big throng of people. There was a man in a red jacket who shouted through a megaphone at the crowd. He was saying, again and again, "This is not a medical emergency. Please return to your homes. This is not an emergency." I went back to the receptionist to ask what was going on, and she told me about the virus. She was surprised I hadn't heard the news. I returned to Isoke with a tray of buffalo stackers and tried to pretend there was nothing out of the ordinary, but she could see right away that something was up.

We were released two days later, and things had calmed down a bit. Truthfully, I wasn't paying that much attention to the outside world, because I was so taken with my boy that nothing else mattered to me. That first month went by in a blur of dissolvable diapers and nutrient bricks. And then my brother called with the news of my father. I had just nodded off in the bedside chair next to Akintunde's crib, where the boy lay exhausted after hours of twisting and screeching in the heat. The buzzing of the phone shook me from my dream and woke Akintunde, who started screaming again immediately, as if he had never stopped. I could hardly hear my brother through all the noise as he told me that our father was coming down with the silence. They'd just been in to Lagos to see the doctor, and he said that our father had maybe a week left to talk. Isoke took the boy into our bed to feed him while I looked at flights. I had not seen my father since I left home. We had not parted on good terms. He'd wanted me to help him run the women's clothing store he'd built from nothing, and he begged me to stay. He said, "Kenule, I have such a bad feeling about this. I fear that you are going to fail in America." He did not attempt to hide his disgust at my proposition, and I hated him for saying it. These words my father put on me were like poison running wild in my blood. But they were also the thing that kept me going. Without those words, I would not have my own business, my home. I would not have Isoke in my life. I felt the need to tell this to my father. While he could still understand me.

Forty-eight hours later we were in my brother's car, slowly

coasting out of Lagos in a sea of vehicles. In Manhattan you could see people everywhere who were worried about the virus. In the airport some workers were wearing those surgical face masks. The man behind me in line for the pretzel hammer was reading straight from a dictionary, trying to cram his brain with words, as if this might help him. His son held a ticker to count how many adjectives he was using. But in Lagos, nobody seemed very concerned. It was still the city as I remembered it. Jam-packed, filthy, but pulsing with energy. I asked my brother about why nobody seemed worried, and he shrugged. "Those who are worried have enough money to hide from the rest of us," he said. "And we are used to it anyway. Yoruba, Hausa, Igbo, Fulfulde—half the time we are communicating without words already."

We pulled into my father's house at dusk. My brother's wife, who I'd never met, came out to embrace us all. She took Akintunde and held him high in the air, and the boy calmed down immediately, even after the hell he'd been through in getting there. Isoke looked amazed and relieved. We went inside and there was my father, sitting in a recliner in the center of the living room, with all of my family around him like a portrait by one of the great painters. I approached him cautiously. Through all the chaos of the travel arrangements, I had not prepared myself for our actual meeting. I kept trying to rehearse something in my head, but Akintunde's ever-present needs always won out in the battle for my attention. So there I was, standing like a little boy in front of my father, who stared at me with a curious look on his face. You know how sometimes a person you know will make an expression you've never seen before, and it is as if, just for a split second, you are looking at a stranger? That was what it was like. He opened his mouth to say something, but all that emerged was a soft tone. A single note, almost musical. He turned away from me, as if he was ashamed to have made the sound. Nobody in the room had to tell me that it was too late. That it had already taken hold of him.

And yet this did not stop me from kneeling at his side, taking his hand, and telling him that I had returned to him as a successful man. I told him about my business, about how I had built it up from a single, broken-down cart to an entire fleet. My brother put his hand on my shoulder to try to get my attention, but I did not stop. I kept talking to my father, going on like an idiot about all of my accomplishments. My brother shook me again, and I looked into my father's eyes. They were like the eyes of a rabbit that's just been snared in a trap. Terrified and bewildered, darting back and forth from me to the rest of the room and back. He was backed up into his chair as if I was threatening him with a knife.

I stopped. I had come all that way for no reason. Pride had kept me from my father, and now the door was closed forever. There was no way for me to tell him how, as much as I hated him for saying what he said, he was responsible for my success in the world. I knew he was not dying, but it did feel like a sort of death in that moment. It felt like his soul had left his body, and his spirit would wander the earth forever, hurt and betrayed that his son had abandoned him, always wondering why.

I stood and backed away from the recliner, apologizing to everyone in the room. I hadn't come thousands of miles just to make him feel worse, I said, which made nobody laugh. I wanted to evaporate in that moment. I wanted to crumble and be carried away on the wind.

But then Isoke approached my father. She walked up to him very slowly, staring at him intently. He had never met her—he knew her only from pictures my brother had shown him. But she came forward and stood at his feet. And as he watched her, his face softened. He relaxed his grip on the arms of the recliner. The creases along his forehead disappeared. Everyone in the room saw this happen. My aunts and uncles, cousins and siblings, all watching my father, who was staring at my wife's face as though it held the secrets of the universe. She extended her hand and he took it. He rose slowly from the chair. My family is not generally superstitious, but I could tell that they were thinking to themselves that she had performed some kind of enchantment on my father. But this is just who Isoke is. She sees into a person's soul and reflects it back to them in some way I cannot even describe. To look into her eyes is to relive your childhood, the whole thing, in a single moment. And my father, he was standing, now more steadily, still wearing his old robe. He and Isoke were an arm's length apart, seeing nothing but each other's face, and his eyes narrowed and his features sharpened and he almost began to smile. It was as if he just then remembered that he was still Beko Mitee, even if those words had no meaning for him. Even if he could no longer speak his name.

Isoke guided my father toward me, and I took him into my arms. I felt his stiff, bone-thin arms cross my back and the mat of his beard scratching my collarbone, and I knew that I was home.

FRANCINE CHANG

OAKLAND, CA
2041

At the hospital, I watched as the doctors hooked Nancy up to a dozen different monitoring machines, and I knew immediately that something was wrong. All that scrutiny and pinpoint industriousness, it was scary. I wanted to stay behind, be there for Nancy, since everyone else had disappeared. But a hospital administrator found me in the cafeteria and told me I could no longer hang around. I think her precise words were, "Our liability exceeds your utility." Nancy was now in an isolation ward, so I couldn't even say goodbye. I boarded a train for Oakland.

The trip started out fine, but by Utah just about everybody in my train car was in an uproar over news of the virus. I just wanted peace, the solitude of my own inner reverie, and after that a bath and my own single bed, but I couldn't help listening. Everybody had heard or seen or read something, and they were all trying to outshout one another, eager to share what they thought they knew. Something like seventy-five percent of the test group had come up positive for the virus, but so far there were only about two thousand cases of people who showed Nancy's symptoms. This sounded perfectly scientific, verifiable. Rooted in numbers. Then someone behind me said, "Government doesn't want you to know this, but the virus actually originated from an infected satellite. They're trying to manually override it, but the satellite's outsmarted them. It's gone rogue. Only recourse now is to blow it out of the sky."

By the time we passed Reno the landscape had turned green again, and everyone around me seemed angry and forlorn. Some kept their eyes closed. Others stared into the seatbacks. A woman announced that the proper linguatherapeutic method for delaying the onset of the virus was to ration how many words you used per day, to save them up. But then somebody on the other side of the train found a neuroverbalist in Germany who said that the only way to combat it was to maintain a constant chatter, so as to keep the brain's language regions perpetually stimulated.

A teenage boy let loose a string of profanities. A woman in the seat across from mine held a sleeping baby and stroked its head and cried as softly as she could.

I just sat there, stunned. Someone on the train should've taken control. Someone should've stood up and said, "Listen, even if the worst happens and we're all stricken, who's to say what being silent will be like? Maybe it's like a purge, or a clarifying cleanse. We can't begin to know, so the only thing to do is just stay calm, keep our heads, and wait." It should've been me.

But not now. No. For the rest of the trip I could feel panic edging in, I could taste it easing upward in my throat. As a way of distracting myself I started to name everything I saw, outside and inside the train, trying to find the most precise word I could. *Espadrille, briefcase, pistachio, sequoia.* It wasn't a strategy, just something my brain started to do on its own. And kept doing.

When I arrived home, my toilet was backed up again, and a pair of raccoons had broken in through the crawl space and made babies in my bedroom. I went to work right away. Stripped the bed, the couch cushions, scrubbed the entire place, went on a trashing spree. Eight big bags of artifacts I named as I threw them away.

For the next few weeks I pecked around for something else to do. I watched the news. I stayed inside. I chattered to myself. I thought about volunteering at one of the makeshift transitional centers by the shipyards on Alameda. Some church had set up beds and a cafeteria and were trying to help ease the shift into silence. On the news the centers looked to be already brimming with patients. There was footage of two placid-looking women painting circles on a giant sheet of paper. I watched the women and tried to imagine myself in their place. Sitting with a brush in my hand and not a single sentence in my head, just some murky geometry. Would I still remember things? Would I think? Would I feel? Or would I just be a loose stew of inner spasms and urges, lurching around from room to room in my house? I couldn't imagine it. That's the thing that made my neck shiver—no matter how hard I tried, I simply didn't have the imagination to picture what it would feel like when the virus started to work its way through me.

One night, after too much red wine, after going on a visual dictionary site and memorizing the names of different kinds of bulldozers so I could identify them out loud whenever I passed the construction site on San Pablo, I recorded a video memo for myself. It started as a pep talk, like, "Francine, sister, you really need to marshal your inner whatever and come to grips with your *destiny*." The way it came out, I sounded like one of those old bouffant-haired Motown singers. I liked it. So I kept going. "Your sugary, lovelorn, hard-timing destiny. Dreamcatchers and wildflowers in your rearview. And old men coming at you with parking tickets in their wallets and bags under their eyes. Wanting to spread their love all over your new pillowcases."

I then began to record a reverse list of all the men I'd ever slept with, starting with Donald, in the back of his refrigerated truck in Rock Island. Donald, Briden, TJ, Klint . . . and then I blanked on the name of a man I'd dated for at least three months. Jesus. I mean, Jesus wasn't his name, it was what I said out loud. I could name the guy's dog, his ex-wife, I could recite the catechism tattooed in Latin below his navel. But his name was gone. It was something like Sam. Or Mike or Bill, Paul, Vic, Chuckie . . . I felt my heart speeding up, panic edging in again. I knew this is how it'd hit me, a bloodletting, a reverse acquisition, one word at a time. First it was his name, then it would be his dog's name, then his ex-wife's, and pretty soon the catechism. Sure, who cares about what's-his-name and his tattoo, but pretty soon I'd start losing things I did care about. And once the names were gone, how would I know what the names were attached to? Without names, all the men I'd ever slept with would be a sloppy pile. Not even that, because I wouldn't know what sloppy was, or pile. Without names they'd be gone.

Already a steady snow was starting to fall on my mind, removing all color and contour, whiting everything out. I could feel the first flakes coming to rest.

Theo and I met downtown and walked around the lake. Sometimes we talked and sometimes we just matched each other's stride and listened to the birds and kids. When there wasn't anything around to name, I counted each step in a whisper. Theo laughed at my word games. When I asked if he was worried about the virus, he shook his head and said he hadn't exactly decided what he was about the virus, but he definitely wasn't worried. He said, "I just wish it'd happened sooner."

That night we sat in my apartment watching a Danish movie about a twelve-year-old dogfighter whose favorite dog runs away and then the boy becomes a lonely shepherd but for goats. I think that's what it was about—I couldn't really follow what was happening on-screen, because whenever the subtitles appeared I couldn't help but read each word aloud. I did it as softly as I could, but Theo and I were sitting close enough for him to hear me. At one point he paused the movie and asked if I really needed to do that, and I thought about it for a minute and told him no, I didn't *need* to do it, but it made me feel better. It soothed me.

He unpaused the movie and we watched for a little while longer with me whispering the subtitles to myself. The boy met a man who said he'd seen the boy's dog, but I wasn't sure whether this was true. All I had were the words. I kept reading, and Theo paused the movie again and smiled. He fiddled around with the menu, and when he restarted the movie the subtitles were gone. Just the action on the screen and the indecipherable dialogue. I didn't know what he was up to, but I studied the boy's face as he's tending the goats, and all of a sudden I could tell he's pining for the lost dog. And the man comes back, and now I knew he was lying to the boy, I could see it in the way his mouth smiled but his eyes didn't.

We watched the rest of the movie without subtitles, and I still felt those flakes falling but they weren't so loud.

GORTON VAHER

PHILADELPHIA, PA
2041

After the riot the *Muir* was dry-docked indefinitely, while the kids on the streets went mental. I drank lukewarm tea and sulked all day in my apartment. It was more a room than an apartment—actually, more like a shared kitchenette. I laid my sleeping bag next to the minifridge and thought of Persephone while clenching and unclenching each muscle, starting with the scalp down to my feet. I dreamed of her floating away, trapped in prehistoric ice. While I slept, the other boarders, mostly nocturnal Laotians, slid open the curtain and used the sink to animate their powdered vodka, then turned on the screen to watch badminton. They chatted along with the action, but it didn't bother me. They urinated in the sink, which did bother me.

I knew the virus was sending people haywire, but I needed to get out of there. I looked for work, but there was even less call for ice sculptors. I tried selling whimsical tinfoil carica-tures on the street, but no one would look at me—they didn't want whimsical, they were too busy buying water and propane, preparing for their personal typhoons. I studied the crowds for Persephone, scanned city buses when they went by. I peeked in the Mexican pastry shop on South Eighteenth, because I knew she liked Mexican pastries.

After a week of nothing I walked across town to the *Muir*. Captains are supposed to go down with their ships, so I thought maybe some night manager would still be there sifting through the rubble. Maybe he could tell me where Persephone was. The back door was open, swaying on its hinges, so I made my way through the pretend boiler room and into the darkened building. Three engorged rats were munching on the remnants of that last dinner, straight off the dusty china. My ice station lay on its side under a table.

In the break room I went straight to Persephone's locker. I knew it because I used to leave stuff in there—acorns, flowers, bits of agate I found, anything I thought she'd like. Inside was a spare apron, her ID keycard with her home address on it, and a red felt-tip pen. Seeing the pen gave me a jolt. Persephone often kept it behind her ear. It would sit there all shift, going where she went, never wavering. It was her pen. She needed that pen.

I tied the apron around my waist, put the ID card and pen in the front pocket, and set out for the address on the card. I was halfway to her apartment before I realized I hadn't even bothered to clean out my own locker.

She lived in one of the studio warrens along Shunk, apartment 14FP. There was no answer when I knocked, so I tried the apartment next door. A man wearing a yellow neoprene face mask answered. When I held up the ID card and asked if he knew where this woman lived, I needed to give her something, his jaw moved and a thick reddish fluid dribbled out from under the mask, onto his sweatshirt. I reared back, but he just brushed at his sweatshirt, pulled the mask away from his face, and said, "Antibacterial toothpaste."

The man told me Persephone was out, and did I want to leave whatever it was with him? No, no, I told him, patting the front of the apron, what I wanted to give Persephone was far too valuable. The man raised his eyebrows. In retrospect, probably where I patted gave it a lewd connotation. He said Persephone spent all day every day at the Center City Transitional Facility, up on Broad Street.

I walked to Broad and found the building. An old hotel with a big pulsing sign out front. As I entered the lobby I rooted around in the apron to make sure the ID card and pen were still there. I held the pen tightly so it wouldn't jostle out. I needed to look casual but not uncaring, needy but not desperate, like a man of dignity, scruples, grace, gratitude, et cetera. Mostly I worried Persephone would be able to tell, by my stunned look, that I hadn't gone more than two hours without thinking about her since we parted over a month ago.

At the front desk some men and women were asking questions to the crowd that had gathered—things like, "Can you talk? Are you frightened? Alone?"—and then gathering them into groups. A boy brought the hungry and thirsty ones food and water. Another boy brought the cold ones bathrobes. A woman said, "Soon we'll all be going to the ballroom." I liked the sound of it. I liked how everyone was reined together calmly, efficiently.

I walked past them to the elevator, which was stocked with hastily made government pamphlets, *20 Reasons You Shouldn't Panic* and *100 Essentials for a Fully Prepared Home*. At the ballroom level, the elevator doors opened onto an enormous, dimly lit room, with crystal chandeliers and wallpaper bruised in water stains. People all over, some alone and some in clusters—holding hands, talking, playing cards, scribbling on large pads of paper. One couple seemed to be slow dancing. In the center of the room was a circle of seated people, men and women, all ages, all with their eyes closed, and at the head of the circle was Persephone.

I started toward her, my insides expanding with each step, but then I paused. The circle seemed united somehow, un-breachable, maybe holy, and I didn't want to interfere. I lingered at the edge of it, my hand still clutching the pen, and tried to think about anything except the fact that I'd been thinking about Persephone. She would see me and know with a glance what my intentions were, and then she would be burdened by it and have to walk me to a different circle, the one for men who were sad and pining.

So I thought about my sister in Lithuania, wondered if she was okay. Then I thought about Persephone. I thought about how it would feel when all the words were pulled out of me. Then I thought about Persephone. I thought about her red pen. I thought about her again. Then I kept thinking about her. It was hopeless.

I closed my eyes like the people in the circle. It didn't help, but it felt nice to stand in that big rustling space and for a minute not fret over what I was going to say next. When I opened my eyes again, the circle had opened in front of me. I looked at Persephone and she had her eyes open and was smiling at me. I didn't try to untangle the smile. Whether it was happy or happy plus a little pitying or real or not real. I just stepped in and filled the space and smiled back.

I spent hours in the ballroom, standing, playing cards, even dancing. The later it got, the dimmer the room became. I felt unstable, like my heart was pulverizing itself to mush. I picked up some spare government pamphlets and, on the back of them, started quickly sketching portraits with Persephone's red pen. I handed them out. When I came to Persephone, I didn't need to look at her face to do it. I drew the image that was in my head.

I gave it to her and she smiled again. She put her hands on my face and stared, alertly, patiently, with bright eyes. She kissed me. I kissed her back. Mostly I inhaled her breath and froze and didn't exhale for a long time. When we were done, my lips, cheeks, everywhere she had touched, pulsed.

I reached into the apron and pulled out the pen. Persephone studied it carefully and then put it behind her ear.

PATTI KERN

SPINDLETOP, KY
2041

Released at last, I had a vague notion of returning to the silo, but the first ride I caught was with an old man with swimming dentures who was hauling Slush syrup to a fair in Spindletop, Kentucky. So that's where I went. Another temporary partner. He was foaming to talk—said all he wanted to do was tell as many people he could that he loved them before he couldn't speak anymore. He had an aggressive gleam in his eye. By the time we crossed into Kentucky he was begging me to come live in his house with him, which he described as we drove—straw bale, vine fruit in the backyard, handmade porticos. Sounded nice, but I wasn't about to be pinioned. I, too, had some things to do before I couldn't speak anymore. I didn't know what things, but it didn't matter. Out of gratitude I let the man rut with me five or eight times on the top bunk bed in the back of his cab, which he'd parked in a clearing a few miles from the carnival. I quietly slipped out before he could tell me he loved me again. In the raw dawn I walked until I came to the midway, a blossoming of bright metal and primary colors.

Leo Kornblatt's Traveling Carnument, it was called, but it didn't look like it had been anywhere or was going anywhere. Already it was crowded with customers. And *loud*. As I approached, the roar of dissonant voices, pleasant at a distance, became overwhelming. I walked past open stalls where carnival workers hawked games of chance, one pitch trampling the next. Every step I took I entered a different strain of chatter. People asked directions to the roller coaster, but I didn't see a roller coaster. A woman told me she was sick and tired of being dishonest and did I know I should really wear a bra in public and pants without a tear near my muff? Others seemed to be reciting monologues, singing.

A young female carnie wearing a zipper-back sweat suit blocked my path as I was walking by. "Try your luck here," she said. "Try your luck before you go vegetable, if you ain't already? Acknowledge me, medicine woman. Come try the Beaver Dozer. If you can build your minibridge before my beavers and their studded tails come and tear it down, you'll walk away a winner." Her breath was a hot mask on my face. When I sidled around her and continued past, she yelled, "Pox-having hag. Broke-ass muted mark. My beavers would slit you up and feed their young on your feeble carcass."

I needed peace. I walked past Thunderball Blitz, Whale Worm Grab, loud games with louder attendants commanding people to test their wits, or strength, or luck. At the end of the midway, among defunct stalls with crooked dartboards and scummed-over water tanks, I found a stall with just a card table and a chair. No lights, no sign. Under the table was a big pimiento bucket filled with teddy bear key chains, and on top of the table was a scattering of playing cards. I sat down. There was nowhere for me to go. I was leashless, destinationless—finally I wasn't following anyone and no one was following me. I liked it.

I began fiddling with the cards. In my twenties I spent six months living on the Morongo Indian reservation—I was trying to learn their language, share their embrace of the ghost kingdoms of the hereafter, but they ended up giving me a polyester tuxedo shirt and putting me to work in one of their casinos—and the muscle memory was still there: blackjack, the Dollar Store, Jamaican Switch, three-card monte. I slid around two kings and a queen, seeing whether I still had the old moves, giving a peek at the queen before losing it again in the swift back and forth.

I did this for hours. All around me the other carnies screamed into the abyss from their booths. "Get some before we all die!" and "Christ almighty, everyone shut up a sec and come win a prize!" One voice shrilled above the others: "Save your words to challenge my beavers. Y'all are wasting everyone's *time*."

Around dusk a tent church from an adjoining field let out and a new crowd came streaming in, the men in ties and jackets, women in floral dresses. They fanned out in formation. At the edge of the group I noticed a single woman with close-set features covered in ruddy freckles wandering around the midway, looking bewildered and gesturing when people approached her. Beaver lady was on her right away. She gripped her arm and said it didn't matter what virus the woman had, her beavers were silent too, and they were equal opportunity. Then the triplets who ran Whale Worm Grab— they couldn't have been older than twelve—blocked her path and shouted that if some lost-tongue wanted to test her strength, it'd be absolutely free. The first time. The woman looked back and forth from triplets to the beaver lady, who was barking even louder, and her eyes grew more and more panicked.

She freed herself and pinballed down the midway toward my booth. She paused to catch her breath. I looked at her and she looked back at me. I was still working the cards, and the woman looked down at my moving hands as they went round and round. I stopped and waited, gave her time to pick a card. She didn't, so I ran through it again, showing her the queen a few times then shuffling the cards side to side.

She picked the card on the left: king of diamonds. I shook my head, shrugged, and began again. She squinted at my hands, the table, the left cuts made to look like right cuts, until her eyes showed a kind of mesmerized stillness. This time she picked the queen, and again on the third round. I pointed to the bucket and she looked inside, took a key chain, and set it on the counter. She played for the next hour, winning more and more frequently, then picked up her key chain and left.

I covered the table with an old tarp and spent the night underneath the makeshift tent. The next day, after evening service, the woman returned with an older man. She played first, to demonstrate. The man followed, and picked kings the first six times. I shuffled the cards, spun them around, watched, waited. The man concentrated on the motion of the three cards, my two hands. I stared at them too, stared until they were the noisiest thing in that hive of sound. The carnies, fairgoers, loudspeakers, all fading to a murmur. He chose the queen.

I stayed at the booth, and the group began to grow. The woman brought jugs of water and someone else donated a box of lutein bars. Earplugs, a first-aid kit. Leo Kornblatt's great-granddaughter came by one afternoon with some paperwork to tell me that I'd been officially hired.

One of the triplets spread a rumor I was trading sexual favors, the key chains were like tokens for later—two for a blow job, three for something else, et cetera—that's why my booth was so busy. Because why would somebody want to play the same damn card game over and over again? Twenty years ago I would've told you silence is a river with many branches, its channels to be eyelessly navigated by fingerless touch. I was rotten with the sound of things. Today I'll tell you that we are endowed with many gifts. And often the only thing that makes you do a full inventory is to be robbed of one of them.

One day after drifting off for a fifteen-minute nap, dreaming I was covered in shale at the bottom of a mine shaft, I awoke to a knocking on my table, hard and impatient. I opened my eyes to see the beaver lady standing there. Still wearing the sweat suit, still angry-eyed. We both listened to the distant drone of pivot-sprayers before she opened her mouth . . . and closed it again. She shook her head and sighed, and then pointed to the cards.

I started shuffling them around.

I'm not oblivious to the circularity but I'm not about to be mesmerized by it. I spent my whole life like a hermit crab, side-walking from notion to notion, trying them on like shells, finding them cracked or cramped or flimsy. Now I shuffle my cards for anyone, no one. I'm open for business for the brief spell until time makes me otherwise.

THEODORE GREENE

OAKLAND, CA
2041

I don't remember who took care of the arrangements for Mel's funeral. I don't even really remember it taking place, and I have no evidence that it did. I blocked it all out, permanently, I guess. The only memory I have of that time is coming home from the hospital with Flora. I carried her in her car seat up to the front steps and put her down next to a condolence vase that had been delivered the day before. The flowers had withered to a crisp in the heat. I fished in my pocket for the keys. Flora thrashed and grunted, swatting at the hospital blanket. It was midmorning, and already the air was heavy. Everyone I knew was at work. I thought of each of them, sitting at their desks, running numbers or watching silly amateur videos or tending their personal networks, and I wanted to end each of their lives. I found the key, attached to an oblong fob that advertised the karaoke bar where Mel and I had first met. *Kama Lounge*, it said.

I opened the door and stepped over the flowers. Inside, nothing had changed. Everything stood just as we'd left it, like a museum exhibit of our last hours together. The dinner

I'd made for her, hardened into a solid mass, rotting in the heat. The pillows Mel had propped up on the couch to make herself comfortable. The television was still on, muted, showing *The Price Is Right*. A fat man clapped his hands on the screen as the announcer revealed the prize he had just won. The light streamed in through the windows, and even Flora stopped fidgeting, as if she too was awed by the sickening stillness.

Mel, like I said, we met at this place called Kama Lounge. The karaoke setup was a total disaster, a tiny room in the back of the bar, with no printed catalog, so you had to navigate songs one by one using a DVD remote. It was the last night of the semester, so all the college kids were out, ripshit drunk. There was an awful guy in a lavender dress shirt hogging the mic, and my buddies were goading me to swipe it from him. I squeezed through the crowd to shut the guy down, but when I made it over to him Mel was standing there with the mic in her hand. She'd beaten me to it. Before I could think of anything to say, the guitar intro to "Purple Rain" started. I stood dumbfounded as she sang the song by heart, just tearing into it, killing every note. Staring directly at my face the whole time—like, deeply into me, shearing through all of my defenses. It was like we were the only two people left in the world. This person I'd never even seen before, I knew at that moment I could never live without. Until I did. Until I had to.

In the hospital they knew she was going to go. They had her hooked up to some machine, connected to a mask covering her mouth. Mel pulled it aside with a crooked finger and said, "You're going to take care of her." I said of course I would. She said, "I don't want you passing on any of your obsessive habits." I promised I'd try. "I will be so pissed if you turn her into a nerd," she said, and I croaked out a half laugh, because I had already painted her room to look like a *Portal* test chamber. "Theo," she said then, "Please. You've got to give her everything. Everything twice. She'll be starting out with only half, so you need to give once for you and then again for me. Promise." I said I would, and that was the last thing on this earth she ever heard.

And I tried. I did whatever I could. But I was so consumed with giving Flora *more* that I never stopped to consider what she actually needed from me. Not until I let her slip out of the hotel suite that night.

When I got back to El Cerrito, I drove out to that house—the house that Mel and I lived in. I asked Francine to go with me. I sensed she was slightly uncomfortable when it came to the subject of Mel, but I risked it anyway. I think I was still a little frightened of the place and I wanted a human shield in case things got out of hand. In my mind it loomed over everything around it, a stabbing column of black smoke that threatened to consume the whole neighborhood. But when we pulled up, we saw that the whole street was nothing but a cordoned-off pile of rubble. Where the house once stood, there was just a cushionless pink couch sagging on a heap of pulverized bricks. A sign posted on the fence around the property said that the area was being converted into a silent transitional center. Which was amusing and sad. I thought about all those videos I'd made of Flora as a child, where I'd held up a cucumber and said, "Cucumber," in an exaggerated voice, and she'd just watch my hand like I was about to perform a magic trick that never happened. What will those videos look like when all the words have been sucked out of us? Will future people think of them as avant garde theater pieces, or will they see them for what they really are—desperation at sixty frames per second?

We got out and approached the fence. Francine said, "This must feel weird." I agreed. I took the key out of my pocket and said, "You want to take a look around inside?" She laughed a little. I ran my finger over the Kama Lounge logo and she said, "You know, you did a pretty good job, all things considered." I had no idea what she meant. She said, "You walk around like you caused all this suffering yourself. As if you had anything to do with it. Bad things happened to you. There's nothing you can do to change that." My eyes stung, and I realized with some embarrassment that I was crying. And then I really gave in—I couldn't remember when I'd last been able to weep, and I was glad to finally be rid of the tears. I flung the key in a high arc over the fence. It glanced off the arm of the couch and landed in a shallow puddle.

My daughter was who she was not because of anything I did or didn't do but because she was part of me and part of Mel. Everything that could've been done had already been done. By the time our kids are born, the fire is already lit. All we are doing as parents is helping them find the kindling. For the first time, I allowed myself to feel that I'd done a good job raising Flora. It wasn't the job I thought I was doing. It wasn't the thing I was so focused on—the healing, the fixing. It was something else that happened when I wasn't looking. It was, maybe, that other half that Mel had asked me to give.

The ride back was quiet. The billboards along the highway displayed public service messages in pantomime. How to care for a newly silent loved one. How to deal with the trauma following the onset of symptoms. Where to go to have medical records translated to pictographs. I could tell Francine wanted me to talk about the past, but I wasn't ready to say anything, not yet. So I turned on the music service and told her to pick whatever she wanted. I told her to surprise me. She scrolled through the playlists while I drove.

A pregnant pause, is that the expression? Something taking shape in the spaces between words, something growing there, waiting to take on a life of its own. Like the silence that's now coiled up inside us, biding its time. I'm not missing the irony that after all my attempts to get Flora to talk, to bring her over to my side, it's me who'll eventually cross over. That's the big cosmic joke. But I'm ready. I'm ready for that morning when I answer the ringing phone and instead of words I'll hear staccato tones, rising and falling, the tumbling incomprehensible streams. The silence, when it comes, will bring me closer to Flora than I've ever been. I'll hear what she hears, see what she sees, and I will finally know her for the person she is instead of the person I tried to carve her into.

Francine found a song and said, "Oh, I haven't heard this in forever." She tapped the screen and a single guitar chord rang out, sending a jolt down my spine even before I recognized it as "Purple Rain." I immediately reached to turn it off, like a reflex, a physical thing. But halfway through the motion I stopped. "What?" she said, looking slightly alarmed. I said, "I just like to listen to this one superloud," and I turned up the volume until the snare hurt my ears. I reached out and dared to take Francine's hand, and the world didn't end.

EPILOGUE

CALVIN ANDERSEN

TERLINGUA, TX
2043

There is a dog that follows me around the property, so I feed him. Or does he follow me around *because* I feed him? I don't remember how it was that we were paired up. But now we are a pair. We get up early. Find the goat. Milk the goat. Drink the milk. Check the cables on the wind turbines. Hunt for snakes and beat their heads with the knotted pole. Skin them and boil them. Eat. Drink snake wine from a hollowed-out cactus trunk. Drink until the stars begin to blur. Sleep.

The dog is orange and white and he makes no demands on me. He barks when he is scared, but otherwise he is quiet. He pants by my side as we go looking for the goat. It is really all the companionship I have ever wished for. We live in a wooden hut that once housed miners. The ceiling is broken in half. A big crack that would let in the rain if it rained here. I sleep on the packed-dirt floor. The dog eats the scorpions that are drawn to the heat of my body in the night.

They left the hotel first—the boy with his parents, led by the old woman. I watched them leave, then watched the man, my drinking friend, still grappling on the floor. I moved to help him, but his face told me to go. I walked to the table, picked up the calibration helmet, and went down the hall to the emergency stairwell. The helmet was never mine, but I took it. I brought it with me to the desert. It still works the same as it did—there is no PhonCom network anymore, but I can send signals to my own implant. I can still speak. But I can only send signals outward. Without PhonCom there is no language processing. No comprehension. I can make words, but I cannot understand them. I have been recording this testament in pieces. I listen back, and it sounds like a long, tuneless song. But I can talk if I need to. If I want to. I do not know where Dr. Burnham is or what he is doing, but I know that someday he will lose his words and I will have mine. One day, perhaps, I will be the last talker on earth. This amuses me.

I don't often think about the past. But when I do, I think only about my boyhood. My parents drove me to Dr. Burnham's office twice each week, every week, from the time I was two until my twelfth birthday, but I remember very little about the office visits themselves. I can remember the posters on the walls, which showed the brain sliced and exposed in various ways. I remember the smell of the nurse when she leaned in close to apply the monitor nodes, a scent like a crackling beach fire. But what I recall most clearly is being in the car. I would sit in the backseat and look out the window at the passing trees while my father drove and my mother embroidered monograms on satin baseball jackets. I felt safe in the car. It was the only time in my life that nothing was expected of me that I couldn't deliver.

My parents wanted a boy who could tell them he loved them. My doctor wanted a success story. The rest of the talkers wanted to see the handicapped man struggle to rise to their level of perfect health. I tried hard to be all of these things. I did whatever they wanted. But I couldn't rid myself of this feeling of being somebody's experiment. Not until I came here. In the desert you are who you are simply because you choose to stay. There isn't anything beyond this choice.

This dog will not fetch. I throw a stick out into the desert as far as I can, and he just looks. I clap my hands and whistle, pointing in the direction of the stick, and he sits on his haunches and stares at me. I go to fetch the stick myself, and he follows behind me. I throw the stick again, and again he sits and watches it sail through the sky and scuff the dry earth in the distance. I don't know why the dog won't run for the stick. Maybe it wants to show its loyalty to me by staying close. Maybe it is just not interested. I cannot begin to guess, and I do not need to. Let the dog have its thoughts, whatever shape they may take. Let the unknown be unknown. The things we need will reveal themselves in time.

ACKNOWLEDGMENTS

Our thanks to Russell Quinn, Chris Ying, Richard Parks, Chris Adrian, Rachel Khong, Max Fenton, Corinna Vallianatos, Mary-Kim Arnold, Max Winter, Ben Marcus, Simon Huynh, Amity Horowitz, Kathleen Alcott, Skip Horack, Chris Flynn, Josh Tyree, Sean McDonald, Andrew Wylie, Kristina Moore, Luke Ingram, PJ Mark, Kassie Evashevski, Lauren Meltzner, Owen Shiflett, Ivana Schechter-Garcia, Jenno Topping, Scott Bromley, Keleigh Thomas Morgan, Kat Jawaharlal, Michelle Satter, Cullen Conly, Carrie Beck, Mark Bomback, and Marge Lafferty.

www.vintage-books.co.uk